LAST TO THE FRONT

LAST
TO THE
FRONT

GEE SVASTI

RIVER
BOOKS

First published and distributed in 2020 by
River Books Co., Ltd.
396 Maharaj Road, Tatien, Bangkok 10200
Tel. 66 2 622-1900, 224-6686
E-mail: order@riverbooksbk.com
www.riverbooksbk.com

Editor: Narisa Chakrabongse
Production supervision: Paisarn Piemmettawat
Design: Ruetairat Nanta

ISBN 978 616 451 040 1

Printed and bound in Thailand by Bangkok Printing Co., Ltd.

Gee Svasti, born in the UK to a Thai mother
and an English father, has worked in television,
design and technology. Founder of several successful
companies in publishing and new media,
he currently lives between London and Bangkok.
He is the author of the novel *A Dangerous Recipe* and
Rabbit Cloud and the Rain Makers.

Dedication

To my wonderful wife, Narisa,
and our lovely sons, Hugo and Dominic.

Part I

Chapter 1
PROLOGUE
Bangkok 2016

Spun by the wind, an angry vortex of dirt rose above the uneven ground, twisting for seconds into the coils of a dragon, before atomising once again into dust. Behind lay the empty building site.

Traffic had delayed the transporters carrying the six ton Komatsu bulldozers. Having waited since dawn, Sutin stood down the twelve men of his demolition team and told them to take a break. Putting a call through to the developer's office he spoke with the director's secretary. Her boss was in an important meeting, she told him; the investors flown in from Hong Kong and Shanghai, he couldn't be disturbed. It was urgent, Sutin insisted. She remained adamant: with the boardroom doors closed no one could enter. The Director hated interruptions.

'Dared' was the word she had actually used - she had said it with some trepidation, her tension, even down the erratic connection, betrayed by the timbre of her voice.

Sutin cut short the call, dropped his mobile to the desktop and venting his frustration, kicked the side of his filling cabinet. Close to the wall, it shook the thin sides of the portacabin, making his staff jump. A management roster fell to the floor, causing an accountant to break from her spreadsheets to retrieve the pages, further shaming his outburst.

In truth he was more than relieved not to have been put through. From the site crew he'd heard rumours of Damrung's wilful and volatile temperament. With a mouth, boxy like a megaphone, he shouted at everyone and everything, from senior executives to junior cleaners, even his Amazon 'Alexa' assistant. So early in the morning, Sutin wasn't sure if he could take such a verbal battering. He remembered gossip before he had accepted his position. The former site manager had been sacked for a relatively minor transgression; being a vegan.

Needing air, Sutin put away his mobile, left the Portacabin and walked out across the parking lot between the rows of closely packed pickups. Shading his eyes against the violent glare from the sun, he glanced across the site in the vain hope that some benevolent being might have conjured up the tractors during the space of his call. He was disappointed. Only flea bitten dogs and stray cats populated the litter strewn dust bowl.

It was the second time the bulldozers had failed to turn up. The contractors had promised them before six, it was already past nine. Thinking that his team wouldn't be tough enough with the booking agent, he had spoken with the hire director himself the night before. From the deep base rumble it sounded as if the manager was reclined on cushions in a subterranean nightclub. Confident and relaxed the man had reeled out all the usual smooth talking assurances, the cadence of his words matched to the thud of the beat, "the booking was number one top of his list, highlighted in bright orange glow pen... he would personally take care of it... drive them there himself if necessary... he had a truck drivers licence, he had driven fuel tankers with the military in Khorat".

Wise to his bluster, Sutin hadn't trusted a word he had said. Wanting to be there himself to check through the paperwork and see the equipment with his own eyes and check their condition, he had set his alarm for five. A storm had rolled in. Rain, drumming on the corrugated iron roof, had muffled his wake up call and he hadn't heard the alert. Late and knowing it would be unlikely to find a taxi so early, he had had to run to the bus terminal at Nakhon Pathom, three miles from their home. The last stretch was a muddy shortcut through a neighbour's plantation, the red silt, sticky and clogging his soles. Passing a grove of trees he had reached out to some low hanging branches and snatching some fruit, tried eating them on the run. The papaya was ripe, easy to break open, deliciously fresh. The banana, still young and green, was harder to peel. Crunchy between his teeth, he found it fiercely bitter and spat out the residue. More than an hour later its sharp astringency still lingered.

He blamed his mother. She was the one who usually prepared his breakfast. A rice soup was his favourite, a Tom Luad Moo, if he was lucky; the chunks of pork generous, crispy and meaty. The whine of his electric shaver was the cue to get her out of bed and into the kitchen to prepare this special broth. On that particular morning, his step father had been the weak link in the chain. It had been on his 'to do' list for a month to replace the gas cylinder. At that crucial point it ran out. His mother was scrambling to fill the charcoal burner with newspaper and coals when Sutin made the mad dash down the stairs to the door. She was five minutes too late.

Turning away from the construction office, Sutin walked across the rough ground to the river front. The waves, turbulent with rush-hour bus boats and barges, mirrored his own agitation. New on site and still on probation, he'd hoped to have made a better impression with management. And it wasn't as if the demolition delay had been his only setback. A diesel generator had been on site for two weeks. But with clogged glow plugs and a faulty magneto, no one could get it to start. A helpful technician from a back street garage, had dismantled the engine and found the fault; a clogged air filter - but a new one could only be sourced in Taiwan. Without electricity for the arc lights Sutin had had to cancel the night shift. A second failing that had further compromised their chances of making up for lost time in a timetable that had already drifted wildly off schedule.

With hunger still pressing, Sutin drifted towards the skytrain intersection. The covered shopping arcade was crammed with fast food shops; pancakes, doughnuts, waffles or mac-muffins - poor, but still acceptable alternatives to his mother's coveted pork soup. He was weighing up these alternatives and close to the site exit when he saw a car swerve in from the expressway. At first he suspected an impatient commuter, using the parking lot to make an illegal u-turn, before slicing back into the traffic a block further down the main road (such a move could easily shave off ten minutes). But it didn't pass through as expected. With a certain dread Sutin recognised Damrong's distinctive gun metal Audi. The trial of dust kicked up behind the big German saloon and the fierce flare of its brake lights suggested that its driver had approached the parking ground at some speed. A security guard raced out to raise the barrier. He was too late. The gate's lower edge grazed the perfect curve of the car's gleaming aluminium roof, carving a slight, but expensive flaw.

How the Director had made it to the construction site so soon after his call amazed Sutin. Even if Damrong had wrapped up the investor meeting early, said his abrupt farewells - his social ineptitude would expedite such haste - it was over thirty floors to the basement carpark, itself an unearthly labyrinth of levels, ramps and exits. From the Chitlom district, its main roads bedevilled with roadworks and diversions, there was never a good time to fight through the near constant traffic, no short cuts to avoid snarl-ups and gridlock. Some of his workers claimed to use a rat run across the St Joseph Convent Campus, but they were on scooters, at most catching a Tuk Tuk, its shape slim enough to squeeze through the thin alleys and footbridges at the back of the Catholic church.

As the large executive car came to rest, a cloud of dust settled on the parking lot, covering the matted fur of the dogs too lazy to shift from their day beds. At the tinted rear window of the Audi, Damrong's podgy round face appeared, sweaty nose marking the tempered glass, hot breath misting the surface. Too fractious and impatient to deliver his reprimand in person, he ordered his assistant, the twenty four year old, Bay, out of the front of the car.

Tottering in elegant shoes across the dried, rutted earth, Bay had already broken a heel on a rock before she had even got half way to the shelter of the foreman's office. Stuck in the open, in the dirt, in the insufferable heat, collapsed designer heel clutched to her chest, the young girl looked a forlorn figure, like a shopper marooned outside a mall beseeching an Uber.

Bay, thin, suave and elegant; creature of climate controlled and carpeted high rise, hated site visits. Deftly avoiding building sites and land inspections where she could, she kept a pair of Nike trainers under her desk for days when she failed. But she had stayed with old college friends the night before - a long evening of cocktails in a newly opened bar to celebrate a colleague's promotion. Accepting too many mojitos and negronis from both friends and strangers they had been the last to leave. Waking, somewhere downtown, her delicate high heels had been her only footwear of choice. But these coveted shoes weren't the only casualty of the harsh terrain and stifling humidity. Caught under the full glare of the sun, she could feel her carefully layered eye shadow melting, her spa pampered curls frizzing in the sticky, super heated air.

With no mercy forthcoming from Damrong's chilled, purring Audi, Sutin relented. Wrun, one of the strongest on his team, sprinted out to the girl. The boy offered to carry her. He was certainly strong enough but Bay was fussed his rough workmanlike hands would leave marks on her dress. The material was silk, Huzhou silk - fine filaments rolled from over three thousand cocoons, susceptible to creases and stains. In the end she rolled up the hem of her skirt, took off the remaining shoe, wrapped her arms around Wrun's neck and jumped on his back. She was light; he smiled.

"Why are you smirking?", she snapped.

"Because you're lighter than my daughter" he replied.

"How old is your daughter?"

"Thirteen, last month."

"She should eat more cakes," she snapped, with little thought that her own frame was wafer thin.

Wrun cleared the open ground and reaching the shade of the portacabins, put Bay down on the firm astroturf. With brute force he was even able to straighten out her bent heel. Gratefully she put them back on again, tentatively transferring her weight to the damaged shoe to test its strength; it held.

Smoothing down her pristine contoured dress, she searched the circle of men, their grinning faces looking cheeky, still ragging Wrun for his galant 'damsel in distress' rescue.

"Which one of you is ...," she checked the screen of her smart phone, "Chanavit?"

Sutin nodded.

"I take it you're in control?"

"I am, yes", he replied, removing his safety hat and brushing back his ruffled hair.

Bay eyed him more intently; a drill screamed, a steam hammer thudded. She waited for the interference to subside.

"I've a message for you from Khun Damrong, the development director".

"DamRonG", there was a hint of bitterness and repugnance in the way she said it, as if she'd been asked to order tinned peaches in a Michelin-starred haven. A sideways glance at the Audi confirmed these sentiments; her bottom lip lifting, nose wrinkling, close to a sneer.

Bay had been Damrong's personal assistant for nine months, her first job since graduating from a Business Management College in Boston. Used to collegiate American ways, where every opinion however crass and ill-conceived was needlessly debated and aired, she had found his dictatorial style blunt and outdated. His attitude to the junior staff, especially women, was particularly offensive and archaic. Hating his over-familiarity and wandering touch she had begun to resent and despise the man, longing for those moments when he was hauled off to some far-flung corporate golfing convention, so that she could manage on her on. But Damrong was family, her father's cousin; a cousin, she was endlessly reminded, from the more salubrious and moneyed side of the clan. Discord could and would wait. Obedient and prudent not to ruffle or vex, she delivered his words as instructed.

"Why the delay Chanavit?"

"Traffic. It's not unusual."

"That was your excuse yesterday. A second day the site has stood idle," she snapped as she twisted around, hand swinging out as if marshalling an army of amazons. In a circle of trees, an abandoned teak house remained an obstinate last impediment before the bulldozers could roll in.

"Everyday that shack still stands is costing us more."

"We're doing everything we can."

"Then get that house down now unless you guys want to do a whip round and pay out of your own wages."

"Without the right equipment," Sutin explained, "We can't start".

"It's just a stupid wooden wreck. A tuk-tuk could take it out."

"Your Uncle's Audi?" Sutin suggested.

Bay broke a smile, liking his insolence. When she'd first seen Sutin's name on the job sheet as foreman she'd expected someone older more experienced. Wearing a worn Carabao T-Shirt and scuffed jeans he looked like a DJ from a nightclub or a moody messenger courier.

"Get me the keys and I'll do it" she whispered with a devious grin, the thought of levelling two objects of distain with one stone, inciting her mischief.

Sutin was impressed; he'd thought her compliant, a corporate stooge.

"It would be an expensive way to take down something so worthless", he added.

"That worthless something stands in the way of a multi-billion baht development project and my promotion", was her parting line, fluffy auburn hair lifting in the breeze as she turned.

Wrun lifted Bay back across the waste ground, even though, with her heel fixed she didn't need it; she'd grown used to the idea of being carried around. Walking back to the far side of the car, Bay gave a last wave and a mischievous smile before opening the passenger door and sliding back into the car. Sutin could see her inside, dutifully turning to the back seat as she recounted their conversation. Damrong, shifting restlessly in the back, didn't look pleased with her account. At some point he pressed his face close to the glass like a petulant frog, angrily grimacing and shaking his fist.

Seconds later dirt again kicked up from the rear wheels of the car. The silver Audi sped off across the dust bowl at the same furious pace with which it had arrived, bleating horns greeting the car as it cut back into the mid-morning traffic.

To escape the coming midday heat several of the work force had already drifted into the shade of the defiant oasis, grateful for the cool from the leafy acacias. This modest glade encircled the old teak house, its timber boards bleached grey by the overhead sun. Thin reed grasses and gnarled roots had broken through the crumbling laterite paving that surrounded the plot. A stone statue of a dove and a mouse crowned a marble column at the centre of a dried-up fountain, its font lined with chipped iridescent tiles. Under a collapsed trellis, trails of bougainvillea had looped their tendrils through the open windows of an abandoned Datsun sedan, now so old and battered few even recognised the badge.

The 'Green Gecko' house, as it was known to locals in the area, was the home of an old school teacher. It had been in his family for more than forty-five years. Built in the 1960's by a retired army Captain, the house and garden was one of many residential compounds dotting the backstreets and klongs of the old Silom district. At the time most of the grander residences were owned by large trading companies and foreign diplomats, their lawns daily watered and manicured by small armies of gardeners. Although built in imposing colonial styles with covered porticos and shaded verandas, it wasn't unusual to peer through wicker gates to see buffaloes and villagers still ploughing waterlogged paddy fields. Monitor lizards, pythons and cobras, keeping in check the rats and stray dogs, were also close neighbours.

Such dreamy Arcadias rarely last. The city, chasing Western ways, shook off its humble, parochial past and fuelled by a rush of development sprinted from sleepy low-rise to frantic high-rise in less than two decades. A skyline previously graced by temples and stupas, took on the messy, crenelated profile of faceless modernity. Along the main arteries of Silom and Sukhumvit, families, pulled by the material needs and avarice of sons, daughters and grandchildren, sold up, their creaky, uncomfortable houses torn down and burnt. Stealing the light and stifling the air, glass towers and concrete blocks, loomed over the small lanes, gardens and squares, now choked with scooters, trucks, cars and buses.

The 'Green Gecko' compound was the last house standing in the previously verdant, Soi Phiphat. Bundled together with nine other abandoned buildings and gardens, it had been bought by a Chinese

Singaporean conglomerate, its land earmarked for one of the most ambitious and luxurious condominium high-rises in the city, the Kingdom Royal Crescent, its legend, "Your Paradise in the Sky".

Standing at three hundred metres above the smoggy city streets, the Kingdom's luxury 'village' apartments, each with roof gardens, open-air kitchens, lap pools and jacuzzis, looked west over the snaking river and the old residential district of Thonburi. On clear days, the glossy sixty-four page brochure proclaimed, one could see the distant mountains of Cambodia – although clear days were a rarity.

The delay of the bulldozers had brought the old teak house a reprieve. They said it was haunted. At least that's what the survey team had claimed. Marooned a month before on site because of monsoon floods, several of the men had been forced to spend a disturbed night in the back rooms. They had lit a fire on the open boards of the veranda, got drunk on cheap Laotian rice whisky and tried to sleep on the creaky iron bed frames.

Doors opening and slamming had shaken the walls. At four in the morning they had been woken by a piercing scream. Glass in an upstairs window had broken, the brittle shards scattered down the staircase. From a roof space above they heard footsteps labouring across the rough planks. The heavy shuffling of feet came back every half hour as if whatever it was, or whoever it was, was rearranging the furniture for a gathering of fellow ghouls; wasn't the third Sunday after Songkran such a portentous day, a gathering of the undead?

No one dared go upstairs. It was clear it was bad spirits. And the locals confirmed it; Phi Krahang – a shirtless ghost, with long stringy locks, that flies through the trees astride a long wooden pestle. Often they had seen such shadows dancing across the telephone lines and electrical cables in the moonlight.

More chilling tales came from the nightwatchman. Patrolling the site late in the evening he was relieving himself in the bushes when he noticed a glow in the stone fountain. A pale face, the face of a woman, half shrouded in flowing silver hair, slowly emerged from beneath the milky waters of the ornamental pond; a pond that by day was as dry as a bone.

Not that such tales rattled Sutin's team. Old spirits held little sway over minds inured by Playstation or Netflix. Besides it was broad daylight, they were restless and needed a break from the heat. A small door secured with a padlock was found at the back of the building. Wrun wrenched the latch from the surround with a crowbar, then kicked the door in with his big steel-capped work boots. Weakened by termites, the whole frame pulled away from the wall and fell crashing to the floor kicking up a fine cloud of wood dust and bug droppings.

A stray dog, curled up asleep on a trunk, was startled – it must have considered the home a safe haven. Scrambling from its bed, the panicked mongrel caught his hind legs on the mosquito netting pinned over the window in his haste to be out.

The shattered entrance door led through a thin kitchen into a living room that looked out over the broken veranda, its rotten, water-logged boards shaded by a last leafy tamarind tree.

No wonder the surveyors had been spooked. There was still furniture in place; a rattan sofa with faded silk cushions, two wooden arm chairs, a large, carved oak sideboard, shelves stacked with dusty ceramic cups and a row of carved mahogany elephants. Shredded, moth-eaten curtains hung limp over the windows. On the walls, frames showed faded photographs of family and work colleagues, standing formal in suits. A coffee table was broken, probably intentionally by the survey team, the pieces used to start a fire. Within the black ash and broken whisky bottles, its charred legs were still visible.

At the side of the room a door opened into a study. There was a rusting steel office chair, its wool stuffing seeping from its seat, pushed under the front of a large roll-top desk. Its lock had recently been picked and the drawers forced open. They must have used the letters inside as tinder to light the fire.

After a further abortive call to the hire company, Sutin joined his team. They found more stools and chairs and arranged them in a semicircle around the charred coffee table. Beers and instant noodles had been bought from a 7 eleven store. Wrun used his lighter to restart the fire. In the kitchen they dusted off an old sauce pan and filling it with water, hung it from a makeshift tripod over the fire.

In a hunt for more fuel, one of the men returned with an armful of papers, telephone bills and bank statements. Kneeling by the fire he started to feed the sheets one by one into the flames. An envelope sliding of the pile fell at Sutin's feet. He used a cane walking stick to flick it out from the smoke. Bending to the floor to throw the package back to the flames, the fussy character of the script on the front caught his eye.

Brittle with age, the envelope had two distinctive postal stamps on its cover. The image was of a foreign city port, its harbour front lined with steam ships, most likely European. In the sky a twin engined bi-plane flew over a bay, the word 'Postes' painted across its underwing.

Sutin put a finger to the corner of the envelope to open it, but the paper, thin and fragile, came away in his hands. Its contents, postcards, old rail and boat tickets, yellowed newspaper cuttings and a set of sepia photographs bound with a string, fell into his lap.

Chapter 2
Bombay 1919

Alaia took her uncle's bicycle into town. It was a heavy, ungainly machine, the mythical name Pegasus crowning an enamel badge on which perched a winged horse above the roofline of its glowing Birmingham factory. The cycle's original owner, a retired Scottish rail engineer, claimed to have bought the machine direct from the works, its front forks and crossbar painted in the family's Royal Stewart tartan, the chips in the design painstakingly retouched by Alaia's ever fastidious uncle.

Two frame sizes too large for her, Alaia found the cycle cumbersome and difficult to manoeuvre through the winding alleys of thatched huts and homes. Hemp lines, pegged out with drying fabrics and cloths from the indigo dyers, criss-crossed the thin passageway. Several times she had to drop her head to the handlebars to prevent her hair getting snagged in the blue, violet yarns. She'd done it before and been screamed at by the old ladies hanging the fabrics, as she weaved through their baskets.

Reaching the outskirts of her village Alaia took a shortcut behind the water baths and dying vats, which passing the grazing fields where cattle still slept, dropped through the misty Chembur Hills. The track ran past mango plantations, their bushy branches heavy with ripe fruit, leaves silvery with overnight dew.

Dim lights flickered in the hearths of the outbuildings at the edge of the Badar estate, as women, veiled beneath coloured saris, knelt over dusty floors stoking charcoal fires and baking fresh roti. Young girls, goat skin mashaq's slung over their shoulders, toiled up through the slippery banana groves bringing fresh water up from the stream.

A train of bullock carts approached on the way to the fields. Alaia slowed and lent into the bushes to allow the animals past. Proud horns, dusted with cobalt and vermilion powder, inched by. Crushed together on the rear platform, field workers huddled beneath thin cotton sarongs against the morning chill.

It had rained heavily the night before. The wheels of the bulky carts had left deep farrows in the sticky ochre earth. The thin tyres of Alaia's bicycle, jogged between the rutted tracks, bounced erratically over the uneven surface; she had to ride carefully.

Further down the valley the first bungalows of the European quarter emerged through the trees. A tall golden cross, perched above the pitched roofs of the St Vincent orphanage, caught the first rays of sun. As she wheeled past its white wicker gates, Ravi, a small boy in white shorts and shirt, ran out into the road and shouted "Mata, Mata". Alaia, wise to the ambush, slowed and swung wide to avoid hitting him. Ravi wasn't the stealthiest of hideaways. He'd hidden behind the same privet bush every morning since spring, greeting her with the same woeful cry. Of course she wasn't his 'mother'. Childhood implanting had embedded in his pliable mind, an indelible association with nurses and motherhood. And Alaia, more beautiful than most, was Ravi's angel of choice; the girl's effervescent smile a million miles from the dour authoritarian "sisters" who ruled his every waking hour. Only last night he'd been reprimanded for hoarding ginger biscuits in a tin box beneath his pillow. He'd get a second vicious beating for his rash dash into the road; a matron, watching from an upstairs window, was already primed to scold him with a broom handle when he came back inside.

Passing the end of the white wicker fence, the aroma of wild jasmine spilled over the walls as Alaia rose on her pedals to take in the last lingering scent. An indulgence frowned on by the nuns toiling the garden, enviously watching her elegant silhouette racing by. The walled enclosure had been planned and laid out purposefully by the fastidious elders: twelve regimented rows of herbs and medicinal plants; tulsi, chamomile, sage, arrowroot, calendula – identified by neatly painted wooden stakes. With no room or time to tend fussy blooms, the jasmine had survived despite their endeavours to get rid of the flowers. Only the Abbess, her purity incorruptible by such temptations, had been allowed the indulgence of a single white rose in her flower box.

From the heights of Victoria Gardens above the Port a view through the trees allowed sight of the sea. Local fishing dhows, unfurling long lateen sails, set out for deeper waters, cutting a line between the grubby freighters and western cargo ships anchored in the bay.

Following the coast, telegraph poles marked the harbour line that ran south to the hill station of Kalyan. Steam from the six o'clock train puffed through the low palms, the carriages heavy with their first transit of officials, clerks and office workers, anxious to complete their journey in the cool of the shade before facing the full force of the sun and its life sapping humidity.

For Alaia the final stretch of her journey was simpler; the main road to her hospital, the Saint George's, passing the white washed villas of the foreign diplomat's compound, was now all downhill. Joining Mansion Road, the central artery of the merchant's district, its streets lined with shops, markets and stalls, she was already at the main gates of the hospital before the first rail commuters had disembarked from their carriages and climbed into their rickshaws.

Ali Khan, a striking Pathan in a proud turban with a bright orange beard and a curved 'pesh kabz' in his braided belt, was on guard at the gate. After more than twenty years at his post, old age, lung fatigue and joint pains had seen that duty relegated to a small stool in the shadow of the gate house. Hauling on a worn rope to raise the barrier gate he still called Alaia "naya gee" despite a vague recollection that she had worked there for some time.

Alaia parked the bicycle under the basement arches of the entrance and took the stairs to the first floor. Four wards occupied the main floor of the building; the Montague, Hastings, Curzon and Victoria. A bell in the central atrium marked the change of shift. Night nurses and porters, coming the other way, filled the upstairs corridor. Alaia knew several of the girls. Three were from villages near her own. A small girl, Pani, was a cousin; they often shared their uncle's bicycle. Alaia tried calling out to her to stop and chat, but the surge of staff down the corridor was so strong they gave up. That in itself was unusual; the density of the crowd. And so many were fresh faces. An invasion that induced both disquiet and relief. For the past month the three hundred beds of the four wards had been totally filled. To deal with the additional patients, mattresses had started to spill out into the corridors and landings. Several times Alaia and her friends had had to work through the night. By the weekend they were totally worn out and useless to parents who insisted they help out in the fields.

The unease and tension continued on the second floor. A meeting was taking place in the administrator's office. Doctors, head nurses and managers were pressed up against the glass partition walls, seated on packing cases and cabinets. On the far side of the office, a first row of chairs was taken up by the senior Directors, dark suited and silver haired. And in the centre of this line of seniors sat the Principal, Doctor Hargraves, his face as solemn as a grave slab. Alaia had only ever seen him a few times before; either as a distant, bobbing, smiling head officiating at ceremonies or smoothly steering foreign dignitaries through the maze of corridors and wards. On this particular morning he looked neither smiling, nor relaxed.

The attention of all was focused on the front of the room. A local doctor, Amar Pavan, stood in front of a blackboard chalking up numbers to a set of pre-drawn columns. A 'six' was added to the square adjacent to the day's date; the additional cases of influenza that had been recorded from the previous day. The new patients added to the twenty-one known cases already admitted. For those assembled it was dispiriting news. Alerted to the scale of the European epidemic more than a year ago, they thought they'd got the better of the outbreak. Indeed their work in containing its spread had been hailed as one of the regional success stories, for which Doctor Hargraves had been given a prestigious award. Now the monthly figures were telling a different story, making his award appear both premature and undeserved.

Fearing a recurrence of the disease, the administrators had already imposed restrictions on access and strict quarantine rules; bedding was to be disinfected, gauze face masks made mandatory, electric fans installed in the public areas to improve air circulation.

The new edicts, written both in English and Hindu, were printed and pinned to a wall in the foyer of the public entrance. Families of the hospitalised, barred from seeing their relatives, were directed to a separate waiting room where they were provided with writing materials to pen letters to their loved ones.

The new measures were designed to reassure visitors that the spread of infection was being contained and controlled, but the speed and severity with which they were implemented only incited a contagion of words that multiplied faster than the virus. Hearing gossip from cleaning staff that the top floor had been sealed off and bedding burnt, a reporter from the *Bombay Chronicle* had telephoned the St George's to secure an interview with Dr Hargraves and his deputy. His alarmist headline, 'The Rush to the hills', had caused panic within the European community. An exodus of families to the hill stations of Lonavala and Matheran, three hours away by train, had already started. Overcrowding had seen platforms closed. Hotels and guest houses, their books full, were already turning away guests. A district official had returned recently from the Raigad district to report seeing families forced to camp out in the gardens of a cemetery. At Neral the reservoirs were low. Drinking water was already restricted. Police had been called out to quell scuffles outside markets and food stores where 'profiteers' had been accused of hoarding.

The mounting hysteria only exacerbated the problems for the administrators fighting to contain the crisis. Although hospitals south of Bombay, at Poona and Mangalore, had helped with beds and medical supplies, there was still a shortfall in medicines, equipment and bedding.

A troopship, the HMT Aquitaine had recently anchored in Victoria docks. Carrying three hundred returning soldiers from the Indian expeditionary Force in Egypt, its captain had gratefully donated mattresses, blankets and sheets to the St George's. The grand ballroom of his ship had been converted into a makeshift hospital during the war and the ship's Liverpool owners, impatient to get the vessel back into passenger service, were only too pleased to get rid of the worn bed frames and furniture.

After the pomp and ceremony that had accompanied the main disembarkation of troops, the wounded and invalided had been stretchered off the ship in the early morning, while the city still slept. The West Wing of the St George, a ward normally reserved exclusively for Europeans, had been devoted to returning soldiers since the beginning of the year. The most serious cases, those with head injuries, victims of gas attack and burns, were treated in the basement chapel.

A small group suffering from trauma and shell shock, confounded everyone. The ward they occupied was formerly a children's wing. The nurses thought the bright, cheerful colours and large, playful numbers and letters might prove restful for the mind, encouraging recovery. Instead the primal hues and monstrous shapes, induced the opposite; neurosis and hysteria. After a midnight breakout in which patients elected to sleep under the stars, the maintenance team were called in to paint the walls and ceilings an inoffensive, soothing beige.

The younger European doctors, influenced by the latest advances from home were anxious to try new techniques. Barbiturates for insomnia, draconian milk diets to calm nerves and electroconvulsive therapy to dislodge deeply set psychological disorders and troubles. Few had any effect; the howls in the night, the shaking and bed wetting, testimony to their failures. Small disturbances from the street; loud voices, a car back-firing, a ship's siren were enough to set off a cascade of horrors.

Alaia and four of her friends had been assigned to help with the troops from the start. Wednesdays saw her in the orthopaedic ward, where she assisted the doctors with leg and arm injuries and helped fit artificial limbs for the disabled. A workshop, equipped with drills and lathes, had been built adjacent to the ward, where carpenters and craftsmen fashioned prosthetic legs and hands. From Bombay's notorious Shor Bazaar, clockmakers, locksmiths and lock-pickers, helped engineer articulated knee joints with complicated pulleys and gears.

On the sweeping lawns overlooking the harbour, a training ground of steps and platforms had been laid out, its oval track shaded by a dense umbrella of rain trees. Here, Alaia and her three companions, encouraged the disabled to walk again and relearn movements stiffened by inactivity and surgery.

Despite their calm and perseverance, progress was frustratingly slow. Advances made one day, would without explanation, evaporate the next. Most of the patients were so bored by their tedious, repetitive exercises that they lost all motivation, the suggestion of a last round of the circuit enough to induce violent protests. One dejected double amputee, was so irritated by his painful straps and braces that he tore off his flimsy encumbrances and dragging himself into the ornamental fishpond was only saved from drowning by the collective efforts of a precarious chain of fellow invalids.

For beyond the physical pain lurked a deeper psychological dread. Knowing that without hands or legs they were unlikely to find meaningful work again, the men were ashamed to go back to their villages and families. Coerced round the garden circuit, they endured their rehabilitation in stoic, sullen silence, ever watchful for that smiling, helpful doctor, who would one day stride down the lawn, signed release form in hand, approving their return to the cruel, real world outside.

The exception was Darwan Singh. A captain with the 89th Punjabis, he had been stationed in Cairo and fought in the Mesopotamian campaign. As part of the British forces, Captain Singh had been one of the first to fight his way back into Kut Al Amara, a desolate desert town on a tributary of the Tigris river, one hundred miles south of Baghdad. The surrender of the thirteen thousand strong garrison two years earlier to the Ottoman Turks and their German advisors, had been one of the worst defeats in British military history.

Singh had lost a brother in the original Kut siege. When the garrison had run out of food, cavalry horses had been slaughtered. Hindus, staying true to their religious principles and vegetarianism, had refused the meat despite their desperate hunger. Deprived of sustenance they had been some of the first to succumb to the cold and damp. After a failed rescue mission the remnants of the force were forced to surrender and marched to prisoner of war camps where more than sixty percent died in captivity.

With the British High Command distracted by plans for a far greater catastrophe in the fields of Northern France, it took a further year for a combined force of British, Australians and Indians, to regain Kut in 1917. Singh was part of the relief army. Despite being wounded at the Battle of Sharqat (a trifling bayonet cut through his left shoulder), the indomitable Singh, sailed through every conflict thereafter, culminating with a victory march into Istanbul itself with General Stanley Maude, where he witnessed the fall of the once mighty Ottoman Empire.

With the fighting over, Singh and his fellow soldiers, toured the souks and streets of the capital, overwhelmed by the magnificence of Arab minarets, Byzantine domes and Roman arches. Mesmerised by the spiritual power of Hagia Sophia, Singh climbed the winding stairs to the upper gallery and emerged under the towering blackened mosaics of the Virgin Mary, framed by the four Arabic shields of the great Caliphs. Finding a hidden shrine in the shadow of the great dome, he dropped to his knees and gave thanks for his safe deliverance in the language of three faiths; Hindu, Muslim and Christian.

After the Armistice, Singh and the 89th Punjabis boarded a troop ship in the Dardanelles straits and crossed the Aegean sea around Cyprus. Heading south towards Cairo they hit a mine off the coast of Lebanon. Detonating against the starboard bow, the ship went down in less than five minutes. Singh, drifting at sea for three weeks in a lifeboat with no food and a single container of water, had been one of the few to survive. Seen by local fishermen twenty miles off the coast, he was picked up with three other survivors and transferred to a cargo ship bound for Bombay. One of these men now occupied the hospital bed next to him.

Initially this frail, emaciated figure was mistaken for an Indian from the southern states; Tamil, possibly Sinhalese. It was only later, when perplexed by the man's inability to understand even the most basic instruction, that the doctors deduced that he wasn't of Indian descent after all. The clothes he was rescued in were retrieved. Papers found in a jacket pocket revealed that he had served in France. His name was Chai Khomsiri, his country of origin, Siam.

When Alaia first learned of this obscure country, she had no idea where it was. Neither did the doctors. Wanting to know more, she found a tin globe in the children's waiting room. Painted with exotic animals and fish it was a confusing and inaccurate reference source. Eventually she found the territory; a small land squeezed to the right of the British dominion of Burma, its position marked with the outline of a bright, yellow stupa.

Although the stocky Singh was already making forays beyond the confines of the ward – mostly on foraging expeditions to the cake tin in the basement and to chat up the pretty pantry maids – Chai, still weakened by twenty-two days without food, was too feeble to stand.

Badly burnt by the sun, his face was a painful mask of scarred and blistered skin. At night he rambled, shouted, screamed. No one could understand what he said. Alaia, seated by his side, used cold towels to dampen his forehead and moisten his chapped lips. In the middle of one turbulent dream, he sat up, grabbed her shoulders and stared out, his wild eyes filled with anguish.

Chapter 3

Chai never heard the explosion. His only memory was being in the waves. At some distance he saw the stern of the ship rise high above the sea, its barnacle encrusted propeller and rudder exposed to the air. Loud piercing shrieks and groans echoed from the contorted bulkheads and deck beams, as the ship slowly slipped into the depths, a last plume of steam hissing from the flooded engine room.

Chai, slow to full consciousness, made no connection that the ten year old troop ship, HMT Lancaster, had been his home for the last three weeks and that just half an hour earlier he had been seated on its shaded upper deck drinking tea and eating Fray Bentos sandwiches.

Seconds later the sea was placid and serene. A break in the clouds opened. Sunlight, blazing like a spotlight onto a stage, briefly illuminated the spot where the ship had last laid, as if fate needed to check whether its grim task had been done. There was little left – empty lifejackets, an upturned life boat, shattered crates and drums, a dark circle of sticky oil seeping outwards, its viscosity calming the waves.

Chai could understand the idea of sea sirens and mermaids. Feeling lulled, embraced by the warm, inviting waters, he enjoyed the sensation of being softly pulled down; the world beneath the waves – bright shafts of sunlight dancing through clouds of plankton and shoals of tiny, metallic fish – more entrancing than life above.

A loud, maddening ringing between his ears, (echoes from the detonation that had so violently pitched him into the sea) rose and fell in intensity like the background chorus of a thousand shrieking cicadas. From this hubbub, a single voice came to the fore; muted, difficult to decipher against the discordant, background hum.

His parents made the first appearance. Seated on the wooden steps of their weather worn house on the Mekong river, his mother was crushing nuts, snake beans and papaya in a stone mortar bowl for their dinner, ingredients she'd gathered in the hills, after a morning tilling yams and cassava. Chai's father, fat and lazy like a gecko, on reed matting by the shore, needed most of the day to warm up. Judging by the low golden light flickering through the creaking bamboo grove, it was already late in the evening and he still hadn't reached his optimum operational temperature. He should have been fishing, checking his nets for carp and perch in the lagoon, but his canoe, beached up on the golden mica sands, its planking cracked and holed, hadn't been repaired for weeks. Fractures that would later give him the excuse to take the cart to the village in the evening, ostensibly to buy resin and hide glue for the repairs, in reality to get drunk and play cards.

Chai's most affectionate memories were for his dog, Dang. Rescued from a blacksmith in Chiang Khan who was about to drown the troublesome litter in a well, Dang was exchanged for less than a coconut. When Chai had left home for the war the fluffy, playful, red and white Bangkaew was still a clumsy, mischievous puppy. Now, seeing Dang in his mind's eye running loose on the banks of the river, frightening dragonflies and wagtails out of the long reed grass, the dog, grown tall, lean and proud, had lost his long baby fur and short, stubby legs and for the insects and wildlife was now a force to be reckoned with.

The third face to emerge from this spinning kaleidoscope of light was a surprise. It was Woot; an odd choice for a closing curtain finale. He hadn't seen the boy since they were teenagers at school, where as best friends they swore never to be parted. Smart, sporting and athletic, the two were looked on in awe by their lesser classmates, envious and aggrieved at the favours and privileges afforded them by their doting headmaster. No one dared complain when they jumped queues, stole sweets from the charity jar or dodged compulsory latrine cleaning.

Once, on the way back from lessons, they had sneaked around the back of the gym to spy on the girls' changing rooms. They were caught and chased by the janitor across the rice fields. Woot, the faster runner, escaped, leaving Chai to take the punishment; six strikes with a cane. Although everyone knew Woot was equally guilty, his 'great escape' became legendary, his prowess at running enough to see him rewarded by the headmaster to a position as headboy.

When a visiting prince came to the area on a tour of the provinces, Woot was chosen to stand in the receiving line to present flowers and a gilded inscription. Impressed by the standards of the school and the ability of the boys, the prince had offered a prize of a scholarship to the Royal Military Academy in Lopburi. In the exams for algebra, geography and history, everyone expected Woot to effortlessly surpass them all and be chosen. A paper banner, strung between classrooms, already proclaimed this success. Two weeks later, after the final papers had been marked and returned by the Academy, the results were announced. All were stunned when Chai's name topped the list.

For Chai the first six months at the spartan military barracks were miserable. As the only one from the 'backward' provinces, he received a sharp education into the ways of the underdog, spurned and ignored at the bottom of the pack. Mocked and bullied by the wealthier boys from Bangkok (he only possessed one worn set of clothes and shoes), Chai grew homesick, missing his family and friends. Three times he wrote to Woot, but received no answer. A rejection that hurt more than the battering and abuse from his older tormentors.

Chai persevered. When he returned to Pakchom at the end of the year proud in his uniform, Woot's house was the first place he called at. His mother said his erstwhile friend was out. Returning the next day with presents and Chinese New Year Moon cakes, Chai still found the door barred. It was only after he had paid a visit to his old school that he learned the real truth. Unable to live with his failure, Woot had lied to his family and friends. Packing his bags a day after Chai had left, Woot pretended that he too had been offered a scholarship and took the cart to the station. After four months of uncertainty, an uncle was sent to search distant Khon Kaen. He was unsuccessful. As were two other expeditions to towns further out. Since then no one had heard from him.

As Woot's sad, pale portrait receded into the dark, something more fantastical replaced it; a face so vast that it appeared to fill his entire field of vision and consciousness: the face of a girl, her features still, expressionless and beautiful.

But it was to the eyes that Chai was drawn; the irises pale-blue, radiant and enchanting. Straw coloured hair drifted over her shoulders. Mixed within the golden strands, small luminescence sparks of light swam between the flowing curls. Suddenly the face lost its composure and serenity. With her mouth wide open, the girl took on a twisted, grotesque appearance, screaming as if to a child as if to idiot, "NOOOAHH".

The ferocity of the image startled Chai. Suddenly he wasn't so sure about dying. Instinctively his legs kicked out, as his arms and hands fought against the dull draw of the deep.

Deliverance came from an unlikely source. A hand reached down into the depths and finding Chai's hair, roughly hauled him from the sea. He fell onto the boards of a small dingy. Water, gushing from his lungs, mixed with the residue of a half digested beef sandwich; his last meal on the now departed Lancaster.

The beaming face towering over him, his arm thumping Chai's back, was Singh. The towering Pashtuni, a born swimmer and chosen child of three faiths, had been his saviour.

Part 2

Chapter 4
FRANCE – June 1918

Six Thai faces pressed into the frame, proud in military uniforms and caps, huddled around a ship's bell, its brass face inscribed with the title, *Aeneas*. As the smoke from the magnesium flare cleared, the pretence evaporated. Three broke from the line, staggered to the railings and threw up over the side.

The two months on the troopship had been an ordeal. The small Siamese contingent, having joined the ship in Ceylon, had had to carve out space already occupied by more than two thousand Commonwealth soldiers and officers reluctant to cede space to the timid newcomers. The conditions were tough. Their deck had a single washroom with just five basins and four toilets that from overuse were constantly soiled or blocked. To avoid long queues it was essential to have completed one's ablutions at least an hour before dawn.

Escaping the exercise drills and wrestling matches of the boisterous New Zealanders and Australians, the Siamese had managed to secure a small sanctuary below the quarterdeck in the shadow of the lifeboat davits. There was a reason it was uncrowded. In headwinds, steam from the funnels often layered them in soot. With rains, water, cascading off the lifeboat covers, was like being drenched by a waterfall. Noticing their plight, an Indian sepoy of the Queen Victoria's Engineers Regiment had negotiated with the captain on their behalf and built out a wooden frame with a canvas awning, beneath which they could shelter from the weather and cook rice. Grateful for his intervention, they invited him to share their meals.

Refuelling at a coaling station in Alexandria, the *Aeneas* crossed to Malta, then north to Sicily and the Straits of Messina. Stromboli passed on the port side, dense clouds of smoke by day, a deep, unsettling glow at night.

The bad weather hit west of the Aeolian Islands midway across the Mediterranean. Although the convoy and its escort of Japanese destroyers had been able to shelter in Naples during the worst of the storms, the last leg to Marseille had been rough, exacerbated by the icy Atlantic winds. Each time their ship rolled between alternate crests and troughs, the engines roared, the vibration from the struggling propellers rattling every timber on deck. Prone to seasickness, none of the Thai ate, their misery made worse by the sight of the spirited Australians still running marathons down the covered promenades, despite the slippery boards and the force of the gales.

Nights brought little reprieve. Huddled together in their cramped quarters, they could hear drinking and gambling from the quarterdeck just six feet above. The Antipodeans, lazing on their backs on the starboard bow of the ship, liked to smoke and shoot guns. Hapless gulls that strayed across the face of the moon - their bullseye in the sky - became victims of late night target practice; one blood splattered carcass falling between the Thai beds.

Siting land, the pale limestone peaks of Mt Faron above the port of Toulon, the small Siamese Company were relieved an end was in reach. By the time they had reached Marseilles late at night, their bags and equipment were already packed, anxious to be first in line to disembark.

Dawn brought a shock, the dark receding to reveal the jagged outline of funnels, masts and rigging against a dull, lead sky. This dense armada of ships, battle cruisers, light corvettes, supply vessels and troopships like their own, all converged on the narrow harbour entrance.

With winds punching in from the west and white foam cresting the waves, the *Aeneas* steamed into port. Rolling through the churned up waters, tug boats and fishing skiffs weaved by on both sides. A dredging boat passed dangerously close to their stern, sea water lapping over its cluttered deck, its captain oblivious at the wheel, black from grease and coal.

As the ship edged into its berth and tied up, the Siamese company massed at the guardrail, nervous and filled with unease as they looked down on a dockside teaming with soldiers, dockworkers and ship crew. Fighting through this melée of men, horse-drawn carts, piled high with crates and barrels, moved between the ships and the wharf buildings.

Above the howl of ship's sirens and winches the order they waited for finally came through. Shuffling down the steel steps to their disembarkation point, the Captain of Siam's first Expeditionary Force, the fifty-seven-year-old, Sumet Chantrawong, had envisaged an orderly, disciplined file of men and equipment, himself at the front. He had wanted it to look neat and dignified. The night before he had told his deputy, Chai Khomsiri, to order the men to polish their buttons and buckles and tie Siamese flags to their backpacks. In the end it turned into a mad, desperate scramble, the gangway steps slippery with salt spray and clogged with cases and bags. From the lower decks, three further columns of men all pressed together at the same narrow exit gate, all fighting to be first off the ramp.

Pushed and shoved by larger and stronger, the Siamese found themselves separated. The Captain, seeing his original plan unravelling, shouted out to Chai and his two companions, the twins, Mae and Manit, already mid-way down the gangway, "Find the equipment and cases. Wait near the dock. We'll follow on," his last words lost in the clamour of voices, engines and gulls.

Sandwiched within the crush, Chai and a handful of men made it to the bottom of the ramp, the feel of firm, unyielding ground beneath their feet, both disconcerting and a relief after so many weeks at sea. They had little time to collect themselves. More soldiers poured off the ship, pushing into their backs and propelling them forward into the dense crowd. Chai had to grab the shoulders of his men in front to prevent them being swept away by the swathes of soldiers, bags and dockworkers.

Reversing back to the *Aeneas*, they found a low wall of crates behind which they could organise themselves. Piling up their cases at the centre of this refuge, they were anxiously watching the gangway ramp for signs of the main company, when a piercing whistle sounded, its pitch so deafening it rattled their ear drums.

"Sortez de là, imbeciles!" screamed a burly harbour master, his short arms pointing skywards, "Sortez!"

Moving their cases away they were lucky to heed the warning in time. A platform of crates flew in low over their heads and thumping to the ground, shattered the paving stones.

Chastened by this narrow escape, Chai shifted his men and equipment a greater distance. They found cover in the shadow of an abandoned warehouse, the interior musky with the stench of pilchards and tar. Tired and stressed by the turmoil on the docks, they huddled together on packing cases at the back of the shelter. Manit and Mae shared out some boiled eggs and a handful of biscuits they had saved from the ship's canteen.

"Stay with the bags," said Chai, "I'm going back to the ship to try and find the Captain."

They weren't happy with this, "What if we get pushed out?"

"I'll be back in five minutes," Chai replied, wanting to appear assertive but equally worried they were right and he'd loose them.

"And if you don't come back, what then?"

"Like I said! You stay put and wait," reiterated Chai, irritated by their doubts.

Chai pushed back through the crowds to the quayside. He emerged two berths down from the *Aeneas* where a much larger vessel, the twin funnelled *Orvieto* from Melbourne was being unloaded. Cranes on the dockside were lifting horses from the hold, their gangly legs getting caught in the rigging. Urgent voices yelled up from the landing stage to haul the animals higher, free of the cables.

Further down the harbour front the roar of engines turned Chai's attention skyward. Rising above the bank of dock cranes an extraordinary flying boat appeared, the grace of its wings and tailplane amazing him. The craft, banking to the right, swung so close to the ships masts and the front line of the docks that Chai could see its pilot, light reflecting off his goggles, striped scarf blowing in the wind, a hairy Alsatian dog his unlikely companion in the cockpit seat next to him.

Taking in these scenes, Chai was both enthralled and overwhelmed. Every detail of the operation, from the size of cranes and winches, ropes and chains, was of a scale and calibre that suggested a race of giants.

Humble Nah Dok in Sing Buri Province had been Chai's setting off point. Saying goodbye to his parents, he had caught a lift on a rice barge pulled down river by bullocks. At night he had laid out on the teak deck, struggling to read a French translation of Hans Delbruck's 'History of Warfare' by a single flickering hurricane light. Midway through the journey the boat had sprung a leak and they'd had to beach on a sandbank to make repairs. Chai was given lodgings in the hut of a local village chief. Over dinner, school children had sung folk songs and performed a candle-lit dance. Despite the crew working through the night, it was a further two days before they could safely continue their voyage. The journey, just ninety-seven miles from the old capital Ayutthaya to Bangkok had taken a week – it seemed primitive indeed.

Stood, as he now was, on the very edge of the new world, this memory only stirred Chai's unease. Intimidated by the industrial might that surrounded him, he felt small and insignificant. Yes they had trained hard, learnt from manuals of modern warfare, strategy and supply – yet past such learnings and months of field exercises and preparation, it was still a mystery why they had travelled half-way around the world to be where they were now. What could they possibly contribute that wasn't already being accomplished by legions of supermen?

A loud blast sounded behind as a second vessel pulled into the landing stage. As ropes played out and gangways were lowered, more pale, anxious faces came to the guard rails and peered down. With the first contingents of men and supplies yet to clear, the dockside was now a single seething sea of humanity. Powerless within this tide of solders and equipment, it was a small miracle that Chai and his men were able to rejoin the rest of the company. Captain Sumet arrived angry and flustered. In their rush to disembark, one of the men had slipped on a rope and dropped a case over the side. Born, the Captain's assistant, had raced to the edge of the dock, but the trunk had sunk before he had been able to find a pole to hook it out from the water. Even worse for Sumet's already fractious temper, fourteen of his men had mistakenly attached themselves to a Gurkha regiment that had marched to the North of the port. It was Chai who eventually found them. Retrieving bags that were about to be loaded onto trucks, he dragged the men back to rejoin the main company.

By the time they had regrouped it was already late afternoon. The mist turned into a fine drizzle, the particles forming like a viscous film, soft and clammy over their faces and clothes.

Dragging their kit bags and equipment across the scuffed cobbles, they were directed to Porte 14 in front of the processing halls. The queue they joined was long and moved at a sluggish pace. Hungry, hot and bad-tempered, it took a further three hours of defensive pushing and shoving to reach the top of the line.

The official seated behind the glass partition was filling in numbers in a ledger and looked surprise when Chai stepped up to the window.

"Vous êtes dans la mauvaise file, the wrong line", he muttered, pointing dismissively to the adjacent hall, where an even longer line wound back through the hall behind the harbour front warehouses.

"No," asserted Chai patiently, "We were directed here."

"By whom?"

"By the port officials."

"He said Porte 14?"

"Yes."

"Alors, your papers. Where are your papers," he asked, cross that Chai had had the affront to question him.

Chai passed a file of documents through a slit in the glass. Anticipating this moment, pre-warned of fastidiousness, fussy bureaucrats, he'd been meticulous. For four evenings before reaching Marseilles, Chai had been up late carefully filling in the forms with the correct names, ages and information; there wasn't a mistake to be found. A precision that was both impressive and mildly irritating to the official whose sole satisfaction in life was prising out error, however small and insignificant.

But Chai's modest victory was brief. Although the papers couldn't be faulted, a more fundamental problem was unearthed. Every new arrival in the city had to be notified with the port authorities in advance. A fresh ledger was made up every night and distributed to the relevant gates. And their names weren't on this all important, authoritative list.

"What's the delay now?" whispered the Captain into Chai's ear.

"He can't find our names," replied Chai.

Chai lent back to the glass, "Monsieur, is that a problem?"

"Of course it's a problem. A big problem. If your names are not on the list you cannot enter," he shrugged, as if explaining elementary maths.

"But you have our papers. For two hundred men. They're standing in line behind me. What more do you need?"

"I am afraid it is not enough. If your names are not on the register, the rules are clear, you cannot legally progress. There is nothing I can do," he concluded, blandly re-rolling the document.

Overhearing this exchange the Captain pushed brusquely past Chai and bending to the window, knocked the glass, astonishing the clerk behind the screen.

"We've waited more than five hours," he snapped.

"Yes."

"This is impossible. How much longer is this going on!"

"How long?", the man replied, looking bewildered; such insolence rare from a 'foreigner'.

"As we have already explained..."

"I'm sorry. But I find that explanation unacceptable..."

At this point the Captain's boot slipped and kicked the partition board. A clumsy mistake it sounded intentional and made the clerk jump.

"Totally unacceptable," Sumet continued, "I wish to speak with your superior."

"Superior?"

"Yes, who ever is in charge."

"I assure you that's not necessary..."

"I assure you it is."

"For what reason, may I ask?"

"So that we might have the opportunity to explain our situation clearly without prejudice," replied the Captain acerbically.

"I see," replied the official, scrupulously peering at Sumet over the rim of his glasses, "I will see if Commander Reynard is available."

The junior official got up from the desk and left the hall. Sumet and Chai waited. Five minutes later the clerk reappeared with a fat, bearded officer, his face drawn and tired like a mule. Eying the two 'suspects' suspiciously from under bushy, grey eyebrows, Reynard approached the front desk. His attention was directed to the manifest of names and the folder of papers.

The Captain and Chai weren't party to the conversation behind the screen, but the Commander's brief glances through the glass looked neither intelligent or sympathetic. More than their troublesome, unpronounceable names, he was sceptical of their origins. Used to dealing with North African and sub-Saharan nationalities and places – thousands streamed through every day – he was ignorant of anything beyond the Sinai peninsula. If this claimed kingdom, 'Siam', was East of Turkey, didn't that place the country on the fringes of the Levant, a territory suspiciously close to their enemy, the Arabian Ottomans?

Once again the papers were folded away. Outwardly the Commander was reassuring and placating, "Oui, nous connaissons bien votre pays, mais nous avons juste quelques points à verifier, patience s'il vous plaît..."

Reynard left with a benevolent smile on his face and a brief wave of his hand, as if seeing off tiresome relatives; a thin pretence that left his face as soon as he was out of their sight. Calls were made to the Port authorities and to military officials in Lyon. The answers came back negative. No one had any knowledge or recall of the so called 'Siamese' Company.

The Captain, still aglow with the delusion that his intervention was having a positive effect, was insensitive to the subtle change in tone. Outwardly nothing appeared out of the ordinary; straight-laced secretaries still hammered out reports on tall typewriters, clerks stamped stacks of freshly processed documents and accountants cranked through calculations on ancient arthmometres. But behind the scenes machinations were quickly turning against the unsuspecting Thai company.

A distant whistle sounded; shrill, urgent, reverberating from the back of the hall. It should have given Sumet his first warning that events had turned sour. Too late he recalled a document from the French Legation that proved a direct connection with General Dubail's office at the Foreign Ministry in Paris. He had kept it safely concealed within a secret compartment in the base of his case. He remembered seeing it when he was repacking his belongings on the last night on the *Aeneas*. Stupidly, because of their panicked disembarkation, the case had been mixed with the rest of the bags. If he could retrieve it and the letter inside, it would prove the veracity of their story and they could be out of the way of these fools.

Sumet turned to the window and rapped the glass urgently.

"Excuse me!", he shouted to get the official's attention, "Tell the Commander..."

"Reynard," prompted Chai.

"Tell Commander Reynard, I have the documents. They're in my case. Do you hear me? They're in my case!"

The clerk, pretending to ignore him, returned to his desk tasks.

Sumet, enraged by this slight, thumped the glass harder shaking the frame. "Did you understand me! I have the papers!"

Still there was no response from behind the screen.

The Captain was on the verge of punching the screen, when Chai, stepping forward, took his arm and attempted to steer him from the window.

"Captain," he began, "shouting at these people won't help."

Sumet shook his grasp away, "Believe me, Chai, shouting at these people is the only way to deal with them!" he hissed.

It hadn't been the first time that Chai had been exposed to Sumet's volatile temper. Two days out of Aden, he and the men had witnessed a similar outburst. During one of the Australians' interminable deck games, a soldier had lobbed a tennis ball into their corner, where it had bounced into the cooking pot spraying hot soup into their faces. As they brushed the dried shrimp and sauce from their clothes, everyone had laughed it off treating it as a joke, for it hadn't been the only slight they'd had to endure on the long voyage and it was unlikely to be their last. Indeed, most had returned to their meal, when Chai, looking up, was surprised to see that Sumet was still standing. He had a soup ladle locked in his grasp and was on the verge of making a beeline towards the guilty bowler – a clear twelve inches superior in height – when Chai and Born hastily intervened. Peeling the Captain's fingers from the handle of the spoon, it took more than an hour to fully placate him. Only three weeks into the voyage, it had made Chai apprehensive. If the Captain could get so hot headed over something as trivial as a rounders ball, how would he behave when objects more dangerous than toys were flying around.

Sumet turned from the window and shouted for Born, "Born, find my trunk. Bring it to me now!"

Born, propelled by the urgency in Sumet's voice, rushed back down the line to the rest of the company; but he already knew the answer – Sumet's case had been the one that had gone over the side. It was hopeless. The special papers now languished at the bottom of the harbour.

The cramped enclosure was dark, its rough floor bare earth covered with damp straw and sawdust, the stench acrid and putrid. Barbed wire lined the perimeter of the rough wooden stockade. Without seats or benches they stood; a dirty watering trough in the far corner their only concession to luxury.

"They'll pay for this, damn it… Believe me Chai, they'll pay for this…" muttered the Captain under his breath. But even as he said it, the threat felt hollow and futile. Armed guards locked the gates and took up positions on both sides of the gate.

It was dark by the time the Siamese Company were released. No explanation was given. The guards simply unlocked the gates and melted away. At such a late hour the trains to the staging camps at

Frejus and Toulon were no longer running. They were advised to find lodgings to the west of the port.

A Customs Officer, having witnessed the whole shameful debacle and embarrassed by their treatment at the hands of the pedantic officials, offered to help. He would make some calls. For the lower ranks he knew of a garrison on the edge of the city that would take them in; five centimes a head though without mattresses, bedding or meals. Buses could be organised to take the men and their bags to the outskirts; the last kilometre they could walk. For Chai, Captain Sumet, the two twins and Born, he knew of a small family hotel close to the port.

"Alors, que dites-vous?", said the smiling man extending a hand.

The Captain, still rattled by the ignominy of their internment – his clothes reeking of sheeps piss and dung – hesitantly returned the greeting. The man, jovial and rosy cheeked, appeared genuine enough, yet he could not help but be suspicious. Marseilles might be the imperial gateway to the South, but besides the fools and incompetents they had already encountered, it was also a haunt of villainous rogues and thieves. What if the man was of such a breed? What if he led them down some dark alley, had them beaten and set upon by convicts and prostitutes? Robbed and assaulted before they'd even left the harbour – the idea made him squirm; a fitting end to a day of astonishing reversals and misfortune.

Plagued by these doubts, Sumet thought through his limited options. If they refused, apart from insulting a man who was, perhaps, genuinely trying to help them, they'd lose all hope of finding a bed for the night. For his men, sleeping rough on the streets was hardly an auspicious start to their first experience of 'civilised' France. Their arrest had been mortifying enough. Penned up inside an enclosure that was clearly designed to quarantine cattle, they'd been the brunt of jokes from the North Africans, Indians and Australians streaming by to the exit. "Baaah baah, oink, oink," they'd chorused, pinching their noses as they passed.

What perplexed Sumet most, infuriated him even, was that leaving Bangkok he'd been assured by the foreign office that they'd be met. There was talk of a staff car, an official delegation from Paris, hopes of drinks and a hot meal. General Chalerm's boasts had gone further; knowing of a motion picture studio in Cimiez, near Nice, he had promised a recording of their glorious disembarkation on film.

In retrospect Sumet was relieved the cinematographer hadn't turned up. He would likely have recorded one of the most humiliating events ever in Siam's modest history; second only to General Voradet's ignominy when he'd presented two war elephants to an American Ambassador, only for one animal to break wind with such ferocity as to overturn tables, frightening the ladies back to their carriages.

Chapter 5

The directions seemed straightforward enough: customs hall, columned facade, walled garden with wrought iron gates and a stone statue of a saint with a broken nose. Repeated four times, the harbour master embellished these brief instructions with a simple flourish of his hand as if it were child's play. But it still wasn't easy finding the Estelle Hostel in the winding backstreets and dark alleys of the old city.

The first landmarks, the customs house and the music hall, came up as predicted. It was the turning after the noseless saint where they all went wrong. Outside a bar, so mean and small its only opening was a serving hatch punched through bricks to the street, a crowd of dockworkers and labourers had overflowed into the road. An argument had broken out over payment and angry voices echoed from the alley. A bottle was thrown, the projectile breaking against a wall close to the Thai. Captain Sumet, thinking them drunk and suspecting that the seemingly benign harbour master might secretly be delivering them into the clutches of thieves, abruptly changed direction.

"We'll try further up the hill," he declared.

"You don't think we should stop and ask directions?" suggested Chai innocently.

"From these inebriates? Are you mad? said the Captain kicking a shard of glass back to the gutter.

'Of course, by all means try your French on them,' Sumet continued, "but it's likely the only answer you'll get will be a fist in your face."

Abandoning their original course the Captain marched them higher up the hill and decided on a second turning from where he hoped to double back. But the turning didn't double back. Instead the circuitous route led them deeper into a seedy labyrinth of unlit backstreets and tunnels that ended abruptly at the entrance to an underground coal bunker. The only way out was a winding cobbled staircase, its narrow steps steep, slippery with lignite dust and lively with rats. It took a further hour of painful trunk hauling to reverse back and finally return to their original, instructed route; by which time even the drunks had gone.

They walked by the entrance twice. It was only by chance that Mae and Manit, nervously watching the upper floors for residents emptying pails of soiled water into the gutters, looked up and noticed the faded wooden sign swinging from a chain. Unhelpfully cast into shadow by a flickering gas lamp, the carved name plate for the Estelle was missing its capital letter; a crucial misspelling that had wrong-footed them earlier.

Thin, built over five floors, its crumbling neo-classical facade was streaked black from age and harsh weather.

Taking in the cracked plaster and blistered peeling shutters, Captain Sumet looked discomforted. He wasn't expecting grand Fin de Siecle lobbies and supercilious bell boys, but in his mind he had pictured clean towels, hot water and a modest bath.

"This is it?", asked Sumet hesitantly, looking up and down the street a second time in the hope that a more elegant entrance had escaped them.

Chai stepped forward to the door.

"This is really it", Sumet repeated in disbelief as if beseeching Chai to disabuse him and serve up an alternative.

"Not only is this the only Estelle on the street, it's the only hotel," answered Chai, too tired to prevaricate and reaching for the door handle. He pushed it open. Loud raucous laughter, like water bursting from a sluice gate, broke from inside. Sumet inwardly shuddered.

Parting velour curtains that hung over the door, they stepped into a crowded dark panelled entrance hall, thick with tobacco smoke and fumes from a fire, the density of which seemed to swirl at head height filling their nostrils. Under the flicker of lamps that hung from oak beams, they could make out the walls, their faded floral wallpaper patched over with crumbling, yellowed newsprint. The furniture was crude and drab. Mismatched chairs and low stools surrounded a circular dining table where a group of sullen faces hung hunched over a card game. A decrepit sofa had a rug thrown over its cushions to hide its threadbare seat. On the far wall, an oversized oil painting was crushed above the fireplace, now so smothered with soot it was difficult to read. Under this grime of ages hid the ghostlike figures of Napoleon and his loyal generals, stepping ashore from a boat to the cheers of flag-waving locals. Lurking in the background a ship anchored in the bay, bright tricolour flying from its stern. That part was clearer. A seafarer must have scrubbed the dirty varnish with his sleeve.

Unsettled by these sights, the Thai dragged their bags in from the street, shuffling uneasily to find space in a hallway already stacked with trunks and kit bags from more recent arrivals. Cutting a path through the cases, Chai led the way across the room, skirting the card table where faces looked up as they passed. One took a deep drag on his hand rolled cheroot and puffed a column of smoke in their path. The Captain, lifting his handkerchief to his nose, choked. Mocking laughter broke out.

Backing to the wall to allow others past, Chai took his turn at the desk, where nine people were already waiting in the queue in front of them. An empty key cabinet behind the main counter, didn't look hopeful. Chai, already daunted by the futility of making a request in the light of so many being turned away, was further intimidated by the woman managing the counter. She looked young, assertive and resolute. Her rejection, though polite, wasn't long in coming.

"Je suis vraiment désolée, mais nous sommes…" she began.

And that was it. Sumet, hearing enough, turned his tired and dejected team around, "just as I thought, a complete waste of time, we should never have listened to the fraud…"

Chai stalled him. He'd remembered the Customs Officer's name, "Philippe, Philippe Pruwer nous a envoyé."

"Monsieur Philippe Antoine Pruwer," questioned the manageress, taking in the motley group with a greater, more sympathetic interest.

Chai, who hadn't picked up the second part of his name, nodded.

The manageress's demeanour, previously stern, lifted.

"We are always, always busy,", explained the woman with a smile, "But for friends of Philippe we will try to find something."

Philippe Pruwer had married an Estelle, a close cousin to Marie Pascal, the thirty-five year old who had taken over the running of the forty room hotel. Originally opened in the 1870's when France's imperialist Third Republic had first made moves on North Africa, the hotel was a base for merchants, administrators and Legionaries making the short sea voyage across the Mediterranean to Algeria, Morocco and Sub-Saharan Africa. Near to the harbour (if people paid proper heed to advice), it was now a convenient shuttle stop for officers and men before making the journey to the training camps in Auvergne and Provence. And after three years of war, its rooms had been filled to capacity, bringing Marie a small profit.

The Estelle had been left to Marie by her late father, Henri Pascal. A Belgian corporal in the Army of Chalons during the Franco-Prussian war, Pascal had resigned his commission to migrate south to open his hotel and brasserie. Seeing his country threatened by the same hated adversaries forty three years later, Henri had been one of the first to head north to offer his services. Although his early letters from the front had asked for fresh socks and clean underpants and complained about the insipid food and watered down wine, its brevity couldn't conceal his patriotic glee to be back in the ranks, fighting for a just and moral cause. Stirred by nationalist headlines, those in his corps lusted to avenge the humiliating loss of Alsace and Lorraine and 'finir les affaires non terminees'.

The siege of Leige was both the first battle and the first defeat for Belgium and her Allies. Henri Pascal's body was one of a thousand casualties so macerated by the big 17-inch German howitzers that had pounded the walls of the Fort of Ponisse, they were unidentifiable.

A bell was rung to call for assistance. An old Basque retainer came down from the first floor to help with the bags, but was already wheezing and fighting for breath before reaching the first landing. Chai, feeling sorry for the stumbling servant, took his own bags.

"In these difficult times," whispered Marie Pascal with a sigh, "it was hard finding staff."

Crossing the hall they paused in front of a rounded alcove. The Manageress pointed out a photograph of her late father, encased in an ornate silver frame at the centre of a glass cabinet, shined-up like a shrine. Taken outside the hotel on a bench in the street before he had left for his war, Pascal had a glass of Bordeaux in one hand, the other raised in salute. The sun was bright, the shadow of his cap came down low over his face, where only his eyes were apparent, gleaming with undisguised, impish pride. Despite his tight blue grey woollen tunic, gold braided collar, polished decorations and a proud ceremonial sword at his side, Pascal's portly appearance spoke more hotelier than warrior; the well picked back-bone of a grilled dorade, scattered langoustine shells and sliced lemons, a more fitting memorial to his life than his blunt sabre.

The route to the annex wound through a set of confused passageways. At the end of a dim corridor, steep steps climbed to a fifth floor. Marie Pascal, ahead of them with a hurricane light, warned them to be careful. Three treads near the top were rotten, in places cracked. Woodworm was the cause. The larvae had gorged on the damp timbers, the leak from a shattered tile in the roof gully three feet above. A suppurating stain in the cracked plaster revealed where rain water still dripped to the floor; yet another job awaiting the return of more competent repair men.

At the top of the stairs, Marie Pascal opened a small door into a low attic room. The scent of decay was in turn displaced by deeper, more masculine odours. It had never occurred to them that they would be sharing. Chai, so relieved to have secured the unlikely room in the first place, had been inattentive to the word 'partager'.

Those sharers were laid out on lumpen mattresses near the windows. One man near to the door, was in the process of removing his boots.

His duffel bag was opened at the base of the bed, its belongings, worn socks, vests and shirts, tossed absent-mindedly over the oak boards. A loaf of bread, (the remains of their lunch), sat on a stool, blunt knife embedded in its side where huge chunks had been pulled away by hand, littering the floor with stale crumbs.

Startled by the new arrivals, the man with the boots turned to the door, his appearance so unsettling as to stall them all in the thin doorway. Uneven tuffs of hair, less than a beard, marked a craggy uneven face. On his forehead, a deep scar ran down to his brow. Having just gorged on sticky dates and apricots, he wiped his fingers on his bulbous cotton trousers, then held out his hand in European greeting.

"Mamet," he said, his broad smile exposing black rotten teeth and chapped lips.

The Captain, at the front, flinched. It was left to Chai to shake hands.

Chapter 6

Captain Sumet slept badly. Without the familiar rocking of waves, the comforting thump of boots on steel staircases and the echo of bawdy anthems long into the night, the unnatural calm and quiet had disturbed him, making his sleep fitful.

He'd had the best bed; a real spring mattress with sheets and a pillow, unlike the thin horse hair mats covered in worn sacking that barely filled the sides of the mean wooden bunks. But the stomach complaint he'd caught at sea had got worse and he woke with piercing cramps in his side. Glancing up at the small antic window, he could see sunlight breaking through cloud beyond the rooftops. A pigeon, sooty grey, red eyed, plump, sat on the window ledge pecking excitedly at the stale loaf of bread thrown out by the Algerians, now softened by dew.

Smoothing down his hair Sumet sat up and took in the room. It looked even more run down and mean in the daylight. Across from him he could make out the sleeping forms of his three companions, together with the Algerians who'd hogged the prime space under the window. Mamet, his under shirt so loose that his belly protruded from under his blanket, looked particularly offensive. Deep in sleep, their combined breathing produced an uneven rumble, making the air feel stale, depleted of oxygen.

Needing an escape, Sumet reached for his clothes folded over a chair, pulled on his trousers and jacket and tip-toed to the door.

The landing outside was still dark. Sumet, feeling for the wall, felt soapy water seep through the holes in his socks. It dawned on him that somewhere around his feet on the floor, a cleaning maid was scrubbing the boards. As his eyes adjusted to the dim light he could make out the fringes of her collar and the white cuff of a sleeve as her hand reached out to snatch back her water bucket, afraid he would kick it.

"Pardon, pardon, madame," he whispered as he edged tentatively forward, feet fumbling for the edge of the stairs, the scent of rot a reminder that he was close to the cracked steps near the top.

Gripping the bannister rail, Sumet headed down. He was half way along the first flight, when a shape bunched up on a step caught his toe making him stumble, the jolt so unexpected it nearly pitched him head first down the stairs. A gruff voice shouted out, "Tête de noeud!" as Sumet's boot grazed his face. Something sharp and round ricocheted down the risers and hit an alcove below. There was a tinkle of glass. It turned out to be Pascal's shrine. Sumet glanced nervously at the cabinet as he passed, worried it was damaged. Ten treads further down a glistening object on the carpet explained the man's outburst; Sumet had kicked his false teeth out.

Reaching the ground floor, Sumet, hoping for a clean run to the door, was taken aback by more disquieting scenes in the hall. Judging by the broken chairs and stools, there had been a fight. A vase, that the night before had impressed with its intricate symmetry, had fallen and broken. Sumet could feel the fragments of broken ceramic crunch beneath his soles.

Incredibly, considering the early hour, a handful of players remained at the table, their heads now so low they were inches from grazing the felt. Locked in their dull gaze, their last frayed cards seemed glued to their hands. Sumet, fearful of disturbing them, tried sneaking around the back of their chairs. A careless foot caught the neck of a bottle hidden under the table, sending it spinning across the stone slabs where it shattered against the fireplace.

"Silence! Nous sommes toujours en train de jouer", growled the card players.

Stepping out of the suffocating interior, Sumet was relieved to be out in the open. The sun was warm. Church bells rang in a distant tower beyond the rooftops. In an adjacent alley a cart was parked up, as workmen rolled milk churns and barrels onto its rear platform. Unhitched from its harness, a horse was on the sidewalk grazing on the uncut grass. Three messy boys rushed by, fighting over a rope. A little girl at the back, racing to catch up, cast Sumet a quizzical look as she passed.

Walking away from the hotel, Sumet started down the hill in the direction of the port. A staff car roared up the incline, regimental flags fluttering from stalks on its fenders. Two motorcycle outriders were close behind, their faces hidden beneath leather helmets and goggles, engine exhaust leaving a trail of thick white smoke in their wake.

Between the rooftops a view opened to the harbour, lined with new ships and arrivals. The Captain, seeing the dockside filling with fresh troops, shuddered; the ignominy of their own treatment in the processing halls as unshakable as the acrid scent of excrement that still lingered on his clothes.

Steering clear of the port, Sumet turned off the main road. A side street led to a secluded square shaded by chestnut trees. A café, Le Séjour, was just opening its shutters. Finding a table in the open, Sumet sat down and picked up a menu card. A waiter approached. Ordering a cup of coffee and a roll, Sumet looked out over the empty tables and chairs and contemplated how he'd got there.

He hadn't been the first choice for command. Thamot has got more votes. English educated, a captain in the Cavalry and a fine cricketeer (he had fielded a winning team against British Embassy staff on Queen Victoria's birthday), he was better qualified and popular with ministers. But Thamot, courting a lucrative governorship in the provinces, had declined.

A second choice, Nikom, a commander of the Royal Engineers, had fought with distinction in a minor border clash against the Cambodians in 1897. But approaching sixty, balding, corpulent and choleric, he was deemed too old and frail for the physical demands of the European theatre. Brat Komchai, a young officer in the Guards, bold, dashing, adventurous, fluent in both French and Russian, appeared the perfect candidate. He was hours from being awarded the prestigious commission before court gossip exposed him as a reckless gambler and philanderer. Lewd tales of him making advances on the General's own daughter finally damned his chances for good.

So events contrived that it was Sumet, fourth on the list, who was the one called before the selection committee – a reflection that occasionally rocked his fragile self confidence.

The ten members of the august panel made a lot about serving King and Country. Siam was proud to be fighting for a just and honourable cause, defending the free world against the tyrannical aggressor, hand in hand with the great empires of England, Russia, France and the United States.

If Sumet was to accept the mission he was to command a first contingent of two hundred men. They were to test the waters, size up the situation and report back to the Generals. If their plans went well, Captain Luang Ramarittirong was to follow with a second combat vehicle company and a medical platoon. A Flying Corps, together with a team of mechanics and air-crew, would also be sent. In all Siam would be committing a combined force of over one thousand men.

"This is an unprecedented opportunity to get close to the action", said the War Minister, Chalerm, puffing ostentatiously through a Cuban cigar; a present from the American Legation.

"A chance to learn about modern warfare, guns, tanks, planes and zeppelins. The world is in a state of flux. A new age beckons."

Prone to melodramatics, Chalerm likened it to going to the picture house (he was in fact the owner of one of Siam's first cinema houses in Nakon Kasem). The only difference being that this picture house was just a very long way away – two months at sea and the last scene was yet to be scripted.

"When it's played out," he declared, as if mustering extras on set, "it's essential that Siam figures prominently in the end credits."

The waiter returned with the coffee, a freshly warmed-up roll on a tin dish and a modest teaspoon of damson jam.

Sumet reached for the coffee and over the rim of the cup, scrutinised the faces of those just arriving in the square. Most were local, middle aged or old, somber in dark suits and hats. Taking seats in the sun, they unfolded morning newspapers to catch up with events from the front. Prominent headlines proclaimed outrage over recent German shelling of innocent civilians near Messines – "Les Boches sont des Barbares!"

Watching a young couple hugging and kissing under the trees (yet another fresh-faced recruit tearfully departing for the training camps), Sumet thought of his own wife, Lek, back home in Bangkok. She hadn't wanted him to go. They had just had a child, a boy. Working as a translator at the Royal Pages School near the Palace, Lek was certainly no fool. She had read the foreign papers; *The Times* from London and *The Straits Times* from Singapore and seen the reports and photographs from the war: the Somme, Verdun, Ypres – the loss of life was mindless, incomprehensible. From such madness there could never be victors. What was the point of it all? Why was he going? Thamot had inveigled himself out of it; why couldn't he?

On their last evening together, Sumet, tired with arguing, had patiently explained that their responsibilities were mainly logistics and transport; food, medical supplies and equipment behind the front lines. Boring stuff. In reality, by the time they got there, the war would probably be over, making it unlikely they would ever see action. Stuck with little to do, he'd be more tourist than soldier. He promised to send postcards from Paris; the Eiffel Tower, Notre Dame and the Seine. In the Galeries Lafayette he would buy his small boy a Steiff teddy bear.

Lek wasn't convinced. On the night of Sumet's departure, she had had disturbed dreams and an unsettling omen of misfortune to come. A fracture had opened up in the side of the spirit house. Preparing some mango and pomelo for his voyage, she had found a dead bird in their pantry. Sumet had laughed off her childish superstitions, although loath to admit that his own dreams had been equally dispiriting and bleak.

The sendoff has been a big affair. The King sent his personal guard, members of the elite Wildcat Corps and a military band. A ten-gun salute sounded from the Wichai Prasit Fortress as they weighed anchor. Sumet, standing on the prow, remembered searching the faces in the crowds that lined both banks of the river, unable to find the one face that mattered.

Although the grandeur and pomp of the departure left some cheer, it wasn't long before dull, daily routine set in. With idle days on deck Sumet had written long letters to his wife and son, often with pencil sketches in the margin of the paper, outlining the ports they'd visited along the way – Colombo, Bombay, Aden, Sudan and Alexandria. A more ambitious picture of a monkey riding a camel at the pyramids of Giza he'd coloured with crayons.

He thought he could deal with the long-distance, that the thrill and excitement of his great adventure would stamp out his longings and remorse. But as each day dragged him further away from the small and familiar, the grandeur and scale of alien new worlds, though undoubtedly majestic and impressive, only clouded his melancholia.

To distract himself from these dark moods, Sumet absorbed himself with books and paperwork. On squared paper he drew up an intricate timetable of duties and drills. A star system of rewards was devised for high achievers within his group, the tokens (cork bottle tops), exchangeable for extra biscuits or cigarettes.

In the mess halls below deck, lessons in French and English had been organised by the acting lieutenant for the Commonwealth and foreign troops. Doctors and nurses also gave lectures on health, first aid and the necessary inoculations. In the ballroom of the former cruise ship, a gym was set up. His men, taking to the ropes and vaulting horses, appeared eager and strong. For they had trained well. A month before departure, Sumet himself had overseen military exercises at a camp in Lop Buri north of the capital. A visiting French diplomat had been so impressed by the close formation of their parades he had deemed them more disciplined and fitter than his own countrymen; "Les Allemands devraient être inquiets", he announced as a toast to his hosts at a farewell dinner.

Seventy-five drivers and one hundred and twenty mechanics and assistants were under the Captain's command. To organise his team structure Sumet liked to picture the company as pieces on a chess board. Within those in the centre of his defences, Chai he could clearly rely on. One of the first he had interviewed, his credentials on paper already convinced. But more than the impressive citations from superiors both in the field and high command, including a royal award for gallantry, Chai's qualities were apparent the moment he entered the room. Eager, intelligent and curious, he knew engineering – could work a lathe; logistics – procurement and distribution – and he knew languages – both French and German. As a short test to gauge the aptitude of applicants, Sumet had written out a short list of questions;

1. What was the capital of Austria-Hungary?
2. Who was the Commander of the British Expeditionary Force?
3. How many rounds could a Vickers machine gun fire in a minute?

Vienna, Douglas Haig, 450 rounds per minute – his answers ricocheted back fast and correct; although Chai's additions of muzzle velocity and penetrating power might have gone beyond what one would normally expect, to almost verge on fanaticism.

Whereas other candidates had baulked when they had found out the true nature of their mission (the prospect of the European war enough to instil panic in some), Chai's eyes had gleamed with an incipient glee. And he hadn't disappointed. His aptitude and discipline had been further demonstrated during the voyage. The conditions after Naples had been appalling. Force-nine gales, twenty-foot waves and the constant threat of German 'wolfpack' attack had seen most retreat to their quarters. Chai had been the one lifting the morale of the men and mediating with the often obstructive and obstreperous crew for more bedding and blankets. Sumet would have been lost without him.

The two twins, Mae and Manit, were also solid, loyal and biddable; nephews of a close uncle, he had known them for years. At eighteen he had taken them hiking to Phu Kradueng, one of Siam's highest mountain ranges. The track to the top was a twelve-kilometre climb through dense rain forest and bamboo. Caught in a torrential thunderstorm at the top, it has been a terrible night. Lighting had struck a tent pole, scorching the flimsy canvas of their tent. With their shelter wrecked beyond repair, the twins had descended down through the jungle in the dark to search for materials to fix the tear. Returning with cut stakes and palm fronds they were able to patch together the branches and supports into a passable cover to keep them dry until morning, when the rain finally stopped.

Shifting perspective to review his forward row 'pawns', Sumet was also confident with his choices. Wrun, Lek and Dee all possessed competencies he could depend on and build up. He had a strongman, Darn, who reputably had the strength to lift the back of a truck, a sound clerk with Worarat and scores of well-trained technicians and engineers. Indeed, within this top team, there remained just one niggling doubt – Born. Young, capricious, often sulky, he'd been a concern right from the start. No one could discern whether his moods were simply down to hunger (he refused to touch European stodge), or because he harboured darker, more impenetrable secrets. Unusually, the young man from Trat hadn't strictly volunteered. Colour blind, he'd been confused by the selection process. Unaware of his choice, he was added to the company just two days before they were expected to set sail, due to last minute defections. The Captain wasn't even informed he'd been included.

At sea after Aden, when the hot nights had made it impossible to sleep, the men had got listless. Sumet had called Chai to organise a play to alleviate their boredom. Together they chose an episode from the classic Siamese drama, the *Ramakien*. Their friendly Indian sepoy, Krishnan, knowing the narrative from Hindu mythology had painted a vivid, fiery backdrop on a canvas taupaulin. Born, sitting alone, legs over the side of the bow, was the only one not to take part. In the end Krishnan stepped in to take on the leading role as the monkey god, Hanuman. Donning a mask made from old sardine cases and with a frayed rope as a tail, his magical performance drew such accolades from the bawdy, drunken audience, they were asked to perform a gala night in front of the ship's captain and crew. In this more ambitious finale, staged under the arc lights on the stern deck, Born was reluctantly press ganged into a part as a goat, his grey bed blanket his only concession to costume.

Chapter 7

The big Berber, Mamet, smoked a particularly aggressive cheroot. It was rolled in the Algerian valley of Turkine in the Tell Atlas mountains near his home, where the family grew the tobacco, together with olives, wheat and cotton. The land hadn't always been fertile. At the time of his grandfather, the terrain, deemed worthless and barren, was a scorpion-infested dustbowl in which nothing grew and few ever visited. A French geologist with the Institut National Geographique, breaking his journey to the West coast of Morocco, had, out of curiosity, drilled a handful of experimental bore holes and chanced on some artesian wells in the bed-rock. Realising how this precious water would radically transform the land and wealth for the valley, the geologist prevaricated and downplayed his discovery. The wells were 'pitifully shallow', he claimed, "likely contaminated with methane and unhealthy bacteria". Abruptly changing his plans, the Frenchman had raced back to the land registry office in Algiers, where, knowing the regional director, he secretly planned to procure the valley for himself. Just ten kilometres short of the city he had fallen from his mule and shot himself through the head. The precious map of wells, hidden in the folds of the dead man's jacket, had fortuitously found its way back to Mamet's father.

Mamet's brief family history ended in a puff of smoke; a pall so dense that for seconds it took on the shape of a genie – a fat one that hovered contentedly over the roof beams. As the unsettled Thai absorbed the questionable implications of his tale's finale, the large Algerian stubbed his cigarette out on the floor, wrapped a scarf around his eyes and stretched out on the bunk. Seconds later, as if someone had hit a lamp switch, he was soundly asleep, his loud snores rattling the thin window panes. His companions, following his cue, slumped where they sat. Bassoon and wheezy flute were added to this nasal quartet.

It had taken time for the Siamese to get used to the Algerian's presence. It wasn't just the cavernous scars that were off putting; he was disturbingly ugly – enough to put them off their meals. Initially they had tried to accept his unfortunate appearance as a disfigurement, either from illness or from a knife fight, until they realised that he had been born with his grossly misshapen ears and calloused nose. Yet within this unkind gene mix the Berber had inherited a single positive attribute; he had deep blue eyes that sparkled with a rare, almost childlike vitality, making his personality strangely charismatic; a beguiling, warm glow that penetrated even the densest puff of Turkine tobacco. To the Thais, bored and with little to do, he made an appealing narrator, companion and guide to their first alien city.

The last weekend of August finished with an oppressive heatwave, the temperature soaring to over thirty seven degrees. Opening the windows and doors had little effect. With no breeze to clear the air, the heat and humidity hung over the cramped attic space like a radiating haze, drawing out the cloying stench of sweat, unwashed socks and clothes.

It was the younger of the three Algerians who first noticed the hatch in the roof. Looking to escape the sticky conditions, the men improvised a staircase of boxes and trunks and climbed out onto the roof tiles. Taking with them enough tobacco and dates to last the afternoon, they found a seat in the eaves and looked out over the rooftops towards the sea. Lines of ships fanned out to the key compass points; east to Valletta and Alexandria, west, Gibraltar and Tangier and south to their own homeland, Algiers and Africa.

With fewer bodies left in the room, those left inside had hoped that the conditions might ease, yet with the sun now angled directly through the skylight, the relentless temperature and humidity only climbed. Chai broke first. Peeling himself from his clammy bunk, he walked to the end of the room and stared up at the hatch. Channelled by the roof valley, a breeze flowed through the opening. Lured by this cool stream, Chai's foot lifted unconsciously to the first step.

Sumet, looking up from his book-keeping, checked him, "Do you think that wise?" The Captain, unlike the rest of his team, hadn't fallen so easily under the spell of the large Algerian.

"It's insufferable in here," complained Chai.

"And if you drop over the edge?"

"I'll be grateful for the rush of air in the fall," replied Chai, stepping up and out of the hatch.

Mai and Manit, equally restless, watched him go. The Captain, knowing they were tempted to join his deputy, fixed them with a withering stare, "I wouldn't try it. It's as crowded as a station platform out there."

Despite this reprimand, the two twins nervously edged past Sumet and following Chai's example, scurried up the stack of boxes.

The Algerians, bunching up to make room on the roof, were welcoming. They offered up their sticky dates, a can of salted pilchards and shared a mug of sweet tea. One passed around a small extendable telescope he'd been using to scan the city. Its lens was cracked and it was dented along one side. Embossed in its leather barrel was the emblem of the French Institut Geographique, together with the initials, PJT, lending added piquancy to Mamet's earlier tale.

Training the lens over the harbour side they took in the latest developments. Gantry cranes were lifting crates of poultry and livestock from the holds of two Australian transport ships. Landing on the quayside, goats and sheep were being herded into makeshift pens. Dazed at suddenly being in the open, several made an escape across the crowded landing stage, the screams from dockworkers only panicking them more.

Chewing on his last date, Mamet lit another cigarette and leant back against the roof tiles. He hadn't come to fight. Short sighted and overweight he knew he would never have passed the physical, despite the lax criteria. A month short of forty, he was too old and ugly anyway.

His mission was different. He had come to find his nephew, Rami. The boy, sixteen at the time, had made the mistake of straying too close to the port of Oran on the Algerian coast. Rounded up late at night by the authorities with twelve of his school friends, they had been accused of causing a disturbance and forcibly conscripted. After a months' training marching through the sand dunes of the southern Sahara, they had been shipped to France and the northern town of Arras. Rami's last letter to his parents had been sent from a 5th Army training camp near a town on the Franco-Belgian border. By chance, Mamet and his uncles were in a village cafe reading about the action around Mons, when they received a telegram from the French officials in Algiers. The message, offering their condolences, declared his nephew a casualty; the boy had died bravely in the very first wave of the assault.

The family, knowing not to trust anything from the authorities, especially the military, even less from a General, didn't believe a word of it. Without doubt the French were the most ingenious race on earth; which also made them the world's greatest liars.

Everyone in the family knew that Rami was born lucky; more so than his cousins. He was also protected. His grandfather had given him a charm; a pure white opal from a desert oasis near Ghardaia. Such stones safeguarded the wearer against any danger, natural or man made, that in the modern age included hand-grenades and Maxim machine guns. Mamet's only problem was finding the boy. A small inconvenience, he acknowledged, in a country the size of France where he was a complete outsider and he knew no one of standing or influence. Yet his confidence remained undiminished; the train service was reliable and the proud armies of the Yankees had arrived. As had the Thai, he tactfully added, slapping Chai on his shoulder. And Mamet wasn't the only one to predict that the war would soon be over. Then he would take Rami home. He had already lined him up with work in his father's tobacco factory, either as a truck driver or managing a line of wrapping and packing machines. Mamet had even found him a wife; a cousin from a Zayanes tribe; exceptionally pretty, legendary within her valley, but also domesticated, skilled with tagines, goats and children.

Three blasts on a horn signalled the end of the work shift. The sun, low over the sea, bathed the harbour front in freckles of gold. A last runaway ram was being dragged back across the cobblestones. Even at a distance, his long horns cast fierce satanic shadows across the quayside. As the sun fell ships lights came on, reflecting in the inky waters. Dockworkers streamed out of the harbour gates. A last convoy of trucks crawled up the incline north of the city and headed into the hills.

With the day fading, the attention of Mamet, Chai, Mai and Manit, switched from the port to scenes closer to the hotel. Bars and cafes were opening their doors. In a square nearby a barman was dragging tables and chairs across the courtyard. In a general store, its displays filled with brushes, shaving lotions and soaps, its owner pulled down the shutters and locked up.

But it was an innocuous side street closer to hand and five floors below, that attracted their curiosity. Thin, dark and littered with bins and waste, the alley ended on a single worn, decrepit door. Above this opening hung a weak, flickering lamp.

Deliveries – barrels, bottles and oak casks, brought in on hand-carts – were at the vanguard of sudden activity. As it grew darker, an untidy queue started to form. Judged from their position high on the roof, Mamet suspected black-market goods or illicit alcohol. But the curious mix of people – young, old, tradesmen, labourers, civilian, military, Caucasian, North African – suggested something more covert and clandestine. One man had wrapped a scarf so tightly around his neck he was probably clergy. Another was shod in boots so perfectly polished, he was likely a banker or customs official.

Again the heavy outer door creaked open, emitting a howl like a goose being strangled. The irregular queue shuffled forward. A triangle of light cut through the opening. From inside they could hear the low base rumble of drums from somewhere deep beneath the ground.

Chapter 8

It took Mamet, Chai, the two twins and Born, three nights to summon up enough courage to leave their high perch on the roofline.

The approach to the back alley was around the far side of the Estelle. Initially they went there just to be nosey, hang around, gawp at the faces, perhaps catch a glimpse through the door. But the way into the thin cul-de-sac, shaped like the neck of a bottle, pressed them so tightly together, that by the time they had decided to turn around and reverse, it was too late. Wedged between a group of dockworkers and rowdy Anzac soldiers (possibly the same men they had had to endure on the passage over), they were thrust deeper into the scrum.

"What do we do now?" muttered Chai, straining against the squeeze.

"We'll have to go along with it. See what all the fuss is about," replied Mamet, both uncertain and bemused by their predicament.

"And if they ask us for money?" asked Chai, troubled by Mamet's nonchalance.

"Money? We'll get thrown out way before that," joshed the Algerian.

Borne along through the alley, they were soon at the entrance. A thin, wizened face, appeared at a side window, looked them up and down and nodded to an accomplice. The big oak door ground open to reveal a curious sign, its title, reading "Refection de meubles. Tapissier.", perched over an image of a velour settee, where a redolent toad lay outstretched on the covers with a needle and thread. And as if to add credence to this feint, a stack of worn stools and armchairs, next to an open cabinet studiously arranged with mallets, metal cramps and fabric stretchers, awaited the upholsterer's attention.

Alarmed that they were about to be indoctrinated into some bizarre furniture cult, Mamet and the Thai shuffled down steps into a warren of passageways that appeared to cross under the oak beams of their hostel, where above, Chai sensed, the card sharks still played.

At the end of this subterranean maze, they emerged in a barrel-vaulted hallway. Frayed curtains pulled back to reveal a cavernous, crowded basement, flickering in soft candlelight. An assault of thick, suffocating tobacco smoke, fused with harsher aromas of tar or sealing wax, was overlaid with the scent of an unusually pervasive cologne. Distracted by this olfactory barrage, Chai, Mamet, Born and the twins, were unprepared for the wall of sound that followed.

Music, loud, brash, discordant, echoed from the far end of the space. Three musicians, a violinist, a pianist and a trumpeter, stood bunched together on a raised dais, hot in tight suits and bow ties.

The underground space had originally been used as a wine store. The far wall still held sturdy shelves and barred iron doors where vintages had been stocked. Heavy oak barrels, too wide to roll out down the narrow entrance tunnels, were smothered in decades of cobwebs and dust. To enlarge the space, someone had knocked through sections of the walls with a sledge hammer, the broken bricks left raw and unfinished. Empty wine casks, hacked into stools and tables, were the only furniture.

Before they'd gone out, Chai had thought it courteous to mention their plans to the Captain, still hunched over his desk with his papers. Liberal with the truth, Chai claimed they needed some exercise and might take a walk around the cathedral and fort in the moonlight. Sumet, working his way through yet another angry missive to the negligent staff at the Siamese Legation in Paris, hadn't looked up. Still wary of their association with the swarthy Mamet, he had tried to dissuade them.

"So late in the evening?"

"I don't expect we'll be gone long," replied Chai, "a stroll up the hill, nothing more, enough to stretch our legs."

"You're on your own then. Don't expect help if you're robbed and left lying in the gutter", Sumet had warned. And to reiterate his concerns, he reminded them about the seamier side of the city, "The bars might look jolly and gay, but take heed. Behind every lampshade and curtain hide hustlers and whores."

Now at the centre of such an establishment, Chai reflected on Sumet's matronly caution, surrounded as he was by drunks, lowlifes and prostitutes. Just to his left, a girl wearing little but a fine chiffon dress, lay across a soldier's lap, deep red lips pressed to his cheek, hand stroking his thigh. Sensing she was being watched, the girl glanced up and catching Chai gawping, fixed him with such a withering look, he quickly turned away. A move that jarred the arm of a soldier passing with drinks. The man cursed out loud. Chai felt warm liquid trickle down his neck.

The sensible option, their curiosity sated, was to turn around and leave as quietly as possible. And primed with such an intention, Chai was on the cusp of persuading his group back through the entrance hanging, when loud cheers greeted the parting of curtains at the far end of the cellar. Managing to get Born out, Chai turned back to the room, but catching sight of the two twins starring open mouthed at the events on stage, knew he had left it too late.

The stage was cheap and crude. Fabricated from cut board and finished with plaster, a frieze was painted to resemble a marine scene where corals and shells floated above strange jellyfish polyps. A closer focus revealed a more salacious perspective. Long tentacles and tongues caressed scaly bodies and probed fleshy orifices. This lewd theme continued to the side of the stage, where tall, erect narwhal tusks framed the proscenium arch.

A trumpet blasted. A short, fat man in a top hat, bounced onto the stage and saluted the crowd. "Mesdames et messieurs," he bowed, "J'ai l'immense fierté de vous présenter les jolies filles des sept mers," and with a flourish, hopped from the stage.

Drums rolled, cymbals crashed. A magnesium flare cast a sharp column of light across the boards, into which sprang a line of dancing girls, their pale crinoline dresses so crushed together they resembled prize chrysanthemums in a window box. A haze of dust and face powder rose from the boards, as rows of black-stockinged feet thumped the floor with as much finesse as a herd of wildebeest. Collisions, wrong turns and missteps were frequent. Yet despite this inept choreography, such faults went forgiven. Instead it was small details that stirred; a flash of lace garter, silk underwear lifting to reveal rounded curves, pouting vermilion lips blowing lewd kisses.

One girl, over flamboyant with her kicks, ripped the stitching of her corset. Pert breasts burst free from the tight embrace of her dress, exposing her rouge-powdered nipples. Although a minor transgression and over in seconds, a great roar of excitement erupted from the mob as they surged forward for a closer view.

Mamet, assessing the room faster than the distracted Thais, had secured seats at a small corner table. It wasn't a good position. A wax encrusted escutcheon nailed to a column obscured the essential view of the stage; the reason it was still empty. Chai and the twins, shorter than most, had to prop themselves up on a ledge if they wanted a sightline to the dancers.

"Now we have a table, we will have to order drinks", said the Algerian, anxiously casting around for a waiter. A task that took longer than expected. Only a handful of overworked staff served the cramped space.

The drink, when it arrived, was a smokey opaque liquid in short fluted glasses. Chai, uncertain what to expect, sipped tentatively. The taste astonishingly alcoholic, flared down his throat like a trail of burning gunpowder. Reeling back from its fierce punch, sticky with the heat and stirred by the charged scenes on stage, he flushed red, worried that people on the surrounding tables might read his predicament. Across from him, Mai, Manit and Born, also blurry eyed, were struggling with the same physiological reactions. Only Mamet, unfamiliar with alcohol and finding the taste tame, appeared unflustered.

'What's up?" he asked of Chai, "It doesn't agree with you?"

"Agree with me?" replied Chai, his head throbbing, "I feel like molten lead's been poured down my throat."

"Another glass?", he turned to the others.

Mai and Manit held up their hands in surrender. Mamet looked disappointed. He consoled himself by draining their glasses.

Back on the stage the performance had ended. The dancers were coming down the steps, the girl with the torn dress last in line still clutching her breasts. Exploiting her vulnerability, two men chased after her. The girl's shrieks alerted the doorman. A former boxer he met the pursuers at the door to the dressing rooms, his mammoth fist raised above their heads like a sledgehammer. Meekly they returned to their seats.

A patriotic blast from a trombone signalled a change of tone. Lamps blazed, flooding the stage in bands of red, white and blue. To a loud crescendo of drums, a line of soldiers marched up onto the platform, stamping their boots and shaking the floor boards. Behind them a painted backdrop fell to reveal a melodramatic landscape of billowing clouds and churned up trenches and craters. Over this muddy scene a battered zeppelin, grey like a whale, was winched down from the beams. Crouched inside its wicker basket, a dwarf in a spiked hat lit fire crackers and bombed the bunker below. The soldiers in the cardboard dugout ran for cover and fired back with their pop-guns. In the final act, a handsome aviator in a corrugated tin plane, swung across the stage and took shots at the zeppelin. But his speed was misjudged and the plane collided with the papier-mâché balloon. Entangled within its strings, the flyer bailed out and fell into the bunker. Landing badly he twisted an ankle on a sandbag. In some agony 'the hero' limped from the battlefield, ceding victory to the wrong side – the helmeted dwarf.

The audience, by now drunk and unruly and thinking it a shambles, shouted for the return of the dancers. At a hasty curtain call where flags dropped to the stage and trumpets pumped out a final patriotic blast, the crowd stamped their feet and jeered at the hapless actors to quit.

"Merdeux! Ouste! Assez!" they roared.

"OFF off, off!", bellowed the Australians, rapping their fists on the barrel tables and stools.

From the back of the room a hail of nuts and rough crusts bounced off the backdrop onto the performers. A bottle, thrown at the suspended paper zeppelin, brought it down. Drifting into the path of the stage lamps its brittle paper caught fire. Those in the front row picked up the flaming pieces and threw it back to the platform. The stage hand with the big fists intervened to quell the crowd. A chair swung across his face, shattered his teeth.

With the atmosphere charged and suddenly aggressive, the large Antipodeans were first to their feet. Mamet, well aware where the evening was heading, was quick to rouse the Thais from their table.

"Time to run," he said, finishing the last glasses and pointing urgently to the exit, "Now!"

Ushering Mai, Manit and Born through the entrance curtain, Mamet led the escape back to the subterranean tunnel. Chai, still reeling from the drink, was last to his feet. Colliding with the surge of men for the fight he was slow through the drapes. Emerging into the passageway to find his companions gone, he raced to catch up, took a wrong turn and found himself in a strange hallway – a dead end. Carpeted and hung with red lanterns, half a dozen alcoves were screened by black drapes. Through an opening to his right a slither of light broke out. Chai, curious, peered inside. A man stood in front of a mirror. Short, bald, perspiring, he was unbuttoning the front of his waistcoat that was over tight and causing him problems. A girl in a long lace dress stood behind him. Her left leg was raised on the edge of a mattress, quite high so that he could see her upper thigh. She wore a necklace of unusually bright red garnets, the glow from the stones like flickering flames against her flawless, pale skin.

Leaning closer to get a better look, Chai lifted back the edge of the drape. Unlike the ungainly, over painted stage dancers, the girl was slender and dark haired. She was also alert; smart enough to sense Chai's presence. For a brief second their eyes met. Her look was quizzical; his looks intrigued - she didn't shout out.

The big sweating man, still fighting his buttons, noticed the girl pause and followed her gaze to the curtains. Stunned to see a small Asian face peering in through the gap, he dropped his trousers, exposing his manhood – pink, angry, erect, like a ceremonial baton.

"Sortez!", screamed the man, scrambling for his belt and pants, "Sortez!"

Despite this loud outburst the two young faces lingered. Chai saw the girl's hand deftly fall to the man's jacket to lift three hundred francs from his pocket.

"Sortez! Putain, imbécile, sortez!" the man roared again, his fat fist swinging from inside. Mamet, returning back down the corridor, pulled Chai back. The punch missed him by inches.

"Do you want to end up dead before even seeing a battlefield?", admonished the big Berber grabbing Chai's arm and pulling him away from the cubicles. Rushing for the exit, they passed by the entrance to the main hall where the fight still progressed. Most of the bar stools were already overturned and shattered. Two men had broken into the steel cage at the back of the cellars and were helping themselves to the rare vintages. Across the mouth of the stage, the fire from the burning zeppelin still blazed unchecked. A man running down the tunnel with a bucket collided with Mamet and spilled the lot over Chai.

Outside in the open, girls, soldiers and staff poured out into the alleyway. From the port came the wail of police whistles.

Chapter 9

L'Estaque, south west of Marseilles, had been the home for fifteen fishing families, a blacksmith and a carpenter for more than two hundred years. Bleak and exposed, shadowed by cliffs so steep they appeared to lean over the fragile houses like giant mausoleums, it wasn't sought out for anything other than its natural harbour of rocks that protected its beaches even in the most threatening of storms. A sombre image of its fishing boats placidly beached as fierce waves pounded the basalt sea stacks, had been painted by the realist artist, Jules Breton, on his way to warmer and calmer coasts off Girona.

The workers came at first light. Six men with saws and axes to take down the avenue of plane trees that led up to the village. Buses and trucks followed the wagons of the wood cutters. By noon the fishing families, furniture and possessions had been loaded on board and moved to temporary dwellings above Marignane, a day's drive from the sea.

With the streets empty the demolition began. The wooden houses along the L'Estaque seafront were dismantled, the old watch tower and chapel pulled down and burnt. Along the water front the shingle banks where the fishing skiffs were pulled up, was levelled and concreted over. Days after, the timber frame of a planned coaling station was already erected and being roofed over.

L'Estaque hadn't been the only fishing community consigned to oblivion by a flick from a bureaucrat's pen. Further along the coast on the outskirts of Toulon and Nice, more than a dozen villages and ports had already been sacrificed to the needs of the war effort, their sheltered ports carved up into landing sites for the growing fleets of cargo vessels and merchant ships.

Despite the war edging into its fifth year, France still strained to control the voracity of their foreign invaders. Americans and Canadians from across the Atlantic, British and Scots over the Channel and Colonial troops of all races from the South and the Mediterranean. The hordes of arrivals all needed water, food, clothes, beds and tents. Storage depots, transport parks and railheads, all became the unglamorous and unsung capitals in the Art of War; the craft of moving stuff from where it was made to where it was needed – be that woollen socks, helmets, bullets or coffins. A ceaseless network of supply and demand that in turn needed bureaucrats and clerks, telephones and typewriters to organise and keep it in play.

On the outskirts of Lyons the relocation of the transport and logistics corp to the fifth floor of the signals division, had not gone without mishap. Trunks and t-chests, wrongly addressed, had ended up in a truck park on the far side of town. Worst still, after the delivery wagons had gone home, several filing cabinets and their box files had been left in the street. Ransacked by locals, they'd used the precious index cards to light their evening fires.

Antoine Chauvert, arriving for duty at six o'clock in the morning, was the first to realise the error. Without the correct schedules, the despatch officers two floors above, were operating from timetables a month out of date. Reaching for his handset, he put a call through to the station master at the Gare des Brotteaux. He was too late. The early trains had already left, the most worrying oversight a troop train from platform seven; thirteen companies of Moroccan Chasseurs on their way to Chantilly north of Paris, the wrong front.

Misplacing an entire battalion was embarrassing, but due to the sheer weight of men and supplies crowding the port at Marseilles, it wasn't the first time that soldiers, their equipment, cargo and munitions had been mistakenly directed.

In a leviathan struggle that involved up to thirty-two nations from six different continents, each with their own command structures and rules, confusion and misunderstandings were both common and natural. Beyond the expected bureaucratic slip-ups and blunders, language was chiefly to blame. To address the issue, an academy was set up at the École Militaire and staffed with tutors and linguists. Those schooled in English, Russian and Italian were easy to come by, but it had been a strain finding enough translators fluent in the rarer Asian and sub-Saharan dialects. After an appeal from the Foreign Ministry, diplomats and staff from the Empire's far-flung outposts had been some of the first to volunteer. Priests, nuns and laymen who had worked for Catholic missions, schools and charities across Indochina and Africa, had also offered their services. Although more than capable teachers, their educational methods, touching on the evangelical at times, proved too disconcerting for the Hindus and Muslims who feared covert conversion in the hours before battle. Fears inflamed by recent eye witness reports from the British front line, where the Angel of Mons was seen hovering over the trenches, guiding the faithful to battle.

In a search of more dependable teachers, the military turned to the Universities of Paris, Montpelier and Toulouse, where recruitment centres were set up to attract foreign language students and tutors.

The twenty-one-year-old Pierre Perigeux had spent three years studying Chinese and Chan literature at Langues O. Like his fellow students he attended the recruitment shows in the central lecture theatre, but was so emboldened by the military posters, banners and uniforms, he rejected the call for tutors and enlisted as an infantryman.

Living in a cramped bedsit loft in the shadow of the old chemical works at Grenelle, Pierre, brought up in Brittany, had never been comfortable with claustrophobic city life. Looking back to idyllic summers in tents on the Loire, he relished the chance to return to camp life, even though that camp was the damp, lice-infested trenches of the 47th Division in the Ypres salient near Langemarck.

After a journey of more than sixteen hours, the last half through the night, Pierre's university contingent were ordered to unpack before reporting for inspection. They weren't given much time. As part of an autumn offensive, their sector was being prepared for a coming attack on a German artillery battery that was targeting their supply lines. The battalion sergeant, aware of the students' lack of experience and unpreparedness, judiciously spared them from any dangerous assignments and sent them to dig drains far from the guns. But the younger members, piqued at being thrown such a demeaning task and too excited to let pass on an opportunity to participate in their first real taste of action, lied about the extent of their training.

In truth Pierre's team were no more experienced than boy scouts with the Éclaireuses et Éclaireurs de France, whose highest patriotic achievement had been collecting berries and chestnuts for the home front reserves. Their military training had been minimal, most of it rolling across the soft sands of the beaches of St Malo, wooden rifles and ply swords their weapons, pebbles as hand grenades. The closest most had got to the enemy was marching past the barbed wire enclosures of the prisoner-of-war camps near the ports, where the inmates dug for potatoes in the waste ground.

The sergeant, not wanting to dampen their youthful enthusiasm, sought out a challenge suitable for greenhorns on a first mission. An assignment was created to reconnoitre a high ground for a future observation post. By all accounts the area, locked between the lines, was ignored and unmanned.

Proudly lining up to descend into the trenches, Pierre's boy soldiers could read the low opinion of their chances on the smug smirks of the sentry guards as they were guided down to their forward positions. Not that they minded being mocked by the cynical and battle weary. Being innocent and naive only tempered their ardour, making them determined to prove to the naysayers, more than fortitude, valour. For years they had looked forward to such an hour; boyhood fantasies having stoked dreams of storming defences unscathed, to bayonet and slit the throats of the foul-smelling 'krauts' as they dozed, despite the sergeant's admission that they were unlikely to encounter anything fiercer than rats and that they'd be armed with nothing more dangerous than trench clubs.

Just after two in the morning, when the longed-for signal was made, Pierre jostled with his comrades to be the first out of the trenches. It was a cold night and misty. Hands, arms and boots wrestled for purchase on the slippery rungs of the ladders. He was yards from the rim of the trench, pleased to be out in the open, when he heard a dull thud in the distance. Almost immediately he felt a shell shoot past his head. So close, he later claimed (although aware it might sound fanciful), that with supernatural clarity he could read the batch number of the Krupp armaments factory printed along its side – MTG APR 23 – the date of his birthday. And that was the last of it.

Pierre awoke to the uncomfortable sensation of a doctor's laryngoscope probing his gullet. He was lying in a bed in a convalescent hospital, near Caen. The two-storey building, a former hunting lodge, stood in elegant beech woods near the sea. Windows looked out over newly-harvested wheat fields. He could smell the scent of freshly cut hay. Blackbirds and magpies foraged for loose grain.

The doctors were efficient and reassuring, the nurses young, attentive and comforting. Everyday at four in the afternoon, coffee and almond biscuits were served; in the evening a soup and a square of dark chocolate before the lights were turned out.

Nights were the most difficult. A horrific hammering echoed between his ears; the aftershock of the blast that had first floored him. This irritation got worse when he moved his head on the pillow making it impossible to sleep. These long hours awake found only despair and then guilt. Guilt that he should be out and back with his friends in the trenches sharing in their struggles and trials (their tragic deaths, as yet, withheld from him). At bleaker moments this shame morphed into a deeper, more disturbing angst; he had lost his stomach for the fight. Crowning this mountain of agonies came a more immediate concern – he was recovering too fast. Two young lads opposite with serious hand wounds, had, just that morning, been hauled away by corporals combing the wards for pretenders and fakers. Well aware that his head wound (in truth ear wound), was less dramatic than it looked, Pierre stayed low, out of sight.

Drinking white spirits from the janitor's cupboard to make himself look pale and sickly, Pierre aggravated an insignificant cold into a fever. With the military snoopers kept at bay by the violence of his sneezing fits, he used the precious interlude to write letters to his friends and family to seek out any connections with influence. His father had a tailoring company in the garment district near the Elysée and had cut cloth for a number of minor officials before the war. Several had since risen to prominence in some influential offices and ministries. Using these contacts, Pierre pleaded for a job – clerk, cook, telephonist, driver – determined not to go back to the trenches.

A principal at his former university was his saviour. With War Office recruitment teams still making appeals for foreign language tutors, he remembered his former Mandarin speaker. And with Pierre's father's connections beavering away behind the scenes to approve his transfer from military duties, he was soon dispatched to Arras as a translator for a front-line Chinese Labour Corps. The work, digging trenches, unblocking latrines, clearing barbed wire, recovering mangled bodies from the blood-soaked mud, was both gruesome and (for his still fragile disposition), too close to the front line for comfort.

Working long into the night, a barrage of further petitions to the same henpecked recipients he'd pestered before, begged for a second reassignment – burdening his father with a lifetimes's ledger of promised suits, shirts and ties. A week later he found his salvation. He was transferred as an interpreter to a second Asian unit; a company of Siamese drivers recently arrived in Marseilles.

Chapter 10

Chai woke to a scratching sound near his ear. Turning in his camp bed, he scanned the edge of the tent and saw a thin face peering in under the canvas, its dark beady eyes gleaming out from red and white fur. With its snout pressed between the guy ropes, a fox was busy lapping the sticky residue from the mouth of a jar; the Captain's coveted plum preserve peaking out from the folds of his knapsack.

Chai, curious to see a wild creature in the middle of a camp, kept still and watched. The animal, as yet oblivious to his presence, appeared relaxed, solely fixed on finishing its sugary treat. After a shrill bugle note still failed to dislodge it, Chai, knowing it was time for him to move and get dressed, was forced to get vocal: "Come on fox, enough. Go! Get out of here!"

The animal stole a last satisfying lick and ran off.

Reaching for a sweater, Chai folded back the canvas flaps and stepped out into a field. It had rained during the night. Rows of tents pounded by the weight of water from the storm had sagged and caved in. Boot prints churned up the turf where men had wandered in the dark in search of the latrines. A larger, deeper furrow showed where one had slipped down a bank and taken out a row of tent pegs.

A chorus of groans, coughing and spitting announced that others were stirring. Two Senegalese soldiers, stepping out barefoot into a puddle of muddy water, loudly cursed. Foolishly they'd left their boots in the open. It wasn't their only oversight. Slow to patch tears in their canvas the day before, rain had poured in through the holes soaking their blankets and bedding.

Ignoring the rising babel of discord and blasphemy, Chai hung a mirror from a tent pole and started shaving. Pouring water from his canteen bottle, he used a flannel to wash his forehead and neck and a second meagre cap-full to clean his teeth. Brushing dirt and mud from his trousers and boots, he returned inside and woke the Captain. Sumet, shaking off yet another disturbed night, took a long time to orientate himself.

Two thousand battered tents made up the Saint Amour training camp. Laid out across fields on a bend in a river, it was hemmed in by dense oak woods and scrub. The regimented avenues of canvas surrounded a square that enclosed washrooms, a nursing station and a mess hall. A central hub of essentials that was difficult to locate within the featureless maze of tents still shrouded in mist. By the time Chai and Sumet had found the canteen at its core it was already late. The Captain looked fractious.

"Did you sleep well?", enquired Chai.

"Chai, I haven't slept well since leaving Bangkok," moaned Sumet, fingers kneading his temples as if nursing a migraine.

"Can I get you something to eat?", asked Chai concerned.

"Just a milk... if it's clean, looks fresh, doesn't smell."

"Anything else?"

"Like what?"

"Something to eat?"

"I would Chai, I would, if it wasn't all so tasteless and bland."

"A biscuit perhaps, or some bread?"

"Later Chai, later", said Sumet, waving him away irritated by his solicitude.

On the drive from Marseilles the day before, they'd stopped twice for breaks. Stepping down from the trucks they had found themselves in windswept plains in the middle of nowhere. Hungry and thirsty after the long drive, they'd hoped for and expected some form of refreshment. Indeed a low table had been laid out with cheese rolls, apples and wine, but inching closer to the spread they were told it was reserved only for drivers and the handful of French officers that accompanied them. Chai, his knees stiff from being crushed up in the back, had wanted to walk up a hill to stretch his legs. Even that was discouraged. When a second stop brought further disappointment, they complained to the staff sergeant who headed the transport. Irritated by this intervention, the officer hadn't cared for their 'whining'. Nevertheless he assured them that they would be given soup on arrival at the camp. Reaching Saint Amour long after dark, the Thai had disembarked just in time to see the canteen being packed away for the night, the remains of an onion and potato soup being poured into a trench; a fitting feast for an army of stray dogs.

Chai, by now wise to their empty promises, had already anticipated this setback. Before leaving Macon at the start of the day, he'd chanced on a sack of loaves at the back of a tent and stashed them away in their bags. But morsels of stale bread were scant reward for over two hundred disgruntled, homesick men.

Chai returned to the table with two plates and a mug of milk. Sumet lent over the bowl and sniffed. Whatever it was, was already shrivelled and cold.

"What is it?" asked Sumet suspiciously, sipping the milk.

"Bread and boiled beans, I think."

"Hah?", he snorted, "There's nothing else?"

"All that was left," replied Chai getting started on the bowl.

"I could have done with something hot... a rice soup," he muttered despondently.

"There was no rice to be seen. But actually..." he paused as he chewed a second mouthful, "It's not that bad... actually has some flavour..."

Against all the odds he'd come across a piece of meat – in fact the only piece of meat in the entire vat; real meat, not fat or grizzle – a tender slither of prime cut with a hint of red wine, that can only have got there after being scraped from an officer's plate the night before.

Savouring this rare treat, Chai reached instinctively for Sumet's bowl hoping to find more, "You don't want yours?"

He didn't want it. But the thought of having to watch his deputy gorge himself on a second bowl, his bowl, was too much to bear. Pushing away Chai's hand, he grudgingly picked up the cutlery and took a spoonful, chewing slowly, as if forced to eat worms. Expecting disappointment he was relieved. Chai was right, he conceded; the beans weren't as bad as they looked. In fact there were faint traces of herbs, possibly spices, he actually liked. Launching himself back to the bowl, he was mid-way through a second, larger mouthful when he was overcome by a violent coughing fit. Something coarse and wiry had stuck in his throat. Choking, his eyes streaming, he dropped his head under the table and violently spat. Whatever it was hit the dirt floor and bounced.

Chai looked on alarmed, "Captain… you alright?"

"I'm perfectly alright…", mumbled Sumet, returning upright and still grasping his throat, "Why wouldn't I be?"

Chai, glancing under the table. At the base of the bench he caught sight of the crushed carcass of a cockroach wriggling out from the Captain's frothy saliva.

The parade ground, a battered square of sticky grey clay graced by a single roughly-hacked flag pole, lay in fields below the main camp. Previously a cabbage crop, rough furrows still marred the surface despite years of square bashing and drilling. The night storm had clogged those ruts with rain water.

Eager to cut a favourable impression, the Captain had had his men polish their buttons and brush down their uniforms, before urging them down to the field early. Finding a dry grassy bank out of the wind, they sat back and relaxed.

In the far corner of the field, a staff sergeant and his second marking out squares with wooden stakes, were far from happy with the state of the ground. Noticing the idle soldiers on the far bank they called them over.

"Clear the field of mud and water," ordered the officer, pointing to the muddy furrows, "You have half an hour."

Shovels and trowels were handed over. Seeing that there were only eight usable spades, Chai assigned different teams to the four quadrants and they took turns. It was back-breaking work, the ground they had to cover more than five hundred metres wide and half again as deep.

By the time the job was finished the men looked a mess, their trousers and boots streaked with sticky white clay. The Captain, panicked by their state, was about to rush them all back to their tents, but already the first soldiers were wandering down to the parade ground. With no time to wash, they set aside their shovels and lined up with the rest. A passing drill sergeant, appalled by their slovenly look, banished them all to the outer reaches of the parade ground. Pressed behind a battalion of Moroccan infantry and Senegalese Tirailleurs, the officer thought it unlikely they'd be noticed.

Fierce winds blew up the valley. The temperatures weren't low, but it was the first time the Thai had encountered real cold. Without the thick khaki great coats that shrouded their North African colleagues, they silently shivered.

Half an hour later a bugle note sounded. A line of staff cars appeared over the top of the hill and driving though the entrance gates, rolled into the main camp. Reaching the perimeter of the cantonment, the motorcade turned onto a line of duckboards laid across the terrain into the centre of the parade ground.

General Henri Mercier emerged from the back of the car, smoothed down his windswept hair and lifted a cap to his head. Stern and short in appearance, he walked slowly, deep set eyes hidden like rifle slits beneath bushy eyebrows. Led to the front of the square, he stepped up onto a raised platform and looking out over the ranks of black, brown and yellow faces, stroked a chest emblazoned with medals.

General Mercier welcomed the troops of North Africa, India and Indochina. They should feel humbled, proud, joyful (humilié, fier, joyeux) he announced, to be standing on the rich soil of the Republic.

"It was the greatest honour in the world to wear the uniform of the French army and to fight for the Empire in the most heroic battle ever fought. With such an honour came a duty to their homeland. A duty that many of those who had come before them had already valiantly served in the noble conflicts and battlegrounds of Flanders, Ypres and Picardy."

Pressing his hand to his heart the general looked skyward, his monocle catching a rare ray of light, enhancing his diminutive stature.

"Like them you must show no fear. The French army has no place for shirkers and cowards. If we shrink from our resolve, we dishonour the sacrifice of those who have gone before us. Your courage will ensure that their precious blood has not been wasted, their glorious achievements squandered. The loathsome Boches, cornered and cowering, are on their knees. The end is in sight. Your duty is to speed that victory. Stamp out their vile tyranny for good and let justice and peace return to the civilised world. Soldiers of the Empire, this is your proud destiny!"

A loud cheer went up from the ranks.

"Long live the Empire, long live France! Long live the army!"

The General's call to patriotism ended on a lighter note. He was sorry that they had to endure French cuisine. But if they catered for so many ethnic tastes they'd have more chefs than soldiers and more saucepans than guns.

Saluting the men a last time, General Henri Mercier stepped down from the platform, shook a few chosen hands and raced back to the comfort of his staff car. The black Renault sedan reversed, then returned back down the lines of soldiers. Turning left at the base of the field, the large car momentarily slowed to negotiate a dip in the field. By terrible mischance it came to rest not yards from the grubby Thai contingent. Captain Sumet, timidly looking up at that exact same moment, was mortified to catch the penetrating gaze of the general himself, his piercing eyes widening with alarm as he took in the ranks of mud-splattered uniforms. With his grim profile seemingly etched in the glass, the long sedan, its tires struggling for purchase on the slippery grass, seemed to take an eternity to move on.

The men were stood down. Exhausted and relieved the Captain and Chai led their shabby contingent back to their tents. Sumet, still reeling from the intensity of the general's withering stare, was on the cusp of entering his own shelter for a much needed nap, when he was accosted by a junior officer.

"Captain Chantra...Wong...?", he enquired.

Sumet flushed red. It had taken less than ten minutes for General Mercier's complaint to find them.

The Thai company were ordered to the Quartermaster's store, a ramshackle warren of tents and corrugated iron sheds at the edge of the camp. Squeezed in between the cooking quarters and the nursing station its interior was an incoherent maze of trestles, lockers and trunks, heavy with the stench of boiled cabbage and camphor making them all feel queasy and faint.

Separated into teams of ten they waited, as trench coats, jackets and trousers rained down from high shelves. Finding the right fit was a challenge. There were long delays as grumbling store assistants rummaged through dark recesses searching for boots that weren't the standard ten to twelve-inch caucasian sole. A last table of equipment, filled with helmets, ammunition belts, bayonets and gas masks, left them apprehensive.

"Winter coats, oilcloths and boots I can understand," questioned Chai, "but gas masks, bayonets and ammunition boxes? It's not as if we're being sent to the front?"

"It's probably just standard issue" replied the Captain, his head rattling loose within his steel helmet.

They took them anyway.

Rushing out of the tent, because everyone else seemed to be rushing out of the tent, they were accosted by a staff sergeant.

"Où allez-vous?" he barked, as if correcting a congregation of church goers.

"Nous retournons au camp," said Chai innocently.

"Pourquoi?", he glared.

"Colonel, soyez patient, s'il vous plait, mais..." started Sumet.

"Mais rien!" bellowed the officer, arm shooting out and pointing downhill.

"Les camions sont là. Montez dedans!", as the sound of engines growled from the parade ground, "VITE!"

Chapter 11

No one said where they were going or why. Chai, perched on the bench over the wheels, tried catching the roadsigns in an attempt to work out where they were heading. Bourg-en-Bresse was the first significant town. Driving through medieval streets of red brick and timber houses, the convoy headed east across country towards the Jura hills, the road narrowing as they rose up through twisting limestone gorges.

The last ten kilometres were the most painful. The trucks were so overcrowded, many had to find space on the floor, wedged between people's legs. Several of the Vietnamese, made frail by the rolling motion of the lorries across the rocky, broken terrain, scrambled to the rear, heads hung out over the road like dogs, desperate for air. When they finally reached their destination, there was an untidy scramble for the tailgate and a rush for a bush.

Climbing down from the back, the Thai found themselves in a field at the edge of woods. The men, lulled by the serenity of the setting and thinking they'd been brought there for no better reason than to fool around and throw fir cones, cleared a camp by flattening the grasses and pulling up ferns and thorns.

Sumet and Chai, watching the trucks turn around and leave, were more circumspect. A tunnel of chestnut trees brought them out over a promontory. Walking to the edge they looked down over the valley. On both sides of the canyon, limestone walls and ravines dropped three hundred metres into a gorge. Cut into this hillside, an intimidating obstacle course of trenches, rope bridges, stone walls and climbing frames, scarred the terrain. Crowning this tortuous playground, stood a mud fort, its crenelated walls manned by straw dummies, a tailor's manikin their gallant commander, strapped to its watch tower. Hidden within hollows in the grass banks, fire pits had been dug. Acrid white smoke collected like snow within the undulating contours.

"So that's why we're here," said Chai.

"It could have been worse…" replied the Captain, "It might have been the real thing."

The circuit, twelve kilometres of scree slopes, dense woods, hidden gullies and streams, was gruelling enough. To make it crueller still, the instructors had handed out backpacks, each filled with sandbags and rocks; twenty five kilos each.

Weighed down by these loads the men were assembled in a semi circle at the front of the course. Chalked wooden signs had been nailed to newly cut poles. Crudely marked on these placards were the colours of Morocco, Algeria, Senegal, West Bengal, Indochina and most remarkable of all, Siam.

Chai, staring up at this forest of nations and amazed to see their own red and white flag, was beginning to wake to the devious chicanery of their puffed-up Commanders. Bored by having to watch over yet another tedious training session, the officers had sought out ways to squeeze some extra entertainment from the day's activities. Corralling the recalcitrant Thai into the trucks, knowing they were mere drivers, hadn't been a mistake. They were there as contestants, another rare breed to add colour and amusement to an afternoon's sport; a gladiatorial contest between nations. And the Thai made up ten.

A grandstand for this coming 'tournament' had been built out over the vantage point. On its edge a scoping telescope on a tripod pointed along the length of the course. To its side a canvas awning shaded a set of armchairs and a table spread with fine wines and spirits. As the training officers drank and joshed, Chai thought he could see money changing hands.

The teams lined up on a starting line. The Captain, positioning his men at the front, sidled up to Chai.

"I don't expect to come first Chai," whispered Sumet stretching his legs, "But it would look good if we weren't last."

The first one hundred yards were a straight sprint, the grass flat like a bowling green, cropped short by goats. Despite its manicured finish, the site still claimed a victim. A Sengalese soldier put his foot through a rabbit hole, spraining his ankle. Thrown forward, his backpack, pitched over his head, pinned him like a helpless beetle to the ground. His team, unwilling to pause for stragglers so early, ran on without him.

The front line of climbing frames and rope bridges was the first challenge. The Thai had the strength for the climb, but their rock packs pulled at their shoulder blades, upsetting their balance. Landing in the bog on the far side, the added weight sunk them deep in the ooze forcing mud through their soles, soaking their boots. Emerging from the mire they came up against the main fortification. Although its ramparts and log guns had presented an intimidating outline from a distance, its straw-stuffed defenders offered little resistance. Born punched the shop manikin's head off, just to be bloody minded.

Past the fort they entered a wood where the ground levelled out and they could settle into a jog. The path reminded Chai of a track at the Lopburi Army camp that linked the town with the fields, its surface as firm as concrete in the dry months. Seconds later he remembered the reason it was hard packed...

"Watchout!" he yelled.

The grass parted and a charging bull exploded through the bushes. It was tied to a stake, but to escape being gored the men had to cross a thirty foot danger zone within the circumference of its chain. Wrun, terror struck, froze. Born had to dash back to snatch him up before the enraged beast completed a full revolution of the circle. Its horns missing them by inches.

Recovering on the far side of the bull ring, Wrun, grateful for being saved, wrapped his arm around Born. The big man, hating his touch, shoved him away.

"Do something stupid like that again..." he admonished the small man, "and I'll personally gore you!"

Relief at escaping the crazed beast provided a surge of adrenalin that propelled them on faster, a burst of speed that saw them gaining on the North Africans and Indochinese. Low scrub gave way to long reed grass thick with flies and mosquitoes. Mai was swiping the thick strands out of his way, when he tripped and shouted out a second warning. His alert came too late. Beyond a high bank, the ground fell abruptly to a near vertical drop. The Captain, besieged by flies, was already over the lip. Chai, hard on Sumet's heels, grabbed his shoulder strap as he rolled over, but the Captain's momentum was so strong, it pulled him down too. Once again it was, Born, who leaping forward, managed to catch Chai's arm.

"Damn that was close!" muttered Sumet, heart thumping from the shock and wiping the mud from his front, "What the hell now?"

"We'll have to go down," Chai replied.

"But it's more than thirty feet!" exclaimed the Captain, still reeling from his fall.

Mai and Manit, undaunted by the height went first, kicking out footholds and digging out ledges with flints into the cliff. Chai and Born went either side of the Captain, taking his weight over the most perilous descents. Darn, the heaviest, elected to go last. It was a prescient move. As the large man reached the midway point the ledge collapsed and he landed with a spectacular splash in the ice cold waters of the Ain. Momentarily stunned by the chill temperature, he was close to being swept over rapids before reaching out and catching a rock.

It took five of them to haul the large man from the water. Collapsing on the far bank, Darn, shivering in his underclothes, began squeezing water from his trousers and jacket.

Chai, taking in the walls of the gorge, was dismayed to see that the track was now all uphill.

"The men should take a break," he said.

"Nonsense!" replied Sumet, impatient to keep going, "We've already wasted enough time." He moved to stand, but even before he was back on his feet Chai saw him stumble.

"Captain you need a rest. And you need water," said Chai reaching for his shoulder and persuading him down.

"I'm fine damn it. I drank my fair share of the river," he joked.

Chai uncorked his canteen flask and passed it across. Seeing the open neck Sumet conceded, drinking so fast the water cascaded down his chin and chest soaking his front.

Without an obvious path, the route out was a scramble through a dense jungle of dead branches and thorns. Boulders crowded the incline, their rounded sides slippery with moss. Searching for a way through this labyrinth brought further delays. Yet despite these setbacks, the afternoon wasn't totally without dishonour. In making the unintended diversion, they'd managed to overtake three teams, the Sudanese, the Vietnamese and a Tunisian unit of ten men. The North Africans, having been in the lead from the start, were first through the birch woods and hadn't clocked the chained bull. Catching them unawares, the brute had ploughed through them all, goring a man in his side and rupturing his spleen. Their comrades had had to carry the wounded soldier for more than three kilometres, the last traverse a punishing climb through the gully. Several times the unit had fallen, dropping the casualty and causing him to howl out in agony.

Hearing their plaintive cries, Chai and Manit suggested they go down to help. The Captain, knowing that it would lose more vital time and the opportunity to report a rare achievement to Bangkok, was almost apoplectic with rage.

"Why? We can get fifth, maybe fourth. Isn't that a worthwhile achievement!"

Chai, not wanting to defy his senior in front of the men, looked for a compromise.

"You lead the team to the winning post, Captain. We'll be quick, I promise, I'm sure the French won't even notice we've gone."

Chai and Manit ran back down the track to the Tunisians. The injury to the solder was more serious than they'd expected. The bull's horn had pierced deep and he was loosing so much blood his bandages and clothes were soaked. The North Africans, worried by his worsening condition, were grateful for Chai and Mai's help. With the two Thai to assist, their leader ran on ahead to the finish line to find a medic. Yet no one took his pleas for assistance seriously.

It was almost dark before the French instructors finally intervened. A hospital truck was called and a stretcher team sent down to retrieve the injured man. Sympathy hadn't prompted their action; they'd reserved tables for dinner at an Auberge in St Vallan.

Delayed by the Tunisian casualty, it took more than four hours to crawl back to Bourg-en-Bresse late in the evening. Chai, the only one still awake, heard the engines fall silent and climbing down from the back, followed the side of the trucks to see what the delay was. In a lane opposite a group of soldiers were smoking and chatting. Passing the men he walked to a rail crossing at the front of the convoy. Beyond the closed barrier a locomotive stood in a siding. A team of men with hurricane lamps were coupling the engine to a line of coal trucks and box cars, the sound of their hammers reverberating between the freight wagons and tankers. High on a water tower, a man was leaning over the railings and pointing down the line, yelled instructions to his men to clear the tracks.

Looming out from the gloom, a second, larger locomotive approached from the south. Chai stepped back from the crossing as a line of box cars and flatbeds rolled by. Tied down on these platforms and shrouded in canvas, a mass of tanks and armoured cars appeared, machine guns protruding like horns from their turrets. As the train rolled by, the weight of the trucks on the junction shook the crossing like a malevolent force, setting off an eerie resonance that left him unsettled. Being at the camp, taking possession of his equipment, completing the obstacle course and now seeing the lines of new tanks – of course he felt unease with this foreign, unfamiliar world – but he also sensed a restless elation; an excitement that even tired limbs couldn't dim. He was finally close to the war. Not any war: The War. A battle between giants, empires. Now in the quiet, staring at the last dying lights from the train, he imagined the distant echo of guns.

Chapter 12

It was late in the evening when the young Pierre Perigeux managed to track down the Thai camp. Finding their tents empty a sentry guard directed him to a field at the edge of the encampment. From a distance, he saw the men on the crest of a hill, silhouetted against the flames of a fire lit by the Algerians and Moroccans. To feed this blaze, lengths of deadwood were being dragged from an oak wood. Around the bonfire, groups of soldiers had gathered in the long grass, sharing out food scavenged from the mess tent. It included two small chickens, purloined from a neglected farm (so they claimed), spread eagled and stuck onto spits.

Awaiting the roast birds, a group of musicians had collected around the flames. One played a stringed instrument, another a flute. Others rapped on tin boxes, even an old bicycle wheel, its rusty spokes making a discordant grating sound. Eventually, smoothed by practice and time, an unlikely harmony settled. A voice lifted, almost feminine. Singing of hardship and loss, its mournful lyrics had everyone thinking of home.

The Moroccans, the winning contestants of the olympian obstacle race, had brought with them their prize, a case of Bordeaux, which, because of their religion, few had touched. Pierre, seeing it lie idle in the shadows, made a mental note of its position on the bank as he approached the two Siamese, Chai and Captain Sumet.

"Captain Chan...tra...wong?" he asked hesitantly.

"Yes," replied Sumet, guardedly taking in the stranger's finely cut uniform – rarely had an approach from a French official come without some hidden barb.

"My name is Pierre Perigeux," he saluted, "I have been attached to your company as a translator and liaison with the high command."

Returning the salute the Captain and Chai looked awkward. Was the man in the right place? Neither of them had requested an interpreter, let alone a liaison officer. Would the cold light of day reveal yet another nonsensical back-office mistake?

Pierre, reading their blank faces, looked just as uncomfortable.

"I judge by your expressions that you weren't expecting me?"

"I'm afraid not," replied Sumet.

"Then I'm ashamed to have to offer two apologies. The first that you weren't notified in advance as to my appointment. The second that you were forced to endure the assault course at Thoirette. You should never have been sent there. It's for combat troops. I'm sorry you were inconvenienced."

"We were not in the least inconvenienced," replied the Captain, "In fact we rather enjoyed ourselves…" although screaming pains in his thighs and back reminded him that this was likely a lie, "far better than sitting around all day doing nothing and being bored. We relished the challenge."

"However, I was told that you had issued a complaint?"

"A complaint? No, no, far from it. Merely a suggestion that it wasn't the sort of thing one would want to do everyday… if you know what I mean…"

"I assure you it will be the last time. For you will be pleased to hear that I've been sent with new orders, Captain," said Pierre reaching to his pocket for an envelope, "This will be your last night in St Amour. In the morning your company is to report to Sens where you will rendezvous with your vehicles."

"Finally on our way then," said the Captain turning to Chai.

Reaching for a glass he offered Pierre some wine. The young Frenchman, recognising the Moroccan's Médoc Bordeaux, gratefully accepted.

"Monsieur Perigeux, to our first mission!", Sumet toasted.

Pierre, raised his glass and drank, relieved to have alcohol flowing down his throat. Refilling his glass he proposed a second toast, "To the health and longevity of your Emperor and Empress!" An exaltation that so pleased him, he rushed to repeat it.

Again perplexed expressions stared back. And then it hit him. Emperor? What was he thinking? They were Siamese, a kingdom, not an empire like China. It was a blunder so farcical it was worthy of some crass music-hall act. Of course, technically, they were from the same region – everything beyond India and the Hindu Kush was carved from the same Mongol pot. Surely they would have appreciated the general gist of it? The answer was no. They had looked completely baffled; he must have looked a bit of a goat.

Taking a deep gulp of Bordeaux to calm his nerves, Pierre quickly steered the conversation to more mundane matters; rain, camp life and food, praying they hadn't latched onto his unease. He offered up a cigarette. They declined, a rejection he used as an opportunity to make a subtle and timely escape.

"Until the morning then Captain," concluded Pierre, offering another salute.

"Indeed," replied Sumet, returning the gesture and reseating himself.

Grabbing two spare bottles and loosening his shirt, Pierre made a beeline for the fire. Stretching out on the grass, he lit up a favourite Gauloise and lulled by the flames had time to calm and collect himself. His journey to the camp had been hell. In the station at Amiens, the platforms were swarming with the lost, the disorganised, the dazed and confused; men either heading to, or returning from the front. Finally finding his train, he'd had to fight to defend his place in the carriage – literally fight – his shoulder still ached from the blows. And to what avail? The train, first postponed, was unexpectedly cancelled. Walking across country with his bags he'd had to hitch a ride with a dairy farmer, the last fifteen miles in the rain and dark wedged between farm tools and silage bales. But despite the delays and discomforts, the anxieties that had hung over him like a malodorous cloud, had miraculously lifted; he'd finally escaped the clutches of the Chinese labour force. And although his new wards, the Siamese, appeared of similar complexion and build, they had a relaxed disposition, that was in marked contrast to the dour, sullen Cantonese; he hadn't liked their food and he suspected them of stealing his soap and shaving cream.

With the evening drifting past midnight, a second foraging expedition returned from the oak woods with more fuel for the fire. As the lumber hit the core, a bright fork of flame reached out and twisted into the sky. The musicians, scorched by the heat, had to regroup higher up on the bank. More makeshift instruments were found and joined in. The fuller orchestra in turn attracted more crowds from the camp.

Pierre became part of that motley band, drumming up an enthusiastic beat on a soapbox. He got on well with the West Africans. At his university, Langues O, he'd made friends with a number of Algerian and Moroccan students. He liked tahini paste on French toast and their Berber music stirred his egalitarian fervour. Impressed by his rhythm on the soapbox one of the players offered him a chance on one of their stringed instruments – a ginbri. Managing a handful of chords, even remembering the opening notes of a Tuareg folk song, Pierre improvised a verse about love and romance, that soon had everyone on their feet and clapping along, including the Thai. In this moody ballad he claimed to be infatuated with a Breton beauty; the prettiest girl in the village, if not the whole of Southern Brittany. Her face was so captivating that she'd been chosen as the image for St Agnes in the cheese making festival. Her husband, blunt, obese, often drunk and blind to high virtues, didn't value or take enough care of her. A crab fishermen, he was either cleaning his traps by the shore or out at sea for long spells. When he was away Pierre helped dig root vegetables in her garden and fixed leaks in her roof. On cold evenings he brought her kindling and logs and helped stoke her fire. When the war was over he would go back for her, marry her, have her children and build a home by the sea.

Handing back the ginbri to the Algerians, the subject of his lost ear came up. Pierre, strangely coy over this disfigurement, didn't want to talk about it. They ragged him mercilessly, "How will you hear the sweet whispers of your beloved Breton beauty?" they asked, "If Cupid calls, how will you know his song?"

Provoked by their joshing, Pierre got indignant: rare was the man who returned from the war without a blemish or scar. His petty wound was nothing but an insignificant gnat bite. It didn't need explanation, deserve sympathy, even less mockery. Couldn't they understand the subject was closed?

In truth Pierre was tired of spinning his tale. A story told so many times he'd lost track of the different variants. Much like a preacher looking to spice up a tired sermon, each new version came recharged with fresh elements, primed either to illicit pity, admiration or terror.

It was his mother who first noticed the unfortunate trait. Over the space of a single leave weekend, her son had recounted so many versions of his harrowing ordeal, that those that left their home, went away thinking they had met different people. Doting family and friends yearned for salacious details, of blood, guts and injury. For pretty girls and nurses, he honed more heroic virtues of bravery, recklessness and daring. Elders and officials got a longer, more sombre play; acts of patriotism, grit and self sacrifice.

But Pierre's antics before the North African recruits, bewildering that they were, concealed a deeper anguish. The harsh truth, the honest truth he was struggling to frame, was that these men, these smiling, joking, jovial faces, singing playfully around the fire, were destined for the same mud-fucked hell, that for the grace of God, and a rare injection of luck, he had so narrowly and mercifully escaped. He'd been there. He'd seen it. Although no hero, he was a survivor. His experience, brief that it was, elevated him to a position of privilege. Wasn't he duty bound to tell them how it was? Shouldn't they be awakened to the terrible realities they were soon about to suffer?

Yet every time the conversation veered back to the subject of conflict, each occasion providing an open door for intervention, he'd held back and remained silent, biting his tongue so as not to weaken.

Pierre's resolve was strong, but no match for the waves of intoxicant that assailed him. Already several glasses down, a sip of brandy dissolved his last, lingering restraint. Its fierce bite, even the feel of the flask, wrenched him back to a dismal place ten feet below ground, the air rank with the reek of sweat, urine, rot and decay.

Crouched on the duck boards, waiting for the signal to head out, a similar drink had been passed between his friends. Impressed by its potency they felt emboldened, invulnerable. This was their time, their moment to prove to the scoffers and taunters, that they too had the guts to successfully prosecute a mission; albeit a training exercise to an unmanned position with no tactical value.

When the expected order came, there was no lag, or hesitancy; even the most timid rushed eagerly for the ladders to be over the top. Once in the open their progress was swift – their beach training in St Malo hadn't been completely wasted. And they'd been lucky with the weather. The sky was clear. Moonlight showed the way, with passing clouds providing convenient interludes of cover, where they could pause and catch their breath. A single rifle shot was unexpected. Lying still they waited. Nothing. Thinking it was just a random discharge they moved forward. A spotlight went on, its harsh arc light probing the ground. A voice shouted. More shots were fired. Pressing themselves to the ground they heard the shrill hiss of bullets pass by on all sides. Then, from the horizon, a more ominous rumble from big guns.

To Pierre, still wrapped in his benign cloud of invincibility, these sounds conjured childlike metaphors; the swarming of restless bees on his parents estate in Callac, backed up by the thud of the steam hammers from the forest loggers camp. Yards from the lip of a shell crater this delusional cloud rudely evaporated. He froze. It was as if his veins ran with lead, stifling every cell, every sinew, every muscle in his body. Locked in the open he felt dazed and wooly headed. Peering through a sickening mustard haze he saw the distorted outlines of his comrades, grasping their throats, reeling back and collapsing. Pierre, choking, as if his insides were being seared by hot irons, staggered back and rolled into the bowl of the crater.

Sometime later Pierre found himself back on the floor of the trench. Face down on the base of the dugout, he was violently throwing up onto the rain sodden duckboards. He must have fallen with some force. Mud filled his nostrils and mouth. Mixed with the foul earth he tasted ash and charcoal; carbon granules and asbestos flakes from a shattered gas-mask. He tried lifting himself, but his limbs, shaking uncontrollably, failed to respond. Others were next to him. Writhing in agony, tears streamed from their bloodshot eyes, foam and vomit from their mouths.

An officer stood above them. Emptying ice cold water from a bucket over their faces he howled, "Sons of bitches, pussies, cowards! Did your mother fuck sheep and breed lambs? Get back on your feet and finish your mission!".

Battered by this abuse, every miserable failing from his life screamed in unison, their fierce voices shaking his sanity. A monster transmogrified from this torrent of agonies: shame. Why was he lying there so pathetically, when those younger, weaker than him, were already flying across the ground to be first to the target and the glory to come?

Pierre, appalled by the thought that in his first epic test he had failed, extracted himself from the sticky ooze and reached for his club. Scrambling back to the ladder, he hauled his battered body over the parapet to return to his company. The sickness that had seen him flounder before, was thrust aside by fiercer imperatives. A total, all-consuming determination to show he had the balls to fulfil his orders whatever the cost. Perversely those same priggish voices that had castigated him for cowardice now screamed at him to get down from a second spray of bullets slicing dangerously overhead. Stepping back to the ladder he blithely ignored them, the idea that he might be court-martialled for disobediently charging the enemy with his big baton, bringing a fleeting smile to his previously tortured face.

That stupid, asinine expression stayed with him as he sprinted across the open ground, the enemy, now fully awake to their presence, firing from all sides. Second time around, his progress proved more difficult. There were so many dead and dying scattered across the churned up ground it was hard to find a clear foothold. And not random, unknown corpses. Faces he recognised. Fellow students and friends, that just fifteen minutes before had been laughing and joking over that last fatal drink.

For seconds, for those who still dared peer over the trench rim, Pierre's crazed, demented dash looked heroic. Despite the constant barrage of mortar bombs and the rattle of machine-gun fire, he made a surprising distance in a short space of time. But fate, like a third rate director playing with tragedy, is more often cruel.

Pierre had been the bane of his commanding officers from the day he enlisted. Disorderly and undisciplined, he always turned up late for parades looking slovenly and scruffy. That scruffiness proved his salvation. A length of loose webbing trailing from his ammunition belt caught on a barbed wooden picket. The hook wrenched him sharply to his side. Pulled off balance he tripped. A mortar round exploded close by. The shockwave, punching into his back, upended him, spinning his body sideways in a clownish cartwheel across the terrain. After three spectacular somersaults, Pierre landed in an undignified heap, limbs askew, bleating like a stricken lamb. At first he thought his chest had been pierced, that the ugly whistling sound was his last breath being expelled from his lungs. In blind panic he tore open his shirt to find the reverberation was from a crushed mouth organ in his breast pocket.

Mercifully he wasn't entirely uninjured. A three-inch blade of shrapnel kindly severed his right ear neatly from the side of his head. He'd hit the ground near the trench entrance, head theatrically splattered with a dramatic spray of blood. The effect looked so horrific some thought half his head had been torn off, that the gore of scarlet mush was his brains. The officer who had previously screamed at him for cowardice, now bowled over by his mad, intrepid, Herculean sprint, rushed sympathetically to his aid and screamed for medics.

Recovering in the hospital weeks later, he was still having trouble piecing together what had really happened. The ward he was left in was rarely attended. Few came to visit. Limping to the latrines, it was only by chance that he caught the tail end of a conversation between a visiting physician and the ward doctor. Half his company had gone; Chlorine gas the cause.

Burning logs at the centre of the fire collapsed, spitting a spiral of fiery ash into the sky. Captain Sumet and Chai, perturbed by Pierre's grim monologue, watched the rising sparks as they rose up then faded into the stars. A silence descended.

Born, squatting by the side of the fire, far from the young Frenchman's story, had been roasting chestnuts in the hot coals at the edge of the logs. Having gathered the blackened husks in a neat circle, he should have been peeling them one by one, but the icy quiet that enveloped them all, affected him too. Like the rest he was shaken, but beyond the unease, deeper emotions emerged. He felt rage and betrayal. Everyone had told him – big-wig officials, officers, doctors and desk clerks – his only role would be safely behind the wheel of a truck, far from the front and the action. Encountering guns, mortars and now this, gas attacks, hadn't entered his thinking. Of course, hopeless with language, he hadn't been able to understand a single word of the Frenchman's account, nor had he wanted to. Yet inscribed within Pierre's gestures, facial expressions and the morbid tonality of his voice, Born was able to reconstruct the described scenes in cold, exacting, detail. Ruthless revelations that he was unable to shut out, despite his work peeling the chestnuts. It was as if he was there himself in the trenches; taking in the churned up mud, barbed wire and shattered limbs. Just as the Frenchman had recounted, he saw the crumpled body on the ground, blood gushing from its head wound, with a clarity that left him stunned. What troubled him most was that it wasn't Pierre's face lying there in helpless, contorted agony, it was his own.

Appalled by this vision, Born attempted to shake the nightmare from his mind, snatching the wine bottle from Mai's grasp and drinking in deep gulps. But the alcohol had the opposite affect, the cinema in his head focusing in on his own pallid features with cruel, sadistic intent. More than anything, a single, horrifying idea shook him: what the hell was he doing dying in a foreign field, for a country that wasn't his own, for a cause he didn't believe in or comprehend? How had it come to this?

It was the day after his twentieth birthday. A Tuesday. After a long night of whisky and gambling, Born, confused and lethargic, was in no fit state to navigate the single most important event of his new adult life. The echo of a bell pulled him and his fellow cadets to the parade ground. The harsh sun cutting through the palms, delivered an instant headache. A ringing started between his ears, rendering the barked commands from the staff sergeant into a stream of unintelligible gibberish. Chattering macaques would have been more succinct.

Two flags were planted in the earth. One was red, the other green. A starting pistol was fired. Following the herd, Born stumbled thoughtlessly to the green pennant, with little idea of its significance. Like everyone, he cheered, "Chai yoe, chai yoe," and threw his hat in the air. A week later he was passing through the main atrium on the way to the mess hall, when he noticed a group crowded around a list on the noticeboard. His name, Born Chuan Chern headed the column.

Waiting in line, boarding a cargo ship out of Bangkok, he had no idea what he was doing. Not that he cared. For Born had his own reasons to leave the country in a hurry.

The disagreement had been futile; it was a fit of rage over a dice game. He'd used a blunt instrument, in fact no more than a broom handle and he'd only hit him once. Then he'd run, enough to ensure that he wasn't being chased: he wasn't.

Later, lying low in a bamboo thicket until dark, he wasn't entirely sure if the man had regained consciousness. Getting hungry and besieged by vicious, red ants, he walked home, ate, slept and forgot about it.

It was a week later, when he was waiting for the train to rejoin his regiment, that he'd heard rumours that a man had died. Naturally he was shocked. He hadn't even been that angry at the time, his strike had been mild, as if beating a dog. Worst still, he knew the family and was close to the daughter; he liked the daughter - had vain designs on a romance. He thought about going back to come clean and give himself in. But then the train pulled into the platform and everyone had scrambled for the doors. Born had stalled on the carriage step, torn between returning, confessing, pleading forgiveness, or making a run for it. The station master's urgent whistle made up his mind for him. With no seats on board, he found a space at the back of the mail car, covered his head with a post bag, curled up and slept.

Since then, he hadn't thought that much about it. Distance, the long sea voyage, had taken him far from the scene of the crime and its reciprocal guilt. Until this; this gruesome, perhaps prophetic vision. Was this karma? Had it, like the mischievous gods of old, chased him across the turbulent heavens to this far continent, to exact cruel retribution?

Chapter 13

Wrun kicked the base of the door. The rusted hinges sheered, dropping the barn door face down to the floor of the chicken shed. It revealed a foul interior. Thin beams of light, cast into biblical lances by the billowing dust, etched sharp shapes on the ground. Past these bright columns they could see the trucks, pressed together like broken toys in a box, at the back of the barn. The paperwork described them as 'camions militaires', although the wording was maybe an over-optimistic reading of their condition. The majority were horse-drawn wagons, milk floats and mail vans. Covered in chicken shit and bird droppings, they were in a deplorable state. One, propped up on wood blocks near the door, was topped by an unusual floral awning and a straw donkey, that suggested it had last been used as a float in a carnival.

Sumet turned around and walked out without a second glance. Crossing the yard he shouted for Born and ordered a return to the camp.

Born, foraging for duck eggs in reeds by the pond, heard the distant command and running back to the farm buildings, intercepted the Captain mid way to the lorries that had brought them.

"Pack my bags. I've had enough of their insults!", he exclaimed. "We're going home!"

"Home?" questioned Born, cradling his eggs in a handkerchief.

"Home!" repeated the Captain

"Home where?"

"Siam home, you fool!"

Sumet's full intention was madder still. They were to board a train for Milan and head east as far as they could go. If the tracks ran out he didn't care. He'd walk home alone, across the Levant and the mountains of the Hindu Kush if necessary.

Chai, running out from the barn, caught up with Sumet and cautiously steered him away from the farm exit. Finding a bench under the trees, he encouraged the Captain to sit down, his rage so implacable, it made the planks shake.

"Captain, please, patience, I plead with you," whispered Chai, fire-fighting again.

"Damn their impudence and arrogance! I'm fed up with it! I can't take it anymore!"

"We're all angry… But we've got to stay patient. They watch us like hawks…"

Chai could see two officials leaning over the gate at the farm entrance. Even from afar, he could read their cynical grins.

"To hell with it, I don't give a damn what they think…"

"If we get upset over such slights, it only hands victory to those who deride us."

"So what should we do hah? Roll over like puppies?"

Returning to camp, Pierre took Chai to the divisional headquarters and angry on their behalf, berated the junior officers who had organised the transports, "The King of Siam sends his personal drivers to help save our nation and you offer them shit wagons!"

Five days later the Thai company tried again. They drove west to the town of Sens, its narrow streets locked with traffic. A gendarme directed them through backstreets to a freight yard on the edge of town. Captain Sumet, dispirited by their earlier attempt, was nothing but sceptical. Indeed, the entrance to the rail-yard couldn't have looked less promising. Its main gate, hammered with worn planks, had to be cleared of beggars and tramps. Catching the acrid fumes of burning rubber and waste, Sumet shielded his face, so certain was he of greater ignominy to come. It was only on hearing grasps of amazement and incredulity, that he was persuaded to prise his fingers from his eyes.

Four regimented lines of trucks filled the square. Most were heavy four-ton Berliet's, newly painted in dull military grey and green, boxy in shape and sitting tall on seven-spoked wheels. Their cabs, open at the side, were shielded from the elements by fabric awnings, secured to the front axles with polished leather straps. Canvas frames covered their rear platforms, the interiors laid out with slated, recently varnished benches. Although dents and broken panels showed the vehicles were far from new, lined up in the mid-morning sun they nevertheless looked grand and impressive, moving some close to tears.

Captain Sumet, climbing down from his seat, took on an air of grave indifference, in an attempt to contain his boyish glee. Walking along the front row of vehicles he had Chai instruct their mechanics to do an inspection of the engines, chassis and wheels before fully accepting delivery. Initial impressions were good. Those standing in the front line, the cleanest and most presentable, looked in worthy condition; more powerful and robust than the ungainly and feeble British Austins they had trained in back home in Saraburi. It was only within the far wings, sandwiched between the third and fourth ranks, that they unearthed some, suspect, unusable wrecks.

Of the thirty-four trucks that had been assigned to the Siamese company, two had broken chain drives, three, radiators that needed patching, six were waiting spare parts, and nine, missing their wheels, were completely unroadworthy. In a dust bowl adjacent to the rail-yard, several had been left on brick blocks in the open, their rusty axles exposed. In the back of one rusting hulk, five men were curled up asleep. Hearing the approach of Chai's men, they panicked, grabbed bundles of clothes and some last scraps of food and rapidly made off. Scrambling over a chain fence they landed in a field waist deep with nettles and brambles, cursing as they shredded their jackets and trousers; likely deserters.

Back in the yard, Pierre organised a mechanic near the station to deal with the more serious technical concerns. He was able to supply the basics – fan belts, radiator hoses, chain drives and air filters – with which to make the immediate repairs. Soon the most roadworthy were separated from the wrecks, filled with water, oiled and refuelled.

The Captain, assigning the teams to their vehicles, selected the finest truck for himself, impressed by its fresh paintwork and finely tailored roof. Unlike the rest it had a longer wheelbase and two rows of benches in the front. Reaching for a grab handle, Sumet launched himself up into the cab, only to land on seat squabs so thick with dead insects and grime he got stuck. Furiously brushing the gooey crust from his pants he stepped down and yelled for a wash.

Born took a wire brush to the interior. The steps and floor were layered with mud, grease and cigarette butts. A dead rat was found under the bench seat. It was removed but an offensive stench remained. Born dug deeper and discovered a ball of soft cheese in the toolbox. Wrapped in newspaper and lively with mould, a date on the headline showed it had festered for years. The back needed more work. Unusually resilient stains marked the oak boards and loading ramp. Mai and Manit were called to help out.

By mid-morning, the trucks looked new and surprisingly respectable. A transformation so complete that it had now attracted the attention of the French transport officials and staff, who, taking a coffee break, had grouped on a balcony overlooking the yard. The Captain, deriving a certain satisfaction from their admiration, then grew nervous that they might change their minds and steal them back again. Anxious to pre-empt such a move he looked for a way to stamp his claim on the vehicles.

"We need a ceremony Chai, something to mark the occasion, make a show for the men."

Lek and Worarat, the two clerks, were called for. Knowing they'd been ordained as Buddhist monks before joining the army, the Captain asked them to officiate over a small service, to bless and say prayers for the vehicles.

Scavenging items from across the rail yard, the two improvised a blessing. Birch twigs were used to flick water over the front of the trucks.

Ribbons and small trinkets were tied around the steering columns of the lead vehicles. Digging some clay from a stream, Worarat dabbed a set of Sanskrit symbols onto the newly scrubbed engine cowlings. A Siamese flag was unwrapped and tied to the roof awning of the Captain's truck.

Sumet, overcoming his habitual reserve, appeared unusually animated. He had even prepared a short speech. Written on the back of a postcard he had bought in the cafe in Marseilles, it included a statement from the Palace, praising "the bravery and dedication of the nation's officers and troops, fighting for the honour of Siam in the battle for the world".

Ending the speech, the Captain, choked with patriotism, burst spontaneously into the last four lines of the Royal anthem.

"We, your majesty's loyal subjects, pay homage to the supreme protector, the mightiest of monarchs, under whose benevolent rule, we, your humble subjects, receive protection and happiness."

He wasn't a good singer; the rest of the Corp, embarrassed by his dissonant delivery, had to rush to his aid.

With the ceremony over, the Captain blew a whistle and ordered his men to their vehicles. Chokes were primed and crank handles turned. Clouds of black smoke poured from exhausts, as somnolent cylinders creaked unevenly into life.

Their first orders took them to a concert hall in the centre of Sens. On a loading platform at the back of the stage their cargo awaited; a Steinway grand piano, musical instruments, a wooden rostrum, wardrobe cases and one hundred and fifty audience chairs. The assignment was to be delivered to General Pétain's residence at Château Montraume.

Wrapping the grand piano and instruments with wool blankets and packaging, they set off at four, east towards Troyes. At a junction close to the town, they were met by an open voiturette filled with gendarmes and two motorcycle outriders, who accompanied them the last ten kilometres to the château. Turning into the courtyard the Stars and Stripes flew from a flagpole. American officers from General Pershing's headquarters were visiting the troops. An opera had been laid on; the singer Lily Maria driven from Paris.

It took ten of the men to offload the Steinway and carry it on the last leg of the journey, to the summerhouse in the rose gardens of the Chateau, its lawns sodden with rain.

As they waited for Chai and Pierre, checking in at the adjutants office, Captain Sumet and his men sat on the rear platform of their trucks and took in the aria from the second act of Puccini's La Bohème, "Quando m'en vo".

Chapter 14

The Leger Forey Estate, close to the Burgundian town of Beaune, had been owned by the same Bourbon family for ten generations. The walled estate included hunting forests, fishing lakes and kennels. But it was the vineyards that the estate was renowned for. Adjacent to the Corton hillside, famous for supplying the Emperor Charlemagne's wines, fifteen hectares were laid out with Pinot Noir and Chardonnay vines. The best grapes were grown on the west-facing slopes, their soil rich with layers of clay, limestone and flint. Since the death of the last male heir, Francois Augustus Forey, the estate was run by his thirty-four-year-old niece, Catherine.

Although the demands of the war had seen all the ablest young men pulled from the workforce, reducing the farm team to nineteen, the estate still managed to produce up to eight thousand bottles of red and white wine. The most sought after were the Premier and Grand Cru's. They were on the sommelier's list at Le Montparnasse in Paris, a restaurant much favoured by government ministers and the military command.

General Pétain, who dined by habit in a private room at Le Montparnasse, now demanded the chateau's finest at every meal. His enthusiasm for the label found favour with his inner circle. Fifty-five cases were regularly delivered to the Château de Montraume, another one hundred to the headquarters of the Fourth Army, together with a further fifteen to the elite flyers of the Escadrille 103, based at the Longvic airbase.

Deemed essential to maintaining "Le moral du Haut Commandement", ten trucks were devoted to the operation every week. For the past six months, those trucks had been managed by a Gascogne team from Bayonne. Operating at a comfortable distance from the chaos of the conflict, the 'special mission' was considered a 'privileged' assignment. So privileged that the staff sergeant tasked with heading the deliveries became careless and complacent. Surly, frequently late and suspected of squirrelling away the precious cases in a cousin's bar in Beaune, the Gascogne man had tried the patience of the dispatch clerks too many times. It was Pierre, ever vigilant and solicitous as to the comings and goings of the transport office, who was quick to latch on to the extraordinary nature of their cushy operation. Chatting up the desk girls and plying them with chocolate and lipstick traded from the Americans, he bided his time. When the Gascogne team missed yet another vital delivery, Pierre, seeing them slip, rushed forward to volunteer their services. Thai drivers, he boasted, were punctual and conscientious and being good Buddhists, honest teetotallers.

The days started early. Pierre, in his anxiety to wrest the crucial assignment from the incumbents, had overpromised on everything; speed, distance and quantity. A simple delivery through Auxerre and Saint Florentin, took more than a day. Few made it back before sunset, one or two limped back after dawn.

The Captain, taking it upon himself to rearrange the delivery schedule, was aghast to discover how quickly their best-laid plans unravelled once exposed to the field. They had military maps, yet every road within a hundred miles of the front was chaotic with jams, diversions and roadblocks.

Returning from Rouen after an exhausting twelve hours on the road, they were ten kilometres from their camp when yet another barrier barred their way. Chai and Pierre, worried by the red flags and a brash sign, "interdit, déviation, Halte", still dripping with sticky, red paint, suggested returning to Rouen. But the Captain, infuriated by the needless delays they had already encountered, had the men pull back the barriers and they drove through.

At first it looked like Sumet's rash gamble had paid off. The road was clear and they were soon climbing swiftly into the hills. Reaching the crest of a rise the road levelled out and ran straight along a ridge for thirteen, unimpeded kilometres. The Captain, standing on the running boards and thinking he could see their destination, the Foyer forests in the distance, rapped the engine cowling urging more speed, "Born, step on it. An ox cart could go faster!"

Born tried to accelerate, but the road was no better than a farm-track, its overgrown banks rising up like a tunnel, deep ditches on both sides. He was more than aware that if a wheel strayed into its grip, it would be impossible to dislodge. The light was also failing. No one liked travelling at night.

They were passing beneath a dense canopy of foliage when Born first noticed a curious rain of splinters and leaves. Thinking it was no more than a family of nut hoarding squirrels, he drove on. It was Pierre, hit by harder twigs, who first grasped the true danger.

Shots sounded. A ricochet hit the side of the truck. There was a soft tinkle of glass. The Frenchman, sitting up with a jerk, realised a case of wine had been hit just behind their partition. He could hear the trickle of liquid drip onto the cases beneath, even smell its aroma; regrettably a vintage.

A second volley sounded. Falling from the trees a dark shape dropped to the footwell. The Captain reeling back, looked down and saw bright blood marring his boots; a maimed crow writhed at his feet. Pierre shouted for them all to take cover. Sliding off the bench seat they crushed together in the footwell.

"Born where's my gun?"

"Back at the base."

"What!"

"I was cleaning it."

"Why?" he wailed.

"That's my job."

"This is a war dammit, not a parade!"

The shooting stopped. They waited. Born managed to grab a wing of the stricken bird and flicked it outside. Thrashing around in the dirt it took a long time to die. Eventually the Captain and Pierre struggled back to their seat and peered out. Across on the far side, a figure had scrambled to the top of the embankment and was waving a white handkerchief. Sumet, standing now, was shocked to see it was Chai. Seconds later they heard the thud of horse hooves cantering across a field. The low bushes parted as an officer appeared on a dark charger.

"What the hell are you doing here? The whole area's closed. Didn't you see the signs, the red flags?"

"What flags?," asked Pierre, pretending to look perplexed.

"Back at the Nolay crossroads," he shouted.

"No," lied Pierre, well aware they'd seen the flags and intentionally ignored them, "We didn't".

The officer wasn't convinced, "Fools... all of you... I should have you reported. What company are you from?"

"The Royal Siamese Motor Division," replied the Captain, leaning forward to make himself more prominent.

"The Royal Siamese what?", he eyed Sumet quizzically.

From the far side of the field a hunting horn sounded. The black mare snorted and pulled impatiently at its bridle.

"Well, whoever you are, you have ten minutes to get out of here. If not, I couldn't care less if you're blasted all the way back to..."

"Siam," added Pierre helpfully.

"Yes, damned Siam!"

The officer turned his horse and rode away. They listened as the sound of hooves receded.

"Well, what are you waiting for!", snapped the Captain, "Let's get the hell out of here!"

He'd forgotten Chai. His deputy was just then sliding down the rough bank to cheers from the men. Sauntering back to the truck, Pierre lent a helping hand to help him up into the cab. Looking chuffed and self satisfied, Chai was settling back onto the bench, when Sumet suddenly turned to him.

"I've seen some stupid acts in my past, but that surely takes the biscuit. What the hell were you doing? Live rounds! You could have been killed!"

"I didn't think…" started Chai, taken aback by the scolding.

"Oh you thought alright. You thought like a fool!" glared the Captain, pointing to two clear bullet holes in the fabric of his handkerchief.

The greatest advantage for Pierre's favoured taskforce were the accommodation benefits. Because they could stay on the estate, they weren't compelled to race back to the dire St Amour camp every evening. At first they pitched tents by the lakeside, but the Countess, thinking them unsightly, had arranged her own accommodation. Some distance from the main château, screened by an avenue of tall poplars, stood a quadrangle of farm buildings, framed by two gothic watchtowers. The barns housed stables, grain stores and cellars. To the side of this square a covered yard provided workshop space for the mechanics; they could spend time on the engines that still needed repairs and maintenance.

Most of the company found space on the ground floor. The old olive presses and barrels had been cleared from the workspace to make room for two lines of beds and wash stands. Captain Sumet, Chai, Manit and Mai had more salubrious quarters on the floor above. Ornate wooden bedsteads were made up with spring mattresses and feather filled pillows. In an anteroom they were surprised to find a rare porcelain bath with a stove to warm water.

Food was prepared in the main barn where there was a large refectory table, granite basins, and two charcoal burners. The Countess's farmhands supplied vegetables and potatoes from her own garden, cheese and eggs from the village and when lucky, joints of chicken, even pork.

Entering the last weeks of October it was still warm enough to sit outside. Captain Sumet, overwhelmed and enchanted by this magical Arcadia, had the men arrange the trestle tables in a square in the courtyard. It overlooked a valley where the beech trees were already turning a rusty ochre. They watched the sky larks darting overhead. In the woods they heard nightingales. Several of the men played card games in the candlelight.

Sumet, never known as a profound thinker, lulled by the serenity and quiet, became worryingly poetic: vineyards, sunsets, dragonflies and blue sage; it was the epitome of natural order and perfection – a blueprint of civilisation and culture. Why would sane men, the same enlightened people who had created such harmony, set out to wilfully destroy it?

Chapter 15

Initially the Captain was treated with suspicion by the farmworkers. Having never seen an oriental before, they were unsettled by his swarthy appearance. Some thought his round face Slavic, possibly 'gitan'; and gitan stole livestock. It took a week of early morning sightings and the comfort that he was both trusted and accompanied by the countesses' notoriously unpredictable Brittany gun dogs, to allay their suspicions.

They were surprised by the man's fluency in French. Inquisitive and curious the Captain explored every avenue of the land and pried into their most mundane details with an intimacy that was almost childlike. He walked the fields, orchards and woodlands; an "Atlas des Plantes" in hand – a dusty manual of lithographs and etchings he'd picked up from a bookcase in the watchtower.

Claude Ferraux, the seventy-one-year-old director of wine production, renowned for his taciturn reserve, indeed distrust of outsiders (which he classified as anyone from beyond the four hills), had a curious affection for the stranger. Impressed by Sumet's thirst for knowledge, he took him under his wing, even offering to take him on a tour of the Forey domains.

Four valleys comprised the estate. The higher ground to the north, ringed by forests of dense pine, fell to mixed woods of elm, chestnut and beech. The trees ringed the west valley, the fields containing the main vineyards. The land, originally stretching as far as the Armançon river, was seized from the church just after the Reign of Terror in the late eighteenth century. It was bought by Jean Henri Borneau, then a junior officer in the Revolutionary Army, who, judicious with his allegiances, was careful to back the right side at the height of the bloodbath. His descendants had successfully kept the lands in the family ever since. It was Catherine Forey's grandfather who had perfected the wine growing. The original Pinot Blanc and Gamay vines grown by the Cistercian monks, had been ripped up and replaced by the current Pinot Noir and Chardonnay.

Pointing out the verdant cascades of neatly-spaced Premier Cru and Grand Cru vines, Ferraux patiently described the geography of the most productive fields. The rounded hills faced south-west to get the maximum sun. The slopes had to be steep enough to drain the soil during heavy rains, as well as providing sufficient air circulation through the harsh winter frosts.

Ferraux walked with a heavy gnarled stick which he used to prod the earth. Stabbing its tip through the topsoil of limestone and gravel he exposed layers of chalk underneath; a rare characteristic of the region's geology he called 'la boutonnière'. Bending to the ground the estate manager scooped up a handful of dirt and crumbling the soil between his fingers, revealed its recondite secrets. In the palm of his hand lay tiny marine shells; porous calcite granules, that acted as miniature water reservoirs for thirsty roots at times of drought.

Walking down to the base of the hill, they crouched beneath the canopy of leaves to examine the fruits, their dark skins covered in a fine sheen of dew. Ferraux, picking a grape, rolled the fruit between his thumb and forefinger to show the waxy coating that contained the yeast. He explained the all-important fermentation process, in which the yeast turned the sugars into alcohol. A transformation so miraculous Ferraux thought it spiritual. Wine, he claimed, was truly the blood of Christ. It gave his endeavours a more religious calling, making him feel more high priest than farm labourer.

"In the Book of Revelations," growled Ferraux, "the end of days is presented as a great harvest, 'So the Angel swung his sickle toward earth and gathered the grapes from earth's vineyard and threw them into the great winepress of God's wrath." Maybe that moment was upon us, he mused, gazing up at the high ridge as if expecting the horses of the apocalypse.

The summer had been late that year delaying the harvest. To gauge that crucial moment, Ferraux and his men had to sample grapes from every corner of the fields; the high and low points, then east and west. Ripe grapes were rich in colour, not green, plump so that they crushed easily to give up their juices. Then it was down to taste, a critical balance between acidity and sweetness; "acidité et douceur".

They went back to the estate buildings on the back of a farm cart. Sumet, letting his legs hang lazily over the back, looked out over the orderly avenues of vines. Enthralled by Ferraux's tour, his mind wandered back to his own country. His mother's family was originally from the province of Khorat. The hills were higher and cooler than the rice-growing plains around Bangkok. Would the soil suit the production of wine?

Back in the cellars a bottle of 1898 Grand Cru was opened. Ferraux unwrapped a small Chavignol cheese from his pocket. With a switchblade he sliced it into small chunks. Several bottles later, Sumet, flushed red with its potency.

Chapter 16

In making the great leap from blood-thirsty revolutionaries to blue-blooded aristocrats, effortlessly wealthy on land rents and wine, the Leger Forey family hadn't completely abandoned their forebears' egalitarian principles. Looking to move with the tenor of the times, a factory had been built within the estate to provide employment for local craftsmen, artisans and the families of farm labourers. Following the principles of the philanthropist Charles Fourier, the Leger Forey Foundry produced enamelled cast-iron stoves, cooking pans and kitchen ware for wealthy, urbane Parisians. A display, 'La Cuisine Contemporaine', the first with built in storage cabinets, spice racks, sugar and flour bins, filled a window of Le Bon Marché, Rue de Sèvres, Saint-Germain. To educate the children of the foundry workers and managers, a school was set up in a village adjoining the factory buildings.

The current schoolmaster was the aged, armchair bound, Henri Biset. Hearing of the Thai company quartered at the château, he had asked the Countess to arrange for some of the group to visit the school and meet the pupils. Their Captain was the obvious choice. But locked in an attic, penning a prospectus on the viticulture future of Siam, Sumet was too busy to tear himself from his work. He suggested that Chai and Mai should go in his place.

The event was the idea of a junior teacher, Sandrine Boucher. Sandrine was a geography tutor, now in her third year with the school.

The subject she was teaching to her thirteen-year-old class was the great Imperial powers of the world. A canvas map, hung over the blackboard, filled an entire wall of the modest Castelnau classroom. Three principal empires, the domains of France, Russia and Britain, monopolised the continents, coloured in large swathes of blue, green and pink.

For the children of Castelnau, many of whose fathers and brothers were fighting on the front, their only interest and focus was on the homeland. Blue lines on the map, stretching outwards like the tentacles of a giant squid, reached out to France's near and distant dominions - Grande Terre, the island at the end of its longest, most remote strand, winding around the fringes of the Antarctic. It left the pupils with little doubt that their proud realm was the epicentre and protector of the civilised world.

Gurnard, the mathematics teacher, had military connections. His cousin was a lieutenant in colonial recruitment based in Besier. Four young soldiers, from Senegal, Algiers, Morocco and Tunisia, had been selected to meet the children and talk about their country's geography and culture.

Driven in by truck, the recruits descended from their vehicles and assembled in Sandrine's classroom before the twenty-five boys and girls. Joined by Chai and Mai from the chateau, they lined up under a long banner stretched across the room, its tall letters proclaiming, "Trois Couleurs, Un Drapeau, Un Empire".

Farid Ahmadi, only seventeen, had grown up in the High Atlas mountains of Morocco. His father was the son of a Berber Chief. Although they shared a stone house in a village with other members of their family, they spent most of the year on the move between the mountains and the west coast of Africa. To earn a living they sold goats and mules to the traders in Chefchaouen and Laghdir. And often, if they got a bad price, his elder brother, under the cover of darkness stole them back again. Farid's job was to wrap burlap sacking around the hooves of the animals so that they made no sound on the rocks and left no trail in the desert.

Hossein Mahrez, a Tunisian, had lost both his parents to cholera when he was just four. He had been brought up by grandparents in a village on the coast. From an early age he went fishing with an uncle. The old man had a small wooden skiff with two masts that mostly netted sardines and shrimps. There was a foreign canning factory in Sousse, run by Italians who would buy their haul. But with too many boats chasing too few fish, they were forced out to deeper waters in the hope of finding larger catches. A storm had blown up. After three tempestuous days fighting the waves and close to sinking they came ashore off the south coast of Sicily. Arrested by carabinieri, they were thrown in a jail for two weeks with very little food or water. A fine, imposed on their hard-up families back home, was paid and they were sent back. His uncle, who never got his boat back, lost his livelihood. Hossein, no longer employed and not wanting to be a financial drain on his grandparents, was promised five thousand dinar by the colonial authorities to enlist.

Khalid Aziz was from a village near Merija, Bechar. Casually shrugging his shoulders and shuffling his hands in his pockets, he had to admit that he hadn't had the luxury of volunteering. A petty thief (he had stolen sweets from a street stall because he was hungry and had no money), he had been given two options by the town magistrate. He could either have his hand cut off, or he could enrol with the local militia. His answer hadn't needed much deliberation. Khalid pointed to his country on the map; yet another patch of cobalt at the end of a squiggly arm from the greater homeland. One day he hoped and prayed that his country wouldn't be blue. Bringing giggles from the children, he used white chalk to try to cover over the colour on the canvas. He ended up making a mess, encouraging louder laughter from the class.

Bernard Fouche, deputy headmaster responsible for mentoring Sandrine through her day, was quick to swoop on the unrest.

"Quiet!", he snapped from the sidelines, "Quiet class!"

The pupils, knowing only too well not to cross the authoritarian deputy, obediently fell into line.

Of all the soldiers invited, Bernard had had his eyes on Khalid right from the start and immediately distrusted him. In fact as soon as the Algerian had leapt from the tailgate of their truck, the man had aroused his ire. Dragging his feet through the gravel, Khalid had looked up at the clock tower and made a petulant gesture to the Tricolore. Bernard, having spent most of the previous day stringing the great flag up in the first place – no mean feat considering the fragility of his ladder – had been incensed by the effrontery. After such an act, Khalid's subversion with the chalk had been entirely expected. Forearmed with a feather duster and close to the board, Bernard's intervention had been swift, the offending mark wiped clean before most had blinked.

"The rainfall Khalid?" interrupted Bernard.

Khalid, well aware that he was being called to heel, stalled.

"The rainfall?"

"Yes, God's gift from heaven, nurturer of growth, fountain of life. When does it fall?"

"The rains come in winter, November to January," continued Khalid mechanically, "God willing and if we were lucky. And with enough water we could grow pretty much anything we wanted, fruit, nuts or dates…"

But as far as Khalid could see it wasn't his own kind that grew wealthy on 'God's rich bounty'. It was the idle foreign merchants; "Why, when there was so much food, did villages go hungry, people starve?"

"Thank you Khalid", interjected Bernard, fast to stamp out any further troublemaking, "Time has no master, and we have other continents to travel to before noon", added the deputy, ushering the Algerian impatiently from the stage.

Sandrine, embarrassed by Bernard's heavy handedness with Khalid, encouraged Chai and Mai to the platform. The two Thais, conscious that they were the last to speak and that the children were restless so close to their lunch break, felt rushed. Chai started by asking the class where they thought Siam was on the map. The question brought an embarrassed silence. Few had any idea it existed, let alone where it was. One or two, rightly assuming that they weren't European or African, pointed to China, a third to Japan. Mai ended their confusion by pointing to a small corner of the map squeezed in between pink British Burma, blue French Indochina and the orange stokes of the Dutch colonies in Indonesia. Bizarrely the area was frustratingly uncoloured.

Chai, anxious to hold their attention, told stories of king's, princesses, golden palaces and palm trees, white elephants and streets of water where fruits and vegetables were sold from boats in canals. The class children were spellbound. Of all the countries they had been told about, this strange, mystical land seemed the most magical. Encouraged by Sandrine, Chai and Mai took turns to draw pictures on the blackboard – temples, stupas, palm trees and buffalo. Mai, getting carried away by the classes' enthusiastic response, started on a set of mythical, multi-headed nagas and flying monkeys.

"Those last one's weren't real," Chai added, apologising for Mai's flights of fancy.

The children were curious. Why were their elephants white? Why was there so much water? And most perplexing of all – why hadn't their king surrendered and subjected themselves to foreign rule? Wouldn't they be proud to be part of France? Surely it was better to be part of their noble, civilised realm, than to be yoked to the bossy, badly dressed, beef-eating English?

Chai, ever diplomatic, replied that the Siamese were friends to both the French and British. That's why they were there. To prove their loyalty to all; to fight alongside all the gallant countries of the world to help save France from evil aggressors and tyrants.

Bernard showed his approval of this noble sentiment, by encouraging a cheer from the children.

At twelve the school bell sounded and the lesson promptly ended. Bernard and Sandrine thanked all the soldiers. The class lined up on both sides of the corridor and to the accompaniment of a tin drum and a flute, burst into the opening strains of the Marseillaise as they marched into the garden.

In a covered courtyard outside a lunch had been prepared. Sandrine had asked the mothers of the children to bring what they could. As a result cheese, paste rolls, olives and dried sausage, filled the table; the quantities so generous as to embarrass those grown used to austerity.

The colonial soldiers, uncertain of what to do, or where they should go, bunched into an awkward huddle under a tree. A passing maid handed out plates and encouraged them to the table. At first they picked modestly from the bowls, but then, seeing as no one was watching, piled them high with as much food as they thought they could get away with.

Sandrine, entertaining the local dignitaries, the post-master, church organist and gendarme, was last to the food. She was heading towards the quadrangle where the aged Biset was being wheeled into place at the top of the table, when she changed her mind at the last moment and turned to the trestle table occupied by the foreign soldiers. It caused some commotion. The North Africans, unsettled to have both a woman and a French national in their presence, shifted awkwardly to afford her more space. She took the seat next to Chai, smiling courteously to all in her circle to put them at ease.

Sandrine had made a simple choice; a slither of cheese, some olives and an egg still in its shell. And for a long time she just toyed with the morcels, as if shifting draughts pieces on a board. Chai, glancing across, couldn't gauge the reason for her nervousness. For nervousness it was; she knocked over a glass, dropped her fork under the table and spilt salt over his sleeve. In Chai's mind the morning had been nothing but a success. With the hard work over, shouldn't she be relaxed, celebrating that triumph?

Searching for some explanation for her disquiet, Chai scanned the garden and courtyard. His gaze settled on the top table. At Bizet's end, surrounded as he was by the priest, post-master and gendarme, all were wolfing their food and happy in conversation. But at the far end, several of the remaining teachers had formed into a more shifty and intimate clique. Engrossed in their chatter, furtive eyes crossed the divide; the most critical those of the school deputy, Bernard.

For the Castelnau school it was unusual to invite speakers to talk at the school, let alone for those outsiders to be foreigners. Several teachers, including Bernard, had opposed the idea on the ground that such an intrusion might prove disruptive to the children. They had strict curriculum to adhere to, courses and subjects that all needed preparation and management. If the event went ahead, who would deal with the additional logistics and paperwork? Because of the war they were short-staffed as it was.

Despite these objections, Sandrine had been determined to prove the doubters wrong. Although she took it upon herself to organise the brunt of the event, countering such negativism from the senior staff only added unnecessary stress. She hadn't been sure until the eleventh hour whether the military would allow the North Africans to turn up. Then there was transport. Even the night before she wasn't certain if the trucks to pick them up at the station had been laid on. Beset with anxieties she had not slept.

The headmaster, Biset, frail as he was, had been her only support. The lunch with the villagers and the local dignitaries had been his suggestion. Previously strict with alcohol, he had also allowed a small measure of wine. The Countess, as her contribution to the event, had sent across a case of six bottles. Bernard hadn't liked that at all. Wanting to control their distribution, he had hidden those special bottles in the hedgerow under his study window. Sandrine had found them and taken two. Later, he'd been furious to learn that she had 'wasted' a whole bottle on the young soldiers.

"The children loved your drawings," enthused Sandrine, overcoming her earlier reserve and self conscious she was being a bore. A concern that spread to her appearance. Feeling too uptight and formal within a circle of men with rolled sleeves and loose collars, she undid her scarf and released the tight buttons on her blouse. The cool brought some much needed relief.

"Especially the elephant, though the tiger and the buffalo were also pretty. How did you learn to draw so beautifully. Did you have lessons?", she asked.

"My school, in the country, was simple", replied Chai, "We were only taught languages and maths. No one had any time for art. If we drew we drew for fun. My father bought us paper and pencils. He often spent time in the village temple restoring the old mural paintings. Helping him out, I was allowed to fill in the trees and bushes. But only green paint. No one trusted me with animals, or people, especially the Buddhas."

Chai asked after her own family.

"There isn't much to say", she replied. "I was born in the village. I had an elder brother. He ran away to Lyons. My father, wary that I'd also be lured away, never let me out of his sight. When he caught me reading an atlas, he took it away. That's when I discovered the church. There was a bookshelf at the back of the sacristy. Hidden behind the dusty hymn books and psalms I found a collection of travel books. My father and mother, thinking that I'd found enlightenment in the scriptures of prophets and saints, were unaware of my corruption by arctic explorers and sea captains. Da Gama, Nansen and Henri Mouhot became my childhood heroes. A salvation that might have saved my sanity at the time, but later became a curse. I didn't just want to read about the size of the Sahara, I wanted to feel the grains of sand between my toes, swim in the waters of the Nile, climb the pyramids of Giza."

"Did you ever succeed in getting away?"

"I had an escape plan. Got as far as Nice when the war broke out. Since then those ideas have been shelved. That's until I saw your drawings on the blackboard. The palm trees and white elephants rekindled those dreams."

At the high table, Biset, comfortably wrapped in his wingback chair and surrounded by his senior staff, was in high spirits. Bernard was praised for his guiding role in the day's "Le Grand Projet". They proposed a toast.

The Deputy Head took a bow, "Non, non, vous êtes trop gentils", he replied, affecting modesty, knowing full well he was shamelessly taking credit for a success he had in all truth undermined. Looking around the beaming faces at the table it appeared that all criticism was, thankfully, forgotten; how frail were people's memories...

A visiting curate, also a prominent donor, had expressed his compliments on the progressive nature of the event. "How interesting it was to hear personal accounts from the less advanced corners of the globe". Like many he hadn't cared for Khalid's childish and sordid intervention. "Young minds, susceptible to sensationalism, shouldn't be exposed to corrupting ideas." But much to Bernard's relief he'd seen it as a minor hiccup in an otherwise informative and stimulating morning. The cleric was especially fulsome in his praise for the young and pretty Sandrine. Talking to the soldiers, putting them all at ease, she had captivated and charmed all the foreigners.

And that's what concerned Bernard as he walked down the gravel path to his room after he had seen the 'dignitaries' to their carts and cars. Flicking back through the events of the morning, had Sandrine been too close, too over familiar with her visitors? It was an anxiety that stalled him mid-step. Small details had indeed irked him; her smile perhaps too fulsome, the way she had purposefully sat at 'their' table; a move some thought brazen, even provocative. Yes, it was hot, but had it been appropriate to loosen her blouse? Of course the wine, as always, was partly to blame. Hadn't he warned the committee it was wrong from the start?

Reaching the shade of the tall cedars, Bernard had a chance to cool down and recompose himself. His temper likewise moderated and calmed. In this interim, kinder thoughts returned. She'd been impish for sure, but taken as a whole did her behaviour really constitute a break with propriety? Probably not. Put it down to the exuberance of youth. Dutiful daughter of a respected member of the community, she was smart enough not to let her emotions get the better of her. Clearly he had overreacted.

Laughing softly to himself, Bernard continued down the passageway, in an attempt to wash away his unease. But when he turned the corner of the walled garden, those irritations and concerns were still there, throbbing like a persistent and irritating sore. A vague recollection of an article he'd come across in a doctor's surgery came to mind. Tittle-tattle for sure, but not unenlightening. And certainly, in the circumstances, cautionary.

The subject of the scandal was an Indian soldier, not Asian or Chinese. And again, the guilty partner was a nurse rather than a school teacher. But petty differences aside, the similarities to the episode were striking. The errant couple had got as far as St Remo on the Italian border when the elopement had been discovered. The man was arrested and sent back to a jail in Arras. There was little debate. "Rastaquouère", they had called him in the local press. Court marshalled for desertion, he was found guilty and shot.

Several puerile photographs had accompanied the article. One showed a twisted corpse propped up against a picket fence surrounded by his cheerful executioners, sharing cigarettes and looking insouciant. A recollection that still made him squirm. Not out of sympathy for the dead man, but the girl. Her portrait had been more complimentary. A round, cheerful face was framed by elegant, glossy curls. Not yet eighteen, she had been damned to an asylum.

Bernard forced himself to a stop, well aware he was being irrational and disturbed by how easily he had succumbed to such lurid fantasies. Of course, the young gentleman from Siam was young, dashing, handsome, but there was no evidence, other than good natured girliness, to suggest any form of infatuation. She'd taken a place at their table only because the top table was full. It was true their conversation had seemed particularly animated, but Sandrine, even with the cleaners and gardeners, liked a chat.

Bernard's ruminations ended on a single greater anxiety. They had both got up from the table at the same time. Glancing across the garden after taking leave of the cleric, he hadn't seen them. Where were they now?

The obvious place was Sandrine's room, the geography class. Breaking into a jog, he hurried around the corner of the school to the back of the teaching block. Standing on his toes he was able to look over a hedge into the school room. She wasn't there. Only the children were inside. They were laughing. A large white elephant had been chalked on the blackboard. That was odd. Had it been there before?

Bernard headed to the courtyard. It was empty as was the playground. His pace quickened as he rushed around to the front of the hall. He was speeding through the gothic archway when his 'suspects' appeared. They were walking down a gravel track. A track which led directly from the church. Sandrine, not expecting to see Bernard, looked startled. The foreigner was standing only a pace from her. Their hands, although not actually touching, were close. Bernard inwardly shuddered; had they held hands?

"I've been looking everywhere for you Sandrine", said Bernard brusquely. "It's long past three", he nodded to the noise of children coming from the open windows behind, "Was it right that your class should be kept waiting?"

Sandrine, turned back to Chai as if she had something yet to say, the rose lustre of her cheeks making her hesitancy appear both vulnerable and endearing.

"Sandrine!", repeated Bernard.

She ran off. They watched her go. Bernard, waiting a beat, stepped closer to Chai; uncomfortably close.

"She's a very attractive lady," he said, his eyes searching.

Chai, still jarred by her last glance, took time to collect himself.

"She was showing me the church," said Chai, as if having to explain himself.

"Yes. Spectacular stained glass."

Bernard walked away without offering his hand. Chai, unsure of what to make of his hostile turn, stood there stupefied. Had he said something wrong, behaved inappropriately? Was the school master blaming him for keeping her from the class?

Chai walked back up the slope alone to their quarters near the château. Reaching the crest of the hill, he turned and looking back down to the school, mused on those final seconds. She had beautiful blue eyes. He'd noticed them right from the start, even before entering the classroom. So utterly beguiling that he had difficulty returning her stare. Not since childhood had he felt so helplessly entranced. But more than that there were deeper emotions he couldn't easily explain.

Dislike of Bernard was simple. Treating them all with distain, they'd despised him from the start. But Chai's resentment of the man stemmed less from his own slights than from his treatment of Sandrine.

Bernard's expression when he'd turned Sandrine back to the classroom, was more than petty irritation. He'd treated her as if he owned her; that Chai had no right to be talking with her, even being close. When Bernard's gaze had fallen on him, the man's eyes had taken in every element of his appearance as if evaluating a thief. Hatred certainly, but jealousy? Could it really be possible that he, Chai Khomsiri of Siam, was the cause of Bernard's agitation? That the teacher was angry because Sandrine had paid him, a foreigner, too much attention?

Guilt was natural; he was an outsider in a country that wasn't his own, with little understanding of their ways or culture. The slight, the transgression, whatever he'd said or done, must have been his. But such self-reproach was not without a perverse satisfaction – that there might be some truth to it. Witnessing Bernard's outburst had made his fists shake. He'd felt sudden, inexplicable rage. Why he should feel so fiercely protective over someone, that had just a day before been a total stranger, baffled him. He would never see her again.

Chapter 17

The tram was late, so Pramot Wongsanit, took the footpath along the south bank of the Seine and crossing the Pont Mirabeau, arrived just before eight at 36 Rue Berton, the home of the Siamese Legation. First at the office, he took it upon himself to collect the keys and post from the concierge, Madame Mouret in the basement.

At that hour, Mouret, as always, was full of complaint. Over eighty, troubled by chest pains and arthritic joints, she had trouble climbing the stairs, which, needing both hands on the bannisters, was impossible with letters and packages. And lately there'd been too many letters and packages. Her postbox was too small to fit it all in. She'd protested to the landlord but no one had helped her.

Behind the rise of deliveries to the legation was a sudden influx of new arrivals from Siam. Over the past month, two companies of ambulance drivers and medical staff had been billeted in towns around Marseilles. The men needed food, supplies and transport to their training camps in the north. Several were missing bags and cases after their move from the port. Some were still lost in the port. Sadder news came that two men had died from pneumonia on the passage over from Alexandria. The soldiers' families, both from Lamphun province in the north of the country, needed to be contacted and informed. A task that fell to Pramot and his staff.

Mouret was right about her postbox. Pramot had to use a screwdriver to lever the lid from the wire basket, it was so jammed with mail. Most were letters from the training camps at Sens and Dijon. Of these, one envelope in particular stood out from the plain buff covers. Snow white and edged with a gilt line, it drew attention to itself with its flamboyant, embossed crest; the crest of the Count's of Forey. Intrigued by the fancy insignia, Pramot opened it in preference to the others. He saw it had been sent by the commander of one of their advance transport units, Captain Sumet Chantrawong. A name with which he was, depressingly, all too familiar.

Written in a dense, ornate script across four sheets of paper – each side again marked with the ostentatious estate crest – the message was tiresomely long. The final sheet proved the most baffling. Three carefully pencilled columns were filled with a complex set of headings and numbers. Initially Pramot took them for ballistic statistics; velocity, elevation and range. But a second reading revealed a more mundane understanding. The headings in the leading column appeared to be place names: Pinot, Syrah, Gamay. And aligned against each of these entries were a sequence of fractions and percentages. Pramot was flummoxed. Was it some form of code, perhaps military cipher?

Seeking help to interpret its meaning, Pramot left the small annex room overlooking the gloomy ivy throttled back gardens and climbed the staircase to the second floor. Rounding the corner of the corridor, he was surprised to find the large ballroom reserved for the officers empty. Proceeding across the room, he strode through the swing doors into the adjoining office. A secretary hunched over her typewriter jumped up on hearing him enter, fingers scrambling frantically for her keyboard.

"Where is everyone?" asked Pramot seeing the empty desk spaces.

"All the senior staff are away", muttered the secretary, cross at being disturbed.

"Away where?"

"A military base in Provence".

"Provence?"

Pramot should have remembered the mission. It had been on the agenda for weeks. Chief of the Military Command, General Phya Bhija

Janridh, had travelled south to Istres to meet an aviation Corps of four hundred and fourteen aviators and mechanics, who had arrived on the same boat as the ambulance crews. Taken to a flight school on the south coast, they had come up against a litany of 'complications' from their French counterparts. Although most of the Siamese aviators were already accomplished pilots, some having flown for years from their Air Base at Don Muang, the instructors at Istres had insisted on a full evaluation of their mental and physical capabilities, before allowing them on their expensive French planes. Doctors from the local hospital, together with two acclaimed specialists from the Pasteur Institute in Paris, had been brought in to conduct the necessary medical examinations.

After two days of prodding and measuring, the examining doctors had nothing but praise for the mens' physical health. Only the Institute specialists still harboured doubts. Both were concerned as to whether the Siamese had the constitution for high altitude flying. Because of the stresses of aerial combat they feared the men might black out under the strain. It was a coronary condition, the physicians cautioned. Asians and Africans, having evolved in hotter climates, had smaller arteries and veins than Caucasians.

Two pilots fell at a more fundamental hurdle; measured at under 5', 4" they were too short to reach the aileron pedals.

From then on their reversals and indignities piled up. Awaiting their medical clearances, the flyers and crew had been forced to camp on the perimeter ground outside the air base. This delay had allowed the US 94th Aero Squadron, fresh in from Brest, to overtake them. Ushered through the main gates with grovelling obeisance by the French guards, the 'yanks' had got in first and annexed the best accommodation. Forewarned of Gallic austerity, the Americans had also come prepared. The spartan nissen huts supplied by their hosts, were augmented with their own homegrown luxuries; sprung mattresses, radio sets, and games tables. To the chagrin of the base chefs, they'd even brought their own food. A mobile hot-dog truck was parked up, together with an oven for doughnuts and rolls and a Coca Cola concession.

This bullish voracity moved to the airfield. Anxious to get their hands on the French planes (considerably more advanced than their own), the American air crews had quickly commandeered the newly delivered Hispano-Suiza powered S13 Spads. With the older training Bréguets pressed into observation service over the trenches, it looked unlikely that the delayed Thai pilots would progress beyond the wooden and string airframes suspended from the gantries of the old dirigible hangar.

"When are they due to return?" asked Pramot of the secretary.

"They'd intended to be back in Paris this evening, but couldn't get seats."

"Where are they now?"

"Stranded in Valence."

"Valence?"

"Six hundred kilometres south."

It was far from the news he needed. Two weeks before there had been a flurry of activity from Bangkok. Frustrated by the silence from Paris, the War Ministry had got impatient and agitated. Two months into 'their great war' and on the verge of despatching a larger fighting force to Europe, the general's office had needed some assurance that progress was being made and that they were having a positive effect. And they'd wanted it on a daily basis.

Hence Pramot's anxiety. A report on the successful first flight of the Thai aircrew should have been that buoyant report. But aware of the depressing setbacks in Istres, he only had a single account to fall back on; Captain Sumet's. Ok, it was hardly a push on Berlin, but at least they were on the road and delivering to General Joffre's headquarters, surely the highest office in the land?

Pramot walked up the five floors to the communications room and with the Captain's verbose documents in hand, began dictating the content to the telegraph operators. By midday the text had been transmitted. Hungry from the effort, Pramot left the office and walked to a small inn in the Rue de Maire. A Chinese shophouse had recently opened – the first Asian inn in Europe. They sold noodles with egg and chicken. At least that's what it looked like. Anyway it was shredded, impossible to tell by texture alone what creature it was. Not that he minded. The sauce was the critical highlight. And Pramot found himself greedily ordering two bowls.

Captain Sumet's message, bounced down the line through Malta, Suez, Bombay and Rangoon. It was three in the morning when it finally arrived at the National Telegraph Service in Bangkok. Translated and retyped by the night team, it was dispatched by bicycle to the gates of the War Ministry next door to the Grand Palace. Taking time to permeate the layers of junior staff and officials, it was midday before it found its way into the hands of the War Minister, General Chalerm.

Bad tempered after a humid and turbulent night (heavy monsoon storms had flooded the administration buildings), the general was late for his morning briefing with the king's advisor, Prince Chakrabongse. Wanting a quick meeting – he had parades to attend – he turned into the palace gates dismayed to find the courtyard filled with courtiers, carriages and bands. A new ambassador from Portugal had arrived. Puffed up like a popinjay, he had appeared to present his credentials and gifts, carried by a motley entourage of staff and family. Chalerm, pulling his hat low and taking to his heels, was mid way around the guards' block when he was recognised by an arriving minister.

The ceremony was interminable. Released just after six, it was dark when Chalerm finally got round to opening the correspondence from abroad, Pramot's telegram top of the stack. Tearing open the envelope and taking in its contents, the general was outraged. Calling for a clerk and striding back to the war ministry, Chalerm dictated a reply on the move. A message that was back in Paris within the hour.

Pramot, brought low by stomach pains after his Chinese meal (the 'chicken' he felt sure was the culprit), dragged himself back to the legation, unprepared for the shock that awaited him. The general's reply was simple and caustic, "The Royal Siamese Expeditionary Force was there to make War not wine."

By rule diplomatic exchanges were dry to the bone, expressing little emotion or passion. Here anger permeated every word; he could feel the heat, like chilli powder, pulsing from the letters even after their six-thousand-mile transmission.

Pramot, glancing anxiously at the clock, considered his options. His superiors were due at the Gare de Lyon just after noon. In an hour they'd be back in the office, where it wouldn't take long for his folly to be unearthed. Had he over stepped the mark? Standing and sweeping back his hair, he ran back over his actions. Naturally the cause of his awkward predicament remained the Captain's original letter. And in truth he'd done little wrong; in fact he'd been remarkably faithful to its content. But here was the rub – aware of the misgivings of the War Ministry officials and knowing there might be friction – should he have been more circumspect in the message's transcription, toned down its overblown prose? It would have meant additional work and the deadline was pressing. And to protect the interests of a close friend or colleague, he might have put in that extra special effort and time. But in Pramot's eyes, the jumped up Captain of a second-rate motor unit, deserved neither his affection or loyalty.

Since his arrival in Marseilles, Captain Sumet and his team had been nothing but trouble. His correspondence, coming at them virtually every day, was an endless litany of complaint; not enough food, not enough clothes, not enough transport: "why were we not informed?", "why have our letters gone unanswered?" The man had even had the gall to make dietary demands. Where on earth were they going to find fish sauce in the markets of Paris? A bread roll was hard enough. Then there were calls for more money, envelopes and stamps. The entire legation staff had been treated as if they were his slaves, the blame for all ills laid at their door. And that door – that dumping ground of grievance – was inevitably his. He was the one forced to wade through their paperwork, make the grovelling calls with the dour French officials, sort out permits and suffer their insolence and obstructiveness. And he loathed it.

Pramot, assailed by these base thoughts, must have screamed out. A window opened on an upper floor and a curious face peered down, timorously searching out the reason for the outburst. Pramot, not wanting to be seen, lent back out of sight, bashful that he had been overheard.

Momentarily calming, Pramot's attention returned to the desk and Sumet's letter. They were his countrymen after all, it was his duty to tolerate their demands, however petty or frivolous. But his plan wasn't to kill them. It was merely to teach them a life lesson, provide 'a change of scene', expose them to challenges worthy of the noble Thai uniform. And with Chalerm's angry missive in hand, "War not wine", Pramot realised he now had the means to achieve it.

The French General Staff were surprised by the change of tone from the Thai Legation. Unlike the colonial troops – the Sengalese, Moroccans and Algerians – for whom they harboured few qualms when dispatching them daily to the "meat-grinding machine", they had been given express instructions from the Foreign Office in Paris, that the Siamese Company were there strictly as 'Services of the Rear' – transport and logistics behind the lines. And that usually meant food, medical supplies, sandbags and construction materials. Freed from these 'special considerations', the transport staff were more than happy to redeploy Siam's modest company of thirty-five trucks to more urgent tasks. Called back to St Dizier, the Asians were to be placed under the authority of General Gouraud's Fourth Army, to be used when and where they were most needed.

A new offensive was being planned. Front line troops in the forward positions were being stockpiled with supplies and ammunition. General Pershing's US Battalions were also flooding into Bourgogne; their focus, the forests of the Meuse Argonne.

Chapter 18

By the time a cold morning sun had filtered through the grey autumn mist, Sumet and Ferraux, had already filled the base of their boat with a sizeable catch. The Captain, puffing contentedly on a cigarette in the prow of the craft, sipped liquor from a hipflask despite the early hour. Warming to his new life, of fresh coffee, French tobacco and brandy (Ferraux must have had a key to the Countess's special reserves), Sumet's air of carefree contentment was imperceptibly transitioning into a second phase; unease and trepidation.

All through his life moments of happiness and contentment, however fleeting, had always been overshadowed by some form of mishap or misfortune; a sense of foreboding that conditioned him to expect something bad. At preschool, a class prize for maths was snatched away from him at the ceremony when a classmate had accused him of cheating; he hadn't. A best friend he'd trusted with a rare collection of cards, stole and burnt them. Cycling to an illicit rendezvous with a girl, he'd been set upon by stray dogs and feared he'd caught rabies. The untimely return of his father on his graduation day (a father that had walked out when he was four), was a harrowing and indelible scar that afflicted every gathering thereafter.

Thus with cruel fate as close mentor and guide, Sumet didn't have to search far to find the harbinger of his coming misery. A small skiff was just then pulling out from the shore.

The man rowed with some urgency, the thrust of his oars churning up the waters of an otherwise placid lake. Soon the small vessel came alongside, a letter held aloft in the rower's hand. Ferraux took the envelope and seeing as it was addressed to the Captain, passed it across the boat. Sumet, with his hand already primed to receive it, took it.

"Mr Ferraux, I'm afraid our fishing trip has come to an end," he announced, without even reading its contents.

Chapter 19

With the first week of October the unusually dry autumn came to a close. Overnight the temperatures dropped. Ice, hard as steel, formed over the engine cowlings of the trucks, its chill freezing the radiators. Unused to cold starts the Thai drivers had difficulty cranking the engines. Several, overzealous with the fuel mix, flooded their carburettors. Mechanics, hands numb from the bitter temperatures, strained to still their shaking fingers as they worked to clean out valves and spark plugs.

Wrapped in great coats and wool scarfs against the howling gales, Sumet's small convoy crawled into Saint Dizier. Three kilometres from the outskirts of town they were stopped. Heavy rain had flooded the river, the torrent rising up over a concrete embankment to cover the streets in a sticky layer of shifting brown sediment.

At the centre of this grim quagmire, workers, knee deep in the mud, shored up the banks with sandbags and railway sleepers. Gaunt and sallow, weighed down by their damp clothes and clogged boots, they moved slowly, as if in a dream. From the bridge, a shout went up. A surge of water broke over the embankment, shattering the ramshackle dyke of doors, gates and sandbags. As the workers rushed forward a man lost his footing and hitting the ooze, split his sandbag, spilling the grit. A guard, screaming obscenities, walked over and stamped on the man's back as he struggled to stand, pressing his body deeper into the sludge.

"Is that really necessary?" asked the Captain, shaken by the beating meted out to the labourer.

"They're prisoners of war, Captain. What else should we do? Hand out biscuits and tea?" replied Pierre.

The realisation startled the Captain and Chai. Although they'd seen pictures of this brutal nation, mostly from propaganda posters, where murderous, savage faces glared out dripping in the blood of innocent women and children, it was the first time they had seen the 'enemy' for real. Here, covered in damp coats and rags, they seemed a sorry, pitiful mess.

Behind, a second section of wall collapsed. More water poured from the breach.

"Ici merde!" yelled the guards, "Vite, vite!"

As a second group pressed past hauling timbers and bags, Sumet and Chai could see them more clearly. In their faces they'd expected to read misery and defeat, yet the prisoners eyes told a different story; a perverse glow remained. They'd survived the nightmare. The stinking, mud clogged patch where they stood, was a paradise.

"Emportez ça, et encore des sacs de sable!" yelled the soldiers.

More men rushed forward with sandbags. Bunched up around the flanks of the truck Chai heard them mutter, even detected a wry smile. "Was sind die gelben Männer doch für Narren, daß sie sich für die Weißen opfern," one seemed to joke.

"What are they saying?", asked the Captain.

"I didn't hear," shrugged Pierre.

"He said 'Narren' something?"

"You sure?"

"What does it mean?"

"Fools."

"And the rest?" persisted Sumet.

"You really want to know?"

"Yes, I do want to know."

"He said he thinks you are fools to fight the white man's war."

"Well right now," replied Sumet looking down at the struggling workmen, "Rather a fool than a rat in that stinking mess…"

Pierre turned to the man, "Wo kommen sie hier?".

"Aus dem Elsass", replied the man, startled to be addressed in German.

"Aus welcher Stadt?"

"Obernai."

"Obernai in der Nähe von Rosheim?" checked Pierre, eyeing the man with more interest.

"Ja, nur drei Kilometer nördlich..."

Pierre suddenly pushed past Chai, the speed of the move making him think that he was about to punch the man in the face. But it wasn't a fist that extended out to the prisoner's mouth, but a packet of cigarettes. The German, as surprised as Chai by the gesture, hesitantly took one.

"Ich bin auch aus dem Elsass," rejoined Pierre, striking a match and holding it forward.

"Obernai is close to where I was born", replied Pierre switching to French.

"Who's with you in the truck? Chinese coolies?

"No, your new enemy," replied Pierre, turning casually as if to introduce family to friends.

"From where?"

"Siam".

"Sounds hot and sunny. Why come to this flea-infested shithole?"

"To give you guys a kicking."

"A bit late for the action?"

"Depends how long you last."

"Ahh, we're done for," said the prisoner nodding to his bedraggled associates, "es ist aus und vorbei." He grinned back at the Thai, "at least they've chosen the right side."

The convoy lurched forward. Born, approaching the damaged bridge, edged the front wheels of their truck onto the boards of a makeshift pontoon and drove on. Mid-way across the divide, a wave broke against the iron joists, soaking them all. The Captain, wiping the dirty water from his face and clothes, ruefully reflected on his last hours on the Forey estate. It had been beautiful and warm. Sitting in the stern of the boat on the lake, he had watched as sunlight burnt through the dawn mists, disbelief at landing his first trout bringing tears to his eyes.

Despite taking Ferraux's dog cart over the hills, Captain Sumet had arrived too late to make any difference to the loading of the trucks. Chai, having read the same orders an hour before, had already organised the necessary tasks and teams. Staying long enough to witness the safe packing of his personal effects, soap, flannel and shaving brushes, Sumet crossed the stable-yard and headed to the château. He wanted to leave a note explaining the abruptness of their departure and to thank the Countess personally for her kind hospitality. Taking a more circuitous route behind the walled gardens, he took in a last view of the vineyards and orchards. With the harvest finished, the leaves of the vines now denuded of grapes, were beginning to wrinkle and yellow. Continuing through the beech woods Sumet emerged near the wrought iron gates at the back of the house. The Countess's vigilant hunting dogs, hoping for a morning walk, bounded out to greet him; he had to disappoint them.

A small Peugeot voiturette and an impressive Panhard staff car were parked up outside the entrance of the château. Its driver, wearing a peaked cap, gloves and polished boots, stood at the side of the larger limousine smoking a cigarette, his foot resting lazily on the running board. Three bicycles were lent up against the privet hedge.

Entering through the main doors of the château, Sumet could hear shrill voices coming from the direction of the dining room. The Countess was obviously entertaining guests for lunch. Not wanting to interfere and anxious to be on his way, the Captain looked for the attention of a maid so he could hand over his note and be gone, but the staff were nowhere to be seen.

Sumet was no stranger to the house. Two weeks before he, Chai and Pierre had been invited to an evening to meet local dignitaries. It was there that they had been introduced to the pastor of Castelnau, together with the headmaster of the local school, Mr Bizet, and his two teachers. The conversation with Bizet had led to the invite for the Siamese to visit the village school to take part in Sandrine's geography class.

The Countess, a distant hostess, could only be glimpsed occasionally in a far room. Young, beautiful, imperious (and to Sumet, untouchable), she'd sat on a sofa surrounded by flatterers and admirers. Music could be heard; just out of view a string quartet was playing.

Although the segregation wasn't explicit, the two rooms had assumed a natural order and hierarchy. Grander, more salubrious guests; politicians, officials and generals, surrounded the Countess in the larger, brighter garden room, whose views looked down over the recently cut lawns to the lake. In the more austere, dark-panelled ante-room, where glass cabinets were packed with dusty arachnids, moths and stuffed birds, the second tier were crammed – bureaucrats and station staff from Montaron, local teachers and the two visiting Thai, Chai and Sumet.

Sumet hadn't enjoyed the evening. Apart from their introduction to the local schoolteachers – Chai, he remembered, being especially struck by one of the young school mistresses' – Sumet had been totally bored and uninterested from the start. Too often he found himself serving up the same banal explanations for his colour, creed and country, as if being scrutinised like one of the dried-up specimens in the cabinets behind; "Arrh, Vous avez de si belles plumes," he silently mimicked.

Hearing the clock chime nine, he saw his opportunity and grabbing Chai by the arm, pointed him to the door. "We're getting out of here, now," he hissed in his ear.

Chai, clearly enjoying his time with the teachers, hastily made up a credible excuse for their sharp exit; they had to be up early for a mission to Macon (which was half true anyway).

Winding their way through the guests and maids, they made their escape across the library to the music room. They were inches from freedom and the comfort of the dark, when turning the handle to the outside courtyard, found the door inexplicably locked. Panic struck they looked for an alternative. There was none. If they wanted to get out they faced an ignominious retreat back through the same anteroom they had just left. But then a more unnerving sensation touched them. They weren't alone. In the far corner of the room, shadowed by a leafy palm in an ornate Chinese urn, stood a woman. Adjusting to the low light and looking closer they were astonished to see it was the Countess.

Sumet, appalled at finding himself in such close proximity with their illustrious host, didn't know what to say, how to act. On top of a writing bureau next to the Countess he noticed an inkstand and a photograph in a gilt frame. Sumet took it to be of the Count. Struggling to express something of note to break the excruciating silence, he complimented the Countess on the beauty and balance of the composition, how handsome, composed and regal the subject appeared in the soft, mottled light. He'd seen many impressive portraits, but he thought this one a remarkably sensitive framing and exposure. Midway through this rambling monologue the Captain looked up disturbed to see how pale the lady had turned. Yet more alarming, her eyes had become so watery, he feared she would cry. He was striving to respond, scrambling for words of consolation, of sympathy, when the Countess, snatching a lace handkerchief from her sleeve, covered her face and lurched from the room.

Later, when they had reconvened back in the stable block, a shaken Sumet had recounted the episode to Pierre. The young Frenchman, having spent a more fruitful evening chatting up the kitchen maids and serving staff, was quickly able to decipher the mystery behind the Countess's distress.

Sumet's great blunder was that the person in the photograph wasn't even the Count. The old man had died years before from gout. By all accounts he was a vicious, lecherous brute and few had mourned his passing. Edouard Deschamps, the dashing man in the portrait, was a distant cousin Catherine had known since childhood. Never rich he had made a reasonable fortune managing cane plantations in Martinique and Guadeloupe for absentee landlords. After the Count's death Edouard had returned to help the Countess manage her estate. And that management included dealing with a mountain of broken contracts, unpaid bills and gambling debts left by her late husband. During Edouard's stay, Catherine had furnished him with an apartment in the watchtower of the farm buildings, near the chateau. The staff were well aware he seldom slept there.

Like everyone young enough at the time, Edouard had taken up a commission in the forces and been stationed with the fifth army near Tournai. He was accompanying the general's staff on a visit to the front lines, when returning at night on a motorcycle, had hit a munitions wagon left in the road. Thrown from the bike Edouard had rolled down a ditch, his fall arrested by trees. The injuries didn't look serious; broken ribs and a gash to his chest. Hospitalised in Reims, an operation, to remove a splinter from his lungs, was successful. Within days he had recovered enough to write home to the Countess. The letter was happy to report that the Doctor's had given him leave; he was being sent back to convalesce at Forey.

The Countess, elated that Edouard was coming home, had excitedly prepared for his return. The kitchens at the château had laid on a special banquet to celebrate his home coming.

Waiting at the small station at Merceuil, it was apparent before the large locomotive had stopped that something was wrong. The carriages entering the platform, came to rest at a solemn, funereal pace. Seconds later a door opened at the front of the train. A doctor and two officers descended and walking towards the small party from the château, approached the Countess: Edouard had been in high spirits when he'd boarded the train. He'd shared drinks, a small meal with fellow officers. Complaining of feeling faint, he had been helped back to his compartment. A physician was called. Half an hour later Edouard had lost consciousness. His internal wounds had reopened. With meagre facilities on the train, there was nothing they could do. He had died silently and peacefully.

As Pierre's tragic account ended, there was silence.

Anxiety assaulted Sumet's conscience. In failing to find the right words to console the Countess, he had more than failed, he had offended. The angst needled him until dawn.

Chapter 20

Sixty-five women worked the telephone banks of the Communications Wing of the Commandement des Lignes Arrières in the city of Sens. Every evening it was their task to make the calls from the city out to the field switch-boards in Bellville. From there cables, wired across the battle-scarred terrain, carried the calls the last hazardous kilometres to the gunnery subalterns on the ridges above the Marne. Their orders, processed throughout the night by clerks at the supply depot in Gievres, were loaded onto waiting trains, then despatched by truck to the artillery batteries whose guns would be winging the cargoes west at first light.

Approaching the winter offensive, this faultless machinery of death played out with clockwork efficiency, its rail networks aflow with a near constant traffic of trains and carriages, streaming their way east like the arteries of some mythological beast.

At dawn, thirty-six box cars crammed with one hundred and sixty tons of shells, mortar bombs and rifle ammunition, rolled into the station yard at Saint Dizier, its platforms awash with soldiers fresh in from Bordeaux. Clearing a path through the ranks of recruits, the loading crews lifted the munitions onto waiting trucks; five lines of vehicles that stretched back to the central boulevard of the town.

Captain Sumet's convoy, delayed by the floods over the Marne, joined a queue of late arrivals at a gate at the head of the station. A portly station master, balanced precariously on an oak cask in the thick of the traffic, directed them to the last empty bay. Born backed up his lorry to a ramp adjacent to the freight platform. As the shutter doors on the box cars swung open, a team of labourers arrived to unload the crates. Aged, grey haired, some infirm, they weren't in the best of shape. Two had to stand down after straining their backs on the first box.

Approaching midday and with more than half the trucks yet to fill, feeding the men became the Captain's next concern. Pierre had noticed an army canteen at the entrance of the station yard, but the queue was long and the soup vats almost empty. Chai called Mai and Manit. Handing them ten francs and two burlap sacks, he told them to fill them with as much food as they could scavenge.

Taking the bags, the two hurried into town, with little idea of where they should go and what they should buy. An avenue of poplar trees leading to a colonnaded arcade seemed a good bet, but on reaching the square they found the shops closed, their shutters pulled down and no signs of life. Further up the hill they spied a porter coming out of an archway with a trolley laden with boxes and sacks. Marking the spot they found steps that led down to a market where a row of shops sheltered beneath a rusty corrugated awning. Midway along this arcade, the brief, enticing allure of freshly baked bread, gave way to the acrid scent of fumes. Engines coughed into life as a truck shuffled away down the alley. An American sprawled across the back bench of the vehicle, his big boots on the tailgate, raised his arm in a lazy wave, "Good luck sucker, we've taken it all!".

And he was right. The shelves of the bakery were bare. Mai and Manit could see enough without entering the shop. So they gave up and turned around, already rehearsing excuses to explain their defeat to the Captain. They were already some distance from the shop when a lady ran into the street and yelled after them, "Vous! Arrêtez, arrêtez!" – the command so loud, so stern, they thought they were criminals.

They stalled and turned. An old woman dressed in a heavy black shawl was beckoning to them with a gnarled stick. Obediently they retraced their steps to her door. Waving her baton she marshalled them inside.

The lady had made a handsome return from the Americans and even now was greedily counting their cash. But she hadn't cared for their pushy, showy ways and was sympathetic to the plight of the two hungry Asians.

"Attendez! Attendez! Je vais vous trouver quelque chose," she muttered as she folded her money into a biscuit tin and began rummaging through the lower shelves.

They were in luck. In a store room at the back, she was able to retrieve two crusty loaves from a previous day's batch. Mai offered her money, but she held up her hands as if fending off brigands, "Non, non, non, C'est rien, c'est rien."

Following the two out into the street, the old woman rapped on the doors of her neighbours with her stick.

"Didier, Marcel," she yelled out, "Je sais que vous êtes là. Sortez tout de suite, des clients vous attendent... Vite!"

One emerged to sell them their last shrivelled boudin noir; a dried blood sausage as black as charcoal, tainted with an unsightly green growth – possibly only attractive to Pierre. A third offered cheese as hard and tasteless as candle wax: no wonder the Americans hadn't taken it.

The two twins returned just as the final munitions were loaded. Two cans of British bully beef from a street hawker, supplemented the bread, sausage and cheese they had already bought. The Captain, expecting better returns after such a long expedition, looked disappointed; it was far from enough. Taking the meagre pickings, he wrapped them in a bundle and packed them under the bench seat of his cab. As Born cranked over the engine, Chai and Pierre joined Sumet on the seat and the convoy crawled out. Crossing the river they drove down the embankment, passing a park shaded with trees. People waved, children cheered, a veteran ran alongside blowing his bugle.

The Captain, relieved to be on his way, and hoping to make up for lost time, opened a map and using his fingers as dividers, began calculating the distance to their next destination. But they were barely clear of the first square of his chart before encountering their first serious setback.

The weak link in the convoy was a worn Peugeot van at the rear of the line. Previously a fire truck – the emblem of the 14th arrondissement still visible beneath its crude khaki brushstrokes – its wheel hit a rut in the cobbles, shearing the leaf springs. The break tipped the chassis sideways, swinging its rear platform abruptly downhill. Crates, poorly stacked by the rail workers, came loose and fell. A shell, breaking free from its ply casing, dropped down the edge of the cargo nets. Although caught in the folds of the roof canvas, a gentle nudge was all that was needed to send it rolling into town.

Hearing the horn from the stricken truck, Chai and Born jumped down from their cab and ran back down the hill. Ropes were found. Chai had the ammunition cases and the shells re-secured. With angry traffic building up on both sides, Born climbed into the cab and edged the damaged truck around. Chai instructed the shaken driver to return to the rail depot, then sprinted back up the hill with Born to the front of the convoy.

"What the hell was that all about?" snapped Sumet, irritated by the holdup.

"Charoen's truck broke down", replied Chai getting his breath back.

"But it's only just been repaired!"

"There was another problem. He nearly…"

Chai jabbed Born hard in the ribs, silencing him.

"I told Charoen to return to the depot," continued Chai, moderating his voice to appear calm.

"Nearly what?", enquired the Captain, suspicious of Born's abrupt silence.

"Nearly dropped a sack of supplies…" lied Chai, "potatoes from the estate…"

Sumet rapped the glass of his newly-acquired wristwatch, "A sack of potatoes? And that took fifteen minutes?"

"Some of them had rolled into town…"

"Damn it, Chai, I couldn't have cared less if they'd rolled into the Élysée Palace!"

Leaving St Dizier behind, the road was straight and uncrowded. They passed the small hamlet of Behanne. The Captain, reaching for his clipboard, methodically ticked the name off his list. It was a small, rural community, still some way from the front, but already signs of war marred the landscape. On both sides of the road, farm buildings and barns had been requisitioned by the military, the neglected fields littered with storage dumps, timber yards and oil drums. The army made untidy tenants. Mounds of refuse and rubble lay dumped in the open. Crowning the highest monument of waste sat the tail section of a wrecked biplane, its canvas shredded with bullet holes. At its base, mud-caked pigs patrolled through the sludge sifting for tubers and turnips.

Coming over a hill the rooftops of a château appeared through the trees. The Captain, excited by the architecture, became loquacious, praising its neoclassical facade, the glazed terracotta tiles that graced its gothic towers and chapel. Neat rows of cars and vans filled the courtyard. Around an ornamental lake, clusters of white gazebos graced the lawn. Ladies, attired in billowing white dresses and ostrich feather hats, walked the gardens pushing prams. It looked quaint and lyrical, like a summer ball. It wasn't. But Chai and Born, wise enough not to dent their Captain's enthusiasm, remained silent. It fell to Pierre to dispel the delusion.

"You're certain of that Captain?"

"And why not?"

"Well, for a start, I'm afraid that's no garden party…"

"A wedding then?"

The road dipped and rounding a bend, came out above the estate, providing a raised view. The white canvas marquees turned out to be hospital tents, the rows of vehicles backing up at the rear doors, ambulances unloading the wounded. And it was nurses, not breezy ladies, wheeling invalids around the perimeter of the lake.

Despite the bitter wind a band played. The audience, made cold by having to endure the 1812 Overture in its entirety, were already sneaking back to the warmth of their wards. One man, taking a greater aversion to the thunderous cymbals and drums, was sprinting across a rose garden, hair on end, the palms of his hands pressed hard to his ears. From the back doors, a team of medics ran in massed pursuit across the front lawn.

Rising from the plains, the road wound up the hillside to the village of Chattancourt. Rustic and verdant, neatly-spaced vegetable plots and fruit orchards, crowded the incline. The small timber houses in the village were pretty, the cut fretwork arches and eaves reminding Chai of the teak trader buildings near his home town of Loei. Flower boxes graced window ledges, their frames secured with green shutters. Across their limestone walls, late roses still bloomed, despite the advance of weeds and brambles over the flowerbeds. A playground school was empty, its swings and benches carpeted with copper and bronze autumn leaves.

Crouched in the shadow of a gate pillar, a scruffy Jack Russell waited as a hidden sentinel at the top of the street. Alerted by the harsh roar of approaching engines, his excited yapping brought out his larger, more savage friends. As Born led the convoy into the main street, this feral pack emerged from all flanks to run barking alongside. Pierre threw a rotten apple core at a bedraggled barbet, the act only eliciting a more frenzied reaction from his vicious companions. A jet black mastiff tried scrambling up the sides of the truck into the footwell. Born had to take his foot off the accelerator to kick the salivating brute away. Running from this mob and steering clear of the most obvious troublemakers, the convoy turned the corner of the street unprepared for the shock that awaited them.

There had never been anything very remarkable about the village of Chattancourt. A small entry in an early Baedeker travel guide mentioned a modest church noted for the elegance of its Medieval tower. That spire now lay shattered across the base of a single shell crater, a yawning chasm that stretched the length of the square. Blackened splinters of the choir stalls and oak pews lay crushed beneath the fallen masonry and rubble. Of the original nave only the north wall of the sanctuary remained intact. A marble statue of the Virgin Mary, eerily white and pure, stood out unblemished against the scorched, pockmarked stones.

Chai, sitting on the far side of the cab and still nursing a graze from a crazed dog, was stunned by the burnt-out ruins they passed by; all that was left of a row of elegant shop houses.

The grandest building in the square had been the Hôtel de Ville.

With its façade and roof ripped away by the blast, the upper floors were left exposed, leaving furniture, tables and chairs marooned in the open. On a desktop on its second floor, the pages of a ledger, crisped and mottled by months of sun and rain, fluttered noisily in the breeze.

Catching a low moan, they thought it the wind. A second glance revealed an old woman, slumped in the entrance of the once stately portico. Wrapped in furs and sitting astride a trunk bulging with clothes, her claw-like fingers clutched her last remaining possession of value; an emaciated goat, sipping water from the edge of the crater.

The eerie quiet and desolation silenced them all. Although few had been exposed to such daunting destructive power before, most were familiar with the effects of artillery. Chai had once commanded a gunnery team during a training exercise. For a field demonstration in front of a visiting general, fifty of them had dragged an Armstrong Field Gun up the slopes of a small hill in Ratchaburi. Aiming at a distant rock shaped like an elephant, they had fired six shots from the top. It was a hot day. His senior officer, feeling the heat, had been unwise to remove his cavalry boots. Searching through the long grass for the impact craters (which they never found), he had been bitten by a cobra.

"It happened during Verdun", said Pierre, nonchalantly rolling tobacco from his leather pouch.

"A... a single shot?", asked Captain Sumet, chastened.

"One shell from more than twelve kilometres away", replied Pierre, "from over those hills," he pointed towards the horizon – it seemed an incredible distance.

"They have that range?", enquired Chai in disbelief.

"A single gun. A monster, the Germans call Dicke Bertha."

"But a civilian target?" questioned the Captain.

"Hah, it happens all the time," shrugged Pierre, "Retaliation for our bombing of a field hospital behind their lines. At least that's what they claimed..."

Beyond the ruins of the village the road climbed through pine forests, the trees so tall and closely packed that little light penetrated through their upper branches. Taking in these gloomy surroundings, a graveyard of trucks and carriages became visible in the bushes, their once proud outlines now throttled by the invasive undergrowth. Rusting chassis, twisted like gnarled roots, were covered in moss and layers of damp pine needles. Wheel hubs, their spokes broken and rotten, sat crushed beneath collapsed cabs. The turret of a tank peered out from a hollow; its steel outer shell peeled back like a pierced bean can.

Chai saw shadows shifting between the abandoned wrecks; a misshapen man in black furs and oily rags. Hopping between the bushes, a worn chicken bone clenched in his jaws, he waved to the distant horizon as if jollying revellers to a dance.

Leaving the hills behind, they dropped to a plain and crossing fields, approached a canal crossing. At a roadblock in front of the steel bridge, Military Police were directing trucks onto the rough verges. Several of their drivers had collected in groups to chat and share cigarettes. Chai recognised those that had set off long before them.

Born slowed the truck as Pierre jumped down from the cab to speak with the men at the barrier.

"Not another hold up?" complained the Captain, when he returned.

"Beyond the bridge it's a single track. A convoy is coming down the line. We've been told to wait until it passes" Pierre replied.

"How long?" asked Chai.

"Twenty, thirty minutes."

"Then we'll take a break," said the Captain.

Stiff from being crushed up with the crates and munitions, the men were grateful for the stop. No one more than Wrun. Because of his short build the driving position of his cab had been killing him. The problem was with the clutch, the travel on the pedal so deep, that every time he'd wanted to change gear he'd had to slide off the bench to depress it. Too timid to mention his plight to the others, searing pains shot down his spine as he staggered down from his seat to the bank.

There was a break in the clouds; the sun shone through bringing some temporary warmth. Captain Sumet had one of the men retrieve the bundle of food from the wooden box beneath his bench seat. The rolls, dried sausage, corned beef and cheese were shared out. Pierre produced a bottle of wine from his jacket; a red pinot noir – one of many he had sequestered from the château's cellars. Others contributed peanuts, apples, even chocolate. Late blackberries, from a hedge at the top of the slope, provided something fresher and sweeter.

Born, eager to contribute to the makeshift meal, searched the pockets of his backpack and unearthed a packet of Huntley and Palmers biscuits he'd kept from the troopship. Hoarded too long they'd grown stale and mouldy. Disappointed by the mess and emptying his pack, Born threw large chunks at the swooping sparrows and crows. Competition soon emerged from the woods; a family of squirrels were bolder and faster to catch the precious scraps.

With everyone filled and satisfied, the Captain felt a certain pride, a godlike delusion that from such meagre pickings, he alone had provided enough sustenance for the entire company, even after keeping the rare boudin noir sausage for himself; its taste reminded him of a homegrown variety - a sai krok from Isarn.

The delay wore on. Chai, basking in the sun, felt listless and drowsy. It had been a mistake to have drunk so much of Pierre's wine. Unbuttoning his jackets and falling back against the soft grass, his mind, floating in and out of consciousness, found himself drifting back to the hot plains of Saraburi and the day of the exercise. Thirsty after a gruelling morning wading through the reeds searching for the shell craters, the company had retreated to the shade of flame trees desperate for water. Seeing their flushed faces and sweaty uniforms, local girls had taunted them with slices of fresh mango and pomelo, coaxing them to preform ludicrous dances for even the smallest of pieces. Upping the stakes, a shameless temptress had bartered a whole dish for a kiss. An orderly line rapidly formed, until a corporal, wise to her game, chased the wicked minx down the lane.

Chai was shaken from his reverie by the roar of distant engines. Sitting up and looking across the plain, he saw a growing cloud of dust marring the horizon. Emerging from this haze, a line of trucks appeared, red flags fluttering from their roofs as they started their descent to the river.

Down by the barrier an urgent whistle screamed. Defying the guards a group of farm labourers had sneaked through the roadblock and had started across the divide on their own. Alarmed by their slow pace, two policemen ran out to help them push their carts to the far side. They only just made it as the first of the convoy appeared around the corner of the bend. As the heavy cast iron wheels of the lorries rolled over the loose timbers, they set off a deep vibration that shook dirt and dust from the planks.

From high on the banks of the incline, the Thai looked down on the convoy. The first vehicles in line looked like large furniture trucks, their corrugated sides a matt black, crude red crosses painted on their back doors. Troop carriers followed close behind, their canvas panels rolled up so that it was possible to see those inside. Filling the benches soldiers sat bunched close together, their expressionless faces staring out, worn and grey. The more seriously injured lay on the bare boards, their broken limbs bandaged or locked in fresh plaster. A head-case victim had cotton dressing wound so thickly around his head, he appeared like a giant snowball, three holes pierced in the fabric for his eyes, mouth and nose.

The five flatbed trucks at the rear of this grim procession were yet more sobering. Mummy-like figures, tightly and neatly stitched in fresh grey blankets, lined the floors; fifteen to each vehicle. Against the breast of one of the corpses, a small terrier had nestled its head; a loyal dog of one of the dead.

As the echo of the last truck receded into the woods, a shrill whistle sounded. The barriers went up and the bridge reopened. Gathering the men, Chai called the drivers back to the trucks. Born cranked the engine back into life and waited in line to be called.

Crossing the bridge a cool breeze blew across the waters of the canal, dispelling the dust and engine fumes. On the far bank a meadow of autumn colour stretched up the hillside. Tall purple thistles contrasted with yellow ragwort and bright red poppies. Beech trees lined the avenue, their orange tinted leaves rustling in the wind. Yet folded within the scent of grasses and flowers an unsettling stench lingered, growing in intensity as they crossed the brow of the rise. Stretching out from the edge of the fields, a blackened morass smouldered. Within this charred debris they could make out the shapes of dead horses and mules, their limbs broken and twisted at odd angles.

"The bodies lead east Captain Sumet. You're happy that your men will finally see the front?", muttered Pierre with a shrug, as if pointing out a herd of sleeping cattle.

Sumet smiled wearily as if he'd only half heard the Frenchman. Of course he'd understood him perfectly, he was just too disturbed to reply. Couldn't the man understand how shaken they'd been by what they'd seen at the bridge? And then to treat such a poignant moment with such flippancy only troubled and vexed him more.

Europeans, especially the French he found complex, difficult to penetrate. Their moods and humour was even harder to fathom, as if it were all play-acting designed to conceal their true nature. It got worst with alcohol; all riddles and witty asides, befuddling any true emotion. All these characteristics were there in abundance with Pierre. Being sharp and a bit of a joker only enhanced his insouciance.

Not that he didn't like the young Frenchman. He might have dressed slovenly, rarely brushed his hair or washed, but from the day that he'd joined them he'd found the man courteous and affable, with none of the distain one had come to expect from the likes of the foreigners who lazed, gin and tonic in hand, on the lawns of the Colonial Clubs back in Bangkok.

Professionally he couldn't fault Pierre either. In acting as their liaison with the High Command, he'd been more than diligent, working hard to protect their well-being and interests; although at times – and this had tested Chai's patience – perhaps a touch over protective...

Of course there was nothing ignoble about self-preservation. Sumet was well aware that their small company was a safe choice; every assignment behind the lines, keeping them a comfortable distance from the true horrors and dangers of the war. Yet somehow that safeguard had been broken. They were on their way east, loaded, not with fine wines or grand pianos, but ammunition, mortar bombs and shells. And then out of the blue, that sly aside; "you're happy that your men will finally see the front". Again more tiresome obfuscation. But did such levity veil hidden resentment? Was Pierre blaming him for losing them their comfortable sojourn at the château? And if he was, how did he know?

Pondering these niggling anxieties, it occurred to him that Pierre might have read his private correspondence. The Frenchman was always up first. Sumet, a light sleeper, often heard him nosing about the compound before dawn. Claiming he liked to start his day with a stroll, Pierre usually picked up their letters and packages from the gatehouse during his walk. Chancing across the critical telegram from the Thai legation, it would have been relatively easy to steam open the envelope, digest its contents, then reseal it – a kitchen with kettles, was adjacent to the work sheds.

The reprimand from Bangkok had certainly been scathing. It would have been simple for Pierre to surmise how that anger might have translated into punishment. Of course in retrospect he felt responsible, guilty even, that his letters and reports might have been to blame for overstating the importance of their mission to the war effort. A particular phrase he'd used (and now bitterly regretted), that their wine deliveries played a 'critical role in fortifying the spirits' of the over-worked generals, had perhaps, over-embellished the truth. But surely it was a relatively innocent transgression to which Bangkok, in turn, had overreacted? He blamed Chalerm, the War Minster, an oafish and uncultured man. It was unlikely that his telegram had been read by those at the top. Prince Chakrabongse, the true Commander of the Siamese Expedition, was a man of more discerning tastes. He'd trained with the Russian Hussars, even served as a page for the Tsar in the Winter Palace in St Petersburg. He could certainly tell his Bordeaux from his Burgundy.

Naturally no one would deny that military secrets and intelligence were paramount, but if the long term goal was the modernisation and expansion of Siam after the war, culture, technology and agriculture – and that included enology – were surely just as significant.

Chapter 21

The rain started in earnest just short of the outskirts of Belleville. Turning up the thick collars of their greatcoats and pulling their caps down low over their faces, achieved little. Silently they shivered and endured it. Blankets were found from the back, but being so thin, they were soon wet through and useless.

The road surface, worn out by the almost constant military traffic, was broken and riddled with potholes. As the wheels of their heavily-laden Berliet's crashed into the deep cavities, the trucks swung erratically onto the loose scree that bordered the steep sides of the embankment. Several times Chai had to reach over to help Born steady the wheel. The rain was the problem; the near constant downpour streaking in under the roof making the steering wheel as slippery as Sumet's precious carp. When a particularly tight corner had them running dangerously wide, the Captain, fearful that they would all end up on their heads, reluctantly ceded his luxurious leather driving gloves. Born, stupidly, had left his own behind on the estate, laid out to dry on a shelf in the barn.

At a junction on the edge of town, the convoy again lurched to a stop. Two columns of lorries, ambulances and munitions trucks backed up, as cart-horses were hitched to a broken-down staff car that had flooded its engine. Pierre used the opportunity to beg a tarpaulin from a supply store. He tied the ends of the oilskin to the engine cowling, stretching the canvas over the sodden legs of his companions.

Heading towards the town centre, they turned into an old residential boulevard, its once grand buildings gutted by fire and shored up with sandbags and timbers. Steam rose from a soup kitchen. Chai could make out an obedient line of men and woman clutching their ration books, as ragged children fought in the rubble wielding bannister poles as swords.

At a crossroads in the main square, a telegraph post was hammered with signs, each new addition over-shadowing the other; Commanderie, Hôpital Militaire, GR4, Quai 14. A freshly nailed placard, hung with a lace garter, pointed caustically to the 'Folies Bergère'.

Pierre lent down to ask directions, "La route aux arêtes?"

"Où est-ce que vous allez?" asked a policeman.

"Le 47eme regiment d'artillerie."

"Restez à gauche, et puis tout droit," he replied, waving his arm to the left.

Clear of the town, the road rose steeply to a ridge. Born had to take both hands off the steering wheel to pull back on the gears as he negotiated the sharp bends. On one particularly harsh right hander, he came in too fast and the front wheels locked on the mud. With four tons of shells shifting violently sideways, the rear of the Berliet snapped out of line, drifting so close to the drop it caused a howl of alarm from those in the back. A sharp correction brought the vehicle back under control, but not before the close call had seen Sumet screaming out, "Look out, fool!... do you want to send us all to the grave!"

Pressed hard up against the far side of the bench, Sumet's position provided an unnerving sight line over the barriers into the gorge. At the bottom of a ravine, an American Packard lay on its back, wheels and chassis twisted and bent. Judging from the trail of dead foliage and stumps, it must have rolled through the trees before coming to rest. A circle of muddy footprints surrounded the crushed cab. Around its door, deep cuts had been made with a shovel in the hard clay. Sumet wondered if its driver had got out alive. In fact there was a rounded mound of earth topped with a cross, only feet from the crash site. Looking up from this wreckage, he could make out the shattered barriers where the truck had smashed through. It was the very same bend where Born had lost control minutes earlier. A nudge would have done it; two inches of nudge – less than a hand's width. What if fate had been that nudge, a last, careless shove that would have seen them over the calamitous cliff?

The trucks were French, they lost thousands every day, it would be no great burden and easy to replace. But the likely loss of his crew – of Siamese nationals under his command – would be harder to endure. Although a fleeting image of a gallows, replete with wailing crowds and hawkish street vendors, was way overdoing it, the thought of disaster churned at his insides, "It is with great regret that I inform your excellencies of a great calamity that has befallen the troops of the Siamese Expeditionary Force. And for this I alone accept full responsibility," – a final tearful confession backed up with a great chorus of weeping and howling.

They found the forty-seventh battery at the far end of the ridge. Two tractors were on hand to help pull the trucks the last hundred metres to the top of the rise, its incline a sticky quagmire of churned mud.

Chai had the trucks back up against the concrete walls of the gun embankments, where a gruff gunnery Sergeant was on hand to supervise the shifting of the munitions to the artillery emplacements. A chain of men lined up at the tail gates and began the unloading of the shells cases onto steel trollies. Pulled by ropes along tracks cut through the earth embankment, the crates were dragged to storage shelters below the gun pits.

"Dépêchez-vous, les poilus! Il faut tirer sur les Boches avant la tombée de la nuit", the Sergeant screamed, pushing his men to work faster.

Walking around the redoubt, he saw Chai and Pierre at the side of their truck and came closer.

"Chinois", announced the man slapping Chai playfully on the back, "Chinois!", he repeated with a second comradely thump.

"Siam", replied Chai, knowing the retort would be meaningless.

It was, "Shyam?" questioned the Sergeant, cupping a hand to his ear as if hard of hearing.

"Siam," repeated Chai more forcibly.

Still the big man grinned inanely masking his confusion.

Chai looked to Sumet for assistance, but out of the corner of his eye he could see that the Captain was already distancing himself from the joshing Sergeant.

Pierre came to Chai's rescue, "Le Siam est un très beau pays d'Asie, avec des femmes si belles qu'elles vous font chavirer."

A big grin spread over the man's face – lithe, elegant beauties – this was talk he understood and liked. "A drink!", he exclaimed, reaching for a hip flask, "To Sham and beauty!", he toasted, handing the flask around. Chai took a swig, the drink bitter and cloudy, but fortunately tamer than the corrosive concoction he'd experienced in Marseilles.

A thin mist, caustic with the lingering scent of chlorine and cordite, hung over the ridge. Needing air Sumet found steps in the earth embankment that rose up the side of the fortifications. By luck the walkway came out above the artillery pits. Twelve of the now legendary modèle 75 canon were lined up facing the valley that led to the distant enemy lines.

Seeing the guns reminded Sumet of a meeting he'd had at a diplomatic reception at the Navy Academy six months before in Bangkok. There he'd met a young English lieutenant fresh from training at the Royal Naval College in Dartmouth. Sumet had been drawn to the man, because, like himself, he'd looked uncomfortable and out of place amongst the high ranking dignitaries, spruced up as they were with garish and colourful medals. Hearing of Sumet's imminent departure for Europe and France they'd discussed the war. Sumet had talked excitably about the impact of tanks, planes and submarines, but the lieutenant had declared that they were too late and too rudimentary to make a big difference – in this conflict at least. Artillery, as always – crude, brutal and more than five hundred years old – would decide the outcome. In that, the French were superior. Their great advance was a long-barrel recoil that allowed their guns to be fired and reloaded without repositioning, giving them ten times the fire power of their British and German counterparts. If there was one thing Sumet needed to pack up in his trunk to bring home, it would have to be a modèle 75.

Aside from this covert mission, Sumet had more personal reasons to get away from his men. He felt rotten inside. The weeks at the Château might have brought some reprieve, but the gastric infection he had endured since their time on the troop ship, had revived. This time the culprit had to be the sausage: The peppery boudin noir, bought by the two twins in the St Dizier market; its slimy texture alone should have forewarned him. Obviously he should have passed it onto Pierre, who ate everything, but he was hungry and oblivious to its sour aftertaste, had scoffed it unseen. The churning pains in his stomach had started almost immediately. For most of the drive from Saint Denis, he had shifted uneasily between Born and Chai, breaking wind silently, agonisingly, desperate for a latrine. When Pierre had left the convoy to search for the tarpaulin in town, he toyed with the idea of making a dash to the washrooms in the basement of the Mairie (if indeed there were washrooms in the basement). But Pierre, contrary to his habitually slothful pace, had been annoyingly quick; there hadn't been time. Reaching the artillery position without a major accident had brought huge mental relief, but it was nothing compared to the elation he felt on seeing the one symbol he so desperately needed.

The sign pointed down a long communication trench that ran parallel with the line of guns. At the end of this track a square hut had been cut into the earth bank. It was small, four foot by six, hemmed in by sand bags; dark, squalid and nasty. A single spar of timber, the 'squatting pole', perched over a deep and narrow hole. Despite gripping his nose and holding his breath, the stench was unbearable; how long the mountain of waste had accumulated and festered he shuddered to think.

Coming around the corner of the trench entrance five minutes later, Sumet hoped that his absence hadn't been noticed. He was so busy fussing with the buttons on his tunic and brushing down the creases in his trousers, that he failed to notice that the gun crews were preparing to fire.

Like a great chorus of Valkyries, the twelve guns of the 47th battery opened up in perfect, terrifying unison, the shells screaming out across the sky towards their far targets.

Seconds later, three of the larger 155mm guns followed, the collective muzzle flashes consuming the ridge in a wall of flame, the violence of the shots seeming to suck the oxygen from the air. As the ground shook, a dense cloud of smoke pulsed out from the battery. The shockwave hit the Captain head on, hurling him against the earthworks, where, loosing his balance, he rolled down a bank.

It was a loading boy returning from the stockade, who first noticed the inert legs sticking out from the pile of spent cartridges. He shouted out. Chai and Pierre, who had been watching the guns from a higher position on the hillside, were shocked to recognise the Captain's distinctive black boots. They slid down the embankment and running to the edge of the bowl, threw planks out across the mounds of shell casings to the centre of the dump. Clambering out across the timbers, Chai dragged the Captain back to firm ground.

"Captain? Captain can you hear me?" shouted Chai, alarmed by his dazed looks and lop-sided demeanour.

Wiping the mud from his mouth, Sumet struggled to sit, his eyes staring out blankly at those crowded around him. He could see Chai shouting, but a loud ringing between his ears made him temporarily deaf.

A second barrage opened up from the guns, "BAAWHAM", then a third, "BAAWHAM"; the effect to the still sensory impaired Sumet, strangely muted and hypnotic. Chai, thinking him concussed, wanted to send for water, but Pierre, pointing to the detonations on the opposite ridges, urged them all back to the trucks as quickly as possible.

"The muzzle flashes will have been seen by the German spotters. If we don't get off this cursed ridge soon it won't just be your Captain's ears that will be ringing", shouted Pierre with an exaggerated gesture; as if his fingers were body parts, raining down in all places. He had expressive hands thought Chai; he would have made a good puppeteer.

The track coming off the artillery ridge was rutted and steep. With the trucks now light, unencumbered by their heavy cargoes, they came down fast, the large drum brakes squealing and smoking as their cast iron wheels slid on the loose rocks and mud. Reaching the plains and the safety of trees, Chai leapt down from his cab and ran down the lines of trucks to check they were all present. Yet again the Peugeot had failed. Its brakes had seized on the last corner, causing it to run off the road into a field where it slid and rolled over. Rescuing its driver they were only too pleased to be rid of it. Chai, returning to the front of the column shouted an order to move out.

Driving back through narrow country lanes to Belleville, Pierre turned and scanned the sky above the escarpment. He'd been right to herd them back to the trucks with such haste; the German guns, finding the French battery with their first salvo, started hitting the crest of the ridge. The explosions, though distant, were violent enough to shake the sides of their truck. Chai, looking up at the flashes in the sky, caught the dramatic silhouette of a company of soldiers strung out along the length of a hill, falling like dominoes as they saw the blasts on the heights.

As more shells exploded on the high ground, Chai began counting the intervals between seeing the flashes and hearing the distant detonations. He was reassured; they were getting further away. Thinking the worst was over and they were beyond danger, Chai was turning to Pierre to express his relief, when a round exploded close by. The detonation lit up Pierre's profile with such a furious halo of flame, Chai thought him on fire.

The convoy entered the outskirts of Souilly late in the afternoon. Grey cloud enveloped the town. Under this dense pall, darkness came early, as if someone had snuffed out a candle. The rain started again, returning the streets back to ooze. With the town clogged with vehicles and men, the Siamese trucks were directed down backstreets to the south of the town. The circuitous route was slow and meandering. Born, unable to use the main headlights, peered into the dark, straining to find a course through the maze of ruins and roadblocks.

Rounding a bend, the roar of approaching engines drowned out the noise from their own modest machines. A line of Latil TAR tractors crawled out from the black; exhausts red hot from cylinders at full throttle, steel wheels tearing up the cobbles as they hauled a pair of leviathan howitzers up the hill.

Close on the heels of these monster machines, ghostlike legions emerged from the gloom, the shifting mass surging by on all sides. Chai, straining his eyes, couldn't make out whether there were hundreds, tens of thousands, or whole armies flooding past.

From the black, angry voices yelled, "Bougez-vous!", "Putain, sortez de la route!"

Somewhere in the dark a horse bolted. They could hear shouts as men fought to bring the stricken horse under control. A wagon overturned. Men screamed in agony. Born stamped on the brakes and saw stretchers and bodies scattered across the road surface.

"Dégagez la route, Bougez-vous!", screamed an irate sergeant, hammering his rifle butt onto the side of their cab as his troops raced to recover the injured from the ground.

Surrendering to this relentless tide of shadows, Chai signalled to Born to pull over. They turned off the road, the flanks of their truck scrapping against a wall of rock embedded in the bank. A bough from a tree whipped out from the hedgerow. Born, seeing it coming was able to shout out a warning, but the caution, in Thai, was meaningless to Pierre who was slow to react. It was hawthorn, its branches covered with its razor sharp barbs, slashing deep gashes across his forehead, almost hooking an eye out.

"Merde", hissed Pierre, reaching for his handkerchief and wiping the bleeding, stinging cuts, "Mon dieu ces épines!"

Chapter 22

Sunlight, burning through the damp mists, cut under the low canvas flaps on the side of the truck and woke Chai.

Slipping between the tangled heap of sleeping bodies stretched out across the benches at the back, he jumped down from the tailgate to stretch his aching limbs. Kneeling down to tie up his boots, Chai glanced to his right and saw Pierre. At some point in the night, the Frenchman had abandoned the crowded interior and stretched out under the back of the truck. The axle had leaked. His face was smeared in black sump oil.

The truck stood in the middle of open farmland. Behind it, the rest of the Siamese convoy was scattered untidily in long grass bordering the fields. In both directions, save for a far off mule and cart, the road was empty. Over the trees in the distance, Chai could make out the spire of the Église Saint Charles that marked the main square of Belleville. Further out a plume of smoke spiralled up from the same artillery ridges they had raced down on the previous day.

Walking away from the trucks, Chai pushed through the undergrowth bordering the grass banks and leapt a ditch to a field. Landing with a thud in a furrow, he surprised a deer munching the short stubble left behind by the reapers. As the fawn leapt away across the meadow, a squall rose from the valley, the rush of wind lifting the loose cuttings in a dense spiral that swept away down the plain.

Buttoning up the stiff collar of his great coat, Chai continued along a rough path to a wood. A line of poplars formed a majestic avenue, their last autumn leaves crackling like a thousand paper lanterns in the breeze. In their upper branches a fierce battle played out; angry blackbirds fended off magpies, fighting to take over their territory.

Between the trees, muddy cattle tracks wandered down the incline to reeds and a shallow stream. Deeper imprints in the damp earth revealed where a wagon had recently rolled down to the creek to load up with water. Further down the tunnel of overhanging willow trees the stream widened. A grey heron, standing on a shingle bank eyed him suspiciously, taking umbrage at the human for disturbing its morning's hunt. Chai could see its prey, a school of minnows darting around the shallows near its feet.

Watching the tiny fish play amongst the reeds, Chai caught his reflection in the water. Covered with dust, grease and sweat, he was bemused by how messy he looked. Brushing down his spiky, matted hair, he knelt to the stream and scooping up a handful of water, scrubbed his face and the back of his neck, the icy chill making him shiver.

After the chaos of the roads on the previous night, Chai had been one of the last to sleep. Sumet, next to him on the boards in the back, had made a bad sleeping companion. Snuffling and snoring for those rare moments when he slept, the Captain made several forays out into the dark when he woke. Bruised after his fall on the heights, Sumet hadn't moved lightly between the sleeping men. Several elected to sit up and await his return rather than risk being trampled when he stumbled back in.

But it wasn't just the unsettled comings and goings throughout the night that had kept Chai from rest. Beyond the coughing, sneezing and kicking, the sights and sounds from the day had relentlessly churned through his mind, each replay unfolding with greater effect.

Escaping from the hearty, boisterous gunnery sergeant, Chai and Pierre had taken a more direct route over the parapet. It meant scrambling up wooden ladders and scaffolding on the side of the defences. The steps had emerged on the crest of the embankment, above the guns of the battery. Climbing down the concrete facade, they were trying to get closer to the guns when a warning was shouted by the guards to move back. Retreating back up the trench a wall of ammunition cases provided a vantage point over the sandbags, giving a clear view of the teams as they were preparing to fire.

With his hands tight to his ears, Chai had time to take in the action of the crews as they prepared and loaded their guns. Transfixed by the perfect synchronicity of the team, it was the fine details that had most indelibly imprinted themselves on his memory; the ranger twisting his hand-wheel to set the elevation, the quivering ends of the battery commander's moustache as he howled out his commands, the tight knuckles of the firing boy as he pulled back on his lanyard, dirt kicking out from the giant wheels as they jumped back from their ruts.

As salvo after salvo was dispatched with cold, deadly efficiency, Chai, awed by the brutal power of the battery, was transfixed. In those brief seconds he understood this new war; it was numbers, cold, calculating, inhuman. Just as western minds had so brilliantly manufactured cotton shirts, cutlery and plates, they had manufactured slaughter; shells and bullets went east, broken bones and corpses came home. He was part of that intricate machine. A small, impersonal cog in that great enterprise, oiled by delusions of honour, obedience and constancy. With men as frail as wheat under the scythe, heroism and chivalry were anachronisms.

Chapter 23

Having ridden through the night in torrential rain, the dispatch rider from the 4th army was recovering in the entrance portico of the Siamese Legation and pouring dirty water from his motorcycle boots, when Pramot arrived to open the doors. Caught unawares, his soggy woollen socks draped unceremoniously over the side railings, the rider stuffed his bare feet back into his still sodden boots and snapped to attention.

"C'est ici... the legation... the Légation de Siam?", asked the young Frenchman, fretful over the grubby smears he'd left over the pristine marble steps.

"Oui, ça l'est", Pramot dourly replied.

"J'ai une... a lettre pour vous," he announced, stepping down to his motorbike. Undoing the straps of his saddle bag, he produced an envelope.

"Merci," said Pramot, taking the letter and returning an awkward salute. In truth he felt a touch bashful. More than half an hour late, his own tardiness had kept the man waiting. Unprepared for the downpour when he'd left his basement apartment, he'd begged a raincoat from a neighbour to protect himself from the storm. The old man had lent him a gaberdine waterproof. Green, with floral collars and a magenta lining, he'd been angry with the choice. It might have kept him dry, but he could judge from the looks of passersby that he looked faintly ridiculous; he longed to be rid of it.

The despatch rider, pulling on his socks and boots and tightly buttoning his jacket, returned to his motorcycle. Damp from condensation, a cloud of sticky blue smoke coughed out from the exhaust as it fired up again. Making a parting wave, the rider pulled down his goggles, hit the accelerator and sped back into the deluge.

Pramot watched him go; a graceful arc of spray marking the messenger's impressive speed down the street, weaving like a skater between pedestrians, taxis and buses.

Folding the letter into his jacket, Pramot unlocked the front doors, crossed the hall and took the stairs to his annex office, now as dark as a cave under the grim, leaden skies. Hiding the offensive floral coat under the stairs, he walked to his desk, switched on a lamp and turned his attention to the envelope. Taking in the the brash army postmark his heart sank. Nothing good ever came from the French. Masters of obfuscation and pedantism, every exchange, or demand, however small or insignificant, required a small mountain of form filling. Such conduct came with an almost religious zealotry, as if bureaucratic nit-picking excused the insane barbarity of the front. The Thai, terrorised by these bookish ways, fought a daily tide of rejection; documents incorrectly filled in, paperwork that wasn't stamped, signatures that had gone missing.

Pramot put a paper knife to the seal and slit open the cover. A heading inside revealed a greater surprise – the letter was from the Americans; a 'Colonel Ernest Stoddard', a commander in the American SOS.

Braced for complaint or some stinging reproach, Pramot pulled open the fold reluctantly. It revealed a hand-written message on crisp watermarked paper, signed off with such panache by the aforementioned Colonel E Stoddard, that Pramot marvelled that the man's ostentation carried even to his signature. An exuberance so potent it had clearly infected its contents. Vividly written paragraphs, extolled the valour and efficacy of a company of men on a recent action at the front. Prose Pramot found so startling and colourful, his only reaction was incredulity. Clearly an error. The Legation was in the thick of the Parisian diplomatic zone. Surrounded as they were by embassies and foreign missions, it was common to receive wrongly directed mail. And the fault was his. So anxious had he been to get rid of his florid, soggy raincoat, he had failed to question the despatch rider effectively. When had they ever received anything of note from the Americans?

Folding the pages back into the envelope, Pramot resealed it, scrawled 'wrongly delivered' on the corner of the package and turning to his 'in' tray, focused on the more mundane issues of the day. A food shipment – rice, dried shrimp and soy – had been damaged in transit. It was not a paltry amount; several tons. He would have to coerce one of the junior staff to travel down to Marseilles to inspect it. If he failed, he'd be the one making the journey.

Lunch passed – a comically mean slice of thinly buttered bread and thinner cheese. Still hungry and thinking of making a run to a bakery, he was passing the open door of the communications room, when he overheard a conversation from inside. The switchboard operator, fielding a call, mentioned the same distinctive surname; "Colonel Stoddard". Intrigued at hearing the name again, Pramot returned to his annex and dug out the discarded envelope. Re-examining its contents, he realised his mistake. So impressed had he been by the Colonel's extravagant signature, he had failed to see that there was a second page to the letter.

Colonel Ernest Stoddard's excited prose on the covering page wasn't empty praise. A more detailed report, neatly typed on a Remington Ten, was yet more effusive: In an attack between Soissons and Reims, an American Division had been cut off in woods above Epernay. Heavily outnumbered and low on supplies and ammunition they were cornered and taking heavy casualties with no hope of retreat. Relief trucks had converged at the contested salient, but unable to find a way through the forest, had backed up at the base of the valley. It was a Siamese Company – and here Pramot had to pause to reread the text: "Siamese", not Italian, not French, nor British – "Siamese". And then a greater shock that only further rattled his balance; "the company was commanded by a Captain Sumet Chantrawong". This company, Chantrawong's company, had been the only ones brave enough to break through. Following an overgrown loggers' track in the woods, they had crossed an exposed ridge on the heights in full range of the German guns, before descending again to the cover of trees to relieve the beleaguered division. After unloading their urgently needed medical supplies and ammunition, they had loaded up with the wounded and returned to the safety of their lines.

Pramot, stunned by the narrative, felt faint. Dropping the letter he reached for his coffee. How could that be? How was it possible that this same feckless Sumet, lover of fine wines and fly-fishing and Captain of a hapless company of drivers, had actually made a notable impact to the war effort? And no modest achievement; a mission of some daring no less. They, his countrymen, Siamese, were heroes in the eyes of a senior American officer.

Pramot, assailed by rare emotion, leant back in his seat. Rarer still was moisture in his eyes. Here finally was something extraordinary, something to feel proud about, shout about, celebrate. And more miraculous still for his standing – he was going to be the one to relay it to Bangkok.

Wired across the continents, the same speedy cyclist delivered the telegram to the War Ministry. Hearing it, the officials were such strangers to accolades, they too thought it either a mistake or a hoax. It took a flurry of exchanges between East and West to convince them the narrative was real. General Chalerm was briefed. Aghast, he raced to the palace. The full ministry was summoned, the newspaper editors called. Rushed to the presses, the first headlines hit the streets; "Victorious Siamese troops, break through enemy lines to relieve the American 4th Army".

The unexpected success spurred a wave of patriotism; prayers were said by the abbot of Wat Pho. Garlands of jasmine were strung around the barrels of the cannon outside the War Ministry. Prisoners of war, a small crew of German sailors incarcerated in a walled compound within the Mahakan Fort, were given extra rice rations. The children of Rajani School sang Handel's Messiah (though embarrassingly, as it was later discovered, using the German text). Some bystanders impressed by the celebrations and fireworks, imagined the war had come to an end.

The Americans, true to their reputation of being bigger and brasher, went one step further. Colonel Ernest Stoddard was the younger son of a well-known Hollywood Big-Shot, a chairman of First National Films. A town hall in Dijon was screening a new cinematic production from their studio, "Shoulder Arms", accompanied by a musician on a piano. As a gesture of gratitude, an evening at the venue had been secured for Captain Sumet and his company, together with hotdogs, lemonade and Texan pecan pie.

Chapter 24

Two cotton bed sheets, stitched together and stretched between columns, provided the makeshift screen. The ten rows of seats that usually filled the town hall, were augmented with chairs and stools from an adjoining cafe. In the minstrels' gallery at the back of the building, technicians set up a hand-cranked Pathé projector on blocks to peer over the balcony. And to cut out the light, heavy velour drapes had been nailed across the six arched windows.

After a two-hour drive from their camp, the Thai company arrived in Dijon just before sunset. Stepping down from their trucks into the street, the men looked impressive to the handful of locals that remained in the square. Sumet, worried they wouldn't 'cut the mustard' against the haughty Americans, had wanted them to look flawless, ordering freshly shaved faces, sharp regulation hair cuts and spotless uniforms, even if that had meant persuading Pierre to bribe the camp guards to secure the necessary belts, brass polish and brushes.

Filing into the hall, a pretty red-headed girl, with freckles, showed them to their seats. The lights went down, the pianist opened with a flamboyant flourish and the film flickered, frame by frame, into life.

Although few were so innocent as to be unfamiliar with the conventions of cinema, the film still proved baffling. Its subject was the war, America's gallant and courageous troops in the trenches – a truth all Thai's took for granted and no one disputed. Yet the central character of the tale was a buffoon.

The first reel proved particularly perplexing. In one improbable sequence this curly-haired comic returned from a night of sentry duty to find his dugout so flooded with rainwater it was as deep as a swimming bath. His companions, obliviously asleep on their bunks next him, had water edging up to their nostrils. Undeterred by the depths, the funny man had ingenuously used the horn from a gramophone player as a breathing snorkel.

More puzzling still, this fool, this bungling incompetent, baffled them all by being the hero of the piece. Not only did the comic single-handedly rescue an American spy from a German firing squad, he also managed to capture the Kaiser and his retinue, driving them back across no-man's land in their own Mercedes staff car. The entire American army had cheered his return, as had the US personnel in the hall. Only the Thai remained stoney faced and bewildered by the scenes they were witnessing. The Captain, more than confused, was stupefied. Had he missed some hidden meaning? In a French army journal, "Le Flambeau", he'd read about psychological warfare; a secret weapon of words, designed to influence and demoralise minds. Maybe tomfoolery was part of that emotional arsenal. In which case they were on the wrong side.

The Thai weren't the only ones baffled by the show. The French members of the audience also found Chaplin's quirky antics, 'déboussolant'. A confusion that the executives of First National Pictures had witnessed before and it troubled them that their entertainment hadn't caught on. Hadn't slapstick been been invented in Europe? And it wasn't as if the experience of film was unknown. A picture house in Aniche, south of Calais, claimed to be the first public theatre ever, screening George Méliès, 'A Trip to the Moon'. And that was a comedy.

Needled by these failings, the US movie directors had sought out solutions to help speed an education of their new found humour. Seeding the auditorium with their own covert operatives, they instructed the team to provide robust 'choruses of laughter' at the opportune moments.

Such a team of 'cheerleaders' filled the row of seats behind the Thai, its chief conductor directly behind the Captain. Initially well ordered and disciplined, plied with beer they became over-exuberant. Soon, even the most trivial of appearances by the comedian was greeted with a barrage of hooting and seat kicking. It became too much for Sumet. After a particularly rowdy outburst, he turned around and pleaded for quiet. But his indignant expression, rather than quelling their mischief, instilled an outbreak of hysterics that caused four to fall back over their chairs into the row behind. The military police were called. The Captain, seeing them head his way and concerned he'd be exposed as the cause of the incident, was relieved when it was the loutish Americans who were dragged from the scene.

Sumet's first experience of 'moving images', was with his father visiting his uncle's village in Nakhon Pathom. A travelling kinetoscope was touring the country, offering standing room tickets at less than ten *satang* each. The films were short, composed of unrelated vignettes that had to be threaded through the projector one by one. The first, showed a quiet pastoral scene, where a barge, towed down the Seine by a team of cart horses, was overtaken by children racing by with steel hoops. A following sequence in a barber shop revealed a bearded man having his moustache waxed, whilst street urchins outside stole his bicycle. A last melodramatic scene of a burning barn being fought over by fire fighters, so alarmed the farmers, that they rushed back to their village thinking their own homes were in flames. When two days later, a rice barn was actually torched, the local police, remembering the film, had the showman arrested. Called before a judge his films were screened as evidence on the court room walls. A jury of two was unanimous. The works were denounced as dangerous and inflammatory. Such potent influences, stated the Judge, might well turn the vulnerable to a life of depravity and criminality. A local abbot, who had witnessed the unholy flickering from the safety of his monastery across the river, condemned the 'magical apparitions' as being the souls of wicked demons who fed off the minds of innocents. A frenzied mob broke into the jail, seized the projectionist's equipment and threw it down a well.

The Captain would willingly have damned his present entertainment to the same fate, but he wasn't so strait-laced to ascribe it the same censure; they weren't unworldly, superstitious villagers – they were the Thai army. Yet the distaste he felt for the sloppy protagonist, wouldn't go away. In a scene in a parade ground where new recruits were undergoing training before a drill sergeant, Sumet felt particularly uneasy. It looked light hearted and innocent enough: Walking the parade ground with the careless nonchalance of a drunken sailor, the pigeon-toed comic made a mockery of his commanders and superiors. In fact it got the most laughs even from his own men. Yet if discipline and rank were the backbone of any modern fighting force, was it wise to make a virtue out of insolence? Surely exposing susceptible minds to such degenerates would only encourage defiance?

In his own country, class structures kept such divisions firmly intact. The Buddhist faith endorsed such rigid hierarchies. Scriptures in the dharma taught humility and acceptance of one's place in life. A doctrine that created an automatic and unquestioning servitude and respect. No one doubted that faith. Yet the same couldn't be claimed of contemporary Europe. Unrest was everywhere. Whether in towns, stations, or training camps, one could sense the contagion. People were awakening to a new spirit. Authority and rank were being questioned and worst still, contested.

Sumet and his men had witnessed such hostility at first hand, when returning from a mission. Waiting at a freight depot on the outskirts of Reims, a train had pulled into the platform, its carriage doors opening to unload a company of soldiers on leave from the front. One of these men staggered down the steps in his socks, boots strung around his neck from their laces, a newspaper hat over his head in place of a helmet. A junior officer, young, fresh out of the Saint-Cyr Academy, outraged by the man's scruffiness, screamed at him to get back on the train and return properly dressed. The man refused. The officer, red-faced, repeated his order with a threat to have the infantrymen court marshalled for insolence. An uneasy silence settled. As if on cue, every soldier on the platform imitated the man's act and removed their boots and helmets. Seconds later the whole station, six platforms of troops, ten abreast, stood in their socks in solidarity. The officer, frightened by the scale of defiance, turned on his heels and ran across the yard, arms raised against a hail of gravel and coal. Crossing the tracks, he tripped and fell. A soldier, pretending to offer a helping hand, kicked him hard in the chest. Sumet flinched on hearing his ribs crack.

"Sors du camp, putain!", cheered the crowd, as if hounding a thief.

And then it was over. The officer staggered to his feet and limped off. The soldiers moved on and the platforms emptied as if nothing had happened.

For weeks the incident had shaken the Captain. Needled by anxiety and unable to prevent himself identifying with the shamed officer, he was beset by doubts as to his own leadership qualities. Like many he could appear authoritative and assertive, strutting the parade ground screaming out orders and dressing down dullards and sloths. Yet beneath all the bluster and bravado his motives remained troubled. Hating responsibility, he derived no pleasure from command nor harboured aims for high office. Further eroding his confidence was the fact that his men trusted, respected and liked Chai more; a tripartite of attributes he miserably lacked. Out in the field, with briefings before the men, it hurt sometimes but he was wise enough not to confront it. Besides, Chai, respectful of rank, never questioned his authority, nor even flinched when Sumet might shamelessly appropriate his ideas.

The same couldn't be said of the French. Out on joint operations, when there were important decisions to be made, their officers, even the rank and file, sought every opportunity to undermine his decisions. Several times their junior ranks had gone behind his back and issued orders directly to his men, or appropriated trucks without his permission.

Such conflicts had come to a head at the Soissons salient where the allies had struggled to relieve the beleaguered troops. Seeing no way through the seemingly impregnable forest, the French were all for caution, retreating back to the main road; few showed any real appetite to lay down their lives to rescue the bullish 'Americans', who, unheeding of warnings, had only themselves to blame for their predicament. The Italians, having long come to the same conclusion several hours before, were already half way back to St Dizier. Not wanting to appear so defeatist, the usual bombast from the French ensued. Senior transport officers marched the open ground looking self important, dishing out orders to everyone indiscriminate of race. Bored and petulant they became covetous, out to blag engine parts, even wheels, to replace their own that had become rusted and worn. Impertinent eyes pried under the bonnet of Born's vehicle. Another dropped to his knees to inspect its leaf springs and drive shaft.

The Captain, chary of their meddling and rightly worried they were about to cannibalise his vehicles, saw an opportunity to both outflank and upstage them. Seeking out the commanding officer, he rashly volunteered his own company for the rescue mission. Chai and Pierre were aghast. Neither had been consulted and no one had had the time to think through a plan or consider the consequences.

Two hours later, exposed to the full horror of a near constant barrage of enemy mortars and shells, the experience had profoundly shattered them; even Chai, usually so steady and composed, had looked shaken. Shrapnel from an explosion yards from their cab, had ripped through the partition close to their heads. The Captain, realising his monumental folly had ordered the men to turn back. Coming off the high ground in a disorganised panic they reached the base of the hill, only to stall at a fork in the road. Born, seeing the incoming blasts come down closer by the second, screamed for a decision. With no logic to inform their decision – one way was death, the other salvation – it was all down to instinct. In perfect synchronicity, Sumet said left, Chai said right. Born went right.

Sheer luck saw them blunder into the American camp. Received with open arms by the stricken troops, Sumet never let on they were really making a mad dash back to the lines. Unloading the munitions, they filled up with the wounded. A second nightmarish run along the exposed ridge saw them safely back behind their defences, earning a standing ovation from the American doctors and nurses and later (much later) some grudging respect from the French.

After the ordeal, Sumet took to his tent, desperate for solitude and the chance to settle his nerves. With quivering hands he attempted to write up his report, only too aware of his own questionable motives.

No act of humanity, he had done it for vanity, to big up his image with his men. A confession eked from his psyche like a snail from its shell – and it appalled him.

Loud, raucous laughter wrenched Sumet back to the film. Mercifully it was the dying minutes of the final spool. The credits rolled, the last frame flickered out of the gate and the lights came back on. The Captain, in his impatience to be out, was already standing, practically throwing himself down the aisle and an escape. It was left to Chai and Pierre to assemble the team and lead them out through the exit. At the main doors the red–haired girl was handing out black and white photographs. Chai, aware that the Captain disapproved of vulgar tat, guiltily took two; a portrait of Chaplin and one of the leading lady, the elegant Edna Purviance. He discreetly folded them into his side pocket.

Like all of their team, Chai hadn't looked forward to the show. Expecting some dry propaganda film when the curtains had first parted (they'd been forced to sit through too many tedious newsreels on the long sea passage from India), he'd been pleasantly surprised to see something so light hearted and fun. Liking the comedy, he'd wanted to laugh out loud, but was just wary of appearing so childish to the Captain, who had already shown his irritation and animosity by shuddering with abhorrence every time the shambolic private had entered the frame.

Now through the doors, photographs safely concealed in his jacket, Chai came away from the film with an entirely different and more sympathetic reading of the main character; the comic hero, absurd that he was, was also a romantic.

This sentimental twist was revealed in the fourth reel, by which time the Captain was past paying attention. In between saving the American, capturing the Kaiser and winning the war, Chaplin had also found time to rescue a pretty farm girl from the lecherous advances of a German cavalry officer. The man had broken into the girl's cottage and was about to ravish her when the comic had valiantly come to her aid. Pinned to the bed by her assailant, she was close to tears. But far from being just another helpless victim, the girl had shown both courage and fortitude in the fight that ensued. Tall and captivating, with flowing auburn hair, she reminded Chai of the girl from the Forey Leger estate; the schoolteacher, Sandrine.

Bernard had been right in his suspicions. Suspicions that were reinforced after Chai had left the chalked outline of the elephant on the blackboard. As Bernard had already rightly suspected, they had got close; too close. But the hand-holding was merely a prelude to an incident that was far more incendiary.

After leaving the classroom, Sandrine had wanted to show Chai a view of the school's playing fields from the higher ground. Coming down through the fields they had ended up near the church. Inside she showed him the stained-glass windows above the altar. Three arched vignettes illustrated scenes from the garden of Eden. Excitedly she pointed out colourful palms, tigers, flamingos and more impressive still, asian elephants, recognisable by their distinctive small ears. Like Chai's drawings in the classroom, two were even white.

It was coming back from the church, that her mood suddenly changed. Chai, glancing across, was surprised by the speed of her reversal. At one moment gay and vivacious – talking so fast he'd had trouble catching her words – the next, so dark and distressed he saw tears in her eyes. Without a care for the repercussions, he had held her tight, kissing her on her forehead and then without thinking, lower on her lips. The memory still jarred him. What was he thinking? He'd never done such a thing before. Even before their lips had parted, flushed with shame, he knew it was wrong. Sandrine, equally agitated, felt guiltier still; had she led him on, sent out the wrong signals, behaved like a loose farm girl? For seconds they stood there frozen like lost children, neither knowing what to say, what to do.

The bell from the school hall brought their moment of collective madness to an end. A flustered Sandrine led Chai back to the main building. When they parted, before Bernard had slyly ambushed them in the courtyard, she'd kissed him again – lightly and rapidly – and made him promise to write. And then she'd gone.

The Americans had been generous with the food. The beer, cakes and blueberry pie were soon finished; only the hotdogs remained – too pale, rubbery and insipid for Asian tastes. Pierre scooped up the remainder, wrapped them in greaseproof paper and folded them into his coat pocket; he could sell them later in camp.

Trucks had been laid on to take the company back to the barracks. Pierre, thinking he had seen the red-headed girl from the cinema leave the party, joined the young American projectionist and went onto the town. A bar was still open. They drank red wine and cognac.

Past midnight, they found themselves at the back of a long queue; one hundred and fifty men lined up in front of a bright red door in a side street. Thinking it was the entrance to another bar they patiently stayed. The house was small; inside were just three women, serving men at ten francs a time.

Because of the long wait, most of the soldiers gave up and hitched a ride back to their bases. Only Pierre and the American projectionist remained in the queue. They got to the red door as dawn broke. No one had told them that the girls had long since gone home.

Chapter 25

A newspaper cutting from an American journal, *The Stars and Stripes*, had been pinned to the felt board in the offices of the Propaganda Planning Ministry in Paris. The Director, catching the unusual account of the bravery of the Asian drivers in his mid-morning briefing, had asked for a full transcript from his editorial staff. It was a report that had come at an opportune moment; he was anxious to exploit its success.

At training camps in Artois and Aisne there had been disquieting rumours of unrest in the West African battalions. Callous remarks by a French general, "to make more use of 'indigenes' to save French lives", had justifiably caused uproar, even desertions, within the Algerian and Senegalese ranks. The timing was also imprudent. With the autumn campaigns still struggling to make headway in the sludge of Verdun, there was a pressing need of more of such regiments to stem the haemorrhaging losses.

The relief of the American troops at Soissons by "les braves troupes Asiatiques", presented a more positive perspective to highlight and propagate. It was a story of both daring and initiative; a morale boosting narrative to reverse dangerous mutterings that the Colonial troops were just good for cannon fodder.

George Clemenceau, Prime Minister and Minister for War, was a week away from his seventy-seventh birthday. To mark the occasion his staff had chosen to celebrate the day in some style. A plan was hatched to visit the American 1st Army at Montfaucon, sixteen miles from the front line at a château on the Marne river. General Henri Gouraud of the French 4th Army, together with some carefully selected reporters chosen by the Press Bureau, would accompany him.

Looking to craft a more uplifting image for the carpers and critics, the High Command would use the valiant Indochinese as drivers and waiters at the forthcoming celebrations. Photographers would be instructed to frame images of these "héros célèbres" serving tea and cake to the noble Prime Minister and the First Army generals. What better way to present a picture of egalitarianism and equality to those in the less-developed world?

Pierre, asleep for less than an hour following his abortive night trailing the red headed usherette, had trouble waking and coordinating himself. Passing on breakfast, he was driven with Chai to the transport office in Valcourt to receive their new orders. Prepared for a long wait in the usual cramped, smokey corridor, they were puzzled when shown to a state room on the first floor where gilt mirrors and giant Aubusson tapestries graced the four walls. The appearance of the section Director with two Fourth Army colonels, trailed by smiling waitresses bearing fresh coffee, only added to their confusion and uncertainty. Pierre and Chai, worried that their over-publicised rescue of the Americans might have earned them an honorary seat on yet another suicidal mission, were relieved to hear that their new assignment was a safe one; they were to be the drivers and staff at Clemenceau's coming birthday. So elated were they with the news, that they chose to overlook the War Ministry's lazy, but grave error. Siam, an independent Kingdom, was certainly not part of Indochina; the geography lesson in the Castelnau school room had long established that. But why needlessly complicate? Stand, smile, salute – "stumm", wasn't that the German expression? As long as there were no atlases around (highly unlikely) and the French Military didn't talk directly to the Siamese or probe too closely (they would have to take the necessary precautions to prevent any close fraternisation), they could probably get away with it. Besides, the mistake, thankfully, wasn't theirs.

The chosen tea service – rare Ming Dynasty porcelain originally from the French Consulate in Peking – was laid out on long trestle tables in the staff canteen at the 4th Army barracks. Concerned that the delicate plates, cups and pots might be too fragile for the rough supply routes to the East, a team of army engineers had fabricated spring loaded platforms into the flat beds of the trucks to absorb the worst potholes and ruts. Everything was wrapped in thin tissue paper, nested in sawdust and wood shavings, then nailed shut within stout T-chests. Galette des Rois cakes, Palmier pastries and chocolate macarons, were delivered by a patisserie in Lyons. A set of velvet-cushioned chairs, round tables, three damask rugs and a large canvas tent, completed the load.

Further lifting the prestige of the mission, four near pristine Berliet trucks were delivered to the Thai company at the camp. Newly painted and upholstered with brown leather seats and varnished wood floors, they were barely recognisable to the grimy workaday mules they were used to.

Having loaded their precious cargoes late at night, the company set off at five, before most of the camp were awake. Remembering the chaos on the roads four weeks before, Sumet wanted to be well ahead of the supply convoys that would soon be crawling out from the rail depot at Saint Dizier. The new trucks were lighter and more powerful than their previous machines, but the Captain, ever neurotic for the fragility of their loads, had Born slow for even the slightest blemish in the road. Drifting along like a procession of monks, they travelled at a snails' pace. Sumet wasn't unduly concerned. He'd already factored in a generous margin of error.

After a mind-numbing crawl of seven hours, they reached Bar-le-Duc by noon, remarkably still an hour ahead of schedule. That left an easy and final twenty kilometres to go before reaching their destination, the American base at Montfaucon. Not that their work would be over. Sumet had blocked out the rest of the afternoon for training exercises. Aware that his men knew little about waitering or serving, he wanted the crates, tables and chairs unloaded and unfolded, so that they might practice and perfect their tea-serving, cake slicing and tray-carrying skills. Pierre, Chai and himself, would sit in and act out the parts of Clemenceau and the American generals. On the actual day, Sumet was aware there would be reporters. Their images and words would likely head East. And if that meant they might make the cover of the national newspapers, they needed to look good and their parts be faultless.

Optimistic and making good time, it was at Vavincourt, west of the Rosieres crossroads, that their neatly laid plans started to unravel. The route of the Captain's task force, had naturally been dictated and cleared by transport officials. At every sector, obsequious guards had waved them through without a word. But Clemenceau's staff, over confident in the efficacy of their mission, had failed to coordinate their movements with the general staff at headquarters, which on the morning of the 9th of November was a disastrous oversight.

The Meuse Argonne offensive was fast approaching an 'End Game'. No greater concentration of men and equipment had yet been witnessed in the war; eight hundred thousand men, 4,596 tons of supplies, more than 10 million shells, trucks, wagons, guns and tanks; all converged on a thin slice of land near the small village of Rumont. And it was towards the sharp end of this wedge, that Born found himself careering towards as he cleared the crest of a hill.

Made drowsy and lethargic by their slow pace, Born was late on the brakes. The jolt threw the Captain forward over the hood, hurling his pencil and notebook into the road. Alarmed only for the delicate crockery in the back, he yelled, "Watch out! Watch out for the Ming!"

The rear wheels locked, sliding on the loose grit. They came to an abrupt stop inches from the rear gate of a troop carrier, the American flag on its tailgate falling lazily over their radiator.

Sumet, recovering from his fall, fell back against the bench seat. He'd hit his knee on the facia panel, the impact grazing his knee.

"Chai, go and see what the problem is," he asked, hands massaging his stinging bruise.

Chai and Pierre got down from the cab and walked up the incline. They didn't have to go far. A short push through a coppice of trees, brought them out on a promontory overlooking a valley. What they saw was a shock. Over the open plain below a dense line of wagons and trucks stretched far into the distance. Midway along this congested highway was a crossroads. Converging on this lean junction, two further columns met in a seething swarm of men and machines, all pressed together towards a single waypoint; a distant church spire in a circle of trees.

"What's going on?" asked Chai.

"Looks like everyone's heading for the seaside," muttered Pierre wryly.

Born was bandaging Sumet's cut knee when Pierre and Chai returned.

"Well? Can we get through?," he asked.

"Not at the moment." replied Chai, "The road's totally blocked."

"But we're so close, just twenty kilometres!", said the Captain, pointing desperately to an 'x' on his map.

"And that twenty kilometres is a single line of trucks and wagons," added Pierre, "pressed so tightly together we'd have more luck driving over them, than around."

Sumet, wearied by the Frenchman's witticisms, rolled his eyes. The urgency of their mission seemed to have escaped him.

"Well don't just stand there. See what the hold up is!" he snapped, pointing back up the hill.

With the road blocked they took a short cut down the hill. Boggy and overgrown, it took more than an hour of slipping and sliding to reach the base of the column. The cause of the hold-up was a surprise. A single munitions carrier was buried up to its axles in the sticky clay. Two attempts to pull it clear, first with mules, then with a larger more powerful truck had failed. Having stirred up the already water-logged terrain, this second lorry had itself become stuck, dragging in more mules, rescue vehicles and men. Frayed ropes, cables and broken chains mixed with the sludge, the ground now so finely churned by wheels, boots and hooves it reassembled a goulash.

At the centre of this quagmire, two harassed French MP's were surrounded by irate American officers. They had called for tractors, but due to the sheer weight of traffic returning from the front, they couldn't get through.

"Get help from the goddamn farms! Cart horses would be better than those skinny mules!" shouted the belligerent foreigners.

From the direction of the village, three gendarmes raced to the help of their beleaguered countrymen. Pushing into the circle of drivers and officers, more voices added to the row. Sleeves were rolled and threats exchanged. A drunk Frenchman barged through and had to be restrained in an armlock by a large American soldier. Chai and Pierre, distancing themselves from the fight, stole away and made their way back up the road.

Darkness fell as they trudged back up along the lines of parked convoys. With more soldiers flowing out into the narrow lane, an air of unease permeated the previously disciplined lines. Drivers and officers poured over maps searching for routes to bypass the blockage. One column had already turned off the main road and breaking through a farm gate, found a track across wheat fields. The horse-drawn wagons went first and with lighter loads were soon in the valley. Encouraged by their success three trucks followed. The steep gradients helped, but their heavy cast-iron wheels cut so deep into the farrows, they were soon spinning uselessly in the viscous sediment.

Further up the incline a tank had impressed all by breaking through a hedgerow into an orchard. Cheers erupted as it shattered the fragile trees throwing up a shower of splinters and dead branches. But its advance was short lived. Crashing against a hidden boulder, it bounced like a ball despite its immense weight, landing on edge, shredding its tracks. With smoke pouring from inside and flames flickering from its exhaust, the crew, concussed by the crash, had to be dragged from inside.

Chai and Pierre made it back to the top of the hill, but found their own trucks so hemmed in by troops, they had problems forcing their way through.

"You've been gone for ages, more than two hours!" snapped Sumet, cross but also relieved, "What's going on!"

"It's hopeless," replied Chai, "It's totally blocked. We won't get through."

"What never?" cried the Captain aghast at the news.

"Not as it stands."

"That's not our only problem," said Born, nodding to the restless mob that surrounded them.

From the far bank the hedgerow parted as a larger group emerged from the fields. The troop were led by a tall Texan, who, bullying his way through the ranks, approached the front of the Thai trucks. He looked battle worn. One side of his face was soot black and scarred with gashes, as if he'd been close to a blast. Sliding his colt back into its holster, he rapped the hood of the Berliet as if sizing up a prize steer.

"We're taking over this truck, buddy," he snapped, gloved hand admiring the fresh paintwork.

The outburst stunned them.

"Taking over whose truck?" stammered the Captain.

"Your truck."

"I don't... I don't understand..."

"What don't you understand?", repeated the Texan, "We want your truck."

Pierre intervened, "With all due respect, sergeant, I'm afraid it's you who doesn't understand... You see we are under orders from the Prime Minister's office. Clemenceau himself".

He'd said it wanting to be diplomatic – it wasn't his aim to offend. But Pierre, all too aware of their illustrious patron, was unable to disguise an air of self-righteousness.

"Clemenca ha?"

"General Georges Clemenceau".

"Is that so?" replied the American unmoved, "Is that so..."

Pierre reached to his jacket pocket and finding the official despatch document, graced by the noble Elysée seal, passed them down to the tall Texan. He glanced at the regal crest, but was otherwise unmoved.

"What's your cargo?", he shot back.

Pierre bluffed it, talking up the importance of their mission, its purpose so confidential he could only reveal their destination – Montfaucon.

The American, still unimpressed and wise to bull and bluster when he saw it, signalled to his men, "Check out the back."

"What? Why?" interjected the Captain.

"Because I'm nosey and I'm curious…" shrugged the sergeant.

Two of his men walked around to the rear of the truck. Minutes later they came back having made a cursory inspection.

"A chink tea set, comfy chairs and an oak dressing table… Like I said, we're taking over this truck," repeated the man.

"On who's authority?" questioned the Captain.

"General fucking Pershing."

"And that gives you the ability to steal anything that takes your fancy?", retorted the Captain infuriated by the man's cocky demeanour.

"In this case it does," replied the sergeant simply, "And I need them now… So if you could step down, it would be much appreciated."

Chai, Born and Pierre complied and climbed down from the cab. But Sumet, gripping the side of his seat like a child on a climbing frame, refused to budge, knuckles turning white with the strain.

"Look, buddy, I'm a bad guy. That's what my friends tell me. I could take you down like a gnat. But I'm not going to do that. I want you to see reason. And when you've heard that reason I want you to make your choice far and square."

"No time, Frank, lay him flat, we need to get going," joined a voice from the dark. "Punch his chink lights out," added another.

The sergeant held up his arm for quiet. Turning again to Sumet, his tone was more conciliatory, "I've got six wounded. A head injury, a stomach wound, three broken limbs and a colonel that's been shot in the back. I need to get them to hospital fast."

"There are other trucks. Your own trucks. American trucks," protested the Captain.

"We've lost our transport. We need yours."

"I'm not at liberty to surrender them, our orders are…"

"Look, we can slog this out. Right here, right now. But that wouldn't be a good ending for you or your men. If I were you, I'd step down now while you still have a nice set of teeth."

Chai reached up and took Sumet's arm, "Captain, we need to do what he says."

"No, Chai. You don't understand! No one understands! We've a mission to complete, that's what we promised and that's what we'll do. I will not surrender our trucks!"

Ten minutes later their precious cargo was wrenched from the back and laid to rest in the long grass near the hedgerow. The complicated sprung platform installed by the French engineers took longer to dismantle. Two men had to search the toolbox for some wrenches to undo the bolts. Eventually it came loose and joined the benches, chairs and tea chests in an untidy heap by the side of the road.

Torches shone through the half-light as more troops appeared. Medics, carrying the wounded, followed. The Sergeant, standing by the side of the road, organised their loading into the trucks. The last in line, a large, stocky tank commander, chewed the butt of a cigar, despite bloodied bandages over his face and side. Lifted to the tailgate of Born's vehicle, he didn't go in easily, his arm reaching out to snatch the steel frame.

"Goddamn it! I'm not finished yet! I don't want to end up in some goddamn Frog hospital!"

Four soldiers had to rush forward to help the medics prise the man's fingers from the back. Once safety inside they secured the stretcher to the benches and made their patient comfortable with cushions, thanked for their efforts with a second salvo of expletives.

The Thai's watched this scene from a distance. The large howling American, battering the sides of their truck, unnerved them. More than kicking legs and foul language, he seemed a giant of a man, possessed of some unnatural primeval force.

George Smith Patton, a West Point graduate, first saw action against Mexico in 1916, when he launched the first motorised attack in US military history by storming down the Santa Fe valley in three Dodge touring cars. Nicked named the 'bandito' for his success in hunting down renegades, he joined Pershing's Expeditionary Force in France in the following year. Promoted to a lieutenant colonel in the United States Tank Corp, he took command of a brigade of French-built

Renault FT tanks. It was on the Meuse-Argonne front that he led an assault on the town of Saint Mihiel. On the day of the attack, low cloud shrouded the valley. Walking ahead of his tanks through this mist, he had come under fire from a German machine-gun post. An infantry platoon, pushed into a counter attack, had been instantly killed. Patton fell back on his orderly, an unassuming New Jersey man, Joe Angelo and pointed up the hill; "You and me, we're going to clear those Hun guns!".

"What?", asked Angelo, incredulous and confused, "You've got to be kidding!"

"You and me..." repeated Patton, his hand making a gesture across his neck as if cutting imaginary throats.

Joe Angelo was no coward. Already that morning he had confronted a machine-gun nest single handed and taken out its gunners. But with bullets scything down the rye grass on both sides and shells increasingly finding their mark, he knew the odds of success were on the wrong side of insane.

Angelo screamed his objections but shell bursts stifled his words. Patton, as impervious to reason as he was to danger, continued advancing up the hill, colt revolver in hand, right arm beckoning forward as if leading a house party in a duck shoot.

Angelo, seeing nothing but an encounter with death over the brow of the hill, caught up with the colonel and grabbing his shoulder attempted to pull him back to the safety of a bunker. Patton, enraged by the soldier's 'chicken-livered' insubordination, twisted around. Knocking off Angelo's helmet and grabbing his hair (an annoyingly long mop of unkept black curls), Patton attempted to shake some sense into him. In all truth he shook the sense 'out of him'. Angelo, quickly changing his tune, deferred to rank, shocked that he had ever had the gall to contest one of the biggest egos in the American forces if not its entire military history. Surrendering all caution, Angelo retrieved his helmet, sharply saluted his superior, levelled his rifle and trudged dutifully up the slippery incline oblivious to the deadly rain of shells, mortar rounds and shrapnel.

The private's fears were soon realised: unseen beyond the ridge was a third German machine gun position. As soon as Patton appeared over the rise in the hill, his last round from his ivory handled Colt spent, he was shot.

Despite a bullet through his right buttock, the headstrong commander still wouldn't give up. Angelo had to drag him back down the hill to the cover of a shell crater. As Joe staunched the flow of blood and bandaged the wound, Patton continued to bellow out orders, "Get those goddamn tanks under cover. They're sitting ducks for the Hun guns!"

Recovering in hospital a week after the incident, Patton called Angelo, "a foppish son of a bitch, and the bravest man in the American Army."

Angelo, interviewed by reporters, had blushed; unused to publicity he had little idea of the fame of the man he had saved and even less of an idea, that in no more than twenty years, Europe would once again be on the battlefield, with Patton, Commander of the Third Army, the scourge of the German High Command, cutting through their defences – in his own words – "like crap through a goose".

Years in the future, the extraordinary fate awaiting the recalcitrant patient was no comfort for the disconsolate Thai.

Captain Sumet, crestfallen at the loss of his vehicles, stepped back from the road and surveyed the scene. To his right he could see his precious Berliet trucks being loaded with the last of the American wounded. Restarted, they reversed and crawled away down the lane, the Texan sergeant shouting out orders from the running boards, accompanied by a barrage of swearing from the back.

Chai was consoling, "There was nothing we could do, Captain."

"Nonsense Chai. We have failed. We have all miserably failed. This is a bleak day indeed for our king and our country…" replied Sumet, so forlorn he looked about to plant himself forever in the dismal suppurating earth.

"We should at least save the tea and food. And if we get to the village, there's a chance we can find other transport", said Chai, anxious not to linger and alarmed at how deep the Captain really had sunk into the glutinous ground. He had to get the boys to haul him out. Even that proved a struggle, the soles of his boots already several inches into the ooze.

Giving orders for Mai and Manit to guard the area, Captain Sumet, Chai and Pierre fought their way through the traffic to the heart of the crossroads. Pierre, directed to a command tent, found an official willing to help. He had several dust carts they could use to retrieve the supplies.

The three raced back, but by the time they had got back to the stacked pallets and crates, the precious tea set, cakes and biscuit tins had already been ransacked.

"I thought we told you to stand guard while we were away," howled the Captain in disbelief.

"Believe me, we tried. But they were pigs. Too many for us," replied Manit, nodding over his shoulder.

The 'pigs' were still there; hungry, unshaven, scavenging through the now empty hampers and boxes and shamelessly wolfing down the last slices of almond and cherry gateau. Another group had stretched out across the special sprung platforms, heads nestled comfortably in the velvet seat cushions, wiping their faces with the silk napkins.

Pierre led Captain Sumet's crew back to the village. They found a barn being used as a supply store. One wall was stacked with desks and chairs, together with a piles of office equipment and stationary.

Treading between the sleeping bodies, they found places where they could lay down on the floor. Manit and Mai, carrying tarpaulins and blankets from the trucks, laid them out in a semi circle around an open brazier. The team quickly spread-out in front of its heat. The Captain, still too angry to forgive or forget, walked away from his men and refused to sit.

Pierre, wanting to report the bad news back to base as soon as possible, went back to the command post. He found a telephone, but yet again, the lines, overwhelmed by the constant activity from the Americans, were down.

Chapter 26

It was a chaotic night. In the early hours a soldier burst through the main doors shouting for Étienne. Although Étienne wasn't there, it didn't stop him trampling over everybody who was there to examine their faces, his clumsy boots leaving a trail of messy red sludge. And he wasn't the only one. Others broke in seeking shelter, or scavenging for food. The Thai, fed up with being pushed around and stomped on, shifted their meagre camp to the back of the barn. Pierre found a sanctuary on a bed of upturned typewriters.

Everyone had bad dreams. Sumet, still wracked with remorse for the loss of their trucks, refused to lie down. Wedged upright between a cattle trough and a hay rack, his tortured state offered little peace. Pitched between states of semi-wakefulness and nightmarish thoughts, so vain were his yearnings that the threat of distant shell fire no longer held any sway over his fears. Seduced by these miseries, he played with the idea of taking a direct hit, of being obliterated and dispersed in a puff of atoms as if he had never existed. He had seen such fine grains covering the trees and bushes at cremation sites near his home.

Pierre woke first, the imprint of an azerty keyboard embossed in his cheek. Mai and Manit, now considered the most competent food scouts, went in search of breakfast. Chancing on an American kitchen wagon they entered a tent and were stunned to find tables piled high with fresh rolls and hotdogs. Handed a sack by a passing cook, they felt duty bound to fill it with as much as they could get and returned to the barn.

Reenergised by the meal the team made an early start. Leaving the chaos of the traffic behind, they took a footpath out of Rumont. Pierre had been given instructions by locals, written in pencil in the margins of his map, the rail yard at Verdun marked with a crude cross as their destination. If they were quick and could complete the forty-five kilometre trek in one day, they would still make their rendezvous at Montfaucon and with luck fulfil their duties as Clemenceau's tea staff, hopefully salvaging some reputation from their seniors in the transport department.

The first villages, Erize and Raival, came up within the first five kilometres, both hamlets abandoned, their thatched cottages and out buildings carpeted with creepers and vines. It was a fourth turning past a stone bridge that was missed. The military had taken down a distinctive circle of beech trees to clear ground for a fuel depot; Pierre's crucial signpost to take the road to the right.

The fatal error took them east, the sandy track, winding through low scrub and birch woods. At one point, the trees were so overgrown and the path so faint, that they lost the trail completely. Pierre, compass in hand, previously so sure and decisive, started to dither. He backed up, about turned, changed his mind and found a third direction.

Scratched and grazed by brambles and thistles they emerged in a deep hollow in the woods, its banks so pitted with tunnels and holes some took them for dug outs. The earth mounds turned out to be badger setts. Oak roots, gnarled and twisted, looked like the coils of ossified snakes. And beyond this circle of trees, the path, frustratingly, petered out.

Pierre, troubled by this outcome, checked his compass bearing and was shocked to see it had stuck. And he could see why; the needle was so encrusted with rust it must have been locked up for weeks, months even – maybe it had never worked? Damn the Pole he had bought it from! And it wasn't as if it had been cheap either – more than five packets of Champion tobacco, together with matches.

"Merde!" he hissed, as he dropped it sheepishly into his pocket.

Several were for turning back, but Chai was doubtful; they'd come too far to make it back to the Rumont crossroads before nightfall. And although they couldn't see the sun, the light was already falling.

Chai left the main group and walked over to check on the Captain. Slumped on a stump between Born and Mai, he didn't look in the best of health.

"Has he eaten anything?"

"An apple," replied Mai.

"That was yesterday," Chai reminded them.

Picking up their packs they followed a stream. Pierre thought it certain to lead to some form of habitation. It didn't. The ground, choked with ferns and ivy, was harder to navigate, roots and vines snaring the unwary. Seeing the Captain fall, Chai had two men support him. It made no difference; he still fell and took down the rest with him.

Marshlands opened up. Hidden in the long grasses they could hear mallard and coot. Wrun, stirred by the thought of grilled duck, gave chase through the shallows. Deep in the reeds the ground gave way suddenly and he found himself waist deep in the bog. Manit and Dee swung out a branch to drag him back to the bank.

With the ground becoming more treacherous and water logged, they formed a chain and waded between the islands of reed and bullrush. Unexpectedly the silty estuary opened onto a wide river, its waters turbulent with flotsam and driftwood. The men, grateful for a chance to rest, loosened their boots, sat on the banks and threw stones into the spinning eddies. Chai, concerned again for the Captain, walked back to Mai and Born and helped Sumet to a seat in the clearing. Opening his canteen bottle he offered him water. He took it and silently sipped.

Leaving the men, Chai walked over to Pierre and took him aside.

"We need to talk," he whispered.

"Yes," replied Pierre, troubled by the sight of the water.

They walked to the far corner of the river bank and unrolled the map on the grass.

"It shouldn't take long to regain the track," said Pierre, brushing back his hair and confidently tapping a corner of the paper. Chai was less certain.

"Pierre, the Captain's not well. He needs a doctor. I need your advice. But before I take it I need you to be frank. I don't mind bad news but I haven't the time for deception. Do you know where you are?"

"No."

"Do you know where we're going?"

"No."

"Thank you for your honesty." Chai rolled up the map again and turned to survey the high ground behind them. He was surprised to see a star – possibly Venus – in a break in the clouds.

Despite the men's complaints and Sumet's deteriorating condition, Chai forced a faster pace, which was now all uphill. Knowing how wrong they'd gone in broad daylight, Chai didn't want to take risks in the dark. His aim was to get them to dry ground as far from the river as possible before exhaustion set in. It wasn't long in coming. After the core team supporting Sumet collapsed a third time, groaning in the long grass and pleading for respite, Chai called a halt. Finding a sheltered clearing in the hillside, they trampled down the undergrowth and prepared a camp. Dry leaves and dead wood were gathered for a fire. Pine branches and ferns were cut to make beds. With canteen bottles filled from the river and enough sausage and salami saved from the American kitchen, they sat and ate in silence. The strong winds, that had oppressed them for most of the day, eventually stilled.

It was past midnight when they woke. Some thought it a howl; a demonic moan that seemed to emanate not from the hills but the ground. No one questioned what it might be. A collective terror gripped them all as they panicked and ran. Their escape route was a steep gully on the far side, thick with low gorse and thorns, the barbs slicing their ankles and making them squeal, adding to their fright and flight.

Reaching the base of the hill they collapsed and rolled in the leaves. They were huddled in a group, pale and shaking with fear when Chai and Pierre caught up with them.

Chai walked into the centre of the group and finding a body curled up like a ball, kicked it, "What the hell's got into you? Come on, get up!"

"No way! Are you mad!", Wrun shrieked back.

"Didn't you hear them?"

"Hear what?"

"The voices."

"From where?"

"From the top of the hill…"

"It wasn't one of us?" he asked sceptically.

"One of us? Of course not!" Dee wailed.

"How can you be sure?"

"Because it wasn't human."

"An animal then?"

"No Chai, what's wrong with you, can't you see it, don't you understand!"

"No, what?"

"Bad spirits, ghosts!" Darn squealed back, infuriated by Chai's obtuseness, "the whole place is crawling with them!"

"Not that again," sighed Chai, shaking his head dismissively.

"You don't believe us?" bitter voices hissed back.

"No, I don't believe in that stuff…"

"Stuff! They're not stuff! They're real! Up there! On the hill!"

"About as real as flying monkeys."

"Don't mock them Chai. It will only bring bad luck on us all!"

Chai glanced over the group. Wrun was there, as were the two twins, Manit and Mai. Behind were Dee, Worarat and the previous strong man Darn, now reduced to a quivering wreck. Three others crouched in the shadows, arms tight over their heads. Excluding themselves and the Captain (still asleep at the top), that only made eight. One of the team was missing – Born.

It was past midnight when Born was woken by the need to break from the clearing and find a discreet site in the dark. Feeling his way through the spiky undergrowth, he found a line of bushes at a safe distance from their camp. Unbuttoning his trousers and relieving himself, he looked up and seeing an arc of stars overhead, was struck by their clarity and beauty. Born knew his night skies, especially the familiar faces from home back in Petchabun, where on hot nights he often stretched out on reed mats over the veranda after an evening meal. "Dao Tai", Castor and Pollux in the plough and "Dao Sam Pro", the masts and sails of the boat in the 'junk' constellation, shone with a spectacular and comforting brilliance.

With his eyes fixed on this silvery firmament and his ears filling with the rasp of cicadas and insects, he could almost smell the scent of grilled pork on the charcoal burner downstairs. So enraptured was he with these fond memories, that he was insensitive to the shifting sands beneath his feet. He never remembered the fall.

Recovering consciousness several hours later, Born's head pulsed with such an intense searing pain, he thought his skull had been pierced with a stake. He tried moving, but so deep were his arms and legs locked within the sticky embrace of the earth, he couldn't right himself. A timber block under his neck explained the bruise to his head. It was part of a wooden arch that loomed above him, the air inside its frame, black and foul. Several times he screamed out, "Chuai duai, Chuai duai, Help! Help!" but his cries, muted by the depth of his Piranesian prison, seemed to lose their force in the labyrinth. Pausing anxiously for a reply he was disturbed instead by closer sounds. Behind his head came an unnerving rattling. Dreading the worse he turned, appalled to see the outline of a skull sunk in the ooze, its teeth snapping up and down as if anxious to talk. Rats, a whole family of them, fat and bright eyed, were the rational, but equally repellent explanation. He could see their furry outlines scurrying along a network of rodent highways, dug through the layers of sediment, sandbags and decomposed corpses.

Born let his head fall back to the sulphurous sludge, resigned to its stench. His cries were useless. No one could hear him and certainly no one could see him. A cool trickle of water came off the bank and channelled into his collar, ran down his spine. Sweaty after his frenzied attempts to dislodge himself from the mud, the icy stream chilled and calmed him; a sensation he found perversely pleasurable. As his mind stilled, his eyes had time to contemplate the surrounding scenery – crushed timbers, rusted helmets, a tobacco tin, a shattered rifle butt; all laced with the lost souls of dead men. So this was his purgatory, his tomb, his final resting place? It wasn't unexpected. Hadn't he seen this place before, known it was coming, heard it foretold in Pierre's gloomy monologue at the Saint Amour fireside? And why not. It was fate, it was karma. He'd beaten a man to death with a club. An innocent man, if not a friend. His guilt was clear. Why fight it? Embrace it, let it go.

Comforted by this surrender, Born found relief within his snug cocoon, now closer to the underworld than the world of the living. Such finality was not without consolation. Fear, no longer a malevolent stalker that threatened at every turn or crossing, was now his close bedfellow, rising even now from its sticky underworld over his helpless body, ready to receive and drag him down. Except this gruesome apparition crawling inexorably towards him, through the layers of debris and corpses, was no phantasm, it was Chai – of course it was Chai.

The scramble out was a painful, slippery climb up the walls of the shell crater. It was a traumatic ascent, the path steep, unstable, seething with horrors. Every foothold and ledge crumbled to reveal something yet more gruesome and repellant. A hand grip Born took for a tuff of grass peeled away to reveal strands of hair. The shock made him snatch out for Chai's ankle almost bringing them back down.

Pierre, hanging from a tree root at the edge of the bowl, was there to give them a last helping hand to the top. Reaching the safety of the crater rim, the three collapsed in an exhausted heap.

"You did well to go down there," said Pierre passing his water canister across to Chai, "The stink was unbearable. I don't think I could have done it."

"If I'd known what was down there," replied Chai, still fighting for breath "I wouldn't have gone."

The rasp of engines overhead woke those rare few who had managed to claw back some much-needed sleep. A squadron of biplanes, SE 5's painted with the insignia of the Escadrille 15, flew in close formation, thin wisps of smoke trailing from their exhausts. As they cleared the horizon they heard the sporadic spit of rifle fire rising from the plain. Heavier artillery fire followed, dark cloudbursts punctuating the sky, long off the mark.

"They're flying east over the German batteries," said Pierre.

"At least that gives us a direction", replied Chai – the white trails marking a bearing in the sky more dependable than Pierre's rusted compass.

Setting up camp the night before, an unsettling stench had been their only clue that they might have strayed into a past battlefield. Now, under heavy, threatening skies, its tragic extent was clear. On all sides the foul, torn-up ground looked like it had been stirred by a giant spoon. Shell craters and collapsed trenches, were mixed with twisted metal, barbed wire and splintered posts. Where they stepped, the ground crunched. The most fretful took it to be bones.

Strung out in an untidy line, they navigated a narrow path through the pits and ditches. A shattered octagonal tower appeared on a hill. Commanding the high ground it looked like it had been bitterly contested. Bullets pitted the masonry, two gaping holes were punched through its sides. High in the belfry, an eerie sentry remained, his severed head topped by a spiked helmet.

On a slope opposite the tower, a burnt-out tank lay in a ditch, its broken tracks trailing down the incline. Pierre used a post to lever back a hatch on the side. Inside its blackened hull, the charred remains of the driver were still hunched over the controls. Pierre, skirting around the gruesome remains, edged through to the engine bay. Over the greasy floor of the machine, remarkably unscathed by the fire that likely consumed its crew, lay postcards from home; a windswept beach on the Baltic coast, a chapel surrounded by snow-clad Bavarian mountains. Concealed in a sooty alcove, sandwiched between well-thumbed operator manuals and maps, sat a leather bound book, its author, "Schiller", still perceptible on its gilt spine. Pierre reached in and opened its cover, the frail pages sticky with damp. A message had been written on the marbled masthead; "Mein liebster, liebster Klaus", read the feminine script, "komme heim zu uns" (come home to us).

For a further hour they scrambled over this bleak landscape. A ridge appeared. As they climbed up its slope a cool breeze rose over its bank dispelling the lingering stench. Beyond its apex a verdant plain of open countryside unfolded; fields thick with rye grass, wild barley and honeysuckle. And as if this surreal boundary between life and death extended vertically upwards, the weather also cleared. Currents of warm air punched through the oppressive blanket of grey to reveal cobalt skies etched with crisp cirrus clouds. More elegant than the earlier planes, a skein of geese migrated south.

"Salvation, Chai," said Pierre wiping his brow, "For a time I thought we'd be stuck there forever..."

"If we'd trusted your compass we would have been."

Pierre reached to his pocket, found the defective instrument and hurled it viciously into a ditch.

At the end of a leafy track, a sign in French crowned with rich, orange lichen, pointed to the village of Chaumont bringing more hope. On the hillside approaching them, the spire of a church and the outline of farm buildings appeared in the trees, smoke rising from their chimneys. Climbing a gate they chanced on a stone drinking trough, the water fresh, cool and clear. They stopped, drank and washed. Another fire was started. Born brought out a small tea pot and filled it with water from the basin. He'd kept some tea leaves from the birthday set; black oolong from China, reputably Clemenceau's favourite.

In better spirits, they were preparing to move off when they heard the approach of hooves. Mounted soldiers appeared around the corner of the hedgerow and came to a stop at the crossroads. They were French cavalry, six disciplined ranks of Lancers on black mares, each with a sabre and lance at their side. Their commander, a towering, proud figure, with a curled, waxed moustache, medal of the Grand Croix over his shoulder, trotted close to the grubby and curious circle.

"Where are you headed?", he asked, taking in their tired and bedraggled state.

"We were on our way to Montfaucon," said Pierre.

"From where?"

"Rumont."

"You're a long way off track."

"I know," replied Pierre, "We got misdirected..."

"You've walked?"

"Unfortunately yes. The Americans stole our trucks."

"The American's steal everything… Wine, livestock and women."

He turned in his saddle, "There's a main road just further up. From there it's about ten kilometres to town. We'll be ahead of you. If we find transport we'll direct them back to you."

"Thank you Colonel," replied Pierre, saluting.

Turning sharply the detachment rode off, their hooves throwing up clods of dirt and turf.

The Siamese watched them go. After the horrors they had just experienced, the Lancers looked like something from another era; Napoleonic, elegant, dignified, banners catching the breeze, polished breastplates reflecting the sun. Even the previously sullen Sumet woke to their elegance and beauty: was this the fantasy of war he had aspired to, the allure of which had dragged him halfway across the world?

Eloquent as the moment was, its harmony was fleeting. Fifty yards from their parting there was a distant, dull explosion. The lead horses and riders were thrown sideways by the blast. Slithers of shrapnel flew out, the shards whistling by over their heads. There was a soft, unremarkable thud; 'phoof', like a stone dropping in mud, almost imperceptible.

The Captain, grinning weakly, crumpled to his knees.

Chapter 27

Pramot, starring into his dismal, sunless courtyard, counted the pigeons on the wet cobbles. His attention rested on the last, the eighteenth bird - a thin, bedraggled male at the edge of the group. Every time it tried to break into the centre of the circle, where a handful of stale, but tempting crumbs lay scattered over the flag stones, they closed ranks and forced it away. Pramot was intrigued by the contest – the raw animal aggression and cruel group mentality untainted by pity or compassion. For some reason he felt sympathy for the bird. It had asymmetrical eyes that looked at the world askew, making it look odd and an outsider.

Wrenching himself away from these gloomy descents, Pramot's attention returned to his desk, where once again the cause of his agonies had come with the post. And tiresomely and predictably from the same source; the Thai company at St Dizier.

Its first sentence had stunned, "Unable to complete mission to Montfaucon, STOP, Captain Sumet hospitalised, STOP." But the full horror had come with the day – "Nov 3". A date that made his skin crawl with anxiety – as if malefic worms slithered through his veins.

News of Clemenceau's birthday tea party had created a stir in Bangkok's highest social circles, the excitement of which had been hard to contain. Daily the Foreign Ministry staff had pestered the Legation in Paris for news of how it went and daily General Janriddhi's secretary had come down the stairs and poked his head round the door of Pramot's office.

"Still no news from Montfaucon? he enquired.

"No, still no news, I'm afraid… I suspect our dear Captain is too busy basking in all the glory to remember us," replied Pramot sarcastically.

"Still Bangkok is getting impatient. Something is better than nothing," added the secretary as he scuttled back up the stairs.

And bowing to pressure, that's what he'd done. Penned a telegram to the Minister's staff just to placate them: "Although they had yet to receive an official report from the south, he was sure the birthday event had passed off with great and wondrous success."

Two days later Pramot had been mortified to learn that not only had his innocent words been misconstrued, they had been used as a catalyst to kickstart an extraordinary celebration. To honour the success of the Montfaucon mission, Ministry officials had chosen to re-enact the entire tea party fiasco in the grounds of the palace. Invites had gone out to every foreign diplomat and high-ranking officer. The Royal household had even been able to dig out a similar Ming china tea set.

Now, the alarming knowledge exposed in a telegram on his baize table top, left him floored. Not only would he have to concoct some cock and bull story to recant the earlier message, he would have to explain that the historic tea party with France's glorious leader and the Americans generals had never even taken place.

Waking early that morning, feeling unusually refreshed and warmed by a rare autumn sun, Pramot had looked forward to the day. Newly-baked rolls and fresh coffee at Bellecour had enhanced that sense of well being. Even headlines from the front in the news kiosk opposite appeared more cheerful and confident.

That positivity had deserted him as soon as he'd stepped into his office. For the St Dizier letter hadn't been the only problem weighing on his mind. How transient is optimism, he sighed.

Two weeks before he had been sent a report from the Thai flyers at the Reconnaissance School in La Chapelle La Reine. Fed up with being sidelined by their French instructors, the pilots had lost patience and taken to the air in an old observation plane, a Dorand AR 1. After a perfect take off, the Siamese pilots had performed two low-level passes and a figure of eight, impressing a French ground crew working on a flight of Spad fighters below. Growing more confident behind the controls, the pilots had headed out across country. Crossing the Roubaix canal, they were midway across the Belleroche hills, when they first encountered problems with their engine. Losing power, they turned back and were less than a kilometre from the airfield when the exhaust spluttered and the cylinders seized. Gliding low over farm buildings at the far end of the runway, the undercarriage caught a mast on the observation tower, flipped upside down and burst into flames.

The two young Siamese aviators, Somsak and Winai were pulled from the burning wreckage and taken by truck to the military hospital in Fontainebleau. Both had broken bones and severe burns. Somsak's leg injuries were so serious, there was talk he might loose his limbs.

The French were quick to assign blame; the Siamese aviators had been too impetuous and were too inexperienced to fly without guidance. And the Thais themselves, knowing they had breached regulations, didn't attempt a defence. Expecting to be sent home, they began packing their bags.

Support came from an unlikely corner – the American pilots of the 94th squadron. Damning the Dorands as "antique rattletraps", in deplorable condition after three years on the front line, they put the blame wholly on the French maintenance teams. The same planes had been examined by their own engineers two months before. With loose struts, frayed cables and sheered bolts, they had been deemed totally un-airworthy. In one, a family of voles, nesting in the corner of a wicker seat, had gnawed through fuel lines. Condemned as "worse than junk", they wouldn't have subjected the Germans to them.

Stung by these accusations, the French military set in motion an enquiry. To provide evidence and to represent the Thai flyers, they'd requested an official from the Thai Legation to stand before a tribunal. Naturally, with everyone ducking responsibility, it had been Pramot forced to stand before the inquisition. That injustice alone had tested his heart rate. He knew nothing about law nor trial process. For the past week he'd been up late ploughing through French legal history, his only confidence being that he could rely on the support of the US air crews. And then, just two days before the inquest, he'd been told they wouldn't turn up – the men had been urgently transferred to a base near Ochey.

The French investigators, backed up by a full legal team, had run rings round him. Flummoxed by the terminology Pramot's defence had been useless. The verdict was swift. Yes, the Thai crew were guilty, yes, they were banned from flying; but on the question of costs (considerable), the judge showed last minute leniency; "Sacré bleu, ils sont nos camarades, pas notre ennemi!"

As expected, the fury from Bangkok was intense. Blame, as if it were a festering commodity that came in a bag, was dumped metaphorically at Pramot's back office door.

Hence his present dilemma. A second failing so close to the first would mean his dismissal. He'd be on the boat back to Siam. The thought of that disgrace – having to plead for forgiveness from his family – upset him the most. He would sooner be shot out of a cannon than face the wrath of his father.

Pramot walked back to the window and looked down into the courtyard. A neighbour had thrown a handful of fresh crumbs onto the cobbles, sending the flock of birds once again into a frenzy. The bedraggled pigeon he'd identified before, too weak to fight, had given up. Sitting away from the group it appeared so still Pramot thought it dead.

With a deep sigh Pramot turned to the door, clear in his mind as to what needed to be done. Confession. Honest and absolute. There was no other way. Head bowed, pale and contrite, he headed up the stairs, but on turning the corner onto the landing was taken aback to find the room full.

"What's going on?" asked Pramot, confused by the gathering.

"You haven't heard?" replied an associate.

The room quietened. A side door opened at the far end of the room. The legation chief came through accompanied by General Phya Bhijai Janriddhi and two adjutants.

"Gentlemen," he began, "I've an important announcement to make."

Pramot, slumping to a seat, breathed a huge sigh of relief.

Chapter 28

A lambent glow emerged from the shifting fog as the locomotive pulled into the Gard Du Nord at ten in the morning, front wheels scattering soot black pigeons and rats from the tracks. A whistle sounded as the brakes gripped, bringing the long train of carriages to a stop. As the first-class doors opened, Phraya Suthammaitri, Siam's Minister in London, and his retinue of twelve emerged from a cloud of steam and stepped down onto the platform. Prince Charoon, General Janriddhi, his adjutants and staff were there to receive them, bouquets of red roses clutched in their hands.

Shown to four Vauxhall staff cars, the delegation cruised sedately down the Rue Royale towards La Place de la Concorde, its Luxor obelisk rising above the thin mists. At that same moment Pramot and two assistants were racing from the back doors of the Galeries Lafayette, arms filled with boxes of crystal glasses and a Sèvres dinner service. In a back street behind the store, Pramot chanced on an Italian restaurant and hired its chef. A menu was organised: cold meats, cheeses, together with panettone and cannoli.

Pramot's biggest challenge had been sourcing a conference table grand enough for the many delegates. Their own humble dining table, unvarnished and rarely used, only seated six. A larger one, carved walnut and rosewood, borrowed from the Spanish Embassy two doors away, had needed the entire legation staff to lift it up the central stairs.

Stuck in the ballroom doorway on the top landing, it had had to be sawn in half to get through the opening – an act of vandalism for which Pramot, no doubt, would be the one offering the cringing apologies (and compensation) at some future date.

In the entrance foyer of the legation, the full staff had lined up on both sides of the staircase to greet the diplomats from London. Phraya Bibadh Kosha, Siam's Minister in Rome, a tall, bearded man in a thick fur-lined overcoat, accompanied by two Italian secretaries, had already arrived. They were warming themselves in front of the fire upstairs.

Before the formal introductions, Phraya Suthammaitri was shown to a small parlour to wash and refresh. Furnished with armchairs and a washstand, there was hot water in a jug, linen towels and eau de toilette.

At nine precisely the doors to the conference room opened and the delegates took their places at the table, now ruthlessly hammered back into shape by the resident handyman. With everyone comfortably seated, coffee and tea was served and papers handed out. The junior clerks and maids left the room and the double doors closed. Two of the general's staff were stationed on either side of the entrance to prevent eavesdroppers and unauthorised entries.

A midday bell announced the first break. The ballroom doors reopened and a thick pall of cigar smoke drifted out onto the landing and down the stairs. Pramot, waiting in the hallway below, was called upstairs to help clear the tables, empty the overflowing ash trays and prepare place settings for lunch. Desperate to pry, but careful not to linger, he laid out the cutlery with an obsequiousness that took far longer than necessary. Further tasks – for cold drinks, cigars, a cloth to wipe an ink spill – provided further opportunities to dally and eavesdrop. From such disparate snippets, the wily deputy was able to stitch together a credible whole. As always, the centre of discussions was the war; updates and reports from London and Paris – the latest advances and setbacks on the front. But what puzzled and intrigued Pramot most was the tone. Events were being discussed as if the fighting, if not actually ended, was close to an end.

It was Minister Kosha, still doggedly wrapped in his grand ermine-lined overcoat, who had come with the most startling revelations. A week before, Kosha had been invited to an opera at La Scala in Milan. A special performance of Rigoletto had been put on by the Italian High Command to which all the foreign diplomats had been asked and all had attended. Needing the washroom in the second interval (the Milanese, despite the deprivations of war, still generous with their Piedmont wines), Kosha was passing the royal box when he overheard a heated discussion from the occupants inside. Peering around the edge of the gilded doors, he was aghast to see Italy's Foreign Minister, Sidney Sonnino, there with the Austro-Hungarian Ambassador, Kajetan von Merey. Sonnino, looking belligerent and hissing with undisguised fury, was waving a document over the head of the Austrian. Being so distant it was obviously impossible to read the text with any certainty, but an accompanying map showing the dark mass of the Alps, was unmistakable. A crude red line, cutting across South Tyrol to Trieste, divided the territories.

The interval bell intervened, prompting Kosha to move on. Back in his box for the final act, Gilda, a tiresome soprano, gave him time to reflect. The sight of two high-powered dignitaries from opposite sides in a royal box in Milan was unusual enough, but the presence of official and perhaps sensitive military maps was yet more remarkable. More astonishing still was the stance of the two men. Kajetan von Merey, legendary for his scornful, haughty demeanour, had cowed under the threats from the shorter Italian. For Kosha the implications were clear. Von Merey, his pixie eyes creased up in panic, looked cornered. It led him to question – were the Italians, anticipating the end game, manoeuvring for a land-grab?

The report, extraordinary as it was, didn't surprise General Janriddhi. A month before he and his staff had been invited to Brest to witness the arrival and unloading of an American ship, the USS George Washington. Climbing onto the roof of the court house to get a better view, they'd been astonished by the scale of the enterprise. Supplies and equipment stretched from the estuary mouth to the distant hills. And then there were the men. From the harbour front gates, a constant flow of fresh recruits marched night and day to the station platforms and the trains that would carry them east. Faced with such overwhelming force, it was unlikely the Triple Alliance could survive.

Janriddhi's young adjutant, two years out of Oxford, provided more tangental evidence. Their driver that morning had let on, that himself and three other drivers, had been sent by the British High Command to acquire four hundred cases of champagne from Les Caves Auges in the Boulevard Haussmann. There wasn't enough; they'd had to send out a second raiding party to the Legrande Filles and Le Baron Rouge in Montmartre.

Prince Charoon endorsed the view that a mood of "celebration" was in the air. In London, from shops and inns, to clubs and ballrooms, all the talk was of victory.

"The Germans, outnumbered and outgunned by the Americans, were finished and desperate for surrender." When that capitulation came (weeks if not days away some had speculated), the conditions were likely to be harsh.

Phraya Suthammaitri, with sources close to diplomats in Washington, had heard rumours of an association of nations. Prince Charoon, also aware of such discussions, was suspicious. Although all the high-minded rhetoric was said to be the promotion of peace and equanimity across the world, in whose interests would that peace reign? "Wasn't such an alliance just old school imperialism in new guise, a ruse to maintain the established empires of old?"

There were graver concerns. If Siam were left out of this special 'trustees club', might France and Britain carve up the Asian sphere to their own advantage? The fact that no informal approaches been made either in London or Paris, worried them most, "Had that 'deal' already been done?"

Phraya Suthammaitri thought it unlikely. Knowing how Europeans liked a squabble, an alliance would take time to negotiate. Yes, the fighting was effectively over, that much was clear. But the real battle was yet to come. And in that conflict, fought over tables in conference halls and dining rooms by technocrats and politicians, a single word would mean more than a million lives lost on the battlefield. Siam needed different expertise – lawyers, friendly diplomats, people of influence, especially with prominent British and American politicians. Yes, their own part in the war had been minimal and they had arrived a bit late, but they had joined the right side and right now their flag flew proudly with the rest on masts in the Champs Elysees. Such loyalty alone must surely justify a voice at the table?

At ten a dinner was served. Pramot's Italian chef had prepared vitello tonnato and a choice of mountain cheeses from Savoie. Several bottles of Barolo were opened. A string quartet had been positioned on the landing outside to play Beethoven, but was difficult to appreciate over the loud and spirited conversations.

It was well past midnight when the meeting finally wound up. Phraya Suthammaitri, Minister Kosha, the colonel and the adjutants took their leave and left. Only Prince Charoon and General Janriddhi stayed on, retiring to an oak-panelled room at the back of the ballroom. Sitting close together in tall wing-backed armchairs, they drank brandy and smoked Cuban cigars. Buoyed up by the success of the day, General Janriddhi, joked with the legation staff and complimented the French maids on their elegant uniforms. It was admirable he mused, that ordinary Parisian's despite the deprivations of war, still had time for appearances and fashion. A subject which turned him to more serious concerns – shopping. After the conflict there was likely to be a lot of surplus kit and equipment lying around and going cheap. If they moved quickly they could possibly get their hands on some of the latest military technology; tanks, artillery guns, aircraft and bombs. Adopted by their own forces, such a superiority would certainly overshadow and intimidate their immediate neighbours – the ever meddlesome Vietnamese, Cambodians and Burmese.

"The presence of a single tank at a border, armed with nothing more offensive than jackfruit, would likely send the enemy scurrying back to their buffalos and paddies," scoffed the General.

Prince Charoon, puffing contentedly on his cheroot, agreed, "Put together a shopping list. I will make sure it reaches the eyes of the Minister. They can arrange the necessary funds." Personally he had his eye on a car, a British-built Rolls-Royce Silver Ghost – its chassis high and robust enough to deal with rotten roads in the south.

Chapter 29
December 1918

A weather worn banner, "Gloire aux Vainqueurs", framed by an array of listless French and British flags and shredded coloured bunting, covered the crumbling facade of the Gare Saint Roch in Amiens. The main entrance to the station was still boarded up with planks and scorched timbers after the city had been shelled in the last year of the war. With the ticket hall closed, passengers, anxious for trains, queued at makeshift kiosks to the side of the post depot.

Winding through the piles of sand, cement and stacked bricks, Chai crossed the tracks to the South platform and was directed to a siding at the end of the goods yard. A chalked board propped up against a water pump announced the next departure for Paris. He found the train in the shadow of a warehouse; a tired green locomotive with six battered carriages, a guard's van and a freight wagon. Mounting wooden steps by the track, Chai climbed inside. It wasn't crowded and he was able to find a clean seat by a window. The interior was muggy and damp, its floor scattered with sawdust, the smell of disinfectant harsh enough to make his nose itch. Several windows were cracked and pasted over with paper. Where rain had seeped in (there'd been a heavy downpour during the night), dark pools marred the boards. Higher up on the sides, holes in the pine panels showed where beds and racks had been screwed to the wall, when the carriage had last been used as a hospital train. Patients had scratched names and etched crude cartoons into the woodwork.

The station master's whistle sounded. Steam poured from the funnel as the pistons pumped, making the carriages judder. They'd barely moved more than five metres when somewhere out on the platform a woman screamed, "Non, arrêtez! Arrêtez le train!"

The brakes squealed as the train jolted to a halt. Seconds later footsteps were heard on the gravel track outside. A door opened and a family laden with bags and trunks scrambled on board. Lifting their cases to the luggage rack, they collapsed on the bench. The reason for their delay was a small boy. He'd insisted on going to the bathroom at the last-minute. There was no bathroom. Much to his mother's anguish and shame he'd had to go behind a tram shed in full view of the street, where truculent labourers had taken a break from their digging. Despite their cruel jibes the boy had taken his time and his mother had scolded him. Even now tears rolled down his cheeks. His younger brother, just as agitated, had a more urgent plight. The wreck of a German zeppelin had fallen near Breteuil. It was visible from the track and he was desperate for a window seat on the right side of the carriage. Chai volunteered to swop places. The woman, embarrassed by the offer, shook her head 'no', eliciting further shrieks of protest from her sons.

"But maman, ce monsieur avait proposé!"

"Ce monsieur a seulement proposé pour être poli. Reste-là!"

"Mais…"

"Tais toi!", she slapped him,"Sois sage!"

The train crawled out of the station. Chai watched as the edge of the town rolled by, the rows of tightly clustered houses, their yards hung with washing lines, an indistinct blur through the tarnished, yellowed glass. On the outskirts they passed by the ruins of a pottery factory, a single brick chimney still defiant and unscathed, thick black smoke swirling from a fire that smouldered inside.

The first stop was Beauvais, a town on a river some twenty kilometres south. More passengers came on board; a middle-aged widow, pale and severe, tugging two plump girls in tight navy suits; a party of nurses and a construction crew with four scraggly chickens pressed tight in a sack. A tall, thin man, with a turbulent beard, took the bench opposite Chai. He wore a military coat, with boots high at the ankle, that looked almost new. As the train picked up speed again, he opened a newspaper, its headline, "L'Alsace revient à France," in a hard bellicose font despite the armistice being signed more than a month ago.

The train struggled uphill through a cutting in an escarpment, then relaxed as they started down to the plains. The famed zeppelin came into view, its skeletal nose cone towering over the trees like a giant bird cage, engines and twisted steel lattice strewn over the fields. Eager to see it, the passengers on the far half of the carriage, rushed to Chai's side, the two boys at the front. Chai lifted the youngest to his seat so that he might see better out of the dirty window. Rubbing the glass he cried out excitedly, "Regardez là, là, un mort!"

It got everyone's attention. He was right. There was a body lying upside down in a ditch. Not an aviator as he'd wanted, but a dead cow, its four skeletal legs pointed accusingly to the sky from whence its assailant (airship Z 27) had fallen and crushed him on an otherwise placid night in the last months of the war.

The crash site passed. The onlookers drifted back to their seats and the boys to their mother. The man opposite Chai, tiring of his newspaper, turned to his bag. Finding a box of biscuits, he munched them in silence, hoping his cupped hand might muffle his chewing. He failed. The youngest boy caught his eye first. And once he had made him an offer (greedily accepted), it was impossible to ignore his more petulant brother. Even his mother overcame her dislike of strangers and snatched two. Resigned now to feeding the whole carriage if necessary, he held out a piece to Chai. Not expecting the offer, he hesitantly took one.

"Thank you. It's very kind of you."

"A second? I assure you I've plenty. Another box in my bag in fact."

An overture that didn't escape the ears of the two boys, who soon crossed the divide to take more, stuffing them into their mouths before returning to their places.

"You're heading home?" asked Chai.

"I wish I was. Unfortunately for me, my work has just started."

Girard had had a quiet war. Safely ensconced in an office in the 10th arrondissement, he'd been miles from any front or danger. For his was a desk job. As chief statistician at the Ministry of Information, his trade was numbers – numbers of recruits, combatants, hospitalised and deceased. With the signing of the armistice and the end of the war, his cosseted comforts, and those of his fellow mathematicians, had ended. Issued with slide rules and notepads, it was their time to the trenches. Sent south they toured the battlefields, cemeteries and graves, listing the dead and counting the lost and unidentified.

"We've just had six days in the Bois Faisan near Fromelles. Now we're being transferred to Verdun. I must say I'm not looking forward to it."

Chai glanced at his feet; his boots were unlikely to stay clean.

"And yourself?" he asked Chai, "I expect you'll be travelling back now it's all over?"

Chapter 30

No one thought it was serious – there was no blood, no signs of a wound, even a graze.

Chai and Mai helped prop the Captain up against a wall and loosened his clothing. Although he joked and made light of falling, it was clear he was having trouble recognising who was caring for him or where he was. His breathing, laboured and uneven, came in fits and starts. Mai passed him some water and he drank slowly, thankful for the refreshment.

"Look I'm fine, leave me", he assured them, "Over there…" he waved up the hill where black smoke still lingered over the track, "There are others who are seriously hurt. Go! Get out of here!"

Chai undid Sumet's shirt and noticed a red bruise across his chest.

"Oh come on, that's just an ant bite!," he snapped dismissively, brushing Chai's hand away, "my, my, you're all acting like a bunch of fussy nannies!"

Uncertain, they lingered, which only made him more irritable. Wrongly they interpreted this as a good sign.

"How many times do I have to say this! For the last time, Go!"

"Wrun, stay with him. I'll be back soon," said Chai standing.

"Please... Is that really necessary..." sighed the Captain.

Chai, ignoring him, signalled for Wrun not to move, picked up his pack and ran down the track. Midway along three riderless horses sprinted by, their flanks slashed and streaked with blood. Over the rise two other mounts lay on their sides, struggling to stand and writhing in agony. Within the injured, Chai recognised the commander on his back in the dirt, head thrown back against rocks in a ditch. Stepping over his dead horse, Chai knelt at the lieutenant's side. Shrapnel had severed an artery in his neck, the blood spurting out in a wide arc across the man's face and front. Chai pressed his hand to the wound to staunch the flow, but the pressure was so great it just pulsed through his hands. He screamed for Wrun, "Bandages quick!"

"Where?"

"In my backpack. The side pocket."

It was only a short roll and once wrapped around the wound wasn't enough. Chai removed his jacket, tore a sleeve from his shirt and wrapping the material tightly around the bandages, eventually managed to stem the bleeding.

"We need to get him up onto the path," said Chai.

It was a struggle. The Frenchman was incredibly heavy, there were only two of them and there was so much blood on the bank they kept slipping.

The Lancers at the head of the column had taken the brunt of the blast. Thrown several yards from their mounts they lay unconscious in the long grass, their uniforms shredded, flesh torn and blackened by the explosion. Pierre was there with the two twins and Darn, the strong man able to free those who had been buried beneath their dying horses. Clear of the animals, they laid the casualties out along the side of the path, but their limb injuries and burns were so horrific that without the right training or equipment they felt there was little else they could do. One, with both his legs severed above the knee, called out for water. Pierre lifted his canteen bottle up to the lancer's mouth. The man sipped slowly, his swollen lips trembling so badly most of the liquid poured away down his chest.

A young cadet, fortunately unscathed because he had trailed at the back, was dispatched by those Lancers still conscious to the farm buildings on the hillside to find help.

Leaving Pierre in charge of the team, Chai, ran back down the lane to check on the Captain. At first he thought he must have gone the wrong way for he couldn't find him. It was only after retracing his steps that he noticed a spike of hair sticking out from the crushed grass. Left unattended, Sumet had slumped down the verge into a hollow.

Chai, lifting Sumet back onto the path and wiping dust and mud from his face, was shocked by his frail appearance, "Captain, can you hear me, Captain!"

"His eyes opened weakly, "Yes... I can... Of course I can..."

"I need to get you to a Doctor."

"No," he gripped Chai's arm tightly, "Stupid... No need, really no need."

Chai turned and looked for Wrun. A little guiltily the driver had followed Chai back down the track.

"I thought I told you to stay with him!"

"I did..."

"And?"

"He told me... ordered me, no, yelled at me to go. What could I do?"

The young French cadet returned half an hour later with two horse-drawn wagons driven by villagers. They loaded the unconscious Lancers into the larger covered cart. Into the lighter buggy, they helped the wounded who could still stand.

Chai and Pierre, on either side of the Captain, approached the cart, but hesitated when they saw it was full. The cadet on the back, making no attempt to create space for them, pretended to look aggrieved.

"What's all this nonsense?" interrupted a Chasseur, organising the loading of his men despite blood seeping down his forehead.

"Our Captain's been injured. I was hoping to get him on board, said Chai, already guiding Sumet away.

"This is intolerable behaviour. Can't you see there's a crisis?" he barked out.

Chai flushed, "I'm sorry colonel. I apologise..."

"No, not you, YOU!", his words aimed at the cadet who had turned them away, "Make sure to find them a space."

"There's no room" he complained.

"Then give up your own place, fool!"

"Thank you Colonel," replied Chai, helping Sumet to the back of the cart.

"Enough. I should be thanking you. You and your men have done more than enough." The Lancer hit the side of the wagon with the hilt of his sabre, "Now get that cart going," he shouted up to the driver.

The first half of the journey was swift, along smooth well-worn tracks, before dropping into dense woodland where the camber of the path was steep and uneven. Chai had to reach out along the flank of the cart to keep both the Captain and a Lancer from sliding out.

It took a further uncomfortable hour along narrow village lanes to reach the field station, half a dozen weather-worn tents at the centre of a stone compound. The leading wagon with the dead was led away to a wooden building at the back of the enclosure. Medics came forward to the smaller cart and made a cursory examination of the four wounded Lancers. Stretcher bearers were called. Lifted from the cart they were swiftly moved to tables in an operating tent. Inside, nurses cut away their blood-soaked clothes and began cleaning their wounds with cotton wool and iodine.

Chai helped Sumet down from the cart. They were directed to benches where the less serious injuries waited. A doctor approached with a clipboard.

"Where did it happen?"

"About ten kilometres south of Rumont... I think"

"How was he hit?"

"There was an explosion. A mine."

"Where's he been injured?"

"We think in his side. It's hard to tell. There are cuts. We don't know how deep."

The doctor looked sceptical.

"Do you feel any pain?," he asked Sumet.

"Only when I move," he groaned.

"On your ribs or inside?"

"I can't say for sure."

The doctor didn't like his indecision.

Sumet's jacket and shirt were undone and pulled away. The doctor bent to examine his chest and back. Apart from a handful of faint cuts across his left breast, his skin looked so smooth and unblemished it was impossible to determine an entry point (if indeed he had been pierced by shrapnel), or discern any serious internal bleeding.

The doctor came away frowning. Chai wasn't sure by his manner if the man was concerned or irritated they were wasting his time. He feared the latter.

"It doesn't look serious."

"That's good," nodded Chai, "then we can go?"

"No," said the physician shaking his head and glancing again at Sumet, "Not until he's been properly checked out."

Chai and the Captain were shown outside where other patients waited on a circle of hay bales. An ambulance arrived and they were driven to a hospital in Souilly – the St Vincent. Orderlies helped the men into an annex building adjacent to the main complex. A sanatorium and bathhouse before the war, its walls were tiled with vivid squares of turquoise and cream, the barrel ceiling painted with an imposing art deco mural of statuesque swimmers and bathers. Where the pool had been was been boarded over, the wooden changing cubicles removed. Rows of benches, laid with thin mattresses now filled this space, the seats packed with lines of sick and wounded.

Chai found a position at the back of the hall. Next to the seat was a warm pipe up against which the Captain could lean and rest his head. Chai found a wool blanket and wrapped it around his shoulders.

An hour later a doctor and a nurse came down the line. The Captain's jacket and shirt were again removed. The doctor asked about his diet and using a stethoscope listened to his breathing. The nurse took his temperature and checked his pulse. Notes were made. The doctor came away cheerful.

"Well, there doesn't seem to be anything too serious. You should be back in the field soon."

Sumet complained of a headache. The nurse spooned out a syrup. The liquid proved so sticky and repellant it lodged in his throat causing a violent coughing fit. Undeterred she tried a second time. This time the Captain managed to swallow and keep the concoction down.

It was late at night when Chai woke. In the low light from the overhead gas lights it took him time to orientate himself in the dark unfamiliar surroundings. Coughing, distant sobbing and the ceaseless creaking of benches and seats, reminded Chai of the presence of others; tens, if not hundreds of others beyond the gauze screens. Lifting himself from the cold flagstones he searched for Sumet. He lay bunched up at the head of the bench, shivering in pain, arms wrapped tightly over his chest.

Chai, taking his shoulder, shook him lightly, "Captain, Captain…"

Sumet mumbled, the words so incoherent, so faint, Chai couldn't gauge whether he was speaking Thai, French or something nonsensical. Chai folded his jacket under Sumet's head and pulled the blanket tighter around his shoulders. His trembling calmed, but Chai remained concerned. Standing, he scanned the hall. In a distant corner of the room, he caught sight of a lantern above a desk.

Chai found a nurse. She was a woman in her sixties, tall, saintly in appearance, her silver plated hair tied up neatly under her cap. She gave an injection. The pain receded. Sumet, recovered enough to sit up, feeling both grateful and guilty that he'd dragged the over-worked nurse from her station; he'd already fallen under her spell.

"I apologise. My deputy must have got over excited… He's like that. Overreacts I'm afraid… I'm sure you've more important things to do…"

At first light the shutters were opened and a trolley of hot cocoa was brought round. There was also sugar; a big tin of it. Sumet piled it high in his cup. Still under the soothing effects of his late night injection and revived by the drink he joked about how he'd inherited his mother's sweet tooth. At home they liked sugar with everything – curries, soups even rice whisky. His wife disapproved. She said too much sweetness made him slothful and fat. She didn't want him being a bad example to their child. He was already too chubby.

At midday, a doctor re-examined the Captain. His temperature remained high, but the physician didn't appear unduly concerned. The pain in Sumet's side had also subsided and his breathing soothed.

"I think we should move you upstairs. It's nicer upstairs," said the doctor.

The recuperation ward was a brighter room with windows tall enough to bring in a breeze to dispel the lingering scent of cleaning salts and soap. Chai had arranged for Born to bring some books and newspapers. Propped on his pillows, Sumet was happy to sit up and catch up with events. Pierre also came by. Using his usual cunning he'd arranged a delivery of fresh pears and the Captain's favourite grapes.

"From the Forey estate," he announced, unwrapping the fruit, "Ferraux picked them himself. He sends his compliments and wishes you a speedy recovery."

Initially the Captain was pleased with the stream of visitors and their gifts, especially his books. But as the days wore on and conversation grew thin, his restlessness and agitation returned.

"Shouldn't you get back to work?" he asked Chai.

"I promised the men I'd stay."

"Why?"

"To check you've completely recovered."

"Look, I'm fine. So fine I'll probably be thrown out tomorrow for taking up beds. So, formally Chai, because I can see you're finding this difficult, I absolve you of your promise to stay."

"The doctors are still concerned."

"The doctors are concerned if one sneezes."

"You are sneezing…"

"From a cold. Nothing more. A stupid cold."

"I'll stay one more night."

"Another night? Why? Why waste anymore time. We've jobs to do. That's why we're here. To fight a war, not sit around eating grapes. I want you back at work. I want you back in your truck."

"But…"

"No, Chai. Go. I command you. Do you need me to write out an order?"

Chai tried to remonstrate, but the Captain's words were so explicit, his tone so devoid of sentiment, that to stay seemed more like insubordination than solicitude. Reaching for his bag and coat, Chai said he would return in two days and left the hospital. Pierre and Born were waiting for him outside.

The Thai convoy returned to the rail yard at St Dizier. With rumours of yet another "final, last, decisive" push (une dernière poussée victorieuse), their work took them back to the forests of the Argonne. They were coming back through woods west of Chalons when, predictably, yet another truck failed. It wasn't a simple repair; its drive shaft had grounded on a rut in the road and snapped. Late, in the middle of nowhere and unable to find a farm, let alone a blacksmith, they camped out. A fire was started and they boiled soup. Manit and Mai stretched a canvas between trees, under which they could shelter.

A passing woodcutter woke them, "Fini, fini, la guerre est finie," he grumbled as if announcing the end of a troublesome liver complaint.

Pierre, unsure what the old man had said and thinking him unhinged, ran after him.

"La grande guerre est finie!", he repeated, irritated that Pierre had had the temerity to ask him to say it again.

Pierre rushed back to Chai with the news. Initially excited – punching the air and embracing – they became doubtful; the man's wild-eyed looks and crazed nonchalance hadn't inspired them with the greatest of confidence. Containing their joy and deciding to keep the news to themselves, they waited until they could find someone more reliable to conform it.

Later some hunters appeared in the woods.

Pierre rushed up to them, "Est-que c'est vrai?" he asked, "La guerre est vraiment finie?"

"Oui, c'est fini. C'est la victoire, la victoire totale. Les Allemands se sont rendus!"

The hunters had found a stag snared in a thicket. Although aware they were poaching, they'd killed it; the landowner, considering the circumstances, would surely forgive them.

Pierre produced some bottles – Chai was never quite sure where he stashed them. Approaching the hunters he bartered a deal – wine and a place by the fire for a share of the venison. The hunters readily accepted, shook hands and started to prepare the carcass. They also had a wild boar and six hares. Pierre, forced to up the stakes, returned from the truck with a sly bottle of gin.

After a long morning of eating and drinking they danced in the forest clearing. In the distance they heard church bells echoing across the countryside and the sound of shots in the sky. The hunters answered by firing a fusillade from their own crude Chassepot rifles, making a lot of sparks and smoke.

Sitting with the villagers around the fire, Pierre and Chai fantasised about life after the war. Pierre had his life all mapped out; he would win over the heart of his Breton girl, return to university, then take over his father's tailoring business. A young, handsome hunter had his eye on the landowner's daughter. Once he'd made his fortune – he was banking on an uncle's inheritance – he'd ask for her hand in marriage, even repay the man for his stag and his rabbit.

Pierre asked Chai about his own hopes, knowing full well he harboured secret yearnings for the school mistress in Castlenau; he'd even caught Chai writing letters by candlelight.

"And you really think I didn't notice you spying?" said Chai.

"Well, it was more than once…"

"Unfortunately, being the hopeless romantic that you are, Pierre, you're completely mistaken. They were for a great aunt in Bangkok."

"There's no sin in dreaming Chai," replied Pierre, reaching out for a skewer and the last chunk of boar.

With victory celebrations taking over the towns and villages, it wasn't until the weekend that Chai, Born and Pierre managed to break from their beer and wine deliveries and return to the hospital. Bounding up the main stairway to the first floor, they were startled to find the ward empty. The beds were still in place, but the blankets and sheets had been pulled from their mattresses and thrown into a pile on the floor. Wash stands, cleared of towels and flannels, were stacked up at the end of the room. By the doors, a cleaner was scrubbing the wood boards with a wire brush.

Chai and Pierre went back out onto the landing and made enquiries at a workstation.

"The patients were moved," one said.

"Where to?", asked Pierre.

"We don't know. You should ask in the clerk's office."

Chai and Pierre walked back downstairs to the main hall. A doorman led them to the administrator's wing, where they chanced on a clerk on his way out to a meeting, arms filled with ledgers and paperwork. He led them to his office and reached for a file.

"His name?"

"Chantrawong. Captain Sumet Chantrawong", Chai spelled it out.

"Ahh, long name, difficult name… One moment… I'll have to check that out…"

The man reached for a folder and ran his finger down the list. Eventually he found it. Writing a note on a chit, he passed it to Chai.

"Room 149, at the end of the corridor."

Chai, knowing he was late - a day late - and likely to face an irate boss, ran down the corridor. But room 149 was a small space, without chairs or benches and empty of patients. Instead, a single hatchway filled the far wall, the opening covered by a mesh grill. Chai walked up to the window and peered through the wire partition. Shelves lined the walls of the interior, the racks filled with boxes and files. At the far end of the room he could see a desk. On its table surface lay a grubby coffee cup, a half eaten apple and the remains of a cheese roll.

"Hello, hello," he called through. There was a small ring bell on a ledge near the opening. He shook it. Eventually a grey haired man appeared around the corner of the door, took a passing bite from the apple and shuffled towards the screen.

"Can I help you?"

Chai handed over the slip of paper. The store-man behind the bars took it, went away and minutes later reappeared. Hinging back the mesh grill he passed through a bundle of clothes tied with a cord.

"There's some mistake," muttered Chai.

The man stalled and rechecked the chit, "No, I don't think so. You gave me ticket RL49 and I gave you item RL49".

"He… he won't need it?"

"Who won't need it?"

Pierre, now in the room with him, took Chai aside. Tears streamed down his cheeks.

Chapter 31

St Vincent Hospital
Souilly
Dieue-sur-Meuse
Grand Est, France

My Dearest Mee Grorp and Look Bla,

First some apologies. I haven't been able to write to you for a week, because no one could fine any paper or pens. So I am sorry for the long delay.

The last few days have been quite miserable. Mostly I am alone getting bored. The men haven't visited. I slept very badly. The pain in my side had got worse. It felt as if someone was bouncing up and down on my stomach making me sick. This combination of feeling horrible and unhappy weighed on me. I felt unable to sit up, let alone write.

Luckily this morning I feel much better. I am well enough to lift myself from the bed and sit by the window. The view is very beautiful. I can see gardens at the back of the hospital. A path leads to a gate. I'm sure this track goes all the way up the hillside. There are sheep in the fields. Ten black, five white and some smaller grey ones that are all playful and fluffy. Look Bla would love them. I have drawn him a picture (on the back). When I am fully well it is the first place I will go to. I want to see the river from the top of the hill. It's called the Petit Moron and they tell me joins the Seine, so one can take a barge all the way to Paris.

Yesterday we saw the first signs of snow. Several flakes fell on the window sill. I was able to catch them in the palm of my hand, though they quickly melted. Larger pieces came around lunch time. They say the lake will freeze over. I'm not sure the ducks will be pleased.

They most annoying thing about this hospital is that they keep moving us. Over the past two days, three times already. And its mostly at night. Why do they have to do it in the dark? It's not as if we are anywhere close to the front. Others were also confused. Last night I awoke to find a man going through my locker. He said he was looking for his hairbrush, even though it was obvious that he had no hair – not even a whisker. When I told the matron about it, she said I shouldn't interfere. I know she dislikes me.

The doctor visits most mornings. He is a short man with a huge stomach, with terrible hygiene and breath (would it offend him if I offered him soap). Nevertheless, he is quite jolly and I look forward to his visits. I like him because he treats the foreigners, me included, as well as his fellow countrymen – unlike that battle-axe of a matron. Sometimes he appears a bit foolish, like when he gets his long moustache wound round his stethoscope. He keeps telling us "eat, eat, eat", even though we all find the hospital food stodgy and tasteless like sawdust. The bread is exceptional in that it is almost like rock. I'm sure it will shatter my teeth if I try it. Only the jam – real berries, blackberries (they must be from the hedges at the back of the garden), is delicious.

Of course, the really big news is that the war has ended. It's been almost two days now. In fact it's been such big news, that I almost forgot to mention it. A great fuss was made in the kitchens. A procession of chefs came up into the wards beating pots and pans. Everyone sang songs and danced – at least those well enough to get out of bed and stand. Some doctors dressed up as nurses and made everyone laugh. A special meal of goose and turkey was served. There was also a little beer and wine. I even drank a cup. Of course, everyone is really happy.

Maybe less by the fact that they have won, but the thought that they can soon pack their bags and be gone. Not many had any great feelings for the war anyway. I think I was probably one of the only ones who did. Partly because I think I was so over-impressed by the country in the first place. At least when I arrived. Thinking it was all better because they had telephones everywhere and could make trains run on time.

As for the people – French, British, American or German – some are a bit smaller, some a bit fatter, some redder, but mostly the same. They neither engender great love, or hatred (accept for our dear Pierre, of course), and are all just as bossy, pushy and greedy as each other.

Their "La Grande Cause", the war, has been nothing but folly. Millions have died, villages, towns and cities destroyed and for what? The loss is indescribable. What on earth are they going to tell their children and grand-children? How can they possibly explain the horror and suffering they have caused? It won't be the end of it.

I apologise. I am boring you both. Talking about things I know nothing about, I hear you telling me off.

Now it's all over, I will end on a more personal note. I have seen great things. Great cities, cathedrals and palaces. But I am tired with it all now. I, like the other patients, have only one desire. To be away from this place and be home.

We have been told that we have done great things for our country. Personally I'm not sure that we have made any difference. The only difference I know is that I love you and my boy, with a completeness that wasn't possible before. You two are all I hold precious in this world. I long to see you and hold you,

With all my Love, Sumet

Part 3

Chapter 32

Flecks of snow fell like silver dust over the heights, covering the huts and shelters in a light veil of grey. Bunched around open braziers, soldiers, guards and drivers stood warming their hands and stamping their boots, hoping to return some sensation to numbed legs and feet. At the edge of a parade ground, a field kitchen had been set up, a cloud of steam rising from its vats. A bell rang and the men shuffled towards its serving hatch, mugs held out for a helping of pork and bean stew.

Sixty-five Dodge and Renault trucks had backed up against a low stone wall that faced the border between France and Germany. Loaded with tents, food and water, the convoy was part of a mission to resupply the French 8th Army that had moved into the Rhineland two weeks before.

The people of the Palatinate, worn down by years of rationing and deprivation, looked on the arrival of these self-styled 'liberators', with wearied resignation. Defeated and powerless amongst the ruins of their once proud homeland, occupation was now the latest humiliation they would have to learn to endure. And with winter fast approaching, it was unlikely to be their last.

Aware of the tension and unease between the two former adversaries, a team of liaison officers from the War Ministry had driven out from Sens to join the operation. Heading the relief column in two Delage staff cars, they were there to monitor the behaviour of their men and tame any excessive displays of triumphalism. "Peace keeping" was their role, not invasion; the men were instructed. They were to treat the vanquished peoples with fairness and respect.

Four North African companies of Algerians and Senegalese, made up the bulk of the drivers. The Thai contingent, of thirty-eight trucks, had joined them the night before, Chai, now promoted as their new, but reluctant commander.

The Captain's death had shaken them all. Chai, ever since those last traumatic days in the hospital, had felt especially responsible. Sumet had died alone in a foreign place with people who didn't know or care for him. If he, Chai, had stayed by his side would it have been any different? But could he have stayed? Hadn't Sumet been the one who'd insisted he go. Ordered even – lecturing him about duty, hectoring him to get back on the road, almost as if he hadn't wanted him around.

That, maybe, had been the truth of it – their relationship had always been strained. Other than professional duties, they never spent time together, discussed family, or shared anything personal. With so little affection between them, Chai was confused by his feelings. Regret and remorse crept up on him uninvited. Once, watching something as mundane as puddles calming after a storm, he felt sudden, inexplicable grief.

"Get over it, Chai," Born kept repeating, "We all knew he never liked you. So don't waste time being sad."

But Born was like that; blunt and thick-skinned, never one for the complexities of the soul.

Ground down by this dissonance, the weather and food, Chai had elected to go home now the fighting was over. Having packed his bags, said his goodbyes and organised the transport to the station, only a last minute message from the legation had persuaded him to reconsider.

General Janriddhi himself had penned the letter. No meek plea, it had opened with a full broadside: Patriotism – "Don't desert your nation before the job has been done. Sacrifice – "An honourable man should stay loyal to his men and the army." Concluding with loss – "Myself and all the staff mourn your Captain's parting. May his soul rest in peace." But if he, Chai, "wanted to ensure that Sumet's work and that of his men hadn't been wasted, now wasn't the time to throw in the towel."

As the meeting with Prince Charoon and Minister Phraya Suthammaitri in Paris had so rightly predicted, their nation's struggles were entering a second, more decisive phase. The carpeted corridors and halls of the Foreign Ministry at the Quai d'Orsay were now the conflict zone, pencils and pens their weapons of choice. Until the ink was dry on those agreements and documents, Siam needed to continue to make its presence felt. And for dramatic effect, no better opportunity presented itself than an advance into the enemy heartland itself. Political capital they'd called it. To strike home that message and to highlight their efforts, the general had wanted it recorded and publicised.

The photographer, Jean Jacques Mourier, whose only previous 'al fresco' experience had been photographing couturier collections on the Bois de Boulogne, was horrified by the wintry conditions on the heights. Clothed only in an embroidered velour jacket and waistcoat he felt chilled to the bone as soon as he stepped out of his van. Gathering his equipment from the back, he tried setting up his tripod at the crossing point, but the delicate legs kept slipping on the highly glazed ice. Adding to his frustrations, beads of frost kept clouding his lens. He was a short man and the top half of the glass was just out of reach. Feeling pity for the Parisian, Chai and Born lent him one of their tool boxes to use as a step.

Inspired by a rare Turneresque light piercing the grim clouds, Mourier raced to position his subjects. He'd planned a dramatic composition, the Thai trucks poised on the border line with French and German flags on either side, but the ensigns were too far apart. Aiming to reposition the two poles he sent some men in search of spades. It was slow work, the frozen ground as hard as concrete. Chai, worried it was taking too long, got his team to drag a German sentry box into the frame. The roof ringed with barbed wire, was painted with the Kaiser's black and white cross.

"Surely that will suffice?", suggested Chai. Mourier reluctantly acquiesced.

A second picture was no less ambitious. Mourier wanted to display the Thai convoy driving down a winding track into the mists of the

Saarland valley, trenches and bunkers scarring the hillside behind, but it took more than an hour to ensure the road was free of local wagons and carts. It left little time for the final frame; a shot of the sixty-five drivers and crew in a semicircle around the twisted remains of a burnt out Fokker Triplane. Stoking up a fire within the three-year-old wreck, gave the impression that the crash was recent and still smouldering.

With Mourier satisfied and rushing back to the warmth of his van, Chai ordered a return to the trucks and the convoy moved out. Born, filled with patriotism, had attached a Siamese flag to the roof ties and the pendant fluttered proudly and noisily as they advanced down the Saar valley. Looking out across the landscape, they'd hoped to see chocolate-box villages and Teutonic towers, but were soon disappointed to find the terrain as flat and featureless as the land they'd just left behind.

Appearing in the distance a curl of smoke rose from a fire. At the edge of a field, a circle of men stood in the shadow of trees digging for acorns. Their dog, an Alsatian almost as big as a mule, barked and raced in their direction, despite an uncrossable chasm running between them.

Pierre pointed beyond the huddled group, "See that pit-head beyond the circle of pines. Landen. My uncle had a small farm near the village. We spent a lot of summers there when we were young."

Chai craned his neck to look where Pierre was pointing. He could only vaguely discern the dark lattice of the mining tower flickering between the skeletal trees. The wind, racing across the barren flatlands, was from the same direction and bitterly cold. And when it stopped, the acrid scent of lignite and coal lifted from the dismal terrain.

"Yes," he lied.

Turning from the spits of sleet stinging his face, Chai closed his eyes. A dreamy image of a ship, bright skies and languid seas drifting by, momentarily taunted. By now he could have been sunning himself on the deck.

Before receiving the general's last minute plea (he was seconds from boarding the train), Chai, confident he was finally leaving, had shared out some of his most prized and useful possessions with those left behind. Foolishly that had included spare winter socks and a thick wool scarf. In time he would live to regret the socks, but now, with the chill cutting through every opening, cuff or collar, his scarf was the single item he rued most. Already, only five kilometres into their journey, he was already shivering.

"A stream ran through the bottom of the garden. We made a raft from beer kegs, doors and planks, then fished for frogs and newts," Pierre continued, oblivious to the fierce temperature and Chai's silent despondency, "My aunt's niece was staying with us. Pretty in a virgin white pinafore, my brother and I splashed her with mud bombs. Of course later we were found out and beaten with birch sticks. But knowing my uncle's poor eyesight, we stuffed pillows down our breeches. The canning kicked up the feathers in the goose down, bringing on the old man's asthma. I thought that would be the end of him, but perversely he hit us harder. I still have the scars"

They entered their first German town, Bornheim, late in the afternoon, curious to see its inhabitants. They were hard to find. Most of the houses looked empty, or shuttered. Occasionally a timid shadow appeared through a gap in thick drapes, then disappeared. In one side alley a child waved. Chai was about to return the gesture when an anxious arm reached out and hauled the boy inside.

It wasn't until the convoy had reached the main rail junction that they encountered their first crowds. A mass of men had crushed up against the walls and gates of the station. Wrapped in muddied grey coats, they balanced bags and packs on their shoulders as they pushed against the thin barriers. The uniformed officials, intimidated by the surge of men, chained the gates as a train pulled into the station. More people rammed the entrance. The barrier collapsed. A shot was fired.

"Verräter!" yelled an angry face in the crowd, "Schweine Abschaum!"

A rock hit the slatted sides of Born's truck making them all start. But it hadn't been directed at them, but at a line of red-faced police sergeants running down from their station.

It was after dark when they reached Neustadt. The Algerian company, having left ahead of them, were only now parking up. Chai felt relieved that despite their many delays, they'd caught up with the main convoy.

At the far end of the quadrangle, the French officers got out of their cars and walked towards a town hall where a reception committee waited. Leading this line of dignitaries, the Mayor and Pastor in dark somber suits, hurried down the steps to invite the officers inside. Warming drinks and hot food had been prepared in a state function room.

Left in the cold, the North African and Thai drivers walked the cobbled square by themselves. A fountain adjacent to a Romanesque Church provided an opportunity to drink and wash. Opposite the dark framed town hall, a covered arcade sheltered an alehouse, a butcher's and a collection of shops. Chai and Born, intrigued by a toy shop, pushed open the door and stepped inside. On the surrounding shelves there wasn't much on display, but the few toy soldiers, trains and planes that remained, glowed bright in the candlelight. Chai was drawn to a column of tin animals, lined up in front of an ark. Picking up a pair he asked their price. The woman behind the counter hastily wrapped them in newspaper, but refused his money. With a nervous smile she said she was closing.

In the passageway outside more townspeople had dared to emerge. Wary of the 'foreigners' they kept a discreet distance, pulled their hats down low over their eyes and walked fast. "Chinesisch leute", was whispered as Chai and Born passed, "Von ihnen fernhalten."

Their suspicion and distrust wasn't altogether unfounded. For weeks Neustadt had been besieged by dark rumours. The baker had a cousin who lived in the next door town of Maikammer. Visiting for a week she'd told tales of looting and shooting. A neighbour had added more sensational details. In Elmstein, only a valley away, drunken French and North African troops had gone on a rampage. Statues of the saints had been defaced, a shrine burnt, a voodoo doll wired to the cross. Then came more menacing reports of women being molested and raped.

Back in the main square a clerk had set up a desk oblivious to the bitter winds. Illuminated by an oil lamp he opened a large ledger and began organising the billeting of the men. The drivers circled, anxious to be out of the cold and impressed that the man's pen hadn't frozen with the appalling temperatures.

Two large industrial buildings, a printing works and a leather factory on the outskirts of the town, had been prepared for the Algerians, Sengalese and Thai drivers. The French officials were given rooms in an imposing Gothic hall behind the main square. Pierre and the other interpreters were accommodated in the Zum Adler guesthouse two streets away. Last to be attended, Chai, Mai, Manit and Born, were directed to an alleyway where a driver waited with a horse-drawn wagon, its boards greasy and damp from rotten vegetables. Loading their bags, they were driven down winding cobbled streets to the edge of town. The narrow lane emerged near farm buildings that backed onto fields. Because of the dark, very little of this view was visible save the outline of pines, their trunks shifting and groaning in the restless wind.

The house was oak framed and red brick, built around a paved square surrounding a well. Descending from their cart, the Thai were shown to rooms on the first floor (the family who occupied them, having retreated to an attic space in the barn). Chai's bedroom, large and clean, had belonged to the husband and wife. A brass bedstead held a sprung mattress, quilted eiderdown and feather pillows. On a washstand, a water jug had been filled, together with fresh towels and a flannel folded over its frame. The walls of the room were plain, a line of black and white photographs of family and relatives the only concession to decoration. A more somber portrait of a young man dressed as a navy cadet, adorned with a sash of black lace, was likely their son.

Tired after the eight-hour drive, Chai poured some water from a jug and washed and dried himself with the fresh towel. He tried the bed, its springs soft and squeaky. Next to the headboard was an oak bookstand, the volumes on its shelves neatly ordered and clean. A Bible and hymn books, shared space with a farmer's almanac, an atlas of Greater Prussia and a set of leather-bound encyclopaedias. Chai opened a volume, its pages filled with plants, dinosaurs, mountains and steam engines. White men in pith helmets and black tailcoats roamed the subcontinent and the Americas. In the Arctic a group of Eskimos posed outside the entrance to an igloo, their weather-worn faces shrouded beneath fur hoods. And then there was Asia – India, Burma, China and his own country, Siam, embellished with the headline, "Stadt der Engel", in a foil-embossed font. A coloured lithograph showed an image of a German schooner at anchor on the river in front of a gold stupa. Small canoes had paddled out from the banks to sell fruit and flowers. Officers on the deck, tall and regal in tightly-buttoned uniforms, lent against the railings and gestured at the half-naked sellers as if shooing away starlings. It was a potent image of imperial might lording it over the poor and impoverished. It made Chai reflect on their changed circumstances. When the Thai convoy had first arrived in the square, the town's children had mobbed them begging for chocolate and sweets. "Zigaretten! Süssigkeiten!" they'd pleaded. He'd been the one handing out charity.

They had a dog downstairs; a German Schnauzer, dark brown with white and black paws. Friendly and playful, the dog bounded up onto Chai's lap and licked his face. Chai stroked under the dog's chin and rubbed its furry tummy. Hearing the excited yapping, an old man burst into the room and roared out. Chai flinched, thinking he'd done something wrong. Instead, an arm reached out and dragged the Schnauzer from the room by its tail.

In a timber-framed hut adjacent to the dining room, a grandmother, sullen and austere, hunched over a stove stirring stew. Across from her, a daughter, twenty years younger but almost as lined, grated turnips and onions into a stone bowl. Her father, grey haired and bearded, was out in the yard sharpening his blades for a stack of wood that still needed splitting.

Manit, Mai and Born came down the stairs and joined Chai. Two children, a young girl and a small boy with hair messy like straw, showed them into the parlour. A single candle, stubby and greasy, smelling like it was made from animal fat, gave out more soot than light. Black bread as hard and gritty as stone, was so crumbled it must have been hewn with an axe. Pickled red cabbage (a small spoonful) and a grey, emaciated sausage, accompanied it. Both were impossible to chew, let alone digest.

As the three ate in strained, awkward silence, they could hear the family moving about behind the door in the kitchen. Shifting uncomfortably on over turned beer kegs, they whispered cautions to their children and muffled their sobs.

Chapter 33

Air, piercingly cold like a surgeon's blade, cut across Chai's face, numbing his cheeks. Pulling the blanket higher, he peered out. Between the window frame and the stone surround, rotten wood had crumbled away opening a gap. A crude repair had been made; a wedge of newspaper forced into the crack, but a gust of wind had dislodged it.

Chai was pulling the bedclothes higher over his head, hoping to return to sleep, when a stronger blast blew out a second chunk of paper, exposing a larger break in the frame. Exploiting the breach, a twist of snow spun through the opening and settled over the bed. Chai sat up, wiping the ice from his face.

Scratching a circle of frost from the glass, he looked out. It was white outside, the cloud so thick it smothered the light. Against this colourless canvas, snow was falling in large chunky flakes, some so dense they were like swarming butterflies. And the wind, punching in both from the rooftops and under an arch, blew them in anarchic vortices.

Standing in Herr Fischler's hallway the night before, timid as to what they should be doing or where they should be waiting for dinner – if indeed there was any dinner – they had bided their time taking in the porcelain figures and pictures in the hall. The largest painting hung over the door. Yellowed by smoke, the image depicted a winter scene in a forest in which hunters and their dogs were returning from a chase. Through the trees lay their village, where a circle of men and women in thick coats danced round a bonfire. In the middle of a frozen pond, an older couple roasted chestnuts as children and dogs raced around them. But it was the extraordinary mounds of snow that had had the Thais entranced, smothering the landscape like a sea of rice soup. In places it had fallen so deep that it reached up to the rooftops of the thatched houses. Born thought the depths of snow so far fetched, he dismissed it as a fantasy. He recalled an oak carving of a witch above the bakery door in town. It showed the old hag on the back of a flying goat, not unlike their own spirits back home.

"Folk in this country are no different from our own villagers – one foot in the real world, one foot in make-believe," he claimed.

Recalling the conversation, Chai smiled as he took in the scene from the window. The drifts were deeper than those in the painting. His first instinct was to wake Born and drag him outside, "Look, there is your fairy tale!".

Yet, making such a move, dragging himself from the snug warmth of the bed into the bitter air of the room, was harder than he thought. Luckily Chai had slept with his trousers and shirt on and his sweater and socks weren't far away, folded over the back of a chair next to him. Putting them both on under the bedclothes, they felt stiff and abrasive as he pulled them back on. His boots took longer to fit. Soggy and damp from three days of wet weather, the leather had frozen stiff overnight. It was like trying to wedge his feet into steel clogs.

Fully dressed Chai carefully hinged back the door onto the landing. It was quiet, the silence unsettling. Doors led off the thin passageway, so many he couldn't remember which one was the bedroom that housed his companions. Nervously he glanced at the openings, afraid that one might burst open unexpectedly and he'd be confronted by the wizened glare of the grandmother. A rumble of uneven breathing stilled his fears. It was snoring he recognised. Through a gap in the door he could make out Born's spiky black hair sticking out from the bedclothes. In fact, he was so deep in sleep that Chai didn't have the heart to rouse him. Besides, he was their Captain now, maybe such pranks weren't appropriate.

The room downstairs was unchanged from the evening before. In an attempt to clear the table after their meal, Chai and Born had neatly stacked the cutlery and plates on a sideboard. Since then they hadn't been washed or tidied away. Clearly the family hadn't got up yet; he was free to roam the place at will. Reaching for his greatcoat and spare scarf from a hatstand near the door, Chai softly lifted the latch and stepped out. A rush of snow burst through the opening, the swirling flakes dusting his face and stinging his eyes.

Coming in so late the night before, the square of buildings had registered as nothing more than a blank featureless shadow. Now under the flat light of day he could make out the wood block shingles of the main barn and its heavy stone walls where deep drifts had built up around their base. To his right, timber huts on granite plinths likely housed chickens or geese. Somewhere something larger was stabled; he could hear the low bellow of shifting cattle.

Chai's sneaky escape hadn't gone completely unnoticed. The small Schnauzer had heard Chai lift the latch and rushed from the kitchen where it slept. Bursting through the door as Chai stepped outside, it rolled in the carpet of white and snapped at the dancing crystals.

Following this display of animal exuberance, Chai, dispensing with his usual reserve, scooped up a large armful of snow and threw it childishly into the air. "Wha hah, yah, yaaa," he shouted, as the balls of snow fell back down over his face and he licked the flakes from his mouth.

Seconds later he realised he wasn't alone. Out of the corner of his eye he could see the grim outline of the farmer's family, thickly wrapped in dull woollen coats, starring in his direction. The old man had a sledgehammer raised over his head, his son was gripping a wedge. Behind them the young girl had stacked a neat pile of wood, already several feet high.

Their critical looks suggested to Chai that maybe he shouldn't have let the dog out. The young girl and boy, previously so friendly, looked especially dour. And why not? They'd been up since six performing important household chores – wood for the fire to keep themselves and 'him' warm. What example was he setting, getting up so late and dancing about like a clown?

Brushing the snow from his jacket, Chai quickly sobered up. "Guten Morgen," he greeted them, lifting his cap. They ignored him and returned to their wood chopping. Chai turned around and walked back inside. The young Schnauzer, hoping for a hunt, looked aggrieved.

Chapter 34

There'd been a storm in town. At the townhall reception, a scouting party had been sent in search of oil for the kerosene lamps. Deep in the basement they'd stumbled on the two ingredients responsible for the mayhem to follow. "Die Nacht der Krankheit", was how it became known in Neustadt lore. The first blow was the discovery of beer. Sealed in kegs since the beginning of the war, its fermentation, left unchecked had been brutal, raising its alcoholic content to more than double the norm. The second was the unearthing of cheese. Rauchkaese was renowned throughout Bavaria for its intense flavours. A potency derived from an unusually long ripening period that used the digestive juices of cheese mites to create a distinctive golden brown rind. The basement cheese, having festered for years, was several tones darker; burnt umber - almost black. No one could vouch for its origins.

Hunger and drunkenness make poor states for decision-making. The Rauchkäse cheese, although riddled with menacing blisters, still managed to emit an evocative aroma that was alluring enough to overcome caution. Tentatively tasted, it proved, if not delicious, at least palatable. With nothing better on offer, the cuts were fought over and devoured. It was only at dawn that their chemical effects flared. Of the twenty-five French officials and interpreters, sixteen were bedridden. Pierre, waking with a headache so debilitating that he had difficulty standing, made a valiant attempt to join Chai at the assembly point.

Midway across the square he collapsed and had to be carried back to his digs.

Pierre's absence compounded Chai's problems. His men were only now drifting in from the printing works on the outskirts of town. Blurry eyed and fractious, few had managed to sleep in the appalling chill. Dragging their feet through the snow they searched for the field kitchen, only to find it closed for want of fuel. Feeling hungry, miserable and cold, they tried everything to have their mission postponed.

"The Algerians are still stuck in camp, why can't we?" they moaned.

"The district officer thinks it will clear up," answered Chai.

"Then why don't we go when it does?"

"Because people are starving and it's our job to feed them."

"Who's feeding us?" they shot back.

Not liking their dissent, Chai ordered the men to clear the trucks of snow and ice and load their supplies – flour, grain and animal feed for the Weidenthal valley cut off by the weather.

Fully loaded the convoy drove out of the main square to the suburbs of town, close to their lodgings. Passing the familiar farm buildings, the small Schnauzer, still playing in the snow, recognised Chai. Tirelessly it ran alongside, leaping fences and hedges, sending up great sprays of snowflakes, until Chai threw her a large bite of chocolate as a last gift.

Crossing a bridge, they left Neustadt behind and headed north towards the main highway. A fork in the road took them across fields, the undulating slopes glistening bright in the shifting sunlight. The track climbed. They passed a farm on their right, the buildings so deeply smothered in the wintry landscape they looked abandoned. And then they were deep in the trees, tall majestic pines, their branches creaking under the weight of the heavy falls.

A line of push-carts had come up the track just before them. They could see the wandering ruts of their wheels across the virgin expanse. Where deeper drifts had swept over the road, disordered footprints showed where farm hands had fought to keep their wagons from slipping and overturning. Born looked apprehensive.

"How much further?" he asked, changing gear.

"According to the map, about six kilometres," replied Chai, "Do you think we can make it?"

"It's slippery for sure. But if we take it slowly we'll be alright... It's those at the back I'm worried about..."

The convoy continued, the wheels of the big trucks spinning for grip on the icy, uneven camber. They were close to the crest of the hill when a horn from the back stalled them. Born slowed and stopped. Getting down from the cab, he and Chai struggled downhill through the slush, to a truck that had slid off the road into a thick wall of snow. The men, climbing out of its back, looked shaken.

"What now?" asked the team, looking helpless and despondent in the middle of the road. Chai could tell by their looks that they held him accountable; the late Sumet would never have been so reckless and foolhardy to venture out in such weather.

"Get some men, get it dug out," Chai ordered, irked by their lack of initiative.

A spade was found. One of the drivers started burrowing under a wheel, but, without gloves and chilled by the cold, he made painfully slow progress. Chai impatiently grabbed the handle himself and bending to the back, stabbed the spade's blade under the rear axle where it snapped almost immediately. Looking for a replacement, they searched the remaining trucks. A crowbar, wheel jacks and starting handles were unearthed. Several of the men started hacking at the ice blocks with wooden mallets, but to little effect.

Chai remembered the farmhouse on the hillside they had just passed. If inhabited, he argued, he could ask to borrow sturdier shovels and spades. The men, rigid like tree stumps, were doubtful. The buildings looked deserted they grumbled; he'd never get in. Born volunteered to go with him. Chai declined. The young driver was the only one left with any initiative. Leaving him in charge, Chai went off alone.

The small Dodge van was a relief after the ungainly lorries. Nimble and light, its thin tires cut through the crusts of ice already softening with the warmth of the day. Four kilometres back down the track, the farm buildings came up as expected, its outbuildings and barns cutting a bleak silhouette against the pure white hills. Slowing the car, Chai approached the main gates and looked up at the slope to the compound.

It wasn't steep, but the winding track leading up to the barns looked too rough and pockmarked to drive. He parked up and walked.

Fruit trees, drooping under the weight of the overnight falls, lined the avenue. In their high branches there were still shrivelled fruits, browned and pitted with bites. Across the open fields the carpet of virgin white was dotted with tracks; wandering paw prints from voles and hares, the larger deer or fox. Hawks cruised overhead, eyes vigilant for movement or the unwary.

Despite his thick military boots, Chai found the modest walk up the hill a scramble. Beneath the soft snow, the ice was hard like ceramic. Several times he had to pause to regain his balance and loosen his scarf.

Reaching the top, he took in the surroundings. The central compound of the farm was encircled by high stone walls, the only way in a single gateway secured with a rope. It was a simple knot, but its coils, rigid with cold, were hard to untie.

Walking through the gate, the main farm house stood facing him. It was a black timber-framed building on two floors, its walls inlaid with magenta red bricks. Barns and covered yards ran down both sides of a courtyard. Although slate tiles on these outbuildings were in places missing and the plaster cracked, it appeared a well-off estate. Roofs and balconies were decorated with cast-iron railings, the gates hung with brass lanterns. An imposing oak entrance porch was crowned by a stone carving of St Peter and a date, 1803.

Walking down the side of the main house, Chai peered through the frosted windows. The interior looked undisturbed and deserted. A side block, possibly a kitchen or storeroom, was also empty.

Turning for the barns, Chai looked for a door. In such a large farm, he felt confident he'd find the shovels he needed. He was midway across the square when glancing up at the upper window gables, he was surprised to see a fleeting shadow at the glass.

"Hey!" he shouted up as he ran forward, "Hey!"

The shape had been so brief, that as soon as it had gone, Chai was already questioning his judgement. Was it a trick of the light, a stray cat, a drape blown by the wind? Or should he trust to first instincts – the pale face of a boy.

Chapter 35

Pulling back the oak gate, Chai entered the barn. He found himself in an interior so crammed with farming machinery, cutters and hay rakes, it was difficult to squeeze through. On the walls, rusty saw blades and shears gathered dust. An open landau sat under a canvas sheet, the frame collapsed on one side, the spokes of a rear wheel shattered. But an axe, sitting next to a pile of neatly stacked logs, looked recently sharpened. And next to it lay a small circle of fresh wood chippings. Around the shavings the cobble stones were damp. Melting snow had dripped through the broken tiles from above. Warmth from somewhere had melted it. More evidence that the barn was clearly occupied.

A slatted door to his right led through to a stable block. The stalls were empty, their floors caked with dried straw and dung. Across from the nearest box, adjacent to a wall still hung with bridles and harnesses, steps led to a second floor.

Climbing up their loose treads, Chai reached a landing. In the corner of this stairwell a table with a lamp and a vase stood next to a frayed tapestry leant against the wall. Light entered the space through a square-framed window. It was the opening at which he had seen the pale outline – for he was certain now it had been a face – only minutes before. Stepping up to the glass he looked down into the yard where his own footsteps marked an irregular arc in the snow. More curiously, within a frame grubby with stains, the glass itself was clear; wiped either with a cloth or the side of a sleeve.

Chai turned back to the room. His attention settled again on the tapestry screen. Moving closer he shifted it aside to reveal a hidden door. He lifted the latch.

The hatchway opened into a narrow attic. Cool, dank air brushed by. Taking in the cramped space, Chai's eyes took a while to adapt to the gloom. To keep the light out heavy sacking had been hammered over the window openings. On the floor he saw bedding, blankets and pillows. Next to the door a line of boots filled a shelf, neatly arranged by size. Higher up on the wall a small sparrow hopped in a cage. It looked well fed and watered.

Chai cautiously crossed the room to the far end. Within the timber arch there was a second, larger door. It was stiff, the hinges so rusted he had to kick it hard to open it. Stepping through, his right arm reached out for support and brushed against a tangle of cobwebs. Unlike the previous attic, the room was jet black, impenetrable to sight. Yet, from this dull background, faint signals emerged. A floorboard creaked. He caught a soft exhalation of breath. Following it came the scent of stale sweat. Individually, these tiny, almost imperceptible clues, might have passed unrecognised, yet fused into a whole, they induced a sense of dread as palpable as a fist round his throat. Someone was standing in front of him.

"Who's there?" he shouted.

A face emerged from the gloom. But it wasn't the boy he'd seen earlier, it was the face of a man – bearded, scarred, blood-shot eyes looking leery and brutal.

"What the hell are you doing here?" growled a voice, his knuckles slamming into Chai's shoulder.

Chai, unbalanced by the blow, staggered back. As he collected himself he had time to take in the figure looming before him. He was a soldier, his long slate grey coat covering a dark blue jacket with gold braiding on its collar: French. That much was a relief. Back in the square at Neustadt there'd been talk of German renegades holed up in the hills. Scorning surrender and stealing from farms, they'd refused to hand in their guns. Chai, so close to returning home, didn't fancy a final, farewell bayonet through his guts.

"We were on our way to Weidenfels. Our trucks got stuck in the snow. I was looking for spades," replied Chai uncertainly.

"What, in here?", roared the man, gesturing to the low walls of the attic, "Does this look like a hardware store?"

"No, but downstairs in the barn, I thought I'd find tools."

"The barn, yes, of course, damn it Chinaman, you might be right… the barn… that's true…"

The Frenchman stepped back, his tone softening. A faint smile broke over his face. He offered up his hand. They shook.

"Fleurot, Armand Fleurot. A sergeant in the Fourth Army. What the fuck, we're on the same side," he patted Chai softly on his back as if petting a tame goat, "Who's command are you under?"

"Colonel Brevier", replied Chai relieved the situation had calmed.

"Colonel Brevier is a cretin, a fraud and an imbecile… so are all those in his command. Wankers to a man…"

The exchange gave Chai the opportunity to take in the space. He could see the floor clearly now; an untidy mess of clothes, cushions and bedding ramping up high into the corner. It was then he saw the boy again. He lay twisted up in a heap under the eaves, scornful eyes peering out from a swollen, battered face as Chai's gaze settled on him. He could see blood seeping from the side of the boy's mouth as if his front teeth were broken. More astonishing still, further across the space under a deeper pile of blankets, was the discovery of two girls. He couldn't actually see their faces so tightly were they wrapped in their covers, but lengths of blonde hair spilled out onto the pillows, and stocking feet could be seen jutting out over the floor.

'Thump', came the strike of the man's fist across Chai's shoulder again, playful this time, though still painfully annoying.

"Looks like you and me came in just in time," he nodded behind, "I caught these vermin breaking into the house. Upstairs in the bedrooms, they were looting the place," said the gruff Frenchman, opening his hand to reveal a palm filled with rings and necklaces.

"That little shit put up a bit of a fight…"

Armand rolled up his sleeve and stepped closer. Ugly teethmarks marred his forearm, the blood from the cuts staining his shirt sleeve.

"Fucking animal bit me..."

Armand's uncomfortable proximity betrayed more detail. He had a watch on his wrist with an ornate strap. On an index finger he wore a gold ring. His military aspects were yet more intriguing. Bands on his jacket indicated a lieutenant, yet his hands, calloused and rough, suggested rank and file.

"As you can see", he continued, wiping sweat from his brow, "I had to beat the bastard about a bit."

Chai caught sight of the club he'd used. A gash of crimson ran down its shaft.

"Yeh, smacked him in the face," he said, casually swinging the bat, "Willow wood, it has a nice spring to it..."

He passed the handle to Chai.

"Take a feel... Swing it about a bit... Better still, have a go... Hit him... smack him. I know you want to."

"No," said Chai, backing off, appalled by the idea.

Armand, perplexed, looked disappointed.

"Nervous, hah? Never hit a man?"

"I don't have any reason to hit him," replied Chai.

"Reason...?" Armand pondered this for seconds. "He's Hun scum, isn't that reason enough?"

Raising the club, Armand turned to the corner, "Come on boy! Stand up. Let the man see you... See you for the thieving shit that you are."

Chai's eyes fell to the rags pleading for the lad to move, to obey, to get up.

"Stand!" Armand roared.

The boy reluctantly emerged from the blankets.

"That's good. Very good... Now how about a nice smile for us, hah?"

The boy's expression changed. But far from a smile, he returned a look of utter contempt.

"I said smile, you little rat!"

Again defiance; the boy spat, the spittle hitting the boards in front of the frenchman.

Armand, incensed, leapt forward. But the boy, anticipating his move, was quick and dodged the blow. The club missed his head and slammed into a beam. There was a loud crack, the sharp impact, ringing down its shaft like a bolt of electricity, shocking Armand's arm.

"Yaahhh, Fuck!…Damn that smarts!, Yaahhh!"

The club fell.

"Whhhaah!" he massaged his forearm.

"You little shit!", he turned back to the boy, "You're going to regret that, my god, you're going to regret that!"

Armand's hand fell to his gun-belt and flipped open the holster. Pulling the pistol free, he swung it out towards the boy.

"Last chance boy. Smile or get a bullet in your brains!"

"Bruno, leacheln!" yelled one of the girls, "lächeln!", squealed the other. Yet his insolence remained.

Armand, infuriated, fired two shots in quick succession. The girls shrieked. Incredibly both bullets passed inches from the boy's head and harmlessly hit the rafters.

Armand dropped the pistol to his left hand and nursed his fingers. They were still shaking after the shock from the club; no wonder he'd missed.

"Shit, that little bastard must have fucked up my arm…"

Again his left hand moved to his forearm, rubbing and soothing the muscles. It was no good; he was unable to suppress the trembling.

Armand, grimacing with pain, turned to Chai, "I've a better idea."

Flipping the gun deftly in his hand, he passed the handle to Chai.

"Alors, Chinois… My hand's fucked. Help me out. You know the colonel's orders. Shoot all looters on sight. As Frenchmen, that's our duty. I'm giving you the honour, soldier."

It was the first time Chai had been called 'a soldier', let alone French. He clearly wasn't either. They were Thai and they were drivers. And as drivers they'd never been expected to carry firearms, let alone use them. Was Armand really expecting him to kill someone?

"Be quick, make it merciful. A clean shot, wham, get it over with."

Chai hesitated.

"Soldier!", the man repeated, "What the fuck is wrong with you!"

Again Chai stalled.

"Soldier!" he screamed.

Loosing his patience, Armand grabbed Chai's hand and forced the butt into his palm. Chai couldn't do anything but grasp the handle. It felt warm and sticky from Armand's sweaty grip. Not that he was unfamiliar with weapons. He loved handguns and got a thrill from just holding them. It was the pathetic trembling figure at the end of his sights that alarmed him. A line of sight that zeroed in on the boy's face. Given this focus he could see the boy's bleeding mouth was the least of his injuries. Armand had struck the side of his head; probably after he'd tried to attract Chai's attention at the window. It looked a brutal injury. The three-inch gash had caused blood to seep down the side of his head, matting his hair.

"Come on, what are you waiting for? Do your duty, blow his brains out!"

From the pile of bedclothes to the right, came the muffled sobbing of the two girls.

"Those bitch girls were in on it too. Get it over with. Then we can find your precious shovels, bury their bodies, dig your trucks out of the snow and be gone from this cursed place!".

Bury 'their' bodies. He was aiming to kill the girls too. Why? What had they done? They were so young. It didn't make any sense. None of it made sense. He hesitated. His grip weakened, the tip of the barrel fell. And as the barrel dropped, the menacing outline of Armand moved closer, his face twisted in rage, greasy hand reaching out and grabbing the lapel of Chai's coat.

"You're not getting this. I am ordering you, as your superior, shoot the rats now!"

Again Chai clocked the officer stripes and the silver braiding of his cap and shuddered. Wasn't this everything the army drummed into you – obedience to everything, instant, unquestioning?

A sharp stab in his shoulder refocused his attention. Armand had punched him with the point of his knuckles, the impact so sharp it numbed his arm. But the effect, discomforting that it was, also proved a corrective. Fool, what was he thinking? The boy, the jewellery, the theft, it was all lies. His mind cleared. Turning, he aimed the gun at Armand and clenched the trigger.

For seconds the Frenchman stood frozen, his mouth so wide open with incredulity, no words escaped.

"What... What the fuck! You... you, you're aiming at me?"

Chai remained unflinching.

"Are you crazy, out of your stupid mind!"

Crazy? There was some truth to that. He had lost his grip. Here he was, a nobody, threatening a Frenchman, an ally, a soldier, by rank his superior; the transgressions so numerous he felt faint.

"Chinois, enough hah... joking right?"

Chai cocked the gun.

Armand leapt back, "What the fuck's got into you!".

"I want to speak with the boy first."

"What!"

The word burst out like a projectile, trailing a twist of spit which skimmed past his ear.

"He's a fucking boy. A Hun boy at that. Think you can understand what he says?"

"I still want to talk with him."

"Why the fuck monkey brain?" his foot stamped the boards so hard Chai thought they would shatter.

"Let him speak."

"This has gone too far, Chinaman. Really too far... Give me the gun...", his hand reached out, "for the love of General Gérard, give me the fucking gun!"

"Let him speak!" Chai repeated, levelling the barrel between Armand's eyes.

Armand backed off, holding his hands up in mock surrender, "Ok, ok... You're right, you're right..." he reassured Chai, "Let's hear the boy out, yeh, yeh, let let him speak... for all the good it will do you..."

Having backed down, Armand shuffled back into the shadows, head low, chastened and humbled. His shaking hand reached to a side pocket and fumbled for a packet of cigarettes. He offered one to Chai. Chai declined. Taking one himself, he returned to his pocket for matches and lit one. The smell of burning sulphur quickly filled the space as the flame flared. Chai, both comforted by the smell and flinching with the sudden brightness, was slow to realise a sharp pain in his side. Confused, he looked down and saw a blade glistening with blood, the colour so vivid he had trouble grasping what had happened. There was a second strike. This time Chai was alert enough to twist away. He felt the tip of the blade catch his coat then spin to the floor. Armand's left hand went for his wrist, slamming it hard to the frame. The pistol, knocked from Chai's grip went off at close quarters. The Frenchman roared. The shot had gone through his thigh. A spurt of blood pulsed out across the boards, its velocity powerful enough to reach the girls. Chai, seeing the dramatic spray, vainly hoped that the wound was enough and that Armand would back off. But the Frenchman, impervious to his wound, retreated into the dark to mull his next move. It was crude. A charge, like a bull, that rammed Chai into the far wall. As his large calloused hands found Chai's neck, he pressed down and squeezed. Chai, grasping for breath, grabbed Armand's arms and fought to release his grip, but the man, crazed like a bear, proved impossible to dislodge. In desperation Chai searched the floor. He found a wooden block and swinging it high brought it down on Armand's head. The blow didn't knock him out, but it brought time. Time for Chai to wriggle free and catch his breath. Exhausted, he slumped against the door. His strength was fading; he wouldn't last long. He glanced across the floor. His only hope was the gun. And he could see its handle, not ten feet away under a ledge. He leapt back up, but before he was midway across to the weapon, Armaud was there, his fist swinging out into his ribs and hammering him back to the wall.

This time Chai took longer to recover. Spitting blood and broken teeth, he lifted himself to his knees and saw Armand towering above him. The barrel of the gun rose to his face. It was over.

"God, I hate your kind," hissed the Frenchman, "thinking that because you wear our great uniform you're like one of us… You're not. And never will be. You're nothing but savages!"

Armand pulled the trigger. The hammer hit the cartridge; a dull empty thud returned. A dud. As his finger returned to the trigger for a second shot, Chai saw the cylinder turn. Sweat seeped down his spine; he'd never known such fear. Yet folded within that almost total terror was also hope. Fate had intervened. Its reason might have remained obscure, but the realisation that destiny had deigned to favour him - humble Thai, Chai from Loei – unlocked hidden reserves. A sufficient force to propel him forward and on top of Armand before the man could fire again. The frenchman lurched back, his huge bulk hitting the boards so hard they shattered. Both fell through the floor, landing on top of the cattle stalls below. Chai was lucky; he had the fat Frenchman to cushion his fall. Armand's landing hadn't been so fortunate or graceful. A pitchfork, close to the wall, sliced through his windpipe puncturing his spinal artery. Despite this fatal wound, Armand's fingers clawed for his throat in an attempt to stem the bloody flow spreading out across his chest. An ugly, rasping noise escaped from his lungs, followed by a final, gentle whistle. As his arms dropped lifeless to his side, a cascade of jewellery and coins spilled from his pockets.

Chapter 36

Bruno, born on the 3rd of August, was only nine when the war started, one day before Von Bulow's 2nd Army fired the first shot in the conflict by crossing the border into Belgium. Brought up an orphan in the Bruche Valley in the Vosges, Bruno wasn't even German. Never knowing who his parents were, or where he was from, Bruno was sent to a Catholic School in Landau, a harsh square of brown brick buildings close to a pottery factory on a canal. At weekends they gathered wood for the furnaces, cleaned the kilns and prepared the glazes and clay. When he was ten he was taken in by a farming family, the Hofmanns. They had two daughters of roughly the same age, Heidi and Klara.

With his dark Slavic looks and wild unkept hair, Bruno was never truly accepted as one of the fold. Although he took meals in the main farmhouse and was allowed to play (at certain hours) in the upstairs bedrooms, he slept alone in an attic room the father had built for him over the barn. From Monday to Friday he accompanied the two girls to the village school and carried their books. They sat in different classes.

When a second year of war failed to bring the promised, rapid victory, a call for new recruits saw a further move of tutors and staff to the training camps. The school, unable to find suitable replacements for the teachers who had gone, was forced to close.

The Hofmanns, like other families in the valley, were told to send their children to a second school in neighbouring Lindenberg. The walk, ten kilometres across rolling hills and fields was tough and in the winter months, dark and bitterly cold. Sometimes, if they were lucky, they got a lift home on a milk wagon or coal truck, but soon, even these – the most decrepit of transports – were requisitioned by the military.

After the two girls caught chickenpox and were bedridden for two weeks, enthusiasm for the arduous, mucky walk to school waned. Kept at home, their mother taught them from the handful of encyclopaedias and dictionaries she had kept in her room. Not that the extra time left them idle. Their parents, without field labourers, were grateful for their help on the farm.

As the war ground on without measurable gain except in the length of food queues and rationing restrictions, further pressure for troops forced the government to reverse its exemptions for agricultural workers. Father Hoffman, old, but only too willing to follow the patriotic call, joined two hundred and fifty farmers and field labourers at staging camps at Beverloo in Northern Belgium. After two months of field exercises and weapons training, they were sent to reinforce General Sixt's 4th Army on the Ypres salient. Contributing to a valiant defence on the Westrozebeke Ridge above Passchendaele, their unit was taken out of the trenches and sent to a rest camp. It was mid July, the summer dry, unusually hot. Proud and relieved at having survived howitzers and snipers, their foe was small, almost imperceptible. By the end of the week, three hundred, including Thomas Hofmann, had died from malaria. His wife, deeply religious, who prayed everyday before images of the saints and martyrs, was crushed. A mosquito bite was the work of God, not an act of wanton barbarity. They'd lived their lives chaste and pure. What had they done to deserve it?

Grief-stricken, filled with bitterness and recrimination, Frau Hofmann became ill and took to her bed. Never recovering her faith or her health, she followed her husband to the grave.

Distant Hofmann relatives, saddened by the family tragedy and anxious for the care and safety of Heidi and Klara, took the two girls to live with them in Bornheim. Despite the girl's protests, Bruno was left behind on the farm.

The girls' uncle was a wealthy merchant and investor. As well as owning a mill and a shoe manufacturer, he managed two large garment factories on the fringes of town. The war had been good for his businesses. A number of well placed contacts in the government had been able to secure several large and lucrative contracts to supply military equipment, uniforms and boots.

In retrospect no one could have accused Uncle Hofmann of being inattentive to his nieces. He gave them a large bedroom on the second floor, where there were toys – a rocking horse and a train set – together with a bathroom with hot, running water. With no children of his own, he adored the two girls. And who wouldn't? Their presence alone lit up every soulless corner of his stern "Backsteingotik' townhouse. And they liked him too. They played cards and board games every evening in his study, where they listened to records on his windup tournaphone player. At weekends he spoiled them with new bows, laces and sashes from his many clothing factories.

But Uncle Hofmann wasn't always there to look over them. Business needs kept him away on long trips, his time taken up flattering those of influence in the salubrious dining clubs of Berlin and Hamburg, keeping competitors at bay. And he was expanding; his military lines were going down well in Vienna, where in a luxury suite at the Imperial Hotel he grew fat on fine *mohnzelten* and *sachertorte*.

With Uncle Hofmann away, the house lost its spark and joy. Ruled over by a prudish, puritanical governess, the girls lives became dull and solitary. Devoid of sentiment or art, the woman disapproved of games, even reading. Regarding the gramophone player with especial suspicion, she often hid its steel needle amongst the thimbles and pins in her sewing box. Besides, she had better ideas for gainful pursuit; evenings spent polishing the crucifixes and icons in the hallway downstairs.

Hating Bornheim, with its drab industrial buildings and dingy streets and with few friends to play with, Heidi and Klara yearned for the country with its wild open spaces and pine forests. Early one morning, after yet another stinging rebuke from the governess for staying up too late, the girls stole away from the house and made their way back to Neustadt.

Bruno was repairing a fence post on the high ground above the farm, when he first saw the two girls scrambling up the path from the valley. Downing his tools he ran down through the field and met them at the gates. They looked shattered by their trek – they hadn't eaten since Bornheim – but Bruno, overjoyed to see them, hugged them affectionately and helped them back to the house, where he found them walnuts and apples.

Thinking they were just back for a few days, Bruno boiled up a dinner and made up their beds. Over the meal the girls recounted how they'd hoodwinked the wicked governess by stuffing toy bears under their bed covers and then escaped from the townhouse by climbing out of their window and down a drainpipe. It was only later when washing the dishes and mugs, that they came clean about their true intentions. They had returned for good and had elected to make Bruno their governor and protector.

Bruno, tucking Heidi and Klara back into their old beds, couldn't deny that he was elated to have them back, but he was also filled with misgivings. It hadn't been easy after they'd left. Before their separation his entire emotional life had revolved around the two girls. And then, without a single word of explanation, they'd gone. Feeling abandoned and consumed with remorse he had wandered the farm, unsure what to do, where to go. Eventually he'd got over his sadness and loss by reminding himself that born an outsider he'd never be one of them and was vain to suppose it. Having made this painful psychological adjustment, he was now conditioned to living alone.

Eclipsing his personal emotional issues, there arose more practical concerns. Food was his overriding anxiety. Daunted by the prospect of having to survive the coming winter and half of spring, his stock piles had been meticulously prepared. The four walls of the cellar were stacked with kindling and split logs. Upstairs in the main barn, trays of dried mushroom, sacks of suede, potato and turnip were concealed in the stalls. Pride of place were his jams – two shelves of damson plums picked from the trees that lined the avenue leading up to the farm. He'd calculated two modest spoons of preserve for every day of autumn and winter; five months, twenty-four jars. A small luxury for one, but certainly insufficient for two extra mouths with a special taste for sweet things. It would likely be gone in a single sitting.

For two weeks Bruno kept his secret jam stash hidden. Yet as the days passed he found such fears unfounded. The girls, surprisingly resourceful, proved more of a blessing than a burden. Heidi, good with chickens and geese, showed an uncanny ability to snare woodcock and pigeon. Klara could mill grain, bake bread and craft meals from the most basic of ingredients. When Bruno went fishing on the river and returned proudly with half a dozen perch, the girls gutted, dried and jarred them in brine. Past winter and edging into spring Bruno found his special cellar supplies were still in surplus, even the jam.

Locked in their comparative idyll, the war was never far away. On still evenings they could hear the distant boom of guns over the horizon. Klara swore she had seen Zeppelins cruising east to west like cigar-shaped clouds (Heidi told her they were cigar-shaped clouds). Walking past a neighbour's farm, they noticed that the owner's two sons had recently returned from the front. The youngest, a childhood friend before enlisting, had lost both his legs. The old man took him everywhere in a pony and trap.

Every week Bruno made the long walk into town, carrying eggs, vegetables and woodland mushrooms to barter on the black market for rare sugar or flour. Under an arcade at the townhall, cuttings from a Berlin newspaper, *Vossische Zeitung*, were pinned to a board. Together with the triumphant and stirring headlines, there were photographs from the front; the ruins of French villages, fields littered with slaughtered enemy soldiers, captured guns and most gleeful of all, reports of successful bombing raids on the English seaside towns, Margate and Dover. Gleaned from these news cuttings, Bruno could tell the girls about the capture of Namur, the advance of their brave armies on Paris and their magnificent bombardment of Verdun. His excited account of General Ludendorff's big push, Kaisersschlacht, in the Second Battle of the Somme, was greeted with an outburst of celebration and dance. Bruno, egged on by Heidi, broke the lock on their father's drinks cabinet and they finished the schnapps.

After this run of success, a visiting priest gave them hope that victory was in sight; gallant Ludendorff was knocking on the door of Amiens. By July they would be at Calais, the humbled British dogs forced to swim home across their miserable channel. The French, crippled and on their knees, were desperate for an end. As for the haughty, boastful Russians, hobbled after their chaotic revolution, they had already capitulated. Rumours were rife that Pier Bruckner, master sugar hoarder at the Morgenstein Bakery in town, had been asked to prepare a table long cake, enough for one hundred mouths. Picturing the celebrations, the flags and the brass bands, the young girls were misguided enough to think that their long-lost father would come home.

But the promised victory didn't come. As summer turned once again into autumn, Bruno went back to the town hall to find that the news cuttings, now yellowed and brittle, hadn't changed. Walking the market, disappointed with the meagre bread he had bartered, he saw companies of 'Landwehr' assembling in the main square. Dispiritingly they were far from young. Grey haired, wrapped in sheepskin and puffing anxiously on pipes, the old men lifted muskets to their shoulders and wore curved knives in their belts.

In the pine woods above the farm, Bruno and the girls built their own fortifications – the Hofmann line. Bruno dug trenches, tunnels and dugouts. Heidi and Klara cut branches and gathered ferns to cover the roof. A bale of hay dragged up from the barn and scattered over the dirt, became their floor. On a ledge inside the largest subterranean chamber, fir cones and sticks were lined up; their armoury in case of attack.

Boys from a neighbouring estate made the mistake of wandering too close to the defences. Ambushed in a gully in the woods, a shower of dried horse dung and rotten turnips saw them retreat. Of this invading hoard, one small boy persisted. Lured more by an infatuation for the pretty Klara than an enthusiasm for the fight, he endured being pelted with fir cones and sticks until covered with cuts and bruises. Foolishly he had carved Klara's name into the centre of a heart on an oak tree at the crossroads. His vain crush didn't last. On a moonlit evening they captured the hopeless romantic. Tying him to the barn gate with rope, the two girls tortured him with nettles and barbs until he swore to scratch out the offensive heart – little could Klara foresee that in ten years she would be marrying the twenty-year-old Herr Bauer.

Buoyed up by their great triumph, they built a look out-tower to protect their southern border. Bruno nailed steps into the base of a cedar tree and built a platform in its upper branches. On a hot summer afternoon they drank juice and sun bathed on the top. A squadron of gleaming silver Albatroses, fresh from their factory at the Johannisthal aerodrome, roared overhead. Noticing a salute from the lead pilot they energetically waved back.

To maintain a constant vigil at night, when they were all asleep in the house, Klara tied a favourite doll to the upper branches, telescope and brass bell by its side, to alert them if anything suspicious was sighted.

The cold winds returned. Bruno, aware by now that the bitter conflict wasn't going away, set in motion a plan that had plagued his conscience for months. Working late into the evenings, he made sure that their winter supplies and firewood were more than replenished. On the night of his departure, he checked the girls were soundly asleep, packed a hiking bag with spare clothes and a handful of belongings and stole away into the dark. On the kitchen table he'd left a note explaining his reasons. He knew they would be distressed, but he hoped they would understand and begged their forgiveness. Even though he was probably the wrong age, he was determined to fight.

Bruno got as far as a first day's training at the Kallstadt barracks in Westfallen when he was called to the First Lieutenant's office.

"As the last and youngest recruit to pass through our doors I'm giving you the honour of calling the men," he announced.

Bruno sounded the bugle. The cadets, trainers and officers gathered in ranks on the parade ground. General Major Scheer, decorated at Tannenberg and wounded at Gorlice Tarnow, rose to a rostrum and read out a proclamation.

And that was it. The war was over.

Chapter 37

Bruno was in the work shed filing his saw blade when he heard the scream. That in itself wasn't unusual; the girl's often shouted and messed about. What caught his attention was the tone of the cry. Loud and shrill it suddenly went dead, like a bell being muffled. He knew the girls were inside. Heidi, having found new wool in a store cupboard, was darning his socks. Klara said she would be in the kitchen making new candles. She had begged him twice to find twine for the wicks.

Crossing the yard Bruno saw the main door to the house was wide open. Given the fresh snow that morning it was an unusual and clumsy oversight. The girl's were fiercely protective of their heat and would howl at him if he ever left the door even slightly ajar. Now, perhaps, one of them had committed that grave sin. A sin so rare he jumped at the chance to exploit it.

"Heidi, Klara..." he called out, "Some dumb fool has left the door open..."

There was no reply. He walked to the front porch and listened. Still nothing. Stepping over the threshold, he pulled the thick velour curtain back over the door and entered the hall. On the flagstone in front of him the crust of a fresh footprint marked the floor. It looked too large to have come from one of the girl's soles. Besides they religiously took their shoes off when they went into the house and stored them neatly under the bench; a house rule they'd kept from their departed mother.

Bruno, wary now, took in the room. A picture book, '*Die zwölf Jäger*', was open by the window sill, next to a glass of water and a pocket knife. Heidi's knitting, his own shamefully threadbare socks, lay unfinished on the main table. The rest of the room was undisturbed. Treading softly he crossed the hall to the kitchen door, reached for the handle and hinged it open. A gun pushed into his face. And behind the weapon, mean, yellowed eyes stared down the barrel.

"Who the hell are you?", grunted the man.

"I'm Bruno. I live on the farm", he replied, eyes anxiously searching around the corner of the frame for the girls. They were on the floor, hands tied behind their backs, kitchen rags stuffed into their mouths, their small, alarmed eyes staring out.

"Anyone else on the farm?" the man snapped back.

"No."

"People close by?"

"No. The next door farm is empty. Has been for years."

"Turn around. Hold your hands above your head," barked the man. Grabbing Bruno by his shoulder, he forced him around and pushed him back across the room.

"Show me where the bedrooms are."

With the gun in his back, Bruno led the way across the hallway towards the stairs. Passing a sideboard, he caught sight of the used candles Klara had left out to melt down. Seeing the heavy brass candle sticks, a rash plan flashed through his mind: if he was quick he could grab one of the holders and smash it across the man's skull. He had once killed a fox with such a blow. The animal had broken through the fence into the chicken shed and snapped the necks of two cockerels. Yes, it had needed several frenzied strikes to finally finish the young vixen. And in truth it was just a skinny thing. By mass alone the man behind him was more than thirty times its weight, with a neck as tough as a bull. And he snorted like a bull; a gruff, rasping snuffle that came out of his ugly nose in rough, uneven bursts. Whether it was lungs or throat he didn't sound well. Patience, thought Bruno, get the man away from the girls, put him at ease, be pliant and obedient, then dash his brains out.

"They're up the stairs sir," said Bruno with sly deference.

"Then lead on boy," he rejoined.

Bruno guided the soldier up the stairs. They reached the landing and turned towards a door on the right. Inside was the parents bedroom, an interior that had remained untouched since the mother's tragic death. A lace bedspread covered the bed. At the head of the frame two embroidered pillows rested on a silk shawl. Toiletries, a perfume spray and three framed images of St Ansgar, St Nicholas and St Hildegard were neatly arranged over the dressing table.

"It's not used anymore?"

"Not since they died."

"Who?"

"The parents... our parents."

"So everything has remained exactly as they left it?"

"Yes."

Caring little for the sanctity of the place, the invader put his arm to the table top and swept the lot to the floor. Turning his attention to the drawers underneath, he emptied them, but found nothing of value. Next in line was a sideboard. Dresses, shirts and undergarments joined the lace shawls and scarves on the boards. A wardrobe revealed a carved wooden casket. Frustratingly it contained nothing but dog-eared cigarette cards and old stamps.

After searching the obvious hiding places, the man's focus turned to the obscure. He dug through a hidden compartment inside a grandfather clock, ripped open the base of a knitting box, then turned over a carved trunk full of shoes. Still no success.

Hot and agitated now the soldier reached for the neck of his coat and pulled open the buttons. Wiping his brow, he glanced across the room and caught Bruno eying him.

"You think I'm done, don't you boy? That I'll just give up and walk away..." he spat on the floor. "No way. Done this too many times and I'm wise to the ways... as always... just a matter of time..." Again Bruno caught his laboured, hoarse breathing, "... just a matter of time..."

Sinking back into the soft mattress, the soldier's restless eyes roved round the room again; first to a book shelf above the wardrobe, then to a ledge next to the curtains.

"You see I was born with a sense for fine things," he touched the end of his fat, greasy nose, "I can smell it, see. And right now... I can feel that special twitch... close... very, very close..."

His boot fell lazily to the floor. Rapping the boards a hollow echo returned. He glanced down.

Rolling from the bed, the man crouched down on the floor. The edge of a plank lifted; it didn't take much to prise it free. Reaching inside between the timbers he found what he was looking for – a black leather pouch tied with a bow. Pulling the bag out, he lifted it to the bed, tugged the ribbon around its neck and emptied the contents. Pearl necklaces, silver rings and bracelets fell to the eiderdown. Seeing the hoard, his dull eyes lit up with greed.

"There's more?", the intonation of his voice lifting as he scooped the jewels into his pockets.

"Yes", lied Bruno, surprised by the find. He had no idea the penny-pinching Hofmann's possessed anything of value.

"How much?"

"Much more I think..."

"Think?"

"Yes, I mean for sure. Much more," he corrected himself.

He'd thought of a plan. There was a biscuit tin in the girl's room behind the washstand. It contained a gold tiara, a ruby necklace and sapphire rings. Of course they were all worthless tat; stage jewellery, mostly paste, that Klara and Heidi dressed up in when they played at being Counts and Countesses. More importantly, behind the door he knew was a stout broom handle. Heidi used it to prop open the window on hot summer evenings. Swung with all his force he could possibly knock the man out. That would buy him enough time to rush back downstairs to the kitchen and untie the two girls. Together they would return upstairs, thump the thief again with the broom handle (probably take turns), then wrap him with the horse harness he knew hung in the cowshed. With Bruno standing guard, the girls could then run into town to raise the alarm. And the jewels; not forgetting the jewels. They would turn the pearls and rubies into something more useful like jam and sausages; then have a feast.

"Where?" demanded the man.

"In the next room."

"Show me," he grunted, shovelling the remaining rings and stones into the deep pockets of his coat.

Bruno led the way back to the stairwell. The man, happier now, was whistling a tune, relishing the thought of a second, possibly larger stash. They were about to turn up steps to the back corridor, when the Frenchman, glancing through a small window, suddenly dropped to his knees.

"Get down!", he hissed to the boy.

Bruno knelt on the floor. From his position at the edge of the alcove he could see out over the sill, across the yard and down the hill to the road. A military van was parked up by the gates in the distance. And from it a soldier was walking up the snowy avenue of trees.

"Damn there's someone there! You've been lying to me boy!"

"No, no, I haven't. I've no idea who he is."

"You sure?"

"I promise you…"

"Quick, downstairs."

Pulled by the man Bruno ran rapidly down the stairs. Pausing to carefully close the main door, they crossed the dining room and entered the kitchen. Grabbing Heidi and Klara, the soldier untied them.

"Where can we hide?", he demanded.

"In the outbuildings" replied Bruno, pointing over his shoulder.

Leaving by the backdoor, Bruno led the Frenchman and the two girls around the back of the house to the barn. Entering the stables, they passed by the horse boxes and climbed the thin steps to Bruno's secret lair at the back of the attic. Once inside, the Frenchmen threw the girls to the mattress, gagged them again and began tying them to the roof beams. Turning back to the room, he was enraged to see that Bruno had gone. Rushing back through the adjoining room he found the boy standing at the side window staring down into the yard. He grabbed Bruno by the neck, pulled him down and hit him hard with the butt of his gun.

"One squeak out of you boy and your pretty sisters snuff it!", he snarled as he threw Bruno back through the opening.

Chapter 38

Klara cracked first. The wheels of the barrow were so weedy and thin they cut through the top layer of ice, clogging the wire spokes with grit and snow. She'd chosen to push from the back, but the cart's handles, having lost their leather grips years ago, pressed remorselessly into the soft skin of her palms. When the barrow hit yet another root hidden under a drift, jerking it abruptly out of her hands, the small girl slipped and fell again. Bruno, coming down from the front, lifted her back to her feet.

"Why? Why do we have to do this? Why do we have to freeze to death dragging this man? We don't even know who he is, where he's from," whined the small girl.

"Because he didn't know who you were and yet..."

"He saved us..." added Heidi, brushing the snow from her sister's side.

"I know, I know..." Klara sighed, "But he's so heavy and we're just kids."

"You're just a kid," said Heidi.

"We're the same age," she snipped back.

"There are three of us," Bruno interjected, kicking the slush from the spokes.

It had been a mistake to take the shortcut. Normally the quickest route into town, it rose and fell over several slopes, the deepest snow collecting in the troughs. Worst still, some way back they must have veered off track entirely. Red clay tinted the white, showing that they had strayed into the cabbage patch.

Bruno made a correction and steered a traverse to higher ground. A ridge was found. Being more exposed, strong winds had swept it clear of drifts and they made better progress. But when the ground dipped, the surface became steeper and more slippery. Bruno stabbed his heels into the ice in an attempt to slow their speed, but they were going too fast. Rounding a corner they lost control, the back of the cart ran wide and crashed into the side of the bank. The impact threw Chai's body to the ground where it rolled over a ledge out of sight. Bruno and the girls ran back to where he had dropped. They peered down the slope; only a knee and a tuff of bloodied black hair stuck out from the white.

"Can't we just leave him there?" moaned Klara, letting herself fall back in the snow, her face red with cold and exhaustion.

Heidi too, looked like she'd had enough, "She's right Bruno. He can't be seen from the road. No one will know until the spring," her tone flat, like an undertaker.

"Get Klara to the top of the bank, I'll lift him back into the cart," replied Bruno, not liking their defeatism.

It was easier said than done. Bruno tried getting beneath Chai's body, to swing his legs up from the drift, but every step he made in the gully saw him slip further back in the snow. Heidi and Klara, seeing him struggle, had to shelve their protests and come down to help. They brushed drifts from the bank and stamped steps into the incline, providing Bruno with the foot holds he needed to drag Chai's body back to the cart.

Lifting Chai's last leg into the burrow, Bruno agreed to a rest. The girl's needed it. Breathless and shivering he knew they were shattered. Calling them over he wrapped his arms around them, hugging them tight so that their shared warmth might bring some relief. Now up close, he could see some truth to their complaints. Heidi's hands, reddened by digging the steps, were blistered. Klara, having slipped so many times at the back of the cart, had cut her knees and shins on the ice. Their clothes were also a mess. Both wore elegant town shoes bought by their industrialist Uncle in Bornheim. Flat soled and worn, they provided little traction. And although they were both wrapped in wool coats and scarves, the clothes were several sizes too small, useless against the freezing squalls punching up from the valley. It was also getting dark.

"Heidi, you'll have to take Klara back," he announced.

"What will you do?" she asked taken aback by his sudden change of mind.

"Try and find the road."

"It's over that big hill," said Klara pointing up the incline, "You certainly won't make it on your own."

"Then help me to the woodcutters track. After that you can go home."

"But even if you make it to the road, where will you go. There are no farms or houses. It's too far into town," added Heidi.

They were ahead of him; they always were. He hadn't thought it all through.

"I don't know. If I make it that far I can wave down a truck."

"What truck?"

"I don't know, what does it matter…"

"The only trucks on the road are French. If they look in the back of your barrow and see that a man's been stabbed, who will they blame? Probably you. That's no good. I don't want you arrested, tortured and left swinging from some lamppost," said Klara, letting her imagination get the better of her.

"Klara, where did you get such an idea?" replied Heidi, shocked by her macabre turn, "they're not monsters."

"Not monsters? That's not what Frau Schneider said."

"Klara, you shouldn't believe everything Frau Schneider says. Besides, everyone knows she's really a Czech and secretly a witch. Everywhere she looks she sees demons. Even her black cat is called Diablo."

"Her cat is called Diablo for a reason. She killed and ate a snake. A poisonous viper. How normal is that?"

After a further hour of painful pushing and scrambling, the crest of the hill was reached. Bruno, perspiring and fighting for breath, called a second stop. The two girls, relieved to have made it to the top, collapsed on a log. Heidi, thirsty, pulled down a branch from a fir tree to lick an icicle. When it stuck to her tongue she shrieked, pulling away so sharply as to bring down a cascade of snow over her head and shoulders. Klara, laughing at her distress, threw more snow at her. Surprising them all, the younger sister's mood had lifted; she was beginning to enjoy their adventure.

Bruno used the stop to tighten the chords around Chai's body that had come loose, some frozen so solid they were impossible to undo and retie. He removed his belt, wrapped it around Chai's legs and fastened it firm. On this sharper descent, he didn't want to drop his patient a second time.

"I'm ok now girls. You can go back now."

"What if we get lost?" shrugged Klara.

"With the tracks left by the cart, it's hardly difficult."

Heidi turned and pointed down the opposite side. A recent gale had hit the hillside. The descent, beset with gullies and fissures was strewn with fallen trees and rocks.

"And what do you think your chances are getting through that by yourself?"

"But we agreed," protested Bruno, raising his arms.

"And now we've changed out minds," added Klara, now as adamant to continue, as only twenty minutes previously, she had been adamant to go home.

Bruno, not wanting to be undermined a second time, wasn't going to concede easily. Walking down the incline he pushed through the undergrowth, searching for a safe route down. It was far steeper than he'd expected and the path, where he could find it, was crusted with ice as hard as a skating lake. He took his time, but it didn't need a lot of exploration to realise that the girls were right. The trees were closely packed and those that had blown over, impossible to climb over, let alone with a cart loaded with a body. And in the ravines where rivers cut through, deep chasms fell between the rocks. Bruno looked back up the slope. He could see their pale faces looking down, a touch smug, waiting for him to come back up and admit he was wrong.

Scrambling back up through the boulders, Bruno walked to where they were sitting, "Just to the road then. Then you go back."

They stood up together, shaking their heads in unison.

"No Bruno. We're in this together now. We're going all the way. They can string us all from the lampposts," replied Klara, first back to the cart.

They started on the descent. Bruno took up the rear, the ropes tied round his waist, heels prepared to dig into the ice as a brake. Once or twice the wheels hit a root or a ledge, bouncing Chai's body into the air, the impact causing a loud groan of complaint. Although they hated the sound of his moans, so pained, so macabre, it was a relief to know their patient was still alive.

The far side of the hill ran down to a river, the sharper valley walls channelling the cold artic winds that blew from the north. Gusts, cutting through the trees, shook the upper branches, covering them all in a fine mist of white. Scrambling down a steep bank between bushes they surprised a stag. With its antlers thick with lichen and moss it was so well camouflaged that Heidi almost fell over it. Taking fright the animal bellowed and sprinted off down the hillside. Bruno, ever vigilant for a free meal, made a mental note of their position. When their ordeal was over he'd return with a hunting rifle.

Midway down the valley they came across the entrance to an old tin mine. Inside the cave opening, amongst the rusted shovels and pickaxes, they discovered a bucket that had filled with rain water. It looked clean enough to drink. Bruno scooped a cup and held it close to Chai's lips, "Can you hear me? Water, drink."

There was no reply.

"He's foreign. Likely Serbian, maybe Slav. I don't think he understands us," said Klara.

"Comment allez vous?" tried Heidi.

"Oh, that's hopeless..." said Klara, rolling her eyes.

"Tu comprends?", her voice louder and matronly.

The edges of Chai's mouth weakly lifted.

The way down from the mine was fast. The mining company had built a gravel path that led from the mouth of the tunnel to the base of the hill. Carved out of the rocks to wheel down their trucks, it was so smooth that Heidi and Klara could run ahead of the cart with only the occasional nudge. Bruno, the rear brake on the rope, needed little effort to steer.

Reaching the base of the valley they found a stone bridge that crossed the river. A short track led to the road. Tire marks in the snow showed that trucks had recently passed.

"What do we do now?", asked Heidi looking left and right.

"We leave him in the road," said Bruno, removing the rope from his waist and retrieving his belt.

"What if a truck comes around the corner and hits him. Then he really will die," reflected Klara, "After all the effort we've put in it would be a bit of a waste. I was hoping for a happy ending."

"Nothing's going to hit him," said Bruno, reaching for the branch of a pine and dragging it ahead of the cart. Heidi helped him with a heavier log.

"Look out. We'd better get out of the road," said Klara, pointing anxiously down the hill.

Beyond the distant trees came the growl of approaching engines.

"Get back up the hill," shouted Bruno, ushering the girls back over the bridge. Reaching undergrowth above the road, they crouched and waited.

Within minutes flickering headlights came around the corner. Three lorries laboured up the incline. The one in front, seeing the low wall of branches and logs, slowed and stopped. A shout went out. A man jumped down from the cab and walked up the hill. It was Pierre. Approaching the barrier, his torch alighted on the wheeled cart and the body inside. He was stunned to see it was Chai.

"Chai! What? What happened to you?"

Chai, hearing him, struggled to lift his head.

Pierre pulled back the blanket and saw a dark patch of red.

"Les enfoirés!", he exclaimed as he reached into his coat. Incredulously he withdrew a gun, a German Mauser; the apogee of a year's worth of illicit trading. Looking into the trees he caught sight of small shadows scurrying into the undergrowth. He raised the barrel.

Chai's arm reached up and gripped his elbow, "No."

Chapter 39

Deputy headmaster, Bernard Fouche, woke with a skull-splitting headache, as if a company of rats were mauling his brain. He'd been up late drinking cognac and calvados with Jean-Pierre Bonnet. Jean-Pierre's three brother's had been killed in the closing months of the war after an enemy assault near the town of Cambrai. Only Jean-Pierre had come home uninjured; in fact miraculously and remarkably unscathed.

Bernard had nothing personal against Jean-Pierre returning to the village having survived the world's most brutal and tragic catastrophe. It was just the man's cloying mawkishness that needled him – an emotional incontinence that saw even the simplest of actions, performed with ludicrous sentimentality. He wore a virgin white handkerchief in a breast pocket, flamboyantly deployed to wipe away his crocodile tears. His brothers deaths, regrettable that they were, had become like the cogs of a music box, engaged at the pull of a lever, to crank out sympathy from the soppy village girls as he held court by the fireplace in Mathieu's smokey wine bar. In fact Bernard would rather be gnawed by flesh-eating ants than have to endure another of Jean Pierre's tedious battlefield monologues.

The story, that had the little ones wailing like stricken kittens, was how the eldest Bonnet son, Antoine, with selfless regard for his own life, had vaulted over the parapets to single-handedly rescue a stricken solider from no-man's land. Heading back through the shell craters he had been shot by a German sniper at the last hurdle, metres – no centimetres, even millimetres – from safety. Such an account played well with the callow and gullible, but the miserable truth was that he had died far from the lines in a seaside nursing home in Deauville. All death is distressing and worthy of being mourned, but there was nothing noble or heroic about gangrene from trench-foot.

The young and impressionable Annie Dragonet had proved the most susceptible to Jean Pierre's fanciful tales; "Un homme formidable, si brave et intrepide". And she had paid dearly for her naivety, losing her virginity to the sex-starved oaf on only his third night home. And before the month was out, Bernard was sure that Jean-Pierre would extend his conquests. Marie Fontaine, a dairy girl, and Lilliane Perrin, a pretty red-haired maid on the Forey estate, were clearly in the ex-soldier's sights. Bernard had caught the shy Perrin leaving sugared almonds on the man's doorstep, but the lazy lothario had got up so late the squirrels had scoffed them instead.

Of course, Bernard himself was not above censure. He was part of that fawning circus, readily plying the Homeric heroes with drinks and food to assuage his own guilt at having shamelessly stayed at home. What did it matter that he hadn't gotten himself obliterated because the military had rejected him after a medical examination had revealed a genetic deformity to his feet. Naturally the village had conveniently chosen to forget the humiliating sequel; that he had gone against the doctor's edict, enrolled anyway, been discovered by military police, ignominiously arrested and marched home. Now on the far side of the grand bookend of history, when the valiant and victorious where now coming home, he would be for ever classified within the ranks of the meek and mild, tainted with cowardice for failing to answer their country's' great calling.

Except he had answered his country's calling. For years his own sacrifices had been immense; the clothes and food he had donated, the money he had raised at village fêtes, the National Defence Bonds he had bought after selling precious heirlooms. All now amounted to a paltry credit of nought.

The material losses, painful that they were, he'd learnt to accept.

But subtle shifts in the village hierarchy had also debased his social standing. Bernard and his kind had been quietly relegated to the outer fringes of the community. Now essentially second-class citizens, they were no more than fawning sycophants, there to laugh at lame jokes, swoon over tall tales, wallets to speed the free flow of drinks.

Although Bernard had never been so stupid as to publicly show any resentment of the survivors' undoubtedly noble sacrifices – at unguarded moments, often alone late at night, unable to sleep for the drunken celebrations in the streets – he had let dark thoughts fester; fantasised that the allies had lost, even entertained the idea of a German victory. Warped and subversive maybe, but compared to the psychological hell he was being wrung through, might life not have been better under the Kaiser's cosh?

Bernard's wasn't the only fragile psyche rattled by the end of the conflict. Riding on the wave of euphoria, a surge of patriotic fervour had swept through the foundry factory and school. The headmaster, who had always kept his Franco-German campaign uniform on show despite the moths, had weighed in with this national zeal. Without consulting Bernard or the other teachers, he fired the gardener and janitor; no one could vouch for their true racial origins. Didier Cabrol, no more than a lowly kitchen porter in the "Grande Armée", replaced the janitor. Indolent, permanently drunk, with few practical skills, he was as much use as a horse-brush without bristles.

The celebratory spirit and flag-waving had also invaded the class rooms. Prints of Plato, Archimedes and Copernicus, had been crudely pinned over by pictures of General Foch, General Clemenceau and even the over-rated and puffed-up American, General 'Black Jack' Pershing.

Bernard's own edifying contribution, a meticulous map of the flora and fauna of their village, inlaid with rocks, pressed flowers and small rodent skulls, had been surreptitiously removed and replaced by a vulgar woven tapestry framed with crass bunting. Knitted together by the ladies of Castelnau, the hanging commemorated episodes from the heroic struggle. Yet again the fraudulent faces of the Bonnet brothers were centre stage, as if their actions alone had saved France. The children had cheered the change. Not that he blamed them – they were young and unworldly. Bernard thought it blatant vandalism.

Such was his dour mood when it was announced that there was yet another returning soldier peering in at the school gates. Turning to the hall Bernard cast a suspicious eye through the arched window in the entrance foyer that afforded a view to the drive. What he saw shocked him more than any over-jubilant Frenchman; it was Chai, the Indochinese (he corrected himself), the Siamese soldier.

"Sacré Bleu!", muttered Bernard under his breath, "what could he possibly want?" Although he felt a faint tremor of dread as to what it might be.

His first instinct was to have Didier, the new janitor, deal with it. Morning was never his finest hour, the man was sure to make a complete mess of it – stringing together something so wildly incomprehensible as to be sure to dispatch the Asian on his way.

Bernard took the steps to the basement. He found Didier so covered in grease and bewildered by boiler parts, he knew he'd be wasting his time. Cursing, he returned to the hall and paced down to the school gates himself.

They shook hands.

"I would have come earlier. I thought you might all be at lunch. But I had trouble at the crossing," said Chai.

"I know. The recent storms. The footbridge was swept away," replied Bernard, unashamed that his manner was brusque.

"I came to the school about nine months ago. I was staying at the farm at the château. We talked to the schoolchildren in the geography class..."

"Yes, yes, I remember," said Bernard, eyeing him up. He noticed that Chai, under his great coat was wearing a sling.

"You were wounded?"

"Hit in the shoulder."

He obviously didn't want to talk about it. It was the same with all those who returned with injuries, at least those that were not permanently debilitated. They considered themselves a different breed as if on the better side of some bold initiation test. It vexed Bernard, troubled him, that even Chai, a minor officer in a truck company –

a foreign truck company – might have some gallant tale to recount. When would his persecution end?

"How can I help you?"

"I was wondering if I might see Madame Boucher. Sandrine. If she was still at the school?"

Inwardly Bernard shuddered; his suspicions returned. Women, always women; he was just like the rest of them. They experience history's most seismic cataclysm and come away with a single base yearning.

"No, I'm afraid she's away. Gone to visit relatives in Lyon."

"When will she be back?"

"She said two days, maybe three. The problem, as always, is the trains. Still not back to normal..."

"Can I leave this for her?", said Chai handing over an envelope.

"Yes of course," said Bernard, "I'll make sure she gets it." He took the envelope and slid it into his jacket, curious as to its weight, but even now running through in his mind of how to dispose of it.

"You'll be returning home soon I expect?"

"In two weeks."

"Which ship?"

"The *Lancaster* from Marseilles."

"A British ship?"

"Yes."

"Good luck to you then," said Bernard, extending a hand, relieved that closure was in sight.

They shook hands again. For some reason Bernard followed this gesture with a salute. He had no idea why and immediately regretted it. A foolish Pavlovian habit he'd picked up to 'honour' their own returning men. Everyone did it, the whole village, all the time – but it embarrassed him, he didn't mean it; certainly not to a foreigner.

Chai returned the salute, turned and walked back down the lane.

Bernard rushed back inside. Closing the door he watched from the side window as Chai disappeared beyond the bend. Consciously counting to ten, to make sure, doubly sure he was gone, Bernard tore open the envelope. Inside he found a letter and a small package. Tissue wrapping revealed two tin figures – a dove and a white mouse. Childish worthless tat he thought. Crushing them ruthlessly in his hand, he dropped them to the bin, before turning his attention to the letter. The headline was enough, "My Dear Sandrine..." The impudence. Who was he to use the term "My"?. "My Sandrine!"

Too enraged to continue, Bernard folded the paper in half and shredded it into tiny pieces, letting the fragments fall into the wastebasket. Hot now, he began to perspire. Pulling at the side of his collar to cool his neck, he headed back down the hall. But his anger was not without a certain satisfaction; he had closed the door on the Asian decisively and hopefully for ever.

He was midway across the quadrangle to the masters common room and the prospect of tea, when glancing to the garden he was startled to catch the outline of Sandrine approaching the gate. He hadn't expected her back so early. She said she was visiting her aunt. An aunt, whom Bernard had told Chai, lived in Lyon, but in truth was no more than ten minutes away in Rivau; in fact closer to the station than the school. Embarrassed by his infantile lie and not wanting to be found out – she'd proved so unnervingly capable of reading his guilt in the past – he raced in the opposite direction. Finding an alcove at the end of the corridor, he backed into the shadows. But she was fast across the grass and seeing the edge of his nose poking out from behind a column, accosted him.

"Didier told me someone was asking for me?"

"Oh really...", said Bernard, awkwardly stepping out into the light.

"I was coming back across the field, I saw you were with someone."

"What I meant was, it was no one of consequence."

"He also mentioned a letter?"

"Oh indeed... Didier said that did he... Are you sure?", implying the man had imagined it.

"Bernard?"

"Yes, Sandrine." A trial of sweat broke from his brow and rolled down the side of his face. He knew it was only a matter of time...

"You're hiding something."

The accusation, so sharp, so soon, startled him, inducing an involuntary reflex that had him glance to the hall.

"Sandrine…" he pleaded, but she was gone.

Entering the hall, her eyes fell to the wastebasket, surrounded as it was with the flakes of torn paper. Bernard, in his haste to destroy the letter, hadn't been tidy. The pieces were everywhere. Bending to the floor to retrieve them, she discovered the crushed toys.

"What are these…?"

"Probably something dropped by the children…"

She turned to him, "Oh Bernard, what have you done?"

He tried to take her shoulder, sooth her, placate her. She pushed him away.

"Sandrine, you have to understand," his voice dropping in confidence, "I was only thinking of you, I was only protecting your interests."

She recoiled in shock, "My interests?"

"Listen to me Sandrine. I implore you. Calm yourself and listen to me. No one would deny that it wasn't laudable to fraternise with the soldiers… But enough. One has to respect boundaries, know where to stop. He's not from here. He's not one of us. Never will be. He couldn't care for you, not like people who know and love you could care for you. One day maybe you'll stop gazing dreamily over the horizon and open your eyes closer to home," he pleaded.

She turned to face him, her features fierce.

"I have opened my eyes. And what I see appalls me."

"You're young Sandrine. Young, beautiful, but also naive…"

She cut him short.

"They've been other letters haven't there?"

"No," the word escaping like a whimper, its weakness confirming his lie.

"Tell me the truth!"

"Yes."

"How many?"

"One or two…" he came clean, "Yes… others…"

Turning suddenly, Sandrine rushed from the hall. Bernard watched her go. He knew where she was going. He had a personal locker in the boot room. All the teachers had them. But it was securely fastened, a robust Bayard padlock over the clasp and a chain. He was confident he'd left it locked and she couldn't get in.

But Sandrine didn't intend to break the lock. She went instead to the janitors room, stepped over the now recumbent Didier and took a crowbar from the wall. Hurrying with the steel bar to the boot room, she jammed its head behind Bernard's locker and levered the entire line of cabinets from the wall. They fell with a loud crash bringing a rush of teachers into the room.

As the dust cleared, Sandrine, standing over the shattered remains, reached inside Bernard's cabinet. On a shelf at the back of a compartment she found what she was looking for – envelopes from Sens, Saint Dizier and Neustadt.

Chapter 40

Sandrine ran down the lane in the direction of the village. Bernard, fighting to catch up, was vainly trying to reach out to grab her arm and pull her back. Knowing he didn't have the stamina for a prolonged chase, he made a supreme leap for her shoulder, but was only able to snare a trailing lace from her sleeve. It tore loose. He was left holding the fluttering pink ribbon between his fingers, which unconsciously found its way to his nose. It carried her scent – jasmine.

"Don't do this Sandrine, I plead with you… It won't end well. It will only bring disrepute on us both…" he wailed, anxiously glancing up at the windows of houses they passed in case anyone was watching. Madame Sererin, nosiest of all and bullhorn to the village, lived two doors away on the right.

Deaf to his pleas Sandrine ran on. Bernard was forced to accelerate again. With his lungs gasping for air and limbs burning with the exertion, he came alongside a second time.

"Sandrine… listen to me… this has to end…"

Still she ignored him. Baffled, he glanced across, shaken to see real anguish and distress in her face. And then, from the corner of her eyes, tears, blown by the breeze, that flowed down her cheeks. He was stupefied. How could that man mean that much to her? Had he magicked some mysterious metaphysical hold over her? Could the tin figurines in the envelope have been that spiritual bridge?

Perplexed by her state, he took his eyes off the road for too long. An errant foot hit a rise in the road throwing him inelegantly off balance. Although well able to correct the misstep, he made it appear more severe than it was, pitching himself dramatically into a carefully identified bed of soft grass at the edge of the hedgerow.

Upside down in the undergrowth he lay still and feigned concussion; a last ditch attempt to arrest her reckless dash. A sharp barb in his back made him peer out. Way in the distance now, she hadn't even noticed his theatrics; in fact hadn't slowed. The main bend into the village was coming up. Surely she'd notice he wasn't there, surely she'd turn? She must turn…

She didn't.

A kilometre down the lane Sandrine reached the edge of the woods and paused for breath. With Bernard far behind now she had time to concentrate. Three tracks led off from the sandy junction. The first, wandering across the near meadows was dotted with sheep and goats. The second, leading across the broken footbridge where old man Barthez was hammering the planks, was otherwise empty. From the direction of the third route, the way to the château came the sound of bells. Ferraux, the estate manager, driving the dogcart, appeared through the trees. She ran towards him. Seeing her, he slowed and applied the brake.

"Monsieur Ferraux have you seen a soldier on the road?"

"No, not lately", replied Ferraux.

Sandrine described Chai, the young officer from the Thai company. Ferraux remembered the team, especially his fishing expeditions with their urbane and talkative Captain. Only the other night the countess had enquired after them; whether he thought they had made it through the conflict unscathed.

"He was just at the school," said Sandrine, impatiently curtailing Ferraux's narrative.

"The school? On what business?"

"He came to drop off a letter. I was out at the time. I wanted to see him before he left," she said, anxious not to appear over-agitated.

Ferraux brushed the bench and offered to take her to the main road. If the man was heading to the station at Channay – the only direct line to Lyon and eventually Marseille – it was surely the direction he would go.

With Sandrine now in the seat next to him, Ferraux turned the horse around and took a shortcut across the fields. The track, skirting the vineyards, traversed the hillside above the fishing lake, before descending again to the plain. Passing through gates at the edge of the estate they reached the crossroads to the village. Sandrine, standing on the edge of the cart, searched the dirt road in both directions. Chai was nowhere to be seen.

"He must have gone by the river path," said Sandrine.

"We could try the mill ford. Catch him at Montaron."

Ferraux patiently turned the cart again. As they headed back up the hill, Sandrine, twisting impatiently in her seat, peered down every path, every track, every gap through the trees, hoping for movement, or a recognisable silhouette. As the road entered the thick of the chestnut woods, her mind churned restlessly with the memories of the last six months; torments and misgivings crowding her thoughts.

Bernard's shadow loomed large.

It was the day of her birthday. Although she had told few of the day, Bernard had somehow found out about the occasion and bought her a gift. It came neatly wrapped in coloured tissue, the paper box tied with a bow. To add to Sandrine's discomfort and embarrassment, he had presented it to her in the teachers' lounge during a coffee break. With some trepidation she had opened the box to find an emerald ring (it had belonged to his mother), nestled on a pinkvelvet cushion.

Recalling these details in her mind made Sandrine physically squirm (the rocking of the ungainly dog cart didn't helped). Weak at the time, alone and unhappy, well aware her prospects were low, she had wavered.

At the time the other teachers in the room had applauded and cheered. And why not? Bernard had recently been promoted to Deputy Head of the School, his pay doubled, a cottage on the estate his home.

For many it was considered a fine and enviable match few would decline. Christine Moreau, sniffling into her handkerchief at the back of the room, had, only the year before, been on his list.

How close her life had come to ruin.

Of course, Bernard, too blunt and insensitive to let small obstacles stand in his way, wasn't the kind of man to take 'no' (especially from a woman) for an answer. After all, Sandrine's reply; "deeply flattered but also surprised", with a rider that indicated that she wasn't quite ready "to provide the answer his proposal undoubtedly deserved," hadn't been completely unequivocal. In Bernard's ever scheming, long term game, 'quite' measured by time, was no more resolute than a castle of sand on a beach. Inevitably it would be breached. Confident that cold, heartless logic would prevail – status, position, security – Bernard never wavered. To all intents and purposes his demeanour remained unchanged. He was jovial, he was chatty, even playful. People began to think they were already married. Yet in all his actions, knowing deep down inside that she had rejected him, Sandrine sensed an obsequious insincerity in his behaviour. In staff meetings he appeared all too eager to gauge her opinion; yet he needlessly scrutinised and questioned everything she said.

That obstructiveness came to a head when Bernard first learnt of Sandrine's plan to have the colonial troops speak to the schoolchildren. Initially he had pretended to go along with the scheme, claiming that he had added his enthusiastic support in meetings with the headmaster and the school governors. It was only later, when Sandrine had met with the cleric's wife, that she learnt that he had actively campaigned to undermine the project. Bernard's 'concern', which came quite close to swaying the older, more conservative members, was the suggestion that such an event might be corrupting for young and impressionable minds.

Not content with his meddling before the event, Bernard's acts of disruption continued right up to the day. His aggression against the Algerian, Farid, had been unforgivable. At the time Sandrine had wanted to shout out to stop his needless interference, but had had to be restrained by one of the other teachers. Of course she wasn't so disingenuous as to be blind to Farid's mischief, but if the school children were to learn real insights about people and cultures, honesty, in her mind was paramount. And if ideals, ideas of self determination and independence were part of that mix, that was their life, their struggle, their future. Equality, justice and the fight against tyranny; weren't such values engraved within their own national anthem? Weren't those the maxims the Colonial troops espoused when they were laying down their lives for the Empire?

The special lunch for the visitors had been arranged by Sandrine and a mother of one of the school children. The original plan was to have everyone, teachers and speakers, mix at a single large table. Yet again Bernard had needlessly intervened. Fussing that the ground was too uneven for two tables close together, he had positioned the second at some considerable distance from the first, in a separate, isolated courtyard; almost out of sight and certainly out of earshot.

Protesting against this overt segregation, Sandrine, together with two of the younger teachers, had made a point of seating themselves at the second table. Poetic justice had put her place opposite Chai. Despite a look of obvious fury from Bernard, she resolved to remain, trying her best to animate those around her despite their timidity. As the conversation gradually relaxed, the opportunity to talk more informally with the men, reinforced all the emotions that had welled up inside her when she had first listened to their accounts in the classroom. Siam, with its temples, rivers and palaces, had seemed especially magical. She'd been enchanted by its description. Chai she'd found undeniably charming and handsome. She though his complexion so smooth and beguiling she had wanted to reach out and touch him. And in the churchyard that curiosity had been dangerously rewarded. But she hadn't, as Bernard had so pathetically suspected, been in love with him. Affection, certainly, but not infatuation.

Chai's world, chalked on the board, represented everything that her narrow life wasn't. It was freedom – seeing the unknown – the liberty to wander and dream.

Released from the suffocating behavioural codes of propriety, epitomised by the priggish, uptight Bernard Fouche, there was another world beyond the saccharine prison that was their valley.

They reached the outskirts of Montaron. Ferraux drove to all the approaches and exit roads in and out of the village. They stopped at the post office and made enquiries; the Asian gentlemen hadn't been seen.

After this further disappointment Sandrine asked to be dropped off in the main square. Thanking Ferraux for his help she said she would wait; they were possibly ahead of him.

She found a seat at a tavern. A waiter appeared, and she ordered a lemonade.

Two hours later she was still seated there, her lace handkerchief damp with her tears.

Chapter 41

Pramot never volunteered to stay in the office. But equally, when the subject of the Victory Parade, "Les Fêtes de la Victoire", had first been raised two weeks earlier, in which one hundred of their countrymen would be participating, he was the only one not to raise his arm, or show any great enthusiasm to attend. As numbers were limited, the senior staff decided that he should remain behind to man the building. He wasn't offended. With a hatred of crowds and public gatherings, he was relieved to be left to his desk, finding comfort not in ranks of preening soldiers, but sets of regimented work trays. And it wasn't as if there was nothing to do. Today their men might be marching proud for king and country, but tomorrow that dream would be over and all would be heading home. Then the real work began.

If there was one thing Pramot had learnt from the war, his war, from the commanding position of his lofty seat in the dusky annex office, it was procedure. Any task, however complicated, could be broken down, into smaller, more manageable units; motion study was the theory. Yes, cases and trunks might have filled the hallway downstairs, but who had checked the shipping schedules, indexed the list of departures, prepared the letters of authorisation?

Notebook and pencil in hand, the station chief resolved to start on the ground floor, aiming to count the tea chests and make a note of their sizes. He was heading downstairs and crossing the landing when he noticed the door to the kitchen was open. Pramot had never trusted the food in the larder, but the thought of having the space all to himself was too tempting an opportunity to pass up. Better still, on a sideboard covered by a cloth he discovered leftovers from an official dinner. Helping himself to a cut of ham, pickled cucumber and a slice of cherry gateau, he sneaked in a glass of St Emilion despite the early hour. He didn't really like Bordeaux and the throbbing of a coming headache reminded him why.

Descending to the ground floor, Pramot's forage for documents, started well. He was pleased to find that several of the secretaries had already begun typing up registers of men and equipment. In the clerk's office he found train timetables and shipping departure dates. From such sources it wouldn't take him long to prepare a list of first leavers. Yet despite this favourable beginning, the deeper he probed, small but fundamental oversights remained. Decisions they had agreed weeks ago, hadn't been cleared with ministers in Bangkok. More frustrating still, permissions and forms had yet to be stamped by the relevant authorities; a discovery in itself that was enough to bring on an outburst of expletives. All were painfully aware that in the post-war lull, even obtaining something as simple as a hat chit, needed double stamped consent from high office.

Still too enfeebled to spar with French bureaucrats, Pramot's first instinct was to send a telegram east, to rouse Bangkok and spur the lethargic bureaucrats into action. Dragging himself upstairs, he opened the door onto the now silent communications room and realised that the telegraph girls had also gone to the parade. And even though he was proficient at morse, he wasn't entirely confident how to work the equipment alone. Before he'd used an instruction manual. But without the help of the usually solicitous secretaries, it was impossible to find within the overfilled cabinets.

Descending again to the depths, Pramot slumped down in his chair. The quiet and solitude he'd craved morphed into boredom and irritation. "Go, go and enjoy yourselves, I'll have it done in a day," he had bragged to his associates. Yet the striking of the clock downstairs chided him that already a morning had gone and not a single square of his time chart was filled.

Against his better judgement, it was curiosity that drew Pramot into the street. He heard the boom of the guns at the Porte Maillot that signalled the start of the victory procession, followed by the trumpets of the Republican Guard as they turned into the Avenue de la Grande Armée. His only intention was to get some air, have some exercise, clear his mind, restructure his thoughts, before bouncing back to the fray; he had no intention of mingling or staying.

Although the Legation was some distance from the centre of the parade at the Arc de Triomphe, Pramot was shaken by the amount of people in the road. To avoid them he took a side street he knew behind an apartment block. Running along the Rue Decamps it turned into the Rue Saint Didier before passing a favourite coffee shop, La Petite Marquise along the Avenue Victor Hugo. He paused beside it. In the back of his mind he'd planned ordering a café noir and taking a seat in the sun to watch the passing masses. But it was closed and there were no tables outside.

Disappointed, Pramot attempted to turn around and retrace his steps, but the crowd, already several thousand strong was so tightly packed it proved difficult to move against the flag-waving tide. More alarming still, he realised that his change of direction might be misconstrued as being uncivil, against the 'spirit' of the day, courting a corrective 'patriotic' punch in the face.

Reluctantly surrendering to the mood of ebullience, Pramot let himself be borne along by the throng, their pace, spurred on by the cheers and shouts erupting from the rooftops, becoming more strident.

Reaching the Place de Dome the surge of the crowd doubled. Up ahead, a contingent of cavalry had positioned themselves at the crossroads to calm and control the flow. Piercing whistles blew as they diverted the people away from the square to an adjacent alleyway to ease the congestion. This constricting bottleneck grew narrower before suddenly emerging into the open; the release like unblocked water from a drain.

Chestnut trees lined this central avenue, its lamp posts and telegraph poles heavy with red and white flags. On both sides of the approach, the audience was already twenty to thirty thick and tens of thousands long. To get a better view over the heads, several people had climbed into the upper branches of the trees. Others balanced precariously on newspaper kiosks and bandstands. A dedicated group had come prepared with steps and homemade periscopes. A cavalry Guardsman, elegant in a plummet helmet and silvered breastplate, hoisted a pretty girl into his saddle, giving her a sight line all the way to the obelisk on the Place de la Concorde.

Pramot, recovering from the squeeze at the Place de Dome was yet more horrified by the density of the hordes on the avenue. On his right a line of drummers started up, the militant sonorous beat, "BAM, BAM, BARAM," deafening to his over sensitive ears.

Somewhere in front of him, the first ranks of the procession went past. A deafening roar went up, starting from the first row and rippling to the back like a giant wave.

"Foch! Joffre!, Clemenceau!", screamed the multitudes, "Nos grands vainqueurs!"

The crowd pressed forward, scrambling for a gap in the wall of bodies. Pramot, helpless and crushed up amongst them, felt himself lifted by the collective pack. Rolled within the swell, a chance glance caught a brief flash from a helmet as the French cavalry marched over a crest.

And then from the left a second, louder tumult burst out, "Regardez Les Americans, voici les Yankees, et là, General Pershing!"

The excitement saw another rush from the rear. Arms and elbows jabbed into Pramot's back, then something sharper; the knuckle of an old ladies' cane grazing his ear. Taking cover from a second celebratory swing he didn't even dare to peer out. An army of flags; the eagle of the third infantry followed by the stars and stripes, fluttered by like a distant armada of ships.

And then after the drums, a more fantastical sound, eerie and ringing; the bagpipes of the Royal Scots Fusiliers.

"L'Angleterre, et l'Ecosse!", bellowed the masses. An even louder cheer came from behind. Men lined the balconies and rooftops of the Hotel Astoria, waving Union Jack flags as the Royal Marines appeared at the head of the regal British contingent.

"Tow Row, Tow Row, Two Row", went the Grenadiers, as the British regimental colours passed under the grey arch, their flags, more than two hundred, deep crimson and gold.

And then came the dominion soldiers, the Canadians, followed by the Australians, New Zealanders and Indian regiments; stoic lines of Hindus, Sikhs and Gurkhas.

"Regardez là-bas! C'est qui? Les Indiens ou les Arabes?"

Again more pressure, the constriction unbearable and from all sides. Even below his waist Pramot felt besieged; a child thumped his knees and squeezed through his legs.

Unable to move and suffocating from the press of people, Pramot felt himself shoved to the right. The trunk of a tree reared up; an abrupt and unexpected refuge. Desperately he reached out and clung to its base.

"Là bas les Italiens, et les Japonais!", screamed a young seamstress, a crown of blue, red and white ribbon laced through her curls.

"Bravo! BravOOH," bellowed a fishmonger from Orleans, waving a striped handkerchief.

Loosening his collar and grasping for air, Pramot looked up at the sky, the white frothy clouds spinning dreamily like a child's kaleidoscope. Still the crowd howled, "Les Polonais, Les Grecs." "WHAM, Wham, Bham, BAHWHAM," went the drums, the echo reverberating between his ears and rattling his brain. Pale now, the blood draining from his head, his vision deserted him. As his legs collapsed Pramot slid down the trunk, falling in a heap at its base. With his eyesight gone, his remaining senses, as if panicked, amplified. Dense smells surrounded him; the stifling reek of stale breath, sweat and tobacco smoke especially pungent. Then closer, a more familiar and unsettling stench; someone was pissing against the far side of the trunk, the yellow trickle seeping around the edge of the roots to collect near his boots.

Still the air reverberated with the cries and shouts of the people. More soldiers, horses, bands and flags passed. Somewhere his people were in there, marching ten abreast and ten deep; Captain Luang Ramritthhirong proud at its head, uniforms brushed, belts and boots polished, royal decorations ablaze on breast pockets.

Pramot, arms locked around the trunk - limbs trembling, head throbbing, ears ringing - saw none of it.

Chapter 42

The car, a dark blue, open-top Darracq, nearly hit him. If it hadn't been for the piercing scream from its horn, Chai might not have seen the speeding machine weaving through the handcarts and food stalls of the Arab market behind the old port. Leaping back from the road, he glared at the car as it stopped just inches away, its tyres sliding on the greasy cobbles. A greater shock by far was recognising the driver. For it wasn't a brash, imperious European behind the elegant wheel, but the Algerian, Mamet, he'd met at the Hotel Estelle at the beginning of their tour.

Oblivious to complaints from the passersby, Mamet steered up onto the pavement, the car's front bumper nudging a stacked tray of piled melons, which he then drove over and squashed. A carelessness that brought more howls of condemnation from the outraged fruitsellers.

"Chai!" yelled Mamet, fumbling with the handbrake as he got out from behind the wheel, his face beaming and proud. Walking around to the far side of the car, he opening the passenger door and ushered Chai into the side seat.

"You live!", he exclaimed, wrapping his arm around Chai's back, "You live!" he repeated, pulling him closer.

"You and me," he gestured, "will celebrate!"

They drove to the Hotel Dieu near the medieval citadel and parked up in front of the entrance lobby scattering the bellboys and chauffeurs. Striding into the palatial Belle Époque dining lounge, the flustered maître d'hôtel had tried to persuade the two newcomers to a discreet alcove at the back of the lounge, screened by a partition. But Mamet ignored him and striding outside took a prime place on the front terrace overlooking the waterfront.

"Merci , ici ça va très bien," exclaimed the Algerian, stretching out his legs and nestling back in the silk cushions.

"Mamet, I have to tell you now," whispered Chai, panicked by the affluence of the place, "I haven't a sou. Not even for water."

"Water? We didn't come here for water!" roared Mamet.

Further rattling the supercilious head waiter, Mamet ordered champagne, Tattinger, and a dozen oysters, "Huîtres en gelée, et assurez-vous qu'ils sont frais!"

For Mamet, as evidenced by his new car and his sharply tailored gabardine suit, was now a wealthy man. His family's tobacco business, back in Turkine, Algeria – closed and abandoned since the beginning of the war – had just received a massive 100,000 franc advance for five hundred thousand 'Freedom, Victory', cigarettes. Their village, humming with activity, was now awash with tobacco leaves, drying racks and rolling tables. And in their father's house, a big fat Fichet safe was stuffed with promissory notes from Le Crédit Lyonnais. Their business had enough employment for every home in their valley; even the old folk, women and children from neighbouring Hassi had crossed the hills to help with production.

But as they drank through a second bottle under the languid palm trees in the garden of the majestic hotel, Chai was to discover that it wasn't just money that had brought fortune and happiness to their family. Against all the odds, Mamet had found his lost nephew and brought him home.

"Although, at the time, to be honest, there wasn't much left of him..." muttered Mamet, stubbing out a cigar.

Rami had only been in uniform for a month before being moved to a camp near Amiens. Their company, less that a hundred strong, had been combined with a regiment of Senegalese Tirailleurs and sent to staging posts close to the front lines. Left for two summer months, they sat bored in dry, dusty trenches, ever vigilant of attack, but up against nothing more taxing than fleas, rats and lice. After a third month of inaction, they were pulled from the line. Navigating back to their base they lost their way and strayed into heathland between the French and British zones. Someone shot at them - maybe one of their own. Those at the back panicked and made a run to the shelter of a creek, unaware it was mined. In the string of explosions that followed, more than half were killed. They thought Rami was dead too. He had been laid out on the open ground with all the other casualties. With night fast approaching, only the actions of an indolent gravedigger had saved his life. Impatient to get his last grave dug before dark, the man had knocked a bottle over the edge and heard a pained groan from inside. A doctor was called. Finding a faint but miraculous pulse, medics had Rami lifted out and stretchered back to a field hospital.

Mamet was scouring the camps of Picardy when he eventually managed to track his brother down to a small provincial hospital near Arras. White as a ghost, emaciated, his limbs shattered and in plaster, he was unconscious, close to death.

Medical opinion was pessimistic. They had seen such cases before. Patients might appear 'technically' alive, the doctors advised, but without sustenance, food or water, they quickly faded away. And Rami hadn't eaten anything since he'd come in. Apart from making him comfortable for those last few hours or days, there was little they could do. Offering Mamet their apologies and condolences, they took their leave.

"What could I do, Chai? I sat by his bed, cleaned his wounds and dripped sugared water through tubes into his throat and cried. Of course I never doubted he would make it, but Rami did nothing to encourage my faith. I tell you it was hard. Really hard... The attendants had already lined up his bed for others and every time I turned my back, even for a trip to the loo, they tried to move him to the dead zone.

And then our family came. Of all things, old man Rashid turning up, uncle Adil Rashid who had never seen a pond, let alone a sea, you'd think that would so shock and amaze him, it would induce some kind of reaction? Yet there was nothing. Rami remained as frozen as a block of ice."

Mamet stretched across the table to refill their glasses.

"Then in our darkest hour, when even my hope had started to ebb, came Fatima. With a voice like an angel, singing a verse from a childhood rhyme so coarse it would make you blush, brought the first hope. A small flicker of one eyelid. A movement as fleeting as a fly's antenna," said Mamet, pinching his index finger to the base of his thumb.

"Twitches in his fingers were next. Weeks later, feeling the touch of Fatima's fingers running through his hair, Rami's eyes, Praise to the Lord, opened."

"A long time has passed since those dark days. Six months at least," said Mamet with a big infectious grin, wiping the moisture from his eyes.

"You will meet them both. As a guest at their wedding."

Mamet had chosen the ground carefully. In his new car he and Chai had driven up and down the coast road surveying the beaches. Close to the fishing village of Le Redonne they had come across the perfect location; a sheltered rock promontory perched above the bay, with a view towards islands. On its far side, dazzlingly white limestone rocks fell sharply to the sea, the waters of the cove a deep azure blue as rich as Murano glass. Two tall umbrella pines provided shade over an arena flanked by Cyprus trees, which – Mamet claimed – formed an auspicious circle. Mamet and Chai returned the next day with sickles and spades, to clear the area of thorns and wild lavender and level the ground.

In the city they found a military surplus store. Its owner, having developed a loathing for the mountains of green and khaki he was accumulating, was only too pleased to get rid of some of the tents, tables and benches. From an army canteen, they were able to borrow pots, pans and two portable stoves.

It was a simple approach from the main road; a leisurely walk through vineyards, ending with short scramble down a bank, but Mamet thought it more theatrical to bring his guests in on boats. The day of the event was rougher than expected. To get to the cove, the boats had to round a headland exposed to winds and high seas.

Low in the waves, the men had had to use their shoes to bail out the water.

From the beach, steps led up to a platform where tables and chairs were laid out. From the track near the road, great carts of food arrived. Food that staggered Chai by its breath and colour, inured as he was to scant choice and dull, unpalatable tones. A large steel cauldron, was filled with grilled mutton, rabbit and merguez. On reed mats lay fresh olives, salted fish, flat breads and figs. Either Mamet's home valley was indeed a veritable Eden, or more likely he had clandestine underworld contacts.

Knowing few of the guests, Chai headed for the grill. He took a skewer of lamb, some hummus and flat bread and retired to a quiet seat under the pines. A move that didn't escape the notice of his host. Mamet bounded over to his remote corner and grabbing Chai's plate, opened his arms wide as if offended.

"What is it my friend, that you choose to hideaway in the shade like some miserable hermit?"

Chai was embarrassed that his actions had been misconstrued.

"I didn't want to offend you, Mamet, far from it. Not knowing anyone I didn't want to get in the way of your guests..."

"Guests? Aren't you my guest?"

Hauled from the shade into the limelight, Chai was introduced to a succession of uncles, aunts, cousins and nephews. There was a tailor, a book-keeper, a tax inspector and an iman. A louche man in a peach suit and a fez, traded sugared almonds and gemstones out of Meknes. A short fat man in a ill-fitting djellaba, ran freighters and cargo ships out of Ceuta and was in line for a lucrative Renault concession.

Pulled from the outer circle to the inner court, Chai was both moved and unsettled to be seated close to the wedding couple. Fatima was indeed an extraordinary beauty. Lithe, long-haired, olive skinned, with amber eyes that gleamed like fireflies. She didn't say much, but when she did, her smile lit up with a brilliance that was like a lamp going on; small wonder that her presence had indeed been enough to wake the dead.

Chai congratulated Rami both on his bride and his recovery. He thought his turnaround from deathbed to wedding bed nothing short of miraculous.

"Mamet also tells very colourful accounts of your own experience. What was it again – knifed by a Frenchman, rescued by German children, brought back to life by an Austrian veterinary surgeon?"

Chai laughed it off; it was just a playground graze compared to Rami's horrendous injuries.

"My uncle speaks very warmly of you. He put it down to providence that he bumped into you again," said Rami.

"He nearly ran me down with his car."

"I'm sorry for that. He's only just got the thing. He's better with camels and donkeys."

Rami introduced Chai to Fatima's mother, Aysha. He could see where the daughter had got her eyes from. Despite her older years, the mother's irises glowed with a brighter luminance; an entrancing, penetrative gaze that seemed to bore straight through his soul, instilling both comfort and unease. Chai could see her leaning close to her son-in-law and whispering in his ear.

Rami lent over to Chai to translate, "She says you're also very handsome. Though a bit thin. Back home she has a second daughter. Not quite as beautiful as Fatima, but close."

"I would be honoured to meet her. But sadly, next week, I sail for home."

"She already knows that. And she also knows you would have a better future if you followed her advice, returned to her village and married her young daughter. But such is fate. You will go east not west. She has already foreseen that."

"And I hope she saw an easy journey?"

"Oh yes, an easy journey. Good weather, calm seas. Very calm. But with one last ordeal…"

Chai shifted uneasily in his seat; he'd never felt that comfortable with the pronouncements of seers or prophets – if that was her gist. Near his home, such a man had sat crossed-legged on a rock and accosted those on the way back from school. The warning was always the same; unless he, Chai, devoted his life to the Dharma, he would fall down a hole and be eaten by a giant squid. Seeing as they lived far from the ocean, he never took the omen very seriously. Yet Aysha's words, delivered in a calm, measured tone, proved more unsettling. Skeptical as he was, he still found it hard to resist her.

It took Mamet, catching the lull in conversation, to come to Chai's aid, "Come on Mama, don't give him that look, you know you'll only scare him."

"What's wrong? Is it my fault that I was born with this curse. I say what I've seen! I don't make it up... unlike the shameless cheats who fill the stalls in the Meknes Medina," she snapped back.

"But what you see might not help."

"Oh it will help alright..." she added with a mischievous glint in her eye.

"Then tell me. I was hoping for an easy time of it," replied Chai, an image of himself lazing on the aft deck dispelled by the grim augury, "It's better that I know."

"Oh you will survive," added Aysha light heartedly, "but not without help."

Aysha's stone – opaque, a grubby hue of brown – didn't look that remarkable. Rami folded it into Chai's open hand as if offering him a lozenge to overcome a stubborn cough.

"What is it?" asked Chai.

"A guardian, a protector. It was mine, now it will be yours".

Chai, touched by the gift, broke a smile. He took the stone and rolled it playfully in his palm. The far side was plainer still; comically so. But glancing by Rami to Aysha, he caught a frown of such profound severity that he quickly wiped the grin from his face.

"Just like all the rest..." she signed disapprovingly, "Don't you recognise the beauty inside?"

He couldn't. But somehow the stone felt strangely heavy in his grasp. It was then he understood the magnanimity of what was being offered. It was no small gesture; he would need it.

The tables were cleared, the musicians played, the women danced and the men stamped their feet and clapped.

Chai, rattled by his encounter with Aysha, used the interlude to make a break from the main party. Sitting on the beach, he watched the waves roll against the rough pebbles and listened to the shifting waters in the gullies and creeks. Close by, a shoal of fish, chased by an unseen predator, broke from the water – their fine trails glistening in the moonlight. Further out a breeze blew across the surface, the rough ripples catching the moonlight and morphing into fantastic shapes. Sometimes he saw a whale, sometimes a bird and sometimes the arms of a siren.

A puff of smoke dispelled the magic. Mamet, smoking a massive cigar, fell to the ground at his side.

"You know, when I first met you lot in the Marseilles Hotel, I thought you'd never get through…"

"So you thought we'd just give up and go home?"

"No, no, nothing like that. I didn't want to suggest you guys weren't up to it… It's just that, god in heaven, that war was brutal, the devil himself couldn't have staged it…"

"Well, you'll be glad to know, Mamet, we also took bets on your chances."

"And undoubtedly you foresaw great success?"

"Sadly not. Four to one. We thought your chances were zero."

"Here's to utter hopelessness then," said Mamet, puffing a disc of smoke across the water.

Chapter 43

Chai stowed his kit bag and backpack in steel lockers in the hold. Finding the windowless cabins airless and stinking of coal dust and fumes, he left the men playing cards and took the stairs to the top deck.

Walking to the stern of the ship, Chai leaned on the railings to take in a last view of the harbour. Across the waterfront, fishermen lined the rocks at the base of the old Bourbon fortress, its crumbling walls a soft pink in the evening light. Higher on the hill, a statue of the Madonna crowned the bell tower of the basilica of Notre dame de la Garde, its sooty dome circled by flocks of grey gulls.

Lights came on over the city, the harbourfront glow reflecting in the still waters of the bay. On the quayside below, barrels and sacks of grain were still being loaded. From the back of a horse cart a merchant threw a last basket of chickens. Chai caught the alarmed shriek of the birds as they rolled upside down in mid air.

Chai and his men hadn't enjoyed their last weeks in Marseille. Crammed in a remote guesthouse to the west of the city and out of sight of the sea, it was barren of streets and cafes to walk and explore. Only when the wind ceased its mournful moaning could they hear the ships horns from beyond the hills, reminding them that deliverance, their watery road home, was close. To escape the drab monotony, most made the long hike along the dusty train tracks, or took the one, unreliable bus into town. In was on one of those flights from boredom that Chai had chanced on Mamet in the market. Helping with his party and wedding had provided a much-needed distraction. But it hadn't been the only late night Mamet had organised and he'd needed the rest of the week to recover.

When the Algerians had sailed back home to Algiers, Chai had been there to see them off. Saying their farewells, Aysha had gripped his arm as if he were a jewelled casket and held him with one of her probing, prescient stares. A gaze that was just as formidable as the first time; severe but also filled with unexpected tenderness, bringing him close to tears. Pulling him nearer with her claw like fingers, she rushed through a last interrogation; "Have you kept the stone safe? Is it close? Is it with you at all times?"

Chai promised it was.

"Sleep on deck" was her last ominous admonishment before Mamet stomped impatiently down the gangway, grabbed her arm and pulled her on board.

"Enough of your babble, mother. Either bewitch him and take him with us, or we leave you behind!"

After the long steep walk back to their lodgings – a landscape so arid and bland Chai had started counting the steps – he planned to take a cold bath and retreat to his bed to escape the unbearable heat. Heading to his room he met the concierge on the landing who was coming up with a note. She told him that a French officer was waiting downstairs. Chai's first instinct, dusty and bathed in sweat that he was, was to lie, "Tell him I'm out and won't be back until evening."

The woman was already halfway back down the stairs when Chai reconsidered. French bureaucrats weren't easily put off. Inevitably they'd request a second meeting at a yet more inconvenient time and place; delaying would only prolong the agony.

"I've changed my mind, Madame Sorel. Tell him I'll be down in five minutes."

Dragging himself down the stairs to the basement, Chai was surprised and relieved to find that the 'officer' was Pierre. Out of uniform he was dressed like a bank clerk. In fact in a suit so finely cut and tailored (most likely by his father's Parisian atelier business), it was Chai's turn to look slovenly.

They had to make a furious dash through olive groves to catch the rare afternoon bus. Arriving in town, Chai was able to show Pierre a café in the Arab quarter owned by one of Mamet's inner circle. A fresh catch had come in that morning and was laid out on a marble slab in the café's basement. Out to spoil themselves, they ordered clams, sardine and gurnard. The proprietor prepared and cooked the fish stew on an open fire in the street, leaving street urchins and gulls to fight over the scraps.

Late in the evening the two walked the streets. They chanced on the same subterranean club that Chai had visited with Mamet. Thinly populated by a handful of loyal locals and without the smoke, noise and band, it had lost its decadent seedy appeal. The lurid pink lips of the proscenium were now disguised under layers of thick ochre-brown paint. On stage a fumbling magician dragged cats from a hat and juggled a trio of hamsters.

After his discharge from the army, Pierre had set off west for Brittany to retrieve his Breton beauty. Prepared for an unpleasant showdown with the girl's brutal and abusive husband, he had knocked on the door with some trepidation, expecting a fight. But Cecile, to his relief, was alone. Fate had been kind to the young pair. The drunken fisherman, never one to heed warnings from either family or official, had been out fishing beyond the islands of Belle Ile. Holed by a periscope from a submerged German submarine, his boat had gone down in seconds and he'd drowned.

After a period of mourning – which had been fortuitously brief because few had lamented the man's passing – they planned to get married. In Paris, Pierre had found a studio apartment in Montparnasse. He wanted to continue his studies. His former professor at Paris Diderot had offered him a second chance to study sociology and politics. To help pay the rent his father had taken on Cecile as a seamstress in his tailoring atelier. Partly due to all the interventions Pierre himself had needed in the war, the business still had a mountain of 'favours' to process. After saving enough, Pierre hoped to be sent East. He had connections with a trading company in Hué. From there he hoped to travel to Angkor in Cambodia.

"Come by my door," said Chai, "We can sail there together down the Mekong."

Drunk and filled with mischief they wandered down to the waterfront and finding a bar on the promenade, ordered cassis and anise pastis. It was late in the evening when they finished up. Running to the station, Pierre only just made the last train north. His parting gift was a last bottle he'd kept from the cellars of Chateau Forey. Chai, thanks to the ever generous Mamet, was able to return the gesture with a box of Turkine 'Victory' cigarettes.

Hearing the screams of the dockworkers shouting up to the crane drivers, Chai was thrown back to the days of their first arrival. The memory was now so distant in his mind that it came back faded and sepia tinted as if from a news cutting. Standing at the railings of the *Aeneas*, they'd stared down with nervous apprehension at the uncertain world they were just then about to enter. Now those gawping, frightened faces had been rudely displaced by coarser, tougher, hopefully more sanguine selves, heading back in the opposite direction. Elation and relief were part of that feeling. Dragged through the ruins and horrors of Europe they'd lost any lingering infatuation with the so-called 'civilised' world and longed to be home.

There was talk they'd be received as heroes. Both the palace and the War Ministry had sent congratulatory telegrams, thanking and praising the men for their dedication and service. Chai had been especially commended for his leadership and conduct. He'd acquitted himself well, the men had liked and respected him and even in their bleakest moments – terrorised either by shell fire or ghouls – he hadn't panicked or run.

Of course, Chai harboured darker secrets that few were aware of. Irrespective of the rights and wrongs he'd killed a man. Worst still the act had been outside the sanctioned slaughter of the war and his victim had been a Frenchman. Hospitalised for three weeks after his knife wound, Chai had been lucky that Pierre had been there to cover his back. First on the scene he'd been able to clean up the evidence and wash away the blood. Finding Bruno and the two girls, Pierre had befriended them with canned food and sweets to secure their silence, even though he sensed it unnecessary, as the two girls had already asked anxiously as to the health of the 'Ausländer'. Pierre reassured them that their Ausländer was well and recovering. Indeed recovering so fast, that a fortnight later, Pierre had spied Chai walking to the staff sergeant's office at the entrance of the hospital and intercepted him.

"Where are you going?" asked Pierre, troubled by the wreath of notes in his hand.

"What does it looks like, Pierre? To the staff sergeant."

"Why?"

"To hand in my report."

Pierre, taking Chai by the arm, had taken him aside.

"And you think you'll find reason behind that door, Chai?"

"But if the farm is searched and a body's found, they'll blame the children."

"They won't blame the children..."

"How can you be so sure?"

"Because they won't find anything. I've seen to it all."

And he had seen to it all. With Bruno and Born's help, Pierre had lifted the dead man into a truck, driven to a forest and dumped the body down a mine shaft. Back at the farm, Pierre had been meticulous. All the evidence of the fight – from the broken floor boards, the bloodied pitch fork, the knife and the gun – were either repaired or removed. Assembling the men, Pierre had rehearsed the 'correct' version of events; that Chai had been shot by deserters, who had then escaped through the woods. A simple lie that ensured that no one came snooping. In the light of recent actions against several Algerian renegades, Pierre was well aware of the prejudice against foreigners.

Chai and Pierre had fought with enough bull-headed injustice after Captain Sumet's death. Not only had the hospital staff misplaced his body, but they'd kept no record of where he'd been buried. Scouring the cemeteries of the area, it had taken a week of questioning and searching to locate the mass grave. Chai had been distraught that the Captain hadn't received a last Buddhist blessing. Because of it Sumet's spirit roamed lost. The men still sensed his presence, shifting ceaselessly around outside their tents in the early morning, checking their equipment, buckles and kit. And that had been their lasting impression of him; happiest with his notebooks, fact sheets and graphs. For Sumet, introvert and intolerant, hadn't had the temperament to survive the daily onslaught of setbacks and petty defeats that came with command. His was a more cultivated calling; bibliophile, collector of curio, fossils or rocks. His time on the Forey estates had been his only fond memory.

The company's litany of tragedy hadn't ended there. With the war approaching its close, an influenza pandemic had swept through the camps, troop trains and hospitals. Sixteen members of the Thai team had died. Chai, ever wary of the way the Captain had been treated, had made sure their bodies were given a proper cremation. A depressing end chapter that wasn't so popular with the ministers and news editors back home, looking for a more positive finale to their grand military adventure. Those uplifting headlines had had to wait until the victory parade, where the sight of more than a hundred Siamese soldiers marching under the Arc de Triomphe de L'Etoile, had certainly projected an appropriate image of power and prestige to the world. The foreign journalists and commentators had praised their discipline and order, guided by their now famous white elephant flag. General Janriddhi, in a speech to the press corps, had made much of Siam standing shoulder to shoulder with the 'liberating forces of freedom and justice'. And that spirit of unity and concord rolled out across the capital's great halls, dining rooms and ballrooms over the following two months.

But beyond the canapés, oysters and champagne, the general and his staff had their eyes on more clandestine ambitions.

Three weeks after the Paris parade, Chai and his colleagues had been called to a hotel close to the Legation. It was a fussy interior; all damask walls, tasselled curtains and faded red lampshades. Met by Chief of Staff, Pramot, they were shown to a basement cellar close to the laundry room. Thinking they might have to wade through yet another tray of sugary, flag-bedecked cakes, they were surprised to be introduced to two officers from military intelligence. The conversation, initially light-hearted and frivolous, about shaving cream, zipper jackets and music hall girls, gradually steered towards more searching questions. With Chai specifically, they were impressed he had got so close to the front line.

"What was the bore of the big French guns?"

"How many rounds could be fired per minute?"

"How thick were the gun emplacements?"

"Could tanks out pace horses in muddy terrain?"

After two days of intense interrogation the officers went away happy. Four large trunks, filled with paperwork, notes and sketches (again Chai's drawing skills came in handy) were despatched back to Bangkok. Of course the intelligence officers were military stooges, their interests purely factual and empirical. But being so focused on minutiae – lengths, weights and distances – they'd been blind to greater historical shifts. The established empires of Europe might have been brought to their knees by a revolution in industrialised slaughter, but more dangerous still was a contagion of ideas.

For those who had emerged from the wreckage of five years of barbarity, there was nothing but contempt for the past; its patriarchs, politicians and princes. From town squares and stations to bars and cafes, discord and dissent were everywhere. No one was quite sure where Pierre got his information from – certainly beyond what one would usually find in the established national newspapers, *Le Figaro* and *Le Petit Journal*. Chai had once stumbled on a bundle of subversive pamphlets and journals under the bench seat of their cab. Pierre had immediately disowned them, despite notes in their margins that were clearly his handwriting. It was from these sources that they'd first learnt of the building social and political unrest. Strikes and uprisings had broken out across Poland and Hungary. In Germany, sailors in Kiel had called for a republic. A band of anarchists were arrested in Rome with a hit list of European royalty. In the British Isles, Irish nationalists, rebelling against British rule were hoarding guns and explosives. And most sensational of all, the mighty Russian Tsar had been toppled by a simple bread protest led by women. Inspired by this unlikely Bolshevik victory there was talk of a great awakening, of world revolution. Europe was a tinder box, its capitals ablaze with rebellion. How long, pondered Chai, before such sparks fanned East and found similar tinder?

Voices from the dock below pulled Chai back from his reverie. A late soldier was making a dash through the sacks, pallets and ropes that crowded the landing stage. Way back at the customs gate, he had dropped a kitbag, but didn't seem to care. Again the ship's horn sounded. With winches clawing at the anchor chains, deckhands closed the boarding gate and lifted the gangplank aside. The man with the long hair only just made it. Loud cheers greeted his reckless leap over the divide.

With the ship pulling away from the quay, a single rope remained as a tether between the boat and the shore. As this final mooring was loosened and thrown up to a waiting crewman, Chai felt a great surge of emotion, as if that thin line, a last fragile bond between nations, was finally being severed.

Steam bellowed from the engines as the boards shook and the ship turned. Chai took in the receding harbour. In the modest crowd that had gathered in the shadows of the troopship, small children still cheered and waved patriotic flags. A man had a small boy on his shoulders, his small arms holding up a coloured banner, "Adieu, braves soldats, La France vous remercie".

Born came from below deck to find Chai and coerce him down. There was food, ham pies, even wine. Above the sounds of the ship's horns they could hear chords from an accordion, the echo of a tin drum. But Chai, wanting to stay longer, remained at the railings. At one point a drunken gang came out for air, waving open bottles and singing crude songs. They were in high spirits, punching and kicking the air.

When Chai had met Bernard at the school gates, his obstructiveness had been entirely expected. Distrusting his manner from the start, the malice pervading their brief conversation made Chai suspect that the man had intercepted his letters. Indeed, even before he'd arrived at the school he had heard Bernard's blunt denials that Sandrine was at the school, guessing correctly that he would use an 'aunt', or a relative as a reason for her absence. And to be frank he had felt some release. On the train, on the cart from the station, on the walk up the lane, he had rehearsed a thousand times in his mind, how he would present himself to her - how he would act and what he would say - and every time he had faltered, become tongue-tied and flustered. Being turned away by Bernard without seeing Sandrine was a bitter blow. But mixed with the disappointment and the dread he might flounder, he was secretly relieved not to have to go through with the ordeal.

Anticipating this painful retreat, Chai had written everything that needed to be said in a letter, sealed in an envelope. His best hope was that he would have been able to leave it in her classroom, or in the care of one of the younger teachers who seemed trustworthy. Meeting Bernard had been his worst fear. He knew for certain he wouldn't pass the package on. Just as he was also certain he'd open and read it. And because of that Chai had been circumspect with what he had said. Sandrine had asked him to write and that's what he had done; letters and postcards from the towns and cities he was based in and passed through. His vocabulary and grammar had sometimes let him down. And if he'd used language that might have been misconstrued as being too flowery, even a touch flirtatious, it was only because he'd struggled to find the right words and been forced to take advice from Pierre, who, engaged in his own romantic escapades, was sometimes too bold.

Recounting his experiences, from Chaplin to Clemenceau, the trauma of the Captain's death, to surviving the bitter German winter, there was little that betrayed his true feelings. The real message was in the package: the two tin toys Chai had bought in the toy shop in Neustadt – a small painted mouse and a powder blue dove.

When Sandrine had first taken Chai up to the chapel behind the school, he hadn't liked it. He'd found the interior damp and oppressive, the paintings bleak and a carved figure of Christ above the altar, especially scary and macabre. The stained glass windows depicting the great flood - probably the chapel's only original feature - were its only saving grace. But it was a second set of woodcuts along the south aisle, that Sandrine had steered him towards. The images depicted episodes from a folk tale. The most prominent showed an image of a dove caught in a snare. Rising above the river valley a huntsman was approaching through the woods, a sharp knife in his hand. Hidden in the corner of the picture a mouse gnawed through ropes to free the bird. At the time the image in the frame wouldn't have made such an indelible impression if he hadn't seen it at the exact same moment that Sandrine's hand had brushed against his. He found that he wasn't looking at the woodcut but her reflection in the glass, her pale oval face, her soft pink lips and the jewel-like glow from her eyes. Even now, when he cast back to that memory, finer details emerged: the tip of her nose dusted with fine freckles, a ring of turquoise stones hung around her neck, a scarf with an exotic green Chinese design.

Impressed by that moment, he had allowed himself to waive reality and dwell on the impossible. A fantasy of how things might be, however unrealistic and unattainable. It was like a vision from one of the woodcuts, stylised, romantic and naive. But however fanciful this dream, it was a narrative that was tethered to reality by a single tenacious thread. Sandrine's touch was no mistake. She had brushed against him with intent. Although the area of contact was slight, the effect, magnified by the chaos of his feelings and passion, was everywhere; for seconds he struggled to breath.

Standing now on the deck, looking out across the empty sea, her face returned; beautiful, vulnerable and enigmatic, the power of its radiance like a force that reeled him in despite the ever-increasing distance.

By the time the ship had executed the full turn they were already some distance from the shore. The wind picked up. A tall wave broke against the flank of the ship. As the deck rolled to the lee side, a cloud of spray fell across the boards. From below a cry was heard. A deckhand thought he'd seen something in the sea, possibly a mine. A second crewman sprinted to the bow and hanging over the side, signalled to the wheelhouse. The ship swung right, the decks angled abruptly over, but it turned out to be no more than a barrel.

Chai turned away from the railings and headed below deck. He was stepping down the gantry when he found his way barred. It was the group of men he'd seen earlier drinking and singing songs. At the centre of the group was the tall, lanky soldier who'd made the last foolish jump to the ship from the dock. The man reached to an inside pocket. Chai, his past experience still tender, imagined a knife.

"Are you a Chai Khom... siri?" he asked, defeated by the name.

"I am."

"Had me running half way round the ship for you..." he grunted as he pulled out an envelope.

Chapter 44

Mr Chai Khomsiri
Captain, Siam's motor division
HMS Lancaster
Marseilles

Dear Chai,

As I write this letter, two things plague my mind and cause me the greatest distress. The first is the terrible injustice that has been done to you. Later in this letter I will explain things in more detail. I want you to understand what has happened knowing the circumstances that surrounded the event. It has come at a time of great strain to myself. Secondly, I hope in reading the explanation that you will be able to forgive me for those wrongs.

Since our last meeting I haven't been well. The last winter was unusually cold and it was hard to get coal for the stove. There were floods in Channay making it difficult to get into town. And when we got there we found even less food in the markets despite the war being over for so long. Recovering from the long illness, I was still frail on my birthday. Bernard, knowing I was unwell, used the occasion to propose to me. Although I delayed at the time, pressure from my family and friends saw me weaken. We got engaged on the 25th of March, one week before Easter, to be married in June.

Vainly I thought the interval might sooth my qualms and deliver some form of peace, if not contentment. Instead the opposite occurred. I saw what a mistake I'd made and dreaded every minute that dragged me closer to the day. Hating his presence, even the sound of his voice, I began to avoid meeting him and loathed his touch. To get away I went on long walks and found solace in the woods. It was returning to the village after such an escape, that I learned of a stranger at the school gates. You.

Monstrously Bernard, I later learnt, had already turned you away, but after considerable pressure from me, betrayed the fact that you had written and that he had hidden those letters. I managed to retrieve them from the locker in which he had concealed them and gave chase. Certain that you had headed to Montaron, I caught a lift with Ferraux. But we couldn't find you. After two hours of searching we gave up. He dropped me off in the main square. Finding a seat in a cafe I finally found time to open your correspondence. Reading of your adventures in the Meuse and Argonne I was fascinated, especially the encounter with the pushy Americans, although I didn't envy your cold nights in Neustadt. But your Captain's death saddened me. Too many loved friends and acquaintances have been lost in this senseless conflict. For months, until I heard of your return, I dreaded that you'd be part of that toll. Your survival brought great joy to me. It made me realise the depth of fondness I have for you. But there is more than affection. Your presence in our humble classroom on that day was like a window into the unknown.

A lot of people come to our valley. They tell us it is beautiful, a true paradise. But such comforts can also make one tame, obedient to convention and safe within its walls. Hearing your words broke that spell. I understood the ties that enslaved me. The world wasn't something that could only be lived through the pages of a book, it could also be seen, it could be touched, it could be breathed. That is the invaluable treasure you have bequeathed me.

I am going to Marseille. I hope to find you. I may well do so. But fate is more often cruel and I fear I will miss you. I know your ship, the

Lancaster (more information squeezed out of the reluctant Bernard). And somehow I will get this letter to you. I wanted you to leave these shores with the knowledge that part of you will forever reside in my heart. I will never forget you.

Your loving Sandrine Boucher

p.s. I have broken off my engagement with Bernard. My family tells me I am foolish and will die poor and alone. But I would rather live a spinster in solitude than be cursed by a loveless marriage bonded to servitude. And you gave me that courage.

Chapter 45
EPILOGUE
Bangkok, 2020, present day

Sutin folded the letter closed. As he did so a fold of paper came loose and fell to his feet. Within the brittle fold he found a frayed black and white photograph. It showed a woman, middle aged, European with long hair that fell to her shoulders. She was standing in front of the green gecko house. With cuts of teak lying in the open and the gate posts unplastered, it looked like the building was still being constructed. Children played in a pile of freshly delivered sand. Further back in the frame a man stood in the open, hat shading his eyes, spade at his side, his hand against the bough of a newly planted tamarind tree.

Sutin levelled the photograph and looked out across the courtyard. Ninety years on, the tamarind was still there, leafy, majestic, thirty-foot tall, flanked by two recent lines of cypress trees. The copse of trees stood as the centre of an ornate garden square surrounding the now completed, gleaming 'Kingdom Royal Crescent' tower.

Sutin carefully slid the photograph back inside the delicate folds of the letter and returned them to the envelope. Placing them inside the tin box, already filled with the old postcards and news cuttings, he tied the lid with a cord and walked towards the tamarind. Under its branches he found a hollow between the roots. Reaching for a spade, he dug a hole and pressing down the earth, slid the box inside. Shovelling the soil back over the opening, he stamped it down and covered the mound with loose chippings.

Nearing midday, the car park was filling up. Six large Mercedes limousines had parked in the covered VIP bays, Damrong's silver Audi the last in line, their engines a low purr as cooling vents inside soothed the suited chauffeurs in their seats. Beyond the executive cars a minibus was reversing into a space. The doors slid open. Six robed Buddhist monks, busy on smartphones, descended with their novices and retainers. Met by reception staff they were guided through the main doors of the complex into the brightly lit atrium.

Sutin, realising that the ceremony was about to begin, hurried back to his portacabin, took off his safety hat and jacket and washed the grit from his hands. Only that morning he'd bought a suit from the shopping mall down from the transit station. There'd been a miserable choice. The trousers, far longer than he needed, had to be rolled up over his shoes. Those were also new; black, shiny - an Italian style, thin in the heel, making them painful.

A tie look longer to refine. He hadn't worn one since high school and several attempts were needed to remember the sequence of knots. Ten minutes later he left the cabin and jogging across the car park, entered the main hall. His colleagues from the site office were already there, uncomfortable like himself in tight collars and suits. They'd lined up behind the architectural team and the construction management, shielded by a hedge of pot-plants and loudspeakers close to the stage.

On this carpeted platform, Bay, diva like, towered high on elegant stiletto's; heels sharper than those Sutin remembered she'd lost on the rough ground, now several seasons ago. Looking faultless and resplendent, her eyes and face blazed with bronze mascara and contoured foundation, dreamily layered in Daliesque shades. She wore a McQueen couture dress. It was strapless and had two bands of silvered sequins set off with Swarovski crystals. Around her buzzed her marketing team; three impeccable girls and an intern from Thammasat University. There were last minute changes; additions to the guest list, new timings for the speeches, lighting changes for the technicians.

Checking the overhead screens, Bay's eyes chanced on Sutin in the back row. Walking over she stroked his lapels and pretended to admire the texture of his off-the-peg suit; she could still read the creases left by the retailers' cheap clothes hangers.

"You look good in a suit Sutin. It's a little tight, but still classy."

"The label said Armani," he jested.

She brushed her hand across the polyester lining, "I don't know..." she smiled, "feels more like Gucci."

An echo above drew their attention to the domed ceiling. Twenty metres across, its zenith was crowned with gold leaf. But it was unfinished. Even now a technician in a high rise was smoothing out a last wrinkle. Electric motors whined as the platform raced down and stage assistants hissed into their handsets to have the equipment cleared so the floors could be swept and given a last polish.

"Cutting it fine Sutin..." said Bay.

"The decorators had to work through the night. Your office only approved the drawings on Wednesday. They weren't happy with the design. Too modern. They wanted something more classic. In fact it's the only Thai thing left in the place."

"By the way, whatever happened to that decrepit old house?"

"It was taken down. They were going to junk it. I took it away."

"Come on Sutin, why bother with some shitty old shack?"

"One day I'll rebuild it."

"What ghosts and all?"

"Ghosts and all, with stories to tell."

"Reserve a one-bedroom apartment and it'll come with plenty of tales. Stories of German engineered kitchens, Tuscan craftsmen and hand-painted tiles."

"I don't think I could even afford the coffee machine..."

"We'll give you family rates. We could be on the same floor"

"With a view of Cambodia?" he joked.

"Now you're getting too pushy..." she snapped back.

The room went quiet. Bay joined the executives and investors in the front row seats. There was a hush as Damrong guided in the VIP guests. Incense was lit. A gong sounded. Sutin and his team knelt to the ground and prostrated themselves in front of the monks. The chanting started; prayers for well being, prayers for prosperity, prayers for the clients of the Kingdom Royal Crescent.

With the chanting over they took the stairs to the central atrium, its chrome bannisters wrapped with white orchids. Waitresses were waiting with trays of pink Cristal champagne. Spotlights lit up a stage. Damrong came to the microphone, waving a fluted Baccarat glass in one hand. In high spirits he welcomed the foreign bankers and backers, thanked the architects and construction team and praised those investors wise enough to have put down twenty-five percent deposits on the double-height penthouse apartments in the West wing.

"When I first came here more than five years ago, there was nothing. A family of buffalo and a gang of mad dogs. Only one house was left standing. A Thai house. They said it was historic, that it was wrong to knock it down. That we should respect the past, that it has lessons for us all…"

He shrugged, "What lessons? Leaking roofs, rotten floorboards, snakes and dead trees?"

There was a pause. Damrong waited for the laughter to subside.

"I'll give you a lesson. Forget the past. It's gone and buried. Turn your eyes to the future. Look to power, ambition and vision,"

His arms lifted to the towering dome above them. Projectors came on, their powerful beams illuminating a glittering gold sun at its zenith, "The Kingdom Royal Crescent. A symbol for who we are. And what we can be. Lords of Life with Jacuzzis in heaven."

The End